SKIRTING DANGER

Kay Keppler

SKIRTING DANGER

Acknowledgments

Many thanks to Beth Barany, Patricia Simpson, and Anne Victory, who did their best to help me make this book the best it could be. And a special shout out to that unknown participant in the writers workshop, who, when asked what the young woman in the poodle skirt might do for a living, said, "Maybe she works for the CIA."

Chapter 1

Phoebe Renfrew charged up the blisteringly hot steps of the Las Vegas courthouse and thrust a brochure at the couple hustling toward the door.

"Get married by an award-winning Elvis impersonator!" she said, doing her best to sound cheerful and enthusiastic. "Create happy memories for a lifetime in a genuine 1957 Cadillac! Ten-percent-off Tuesday special!"

The couple escaped into the building, and Phoebe—hot, tired, sweaty, and discouraged—straggled back down the steps. Another customer had gotten away. If she didn't have some success soon, she'd never make grocery money this week, much less rent.

Life sure didn't go the way you planned. Just two weeks ago, she'd had everything she'd worked for since she was fourteen. She'd had the job of her dreams—language analyst at the CIA—where she got to use her skills and, she hoped, help her country. She wore suits to work. She had *benefits*.

Then it all went terribly, horribly wrong. That terrorist threat at the Empire State Building that she thought was imminent? Not so much. When the SEALs and SWAT got there, all they found were tourists.

You'd think the bosses would have been happy about that, but they weren't. Instead, they suspended her without pay—without examining the evidence, without even *looking* at her analysis—pending an investigation. When it was done, if they thought she hadn't followed the correct protocols, they'd fire her.

Without a paycheck, she couldn't pay her rent, and without

options, she'd moved across the country to sleep on her mother's sofa. Now she was working for the Elvis-themed Happy Memories Wedding Chapel, handing out promotional brochures and wearing a uniform, a 1950s-era turquoise circle skirt complete with poodle applique.

But the terrorist threat was still out there. She *knew* it. It hadn't materialized at the Empire State Building, but it would manifest somewhere. Because she hadn't been wrong, no matter what the shortsighted, narrow-minded, thickheaded, bureaucratic half-wit bosses at the CIA thought. So in every spare minute, she checked out the Korean-language websites that she used to monitor, searching for chatter that would suggest a national threat.

If she could pinpoint it, she could avert a crisis, save lives, *and* get her job back.

And if she didn't figure out what the threat was, she might never get reinstated, and all the hard work she'd put in for more than ten years to get that career would be for nothing.

She couldn't bear to think about that.

At one o'clock, Phoebe put away her clipboard of brochures and took her sack lunch and laptop and sat down on a clean spot in the shade, carefully smoothing out her skirt so it wouldn't get wrinkled. James Bond never seemed to worry about his clothes, but he probably never had to do his own laundry, either. Not that she was comparing herself to James Bond. She certainly didn't have a license to kill. She didn't even have a license to *drive*.

As she munched her peanut butter sandwich, she followed up on her usual jihadist websites. Eventually she became aware that something was different. Noisy. Smelly. She glanced up from her reading and saw that a delivery truck had pulled into the parking area, blocking the disability spaces. Diesel fumes poured from its tailpipe.

"Hey!" Phoebe yelled.

The driver ignored her.

"Hey!" Every parking space that a visitor couldn't reach was potentially one fewer customer for the Happy Memories Wedding Chapel. Besides, that area was for disabled people, not truck drivers waiting for whatever they were waiting for. The fumes alone were killer.

She picked up her laptop and dusted off her skirt. Then she ran over to the belching truck and pounded on the door.

"Hey," she said, glaring up at the driver. "Didn't you hear me? You have to move this thing. You're in the disabled parking area."

The driver shrugged and shook his head. He looked Asian. Maybe he was a recent immigrant. Maybe he didn't speak English well. Or at all.

"Go away," she said, waving her arm. She pounded on the door again and pointed to the disabled parking sign. *"Please move the truck."*

The driver ignored her.

Phoebe kicked the tire. "Move the damn vehicle, or I'll whack it so hard you'll sing soprano!"

The driver snorted, still not moving the truck.

Another guy came out of the county building. He looked Asian, too, but he was maybe ten to fifteen years younger than the driver, and his clothes and hair, cut in a spiky style, were more fashionable. He went to the passenger side of the vehicle and said something to his partner that Phoebe couldn't hear. Then he came around to talk to her.

"Lars, send her away!" the driver said in Korean.

They spoke Korean! What were the odds?

Lars took out a cell phone and fumbled with it.

"How can I send her away?" he asked in Korean. "I don't speak English."

"Hurry!" the driver snapped. "We have guns to buy! And she might talk to the cops!"

Cops. Guns. This did not sound good.

While the driver had been talking, Lars had keyed something into his phone. He held it up to her.

"What you want?" a computerized voice asked. She was listening to lousy English through a Korean-to-English language app.

Forget that. Speaking Korean was much simpler. She took the phone from him, turned it off, and handed it back.

"Why do you want to buy guns?" she asked them in Korean. The shock on their faces would have been laughable if the topic had been laugh-worthy.

"You speak Korean." Lars, looking horrified, slipped the phone back into his pocket.

"I do. What do you want guns for? What will you do if you get them?"

"We want to go hunting," the driver said. "This is where we get the permits, yes? We have that correct?"

The county building did issue hunting permits. What animals were in season in midsummer? She couldn't think of any.

"Where are you guys from?" she asked.

"Swe—" Lars began, but the driver cut him off.

"Are you a county official?" he asked.

Crap. He had to know she wasn't a county official because she was wearing the damn poodle-skirt-and-saddle-shoes uniform of the Happy Memories Wedding Chapel. If she'd been wearing a black suit like she wore at the CIA, he'd believe her. This was why she'd mired herself in debt to go to college—so she could wear a suit to work and people would pay attention when she said something.

"Gustav—" Lars said, sounding worried.

So Gustav was the driver's name. Were they from Sweden, as Lars had seemed about to say? If so, they'd be an incredible anomaly. Korean speakers were a tiny fraction of the Swedish population. Just—she did the math—four-tenths of one percent of Sweden's ten million citizens. But the names Lars and Gustav— that sure suggested a Swedish connection.

"Why can't the cops know you want to get a gun permit?" she asked.

"Of course the police can know," Gustav said. "You must have misunderstood. Since you're not a native Korean speaker."

Phoebe felt her teeth clench. She *hadn't* misunderstood what these guys had said, but Gustav had hit a nerve. The CIA had contended that she'd misunderstood the Korean-language communications that had led to the Empire State Building debacle. But she *hadn't* misunderstood, even though no bomb was found and the secretary of state hadn't been hurt.

And now here were two Korean-speaking guys, wanting to buy guns and avoid the cops. The coincidence was just too—well, coincidental. Could a Korean group be planning terrorist acts across the United States?

The connection was awfully thin, but why take a chance? The truck could contain a bomb. She should get them away from the county building.

"You need to leave this parking area," she said. "It's for disabled access only."

"No," Gustav said. "We came here to find out about gun purchases. You can't stop us. You aren't an official, and your Korean is terrible."

And your mother wears combat boots, Phoebe almost added. Instead, she grabbed her phone from her pocket and dialed a number.

"Hello, *police?*" she said clearly and slowly in English. She didn't know if Gustav or Lars would understand anything she said. Maybe Lars. He was younger. He might have some basic English.

"I want to report a truck. I asked the driver to move, but—"

"Gustav, we have to go!" Lars shouted. "She said *police!*"

The truck's transmission squealed as the driver shifted into reverse.

"Hold on," Phoebe said into the phone.

Lars dashed to the passenger door and leaped into the cab.

"Phoebe?" Babette O'Shea, co-owner with her husband Harry of the Happy Memories Wedding Chapel, sounded confused. "What's going on?"

Gustav jerked the truck forward into the driveway, waiting for a break in the traffic.

Now that they were leaving, Phoebe wondered if she'd done the right thing. Should she call the cops for real? Or let them go?

She hated her own uncertainty. But the last time she'd acted quickly and decisively about suspicious activity, she'd been forced into this unexpected and unwelcome visit to Las Vegas, where her life was filled with poodle skirts, peanut butter sandwiches, and her mother's lumpy couch. She didn't see how she could go downhill from here, but she wasn't looking for a one-way ticket to something worse.

"Phoebe?"

"Sorry, Babette. I needed this truck to move away from the

county building, so I called you and said you were the police. Faked it."

"You're a scamp," Babette said. "I have to go. I have the Smith-Crivellos here for their nuptials."

"Carry on," Phoebe said. "Knock 'em dead."

"Phoebe, honey, we do *weddings*, not funerals," Babette said as she disconnected.

Phoebe fumbled with the folds of her skirt to return her phone to her pocket. The truck was just pulling into traffic. It wasn't too late to do something.

But what? If she called one of the law enforcement agencies—the FBI, or even the police—and they didn't find anything, her suspension from the CIA would become permanent for sure.

And if she *didn't* call—if she did nothing at all—and the Korean speakers bought guns and committed a crime or terrorist act, she'd never forgive herself.

A classic lose-lose situation.

However, if she could discover where these guys were going or what they were up to, she'd have more information for law enforcement. Then they could make arrests. And because of her sharp instincts and prompt action, the CIA would have to reinstate her—would *want* to reinstate her.

Yeah, that would work.

She was a language analyst, so she wasn't trained in clandestine work. But that truck was big and white and belching out smoke. How hard could surveillance be? She could decide what to do once they stopped.

Following them, though, was another story. Her transportation was a bicycle. Even now the truck was at the corner light. Soon it would be lost. She couldn't exactly chase it down the freeway on a bike.

Just then a cab cruised down the street, slowing for the light. *Problem solved.* Phoebe waved her arm frantically, and the cabbie pulled over. She scrambled into the back seat.

"Where to, miss?"

"See that truck up there? The plain white one."

"Yes, miss."

"Follow it, please. But not too closely."

The driver looked into the rearview mirror and smiled. Phoebe glanced at the identification in the cab and saw that his name was Sanjay.

"Are we then on a mission of a secretive nature, miss?"

"We certainly are, Sanjay."

She'd be careful. She couldn't get into trouble again, or she'd never get her job back.

But she'd been trained to analyze information, assess the possibilities, use her intuition, and act in her country's best interests. And she'd analyzed and assessed, and her gut was telling her these guys were trouble.

She would not let them get away.

Chase Bonaventure, CEO of Venture Automotive—and former quarterback of the Las Vegas Rattlesnakes—and two of his engineers watched as the crane maneuvered a huge robotic arm into place on the factory floor. He'd hoped to get this robot installed weeks ago so that his potential investors could see it. A group from Midnight Sun Capital, the Swedish investment firm, would arrive two hours from now, and he'd wanted to demonstrate that he could mass-produce energy-saving electric vehicles at a price everyone could afford. If Midnight Sun invested with him, anyway.

That had been the plan. But the robotic arm hadn't arrived last month as scheduled. It had arrived today. And he'd had to scramble—and pay a premium—to get the professional installers, a crane operator and a couple of riggers, to come out on short notice with the right equipment. Now all they had to do was get the robot in place, bolt the sucker down, calibrate it, program it, and start her up. Maybe two weeks' work. And they had two hours to make it happen.

What do you do when you're at fourth and long? Drop back and punt. He'd have to figure out a way to show the investors how he was improving production even if the robot wasn't ready to go.

The riggers waved at the crane operator to lower the arm. The robot, secured by nylon webbing and multiple straps, swayed from the cable as the crane operator edged it toward the steel plate already anchored to the floor. The riggers reached up to help guide the massive arm into place.

"This is it," Chase said, eying the cable, the straps, and the robotic arm. "Take it slow! We don't want to have to move this thing later because we're off on the placement now."

Matt Tinkham, the electrical engineer, grabbed the arm's platform. "Hell, no," he said, his eyes never leaving the equipment. "We can barely move the thing now, when the crane is holding it up."

"We *got* it," one of the riggers said, sounding irritated.

Chase didn't care if the riggers were irritated. He was the guy footing the bills. He was damned sure that nothing would happen to that robot on his watch.

"It's off center," he said. "You can see it."

Tony Minaya, the software engineer, grunted as he pushed the robotic arm more to the left. "Thing weighs a ton," he said. "We gotta get it—"

A sharp blast of desert wind snapped the support brace that held open a roof window vent. The window slammed into the ceiling and shattered, scattering glass across the floor and blowing desert grit and sand into the room.

Chase saw the danger appear almost in slow motion, like when he still played football. In those days, he could see a play unfold in what seemed like microseconds. Even when the defenders rushed him and he scrambled to save the play—or his neck—he knew where his receivers were and how he could connect for optimum yardage.

What happened next was worse than any play on the field. When the glass, grit, and dust blasted across the factory floor, the crane operator flinched, jerking the controls, which sent the cable, and the robotic arm tethered to it, swinging.

The momentum from the swinging robot destabilized the straps that held it to the cable. The robotic arm broke through the protective webbing that secured it and leaned drunkenly to one side. Tony grabbed it, trying to shove it back in.

Chase saw in an instant that his efforts wouldn't work. The robot was leaning too far over. And Tony, who stood directly under the half-ton piece of equipment, was almost certain to be seriously hurt because he was concentrating on saving the machinery, not himself.

"Tony! *Move!*"

Even as he shouted the warning, Chase lunged. He tackled the software engineer, shoving him to the side as hard and fast as he could. Both men fell heavily to the concrete floor. Chase felt a searing pain shoot from his bad knee up his thigh and down to his ankle.

The half-ton robot crashed to the floor, sending shock waves through the factory. Chase and Tony stared at the piece of equipment now occupying the space where Tony had been standing.

"*Jesus.*" Tony rolled to the side and, stretching gingerly, tested his arms. "Man, that was close. Hey, Coach, you all right?"

Chase massaged his knee, waiting to get his breath back. *Hell, no.* That whump on the concrete had to have set back his rehab at least a couple of months. Not that he'd ever say so to Tony.

"Yeah, I'm fine," he said, getting carefully to his feet. "Can't tell a little bump like that from Astroturf. What about you?"

"I'm gonna have some bruises tomorrow." Tony got up slowly. "You know, for a quarterback, you make a damn fine tackle."

Chase grinned. "Let's see if we busted the machine."

They went over to check out the robotic arm. Matt was examining the strap, his face pale.

"You could have been *killed*," he said. "Both of you. This thing would have crushed you."

"Jeez, I hope I'm faster than that," Chase said.

"Coach has good reflexes," Tony said. "For which I'm thankful."

"Did anyone get cut from that window glass?" Chase called out to the floor.

A chorus of noes from the other employees replied.

"At least nobody's hurt," he said. "I'll get someone out here to check out all the windows. We can't have that kind of accident when we're in full production."

The crane operator scrambled out of the cab and hustled over to them. "You guys all right?"

The riggers nodded, looking shaken.

15

"A little bruised," Tony said. "The robot, though—that's what I'm worried about."

"Hell, yeah." Chase nodded at his engineers. "You guys figure out if the robot still works. And you"—he turned to the riggers and crane operator—"can figure out how to get this arm in whatever position we need."

The men nodded.

Chase glanced at his watch. Just an hour now until the investors arrived. He had to get upstairs and get ready for them.

"I have to go," he said. "Let me know your progress by five."

"Will do, Coach," Tony said.

Chase nodded and headed for the lobby, determined not to limp. Couldn't let the team know that the quarterback might be injured. But *damn*. This factory was a dangerous pile of nuts and bolts. He needed cash flow for repairs, and he needed long-term fluidity. He had an appointment to talk to his bank about a second loan, but he'd wanted to show them more progress. He *needed* the money from Midnight Sun.

Once back in his office with his knee elevated and an ice pack taped around it, he finished reviewing the slide presentation for the Swedes. The group of nine businessmen, bankers, engineers, and accountants would spend a couple of weeks with him, checking out the operation, examining at his financial statements, and—he hoped—signing an agreement.

Over the years when he'd earned millions every year playing football, he'd invested in several interesting start-ups, including this electric-car company. When he found out that its initial capital was depleted and it was about to go belly-up, he bought the outstanding stock.

So far, the assets of Venture Automotive included a decrepit factory and a few outdated robots. He employed a motley group of people willing to take a chance on a broken-down football player with no experience in auto manufacturing. But they'd all thrived on the challenge, and in only six months they'd built some fantastic prototypes that had gotten the new company a lot of press.

He was determined to show Midnight Sun that Venture Automotive was the next big thing. He had two weeks to persuade them to put their kronor where their convictions were.

"Coach?" Kristin, his young, no-nonsense admin, poked her head in the door. "I've got Reception on the line. Somebody's in the lobby who says—" She stopped at the sound of shouts from below, then went to the rail of the mezzanine where their offices were located and gazed down at the lobby.

"You might want to see this," she said.

Chase tore the ice pack off his knee and hobbled out of his office to join her. Downstairs, a young woman wearing a poufy skirt broke away from his security detail and sprinted for the stairs.

Note to self: *retrain security*.

The intruder dashed across the lobby and tore up the steps to the mezzanine. She didn't look dangerous, though, just determined. What could she possibly want here?

He moved to the stairway to intercept her. His knee was shot, but he must have a hundred pounds on her. She wouldn't get past him.

She bounded up the stairs, two at a time. Her knees lifted so high, and the blue skirt was so billowy, that Chase thought it might be the first time that security could be called for indecent exposure. Not that he was against indecent exposure. After all, this was Vegas.

He waited for her at the top of the stairs, expecting her to stop when she saw him, but when she leaped up the last step, she barreled right into him. He didn't even stagger, but she bounced off his chest and would have tumbled back down the stairs if he hadn't reached out and steadied her, his hands on her bare arms.

"Whoa! Take it easy, *cher*," he said, blinking as he felt the muscle there and studied her more carefully. Porcelain skin. Direct blue eyes. Straight, light-brown hair pulled back in a high ponytail. And those strong arms.

She flushed as she regained her footing.

"Excuse me," she said, barely breathing hard. "I'm looking for the boss here. Chase Bonaventure, the receptionist said."

"You found him," Kristin said, glancing from one to the other of them like an inquisitive wren.

Chase thought that all of Las Vegas—and probably a lot of the country—knew that he had gone into business when the injuries he'd sustained in the Super Bowl had forced his retirement from the Rattlesnakes. Sometimes it seemed like the entire world was waiting to see how he'd manage—or screw up—his second career. Yet this young woman seemed never to have heard of Chase Bonaventure. That was refreshing in a weird way.

"I'm Chase Bonaventure," he said. "Now tell me who you are."

"Phoebe Renfrew," she said.

"Do you have any ID with you?"

Phoebe sighed. "Yes. Not that it will tell you much." She pulled the Washington, DC-issued laminated ID card from her skirt pocket and handed it to him.

Chase examined it and then her face before handing it back.

"You're a long way from home, Phoebe. What's so important that you had to break through security and run up here?"

Phoebe smoothed down her skirt. He didn't know a thing about women's clothes, favoring the tight and short on the women he dated. Phoebe's knee-length, full blue skirt had a big dog on it.

"Cute poodle skirt," Kristin said.

Phoebe grinned. "Thank you," she said. "I can't take credit for it. It's my work uniform."

"I love retro. With the right bag, you could wear that anywhere."

"You think so? I like it because it's breezy."

"Cotton," Kristin said. "Cool to wear but hard to iron." Phoebe nodded, and Kristin stuck out her hand. "Kristin Seiler."

Phoebe shook it. "Phoebe Renfrew. But you already knew that."

Chase tried to control his exasperation. Honest to God, if he lived to be one hundred, he'd never figure out females.

"Ladies!" he said. "*If you don't mind.* Time's a-wastin' here. Phoebe. What's so damn important you couldn't make an appointment?"

"This is going to sound strange," Phoebe said, and he felt a twinge of premonition. What with the skirt and her becoming BFFs with Kristin in the space of thirty seconds, they'd crossed into strange territory some time ago. "I'm with the CIA."

He laughed. "No, you're not," he said, grinning. That was a good one. The CIA! As if he'd ever believe that. "Nice try, though.

Listen, *cher,* we're busy. Tell me what you're here for, or I'll have security escort you out."

"I really am with the CIA," Phoebe said, sticking out her chin. "Well, technically I'm suspended, pending an investigation. I saw some suspicious people go through your front door a few minutes ago. Their truck is parked in the visitors lot." She glared over the mezzanine railing at the lobby one floor below. "Your receptionist didn't stop them."

"She probably had a good reason."

Phoebe turned glacial blue eyes on him. "I've been following these men ever since I heard them talking about buying guns. They're in a white truck, they drove here, and they went in your front door. Do you have a reason to be hiding Korean gunrunners?"

Chase drew back, all amusement gone. Was she *accusing* him?

"I don't know what you're talking about. There aren't any Koreans here. And no guns, either. Maybe you lost them along the way."

"I didn't lose them. I'm a trained operative. I know suspicious behavior when I see it."

"You didn't see any here." Chase took her arm, turned her around, and motioned to the two guards still standing on the lower steps. "Thank you for your service to our country. I wish the CIA nothing but good luck. Security will see you out."

He watched her jerk away from the guards as they escorted her down the stairs, across the lobby, and out the door. Too bad she was off the wall. She was cute—and she had those amazing arms. He bet her legs were just as amazing.

"Huh," Kristin said as the phone on her desk buzzed. "I wonder what she saw? I think part of that must be true, don't you? She's a trained operative. Plus wearing that cute poodle skirt."

She grinned at Chase as she picked up the phone, and Chase shook his head and went back to his office to get his laptop.

"Yes," Kristin said. "Uh-oh. Uh-huh. Uh-huh. I'll tell him. Right. Thanks, Megan."

"Tell me what?" Chase asked as he came out of his office with his laptop.

"With all the excitement, Megan almost forgot. She says a

19

couple of our Swedish group arrived early in their own vehicle. You were on the floor with the new robot, so she put them in the conference room with the coffee and pastries. And the van driver that's bringing the rest of the group called. He's two minutes out."

Damn. He didn't have time to meet the early arrivals now. He needed to be down in the lobby to greet the main group. He headed for the stairs.

"Thanks, Kristin, I'll—"

"One more thing," Kristin said. "Megan says the early arrivals don't look Swedish. At least, they're not tall and blond. She says they look Asian."

He stopped in his tracks. "What?"

"That's what she said. And they didn't speak English. They used a translation app on their phone to make themselves understood. Think they could be Korean? Like Phoebe said?"

Chase closed his eyes and exhaled. Today of all days, when he wanted to be focused, everything was coming up crazy. He felt a sinking sense of inevitability.

"What kind of vehicle did they come in?"

"A white truck. Maybe they have guns, too."

"I doubt that, but let security know, I suppose, to be on the safe side." He started down the steps.

"Will do. Go get 'em, Coach."

Guns. Koreans. Women in poodle skirts telling crazy stories. Definitely the last thing he needed.

Chapter 2

Phoebe shook loose from the security guards as soon as she was out of the building and headed toward Sanjay and the taxi. As she crossed the pavement, a white passenger van pulled up and a group of men got out and headed toward the steps to the lobby door. Phoebe stopped and smiled at them.

"Hello," she said in Korean. The men all beamed.

"Hello," they responded.

So she was right. Chase Bonaventure *was* harboring Koreans.

The men went into the building, the van drove away, and Phoebe crossed the drive to where Sanjay was parked. He was leaning against the front fender of his taxicab, checking his phone, but he straightened up and put it away as Phoebe approached.

"Any luck, miss?"

Phoebe glanced back at the young security guards still standing at the door, looking like oversized action figures.

"They didn't believe me. But the truck is sitting *right there.*"

Sanjay gazed at the truck. "Perhaps they did not feel that a delivery truck by itself was suspicious. Meaning no disrespect, miss."

Phoebe slumped against the fender next to him. "None taken. And the boss, Chase Bonaventure, swears that no Koreans had entered the building. Of course, he didn't let me poke around." She stared gloomily at the white truck baking in the desert heat. "Well, who could blame him? It does sound pretty far-fetched. Except that the people who just went in there are Korean."

"You *spoke* to Mr. Bonaventure? To him directly? That is

thrilling! Had I known you were likely to meet, I might have dared to ask you to get me an autograph!"

Phoebe dragged her gaze away from the offending white truck and focused on Sanjay. "Why would you want Chase Bonaventure's autograph?"

Sanjay's look of shocked amazement was almost comical.

"You are not a fan of our professional football team, the Las Vegas Rattlesnakes?" he asked.

"I'm from New York and DC." Not that she was interested in professional sports, no matter what city she lived in.

"Chase Bonaventure was the Rattlesnakes quarterback until the Super Bowl a few months ago, when a most unfortunate injury to his knee incurred during the course of the game forced his retirement from the sport," Sanjay said. "But his playing was a thing of beauty, a symphony in motion."

"Ah, okay," Phoebe said. She didn't know a thing about Chase Bonaventure's playing, but he was so strong that running into him had been like running into a brick wall. A warm brick wall with steadying hands. Even the *thought* of bumping into him again made her flush all over.

"Last year, I am in the stadium for the Snakes-Steelers playoff game," Sanjay said, oblivious to Phoebe's uninterest in professional football. "I have season tickets on the five-yard line. I am going always with my cousin Mohan, my colleague at the garage. Mr. Bonaventure took the snap on the fifty-yard line, the Steelers were pressing, he scrambled, and then—most unbelievably!—he is throwing the football, an impossible, last-chance Hail Mary to his teammate Dan Freer, the wide receiver, in the end zone, right in front of us." Sanjay's face was alight with memory as he relived the excitement.

"It was a miracle," he said. "And yet, not a miracle. A ballet of strength and grace. Of skill and determination. And if Chase Bonaventure can throw a pass like that with such power and precision, and Dan Freer can leap in the air as though he were borne on the wings of angels and catch it in the end zone, completing the play like... like heaven intended for them to do it, there is hope still for world peace. That is what I believe."

Phoebe blinked, caught unawares by Sanjay's eloquence. Maybe she'd missed something by not watching professional football.

Yeah, probably not. But Chase Bonaventure had certainly sparked admiration among his fans.

"Well, I'm all for world peace," she said. She considered the hulking building. It was desperately in need of repair. The new landscaping was nice, though, and the windows had been caulked recently, so some effort had been made to spruce up the place. "What kind of business is this, anyway?"

"Venture Automotive is an electric-vehicle manufacturing concern, although as yet it has produced only some very striking prototypes. Under Mr. Bonaventure's leadership, we have high hopes for the company's success."

"Huh." Phoebe gazed at the building speculatively. "You know, this place could be a front organization for a criminal enterprise—money laundering, for instance—if they're not producing any cars yet. That could explain why they're hiding Korean gunrunners. Something else: a start-up that needs a big cash infusion could be susceptible to bribes or other kinds of influence."

"I don't think it can be that, miss," Sanjay said, looking shocked all over again. "If you'll pardon my saying so, you have a very suspicious mind."

"That's the CIA for you." Phoebe gazed at the huge sign perched on the building's roof. "Chase Bonaventure, Venture Automotive. I get it now. Is he from Louisiana?" That *cher* had been a tipoff, not to mention the Cajun accent and his French name.

"He is, according to the official NFL website." Sanjay cleared his throat. "Is it possible that you could have been mistaken in what you overheard?"

Phoebe sighed. First the CIA didn't believe her. Now Sanjay.

"Anything's possible. But I don't think so."

"The other potential explanation as I see it is that we inadvertently confused the trucks in our pursuit and followed an innocent vehicle entirely by accident. I'm thinking that could be a likely alternative scenario."

"You know we didn't do that. We followed the right truck all the way. It's sitting right over there."

Sanjay slumped against the cab. "I was thinking the same, miss."

23

The security guards were still watching them. Phoebe wondered if they were sworn to protect the vehicles in the visitors parking lot. Did they shoot to kill? Probably not. And what was the story with these Korean speakers? Was there a bomb in the truck? Did they have any guns already, and if so, did they want more? She wanted to find out.

"Watch my back, Sanjay." She walked over to the delivery vehicle and pulled on the back door. Locked. But the handle turned on the driver-side door. She swung up into the seat and took stock of the interior.

The glove box didn't contain anything interesting, but in a compartment under the dash, she found a rental agreement signed by Gustav Eklund and Lars Eklund. Who *were* these people? They spoke Korean. They looked Korean. And yet—they had Swedish names. Maybe they were brothers, but more likely cousins. They didn't look that much alike. She folded the papers and slid them back where she'd found them.

She poked around in the maps and paper detritus she found in the door pocket. She didn't think she'd find anything, and she didn't. What had she expected? A receipt from Guns R Us showing that two Korean nationals with forged Swedish passports had bought one hundred assault rifles? Unlikely. What she wanted to find but didn't was a key that would unlock the back of the truck.

Nothing here was inherently suspicious, but the whole setup felt off. Something was up with these guys. She just didn't know what.

But she'd find out.

A car horn blared and Phoebe glanced up to see the security guards bearing down on her. She jumped out of the truck, slamming the door, and dashed over to the taxi, but the guards got there first and held her by the arm.

"You can't go stealin' stuff from a customer's truck," the taller guy said.

"I didn't steal anything!" Phoebe said, yanking her arm away.

"Maybe the boss should talk to her," the shorter of the two guards said.

"You have no legal grounds to hold me," Phoebe said, hoping that was true, "so I'll be on my way. Or I *will* be calling my lawyer and the police."

The guards glanced doubtfully at each other. She planted her hands on her hips.

"Or do you think Mr. Bonaventure wants a lawsuit on his hands?"

Chase gazed down the gleaming conference table at his nine potential investors. Nine expectant, uncomprehending faces gazed back. Nobody spoke.

The silence was sharp and painful. He'd rather be in the middle of a delicate knee operation performed by blind chefs wearing oven mitts than sitting here. The Midnight Sun investors had flown all the way from Sweden to evaluate his company and, if they liked what they saw, invest the millions he needed to expand his plant and keep his people working.

If only they could understand a single word he said.

Just fifteen minutes before, he'd shaken hands with every one of them in the lobby. Seven more Swedish investors. Who, like the first two, were not what he'd expected. Who were, in fact, Swedish citizens of Korean descent.

In less time than it took to ruin your knee in a bad tackle, he learned just how badly things could go wrong, even when you had done everything you could think of to prepare.

"Hello," he'd said. "Good morning."

"Hello!" they'd chorused.

"I want to start by showing you our prototypes so you can see what makes us different from other companies. Is everybody with me?"

"Hello!" they'd all said.

They were from *Sweden*, for Pete's sake. They had Swedish passports. And he'd expected them to speak *Swedish*. And *English*, although to be on the safe side, he had a Swedish translator standing right here, just in case.

How could this possibly be? How had his Swedish investors become Korean? And how did Phoebe Renfrew fit into this? She'd been right about the Korean part. Was she right about the guns, too?

One of the younger guys raised his hand tentatively.

"Yes?" Chase tried to look encouraging.

The guy said something he didn't understand, but Inga, the translator did.

"This is Lars Eklund," Inga said. "He and his brother, Gustav, speak Swedish and Korean. The others speak only Korean."

That wasn't good.

"How will this work?" he asked. "How are we going to communicate?"

"Slowly, it seems. Let me ask them if they had a plan, since they didn't tell you about the language requirements."

Inga said something in Swedish, and then Lars said something to the group in Korean. The oldest guy responded. Then Lars said something to Inga in Swedish, no doubt a translation of what the old guy had said in Korean. They went back and forth a bit. It took a while.

"The president of the group is Sven Eklund," Inga finally said. "Lars and Gustav are his sons. They're the Swedish-to-Korean translators, but they're not part of the Midnight Sun evaluation team."

At the sound of their names, Lars gave a little wave and Gustav nodded brusquely.

"Don't any of them speak English?" Chase asked. "Not even the young guys? I thought young Swedes all learned English these days."

"Not these young Swedes," Inga said. "That's extremely unusual. They must have been very protected as youngsters. And they're not professional translators. We had a couple of issues over some idioms."

Chase shoved his hands in his pockets. If he'd learned one thing playing football, it was to roll with the punches. No matter what happened, you had to play your best with what you had. And people sitting around his conference table speaking Korean was what he had.

"Okay," he said, turning to the investment team. "Any questions before we get started?"

He waited while Inga translated the English to Swedish and Lars translated the Swedish to Korean. Somebody asked Lars something. Lars translated to Inga. They went back and forth again.

Chase tried not to feel impatient. These guys were his future, although the way things were going, his future was a lot farther off than it had been just a little while ago.

Finally Inga turned to Chase.

"They want to know if you could arrange a tour of Hoover Dam for their engineering team on the weekend," she said. "They say it is such an engineering marvel."

"I can try," Chase said. But that was *it*? All that talking, and all they'd asked for was a tour? At this rate, they'd never get through everything they needed to understand in only two weeks. And he didn't want his words filtered through two young guys who didn't understand English idioms, business, or automobiles. How accurate could they be? He needed the evaluation team to understand what his company could do.

He needed an English-to-Korean translator. How long would it take to find that person here in Las Vegas? Maybe he could import one from somewhere. Say, Korea. Yeah, that would work.

"This translation setup isn't adequate," he said. "So here's what we'll do. Our driver will take everybody back to the hotel, and by tomorrow I'll find someone who speaks English and Korean. Tell Lars and Gustav no offense, but I need a pro. Ask everybody if they'd like tickets to a show tonight. And commemorative football jerseys. I bet the young guys would."

Inga translated, Lars translated, and everyone's face lit up.

Okay, then. He thanked them for coming and strode down to his office. Kristin looked up from her computer screen.

"Back so soon?"

"The Swedish evaluation team speaks Korean," he said. "Call that agency where we got this Swedish translator and see if they have a Korean translator. We need to get a behind-the-scenes tour of Hoover Dam on the weekend for the engineers if we can. A Korean-speaking tour. Then get tickets to a show tonight for those guys. A magic show, or maybe a musical. Something not too wordy. And commemorative jerseys."

"Okay," Kristin said. "What happened? Did I make a mistake somehow?"

"You got it right. Midnight Sun Capital is interested in investing in electric cars, and they're Swedes. But they speak Korean. Two of the guys speak Swedish, but they aren't part of

Midnight Sun. Don't ask. I don't know. So I need somebody *right away*. By tomorrow morning."

"On it," Kristin said and picked up the phone.

Chase went into his office dropped into his chair. Where could he get a Korean speaker? Maybe the university. He went online and started checking.

A few minutes later, Kristin stuck her head in the door. "No Korean speakers at the agency," she said. "One of the hotels has a native Korean speaker, but she won't give up her vacation days to translate here for two weeks, not for any money. For your information, this is the first time since I started working for you that just mentioning your name didn't get me what I want."

For a second, she looked so annoyed to be thwarted that Chase had to laugh, despite the discouraging news.

"She's probably a baseball fan," he said.

"*Baseball*," Kristin sniffed. "Who cares about baseball?" She took a deep breath. "Coach, something occurred to me while I was making those calls."

"What's that?" What had occurred to him was that he was spending an awful lot of money wining and dining Swedish investors who might never invest. If he couldn't find a solid translator soon, they'd go away not understanding one thing about his car company.

"Well, Phoebe Renfrew. How did she know that our investors were Korean? Megan told us they looked Asian. But Phoebe said she heard them talking about guns, right? She *heard* them. So either they speak English and they've been lying to us, or she speaks Korean. *She* could translate for us."

Chase's eyes narrowed. *Damn*, she was right. Phoebe Renfrew might be crazy—the CIA, that was a joke—but if she could translate accurately, that was all he needed. And he'd just hope that she was wrong about the guns.

"Is she still here?"

Kristin peered over the mezzanine wall into the lobby. "I don't know. Oh, there's Daryl now." She called down to the burly security guard, and he grinned at them, gazing up at the mezzanine.

"Coach," he said. "You won't believe this. After I took that girl out of the building? She snooped around in their truck!"

"Is she still out there, Daryl?" Chase asked. "Stop her! Don't let her get away!"

Phoebe had hoped to escape the parking lot with her idle threat of a lawsuit, but she hadn't counted on the wholehearted diligence of the security guards. Now she glared up at Chase Bonaventure, who stood in front of her, his broad shoulders blocking the sun.

"Miz Renfrew, I'd like a word with you," he said.

"I can explain everything." She could explain nothing, of course. She was nosy and suspicious, that was it. The sole reason for climbing into the truck.

She'd almost gotten away. But the security guards had barreled out and stopped them from leaving. Then Chase Bonaventure and Kristin came tearing out of the building, yelling their heads off. And now the boss wanted a word with her. No, thank you. She didn't want to hear any words.

"That's what I'm hoping," Chase said. "That you can explain everything."

"Excuse me?"

"I have a proposition for you."

Well, that was a surprise. But whatever kind of proposition he had in mind, she wasn't interested.

"I don't think so," she said. "Anyway, I have to go. I have an appointment."

"You don't know what it is yet."

Too late, she saw that Sanjay had gotten out of the cab and was gazing in rapt wonder at his hero, Chase Bonaventure. She'd have to speak to him about loyalty and the importance of customers who paid the fare.

"Really, Miz Renfrew, I would appreciate a moment of your time," Chase said.

"Phoebe, come inside, okay?" Kristin said. "It's too hot out here. Coach wants to offer you a job."

A job? Phoebe glanced from Kristin to Chase. Chase shrugged.

"How much does Miz Renfrew owe you?" he asked Sanjay, reaching for his wallet. "I'm not sure how long this will take."

"Oh no, you don't!" Phoebe said. "Thanks anyway. Sanjay,

let's go."

"It's a good offer," Chase said.

"Phoebe, please," Kristin said. "Just consider it."

"You should listen to what Mr. Bonaventure has to say," Sanjay said. "I'll wait."

Phoebe shifted her glare to Sanjay. *Football fans.* Why couldn't she have gotten a taxi driver who was a baseball fan?

"Thank you," Chase said, and they all trooped inside.

Once back in the cool lobby, Sanjay took a seat in the visitors waiting area, and Kristin led the way up to the mezzanine. Chase ushered Phoebe into his office.

"Take a seat," he said, waving his hand at the guest chair. "Water?"

"No, thank you," Phoebe said, still annoyed. He'd shanghaied her into coming into the building, and she didn't like it. These rich guys thought they could get away with anything.

Chase opened a small refrigerator behind his desk and took out a pitcher of filtered water. He poured two glasses and put one in front of her. Then he sat down in his own chair, swallowed some of the water, and considered her speculatively.

"I've got a bit of a situation here, you might say."

"Me, too," Phoebe said. "You might say I have to go back to work *right now.* Let me go and nobody has to get hurt."

Chase laughed. She knew what he was thinking: She didn't look dangerous. She bet if she were wearing a suit, he'd think she was dangerous.

"I know, *cher, you*'re a trained operative," he said. "You told me. But I need your help. You do me a favor, and I'll owe you one."

"You'd owe me, as in, you'll help me find the guns that your Koreans have stashed somewhere?"

"Of course. If you can prove to me that the guns exist."

"They exist. Somewhere. Somehow." She didn't know how she was going to find them, however. "What's the favor?"

"You speak Korean, right?"

"Of course. You knew that. I told you." She picked up her water glass and took a long drink.

"You didn't exactly say 'I speak Korean,'" Chase said. "I would have heard that."

"Fine." She set down her empty glass. "You didn't know I speak Korean. What does that have to do with anything?"

"Those two men you saw come into my building—they're part of my Swedish investor group. They have Swedish passports, and they're Swedish citizens, and they speak Korean. All nine of them."

"I know."

"You do? How—Never mind. The point is, my translation setup right now is English to Swedish to Korean, and that's too slow and not accurate enough. I'd like you to translate English to Korean."

She hadn't seen that coming. "What?"

"I want these investors to understand the operation here. I have discussion points prepared. They'll have questions."

Phoebe shook her head. "I'm not a professional translator," she said. "Anyway, how do you know I'd be accurate?"

Chase grinned. "You work for the CIA, right? I bet you got good training. You're a trained operative."

Phoebe rolled her eyes. "I might have exaggerated that 'trained operative' part a little bit. Anyway, you don't believe me about the CIA."

"I believe you speak Korean," he said. "That's enough. I'll pay you anything you want—up to a point—to work for me for two weeks. And I'll explain the situation to your employer. Usually that's worth a few brownie points."

"Really? Why?" She must be missing something.

"Hello? Ex-quarterback for the local NFL team," he said. "Some people would be impressed."

"Oh. Well. I don't follow football, but thank you," Phoebe said. "Of course, it's an attractive offer, but Harry and Babette took a chance by hiring me, and I don't want to let them down. Besides, you're no help. You don't know where the guns are, even if you believed me, which you don't. I'm better off following those guys on my own. Not tied down with a full-time job."

"Wrong. According to you, I've got a couple of gunrunners or whoever they are sitting in my conference room right now. Don't you want to get closer to them? Eavesdrop on the conversations and figure out what they're up to and where the guns are?

Search their truck?"

She felt her face warm at that one.

"I'll call Harry, tell him you need two weeks' vacation," he said. "Is Harry a football fan?"

"Of course not."

"He probably is. I'll talk to him. Give me the number." He took out his phone looked at her expectantly. "Well, *cher*? What's the number? I'm kind of in a hurry here."

This was beyond exasperating. Who did Chase Bonaventure think he was, assuming she'd drop everything to work for him? She wanted to smack him with her clipboard just on principle.

But the Koreans—evidently *Swedish*-Koreans—would be coming to his conference room *every day*. The very people she wanted to follow. They'd recognize her, of course. They might clam up. Or try to run. But if she could find out more—this opportunity could validate her decision about the Empire State Building. And get her back at her job at the CIA.

She had to do it. Didn't mean she had to like his tactics.

"How much?" she asked.

"How much what?"

"How much will you pay me?"

"Name your price."

How much should she ask for? She had to ask for a huge amount so he'd take her seriously. And understand that she knew she was worth it. How much was that? She might as well start scandalously high.

"Twenty thousand dollars."

He raised his eyebrows. "You better be good, *cher*. Done."

Holy cow! She never thought he'd pay her that much. He agreed so fast, maybe she should have asked for more.

"I'm good. I work for the CIA, remember? Although translating the parts of a car in Korean might be tricky. I'm not sure I could translate, um, carburetor, for example."

"First thing: gas doesn't go in these cars, so you won't have to know the word for carburetor. Next thing: right now our translation setup has more kinks than a rattlesnake wrapped around a corkscrew, so you're already way ahead in the game. Can I call Harry, give him the bad news?"

She dug out her phone. "I'll call him. If you're as famous as you say, he won't pick up if he sees your name on the display. He'll think it's a prank."

She tapped her phone screen. "Harry, hi, it's me, Phoebe," she said. "Listen, I know this sounds crazy, but I swear it's true. I'm sitting here with Chase Bonaventure. You know who he is?"

"Greatest quarterback that ever lived," Harry said. "Played for the Las Vegas Rattlesnakes for ten years. Won six division titles and three Super Bowl titles. You should have seen that playoff game with the Steelers!"

"Yeah, that's what Sanjay said."

"Who's Sanjay now?"

"My taxi driver. It's a long story. He—Chase Bonaventure—wants to hire me for two weeks starting tomorrow morning, and he'll do you a favor if you give me the time off."

"Let me speak to him," Harry said.

"Okay." She held out the phone to Chase. "Harry wants to talk to you."

"I don't want to do him a favor," Chase said, not taking the phone.

"*Shh*. You'll hurt his feelings." Phoebe stabbed the phone at him and he took it from her.

"Harry, this is Chase Bonaventure," he said. "I'm putting you on speaker."

"Damn, I thought it was somebody pulling her leg, but you sound just like that guy who always did the press conferences after the games," Harry said. "You got that Louisiana twang."

"Not pulling her leg," Chase said. "I'm really that guy."

"I'm a huge fan," Harry said. "Listen, I can't chat now. I'm in rehearsal. But if you want to borrow Phoebe for a while, that's fine. Phoebe, call Babette and explain."

"I appreciate it, Harry," Chase said.

"Anything for you and the team. I gotta tell you, I'm worried about next season. I don't know about this new guy they got trying out for your spot—he looks like all spit and no polish."

"The coaches and players are working hard," Chase said. "I feel good about our chances."

"I hope you're right. All right, gotta go."

"What does Harry do?" Chase said as he handed Phoebe her

phone. "He said he had a rehearsal."

"He's an Elvis impersonator." Phoebe stuck the phone back in her bag. Harry sure gave in easy. Just throw a retired professional football player at the guy and he caved. For all Harry knew, he'd been talking to an actor pretending to be Chase. A Chase Bonaventure impersonator.

"No kidding. I've never met an Elvis impersonator."

"Harry's part of an act called the Las Vegas All-Elvis Revue. They get work at conferences and conventions, stuff like that. Even movies. They have a big gig coming up. And the wedding chapel has an Elvis theme."

"So the poodle skirt is part of the image."

"Right." Phoebe nodded, smoothing her skirt down over her knees.

"At least working for me you won't have to stand outside in the hot sun all day. Kristin! Do you have that employment contract ready?"

"Right here," she said, bringing it in. "Just sign here, Phoebe."

Phoebe read the one-page document. She didn't see anything tricky, so she signed. Chase took it from her and countersigned.

"That's it," he said. "Glad to have you on board."

"Let me ask you," she said as they headed down the stairs. "Is everybody you invited here really an investor? I mean, did you do background checks? Are you *sure*?"

"*Cher.*" Chase stopped in the middle of the lobby and frowned at her. "These people belong to a Swedish business association that goes back forty years. Midnight Sun has a lot of money to invest. I need that money, so I need you to translate, not go tearing off on some weird conspiracy theory. Forget this guns and CIA thing. Nobody here is a gunrunner or a terrorist or whatever you think they are."

Phoebe narrowed her eyes. "I *said* I'd translate. But if your investors are doing something illegal, I'll find out. And I can't overlook a national security threat, no matter what. If I find something, I'll have them arrested. Just so we're clear."

"We're clear," he said. "But if you do one crazy thing that ruins this deal, you'll be sorry. And you better be clear on that, too."

Chapter 3

Sanjay handed Phoebe a business card when he dropped her off at the county building to pick up her bike.

"Call me if you ever again need any driving of a stealthy nature," he said.

"You'd make a terrific spy, Sanjay." Phoebe dug out some bills—she had enough to pay the fare if she ate peanut butter again all week—and handed them to him. "Keep the change."

"Too much." He handed back one of the bills. "Call anytime."

The marriage license bureau was open almost every day until midnight for the tourists, the deranged, or the alcohol-influenced who wanted to marry on impulse, so the other wedding chapel reps were still pursuing prospects. But as of thirty minutes ago, she didn't have to join them again for the next two weeks. And right now, all she wanted to do was go back to her mom's place, take a bath, and think about the Koreans, the guns, and Venture Automotive.

Waving to the other reps, Phoebe unlocked her bike and, fighting heavy rush-hour traffic, pedaled to her mother's cramped apartment. She'd arrived Saturday night when her mother, Brenda, a cocktail waitress, was already at work, and on Sunday while Brenda slept in, Phoebe went out to hunt for a job, so she and her mom hadn't even seen each other yet. As a roommate situation, except for sleeping on the lumpy couch, it could be a lot worse.

"Mom?" Phoebe called. She pushed her bike into the living room and leaned it against the wall.

"Hi, sweetie!" Brenda poked her head out of the bathroom, mascara wand in hand. "I'll be right out! Help yourself to whatever's in the fridge! *Mi casa es su casa.*" She ducked back into the bathroom.

Phoebe squeezed around the ironing board that Brenda had left blocking the galley kitchen and opened the refrigerator. There was food, if you were willing to call an opened jar of pickles, several fast-food packets of mayonnaise, and a jar of instant coffee "food." She closed the door again.

Phoebe heard Brenda tossing her bedroom, looking for something to wear. That could take a while, so Phoebe took off her poodle skirt, ironed it, and hung it up over the living room curtain rod, which now functioned as her closet. She had just changed into shorts and a T-shirt when Brenda emerged from the bedroom, sticking an earring into her ear and adjusting the backing. She came straight over to Phoebe and gave her a hug.

"It's good to see you!" she said. She leaned back and scrutinized her face. "How are you? Before I go to work"—she checked her watch—"give me the quick version. How did you lose your job? Did you have an affair with your boss? I told you to be careful about that."

"No!" Phoebe pulled back and flopped on the couch. "There was no affair. The CIA thinks I made a mistake, that's all. Except I didn't."

Brenda sat down next to her. "You got fired for one mistake? Must have been some mistake."

"The *CIA* thinks I made a mistake. I don't agree. Do you watch TV, Mom? See the story about the Empire State Building?"

"Don't change the subject."

"I'm not changing the subject."

Phoebe watched as understanding dawned in her mother's face. Brenda hadn't had a good education, but she wasn't stupid.

"Omigod," Brenda said. "You had something to do with the thing at the Empire State Building? It's been on the TV news for *days*! That terrorist attack? They were going to kidnap the president! *You* were involved with that?"

Phoebe closed her eyes, remembering the horror of discovering the plot. The thrill when her boss supported her analysis. Then the shock—and relieved surprise—when it didn't happen. And the shame when all fingers pointed to her.

"That was *awesome!*" Brenda said. "Talk about *amazing!* The SEALs who roped down from the helicopters to the observation deck? I bet *that* took some practice! How tall is the Empire State Building anyway? And the SWAT teams everywhere! And the tanks, or whatever they were, streets closed. And the drones! Did you see the drones? And then it was all a colossal screwup. Nothing happened! Our tax dollars at work, that's what I said to Rudy at the bar. That was *you?*"

"We're not sure that they were after the president," Phoebe said. "We think it was the secretary of state. But otherwise, yeah, that was me, pretty much."

"*You* made it happen? *My* kid?" Brenda said, pride in her voice. "So what are the SEALs really like? Did you order them around? Did you go out with any of them? Having an affair with a SEAL would be a lot better than having an affair with your boss. Those guys are *fantastic.*"

"Mom. I didn't go out with any SEALs. They're—"

"I can't believe that *my kid* can order SEALs around! Could you get them to rope down to where I work? That would be so cool. Wait until I tell Rudy."

"Mom! Don't tell Rudy anything! I don't give the SEALs orders. That's the Navy's job. My job is different. I work for the CIA. I told you that. And… something went sideways. Like I said."

"Well, except for not catching any bad guys, it looked incredible on TV," Brenda said. "Better than any movie. But yeah. I can see how SEALs roping down from helicopters onto the observation deck of the Empire State Building to protect the president when there's no terrorist threat could be considered a screwup at the CIA. What with the tourists and everything."

Phoebe swallowed. When her analysis had predicted an imminent threat at the Empire State Building, the military and law enforcement had gotten involved in a big way. SEALs, SWAT, the National Guard, police, artillery, tanks, helicopters, robots—you name it, they'd been there. Not to mention the press.

But then nothing happened. The Empire State Building

didn't blow up—it had been *crickets* over there—but instead of being happy about it, her boss, Greg Peeling, had blown a gasket. Well, the press was there. They'd had a field day. Some news outlets were *still* having a field day.

"Yeah, probably the secretary of state, not the president. Anyway, that's the story in a nutshell. So for now—"

"*Not* the president? Oh, well," Brenda said, sounding philosophical. "Anyway, don't worry about a thing. The couch is yours for as long as you need it."

"I hope it won't be for too long," Phoebe said. "A couple of months at the most, I think. And in the meantime, I'll figure everything out." *Because the danger was still out there.*

"Of course you will, sweetie," Brenda said, patting her hand. She glanced at her watch. "Listen—"

"You'll be late to work. Can I go to the store for you? Got a list?"

"Get anything you want." She lowered her voice. "And don't wait up for me. I'm going out later. I've been seeing this rancher. Bud Corvallis. I think he might be ready to pop the question."

No, he isn't. Not that Phoebe would say so out loud. Her mom was an eternal optimist, convinced that every man who bought her a drink or flirted with her across the bar was the man of her dreams, the one who'd love and cherish her forever. And so far, all that had happened in more than thirty years of dating was that Brenda galloped off with her latest heartthrob, hoping for the best, and then came home months later when the glow wore off.

Brenda was still looking for eternal bliss, and Phoebe sort of admired her persistence and faith in the likelihood of finding it. She herself didn't think True Love existed, but who was she to burst her mom's bubble? The fact that it hadn't burst years ago from all the wear and tear was a miracle right there.

"If this Bud Corvallis is the right guy, I'm happy for you," Phoebe said.

"He's a keeper!" Brenda said. "You'll see! Wish me luck!"

The kind of luck that Phoebe wished for her mom probably didn't come with guys like Bud Corvallis, not that Phoebe had ever met the guy. But she knew Brenda and what kinds of guys she went for.

"I'll be rooting for you," she said, her best compromise. "Have fun tonight."

"You take care, sweetie," Brenda said as she flew out the door. "Don't do anything I wouldn't do!"

As if. The only things she did were exactly the things her mother *didn't.*

The next morning when the investors arrived at the factory, Lars was startled to discover that their new translator was the woman who'd confronted them the day before in the courthouse parking lot. It seemed awfully coincidental. But it also seemed like the least of their problems.

He wished he hadn't come along on this trip. He was terrified of what would happen. His father, Sven, planned to kidnap the American secretary of state and hold her captive until she agreed to negotiate the release of Sven's father, who was imprisoned in North Korea. They had aborted their first kidnapping attempt in New York at the Empire State Building when they saw a huge police presence there, so Sven and Gustav, Lars's older brother, planned to strike here in Las Vegas while the secretary was speaking at some conference.

They'd been lucky to escape the first time. Lars didn't think they'd be lucky twice.

Lars wasn't unsympathetic about his father's desperate ploy to get Grandfather Ji-hoon released. Grandfather Ji-hoon had sacrificed everything—his job, his family, and his freedom—to smuggle Sven and Gustav out of the North and into Sweden, and Sven was determined to return the favor.

But kidnapping was not the way to do it. Diplomatic channels, absolutely. Back channels, of course. Media channels, certainly. But kidnapping the secretary at gunpoint—that would not end well. The Americans didn't even talk to North Korea. So how could the secretary help?

Gustav was fiddling with his phone—probably uploading more crap to those jihadist websites he favored. How much of all that stuff did Gustav really believe? Maybe all of it—he had lived in North Korea until he was about ten. Lars himself was the product of Sven's short-lived second marriage to a Swedish woman. She'd died when Lars was two, and Lars didn't know her people. But he was sure that something from her must have rubbed off on him.

Gustav put away his phone and came over to join him at the midmorning coffee service. Lars enjoyed the Western-style pastries Chase Bonaventure had brought in for the break. They were similar to the Swedish-style treats he loved so much. The older members of the delegation didn't care for them, but that just left more for him.

"That translator was planted here for a reason," Gustav said, glancing around. Talking about her was complicated, because she could understand everything they said. Lars thought that was pretty funny. "She's a spy. She's working against us somehow."

"How do you know that?" Lars inspected a raisin twist dusted with cinnamon sugar. It looked good.

"How else can you explain her presence at the courthouse when we went to secure gun permits, and again out here at the manufacturing plant? She's following us. Watching us."

"She's probably not a spy." Lars picked up the raisin twist and bit into it. The sweetness of the raisins swept across his tongue, and the buttery pastry melted in his mouth. He closed his eyes to savor the rush of flavor.

"Your dedication to the mission is weak!"

Lars sighed and opened his eyes. "I want Grandfather Jihoon released, too," he said around the raisin twist. "But kidnapping the American secretary won't work. You saw what happened in New York. If we try something again, we'll go to prison forever. We might even be killed! If Phoebe's presence changes Father's mind, I'm all for it." He put the raisin twist down on a napkin and poured himself a cup of coffee from the carafe. The coffee was good here, too.

Gustav clenched his jaw. "I'm telling you, she's a spy! She threatened to call the cops on us! That's what you said!"

Lars took a careful sip of the hot brew. "Yeah, I *think* that's what she said. Something about police, anyway. But she didn't call. Or at least, no cops came. Anyway, she doesn't know anything about your plans. How could she?"

Gustav nodded, considering. "Perhaps you're right," he said. "But I'm worried. Father has so many hopes, and if this plan fails, everything fails."

"I sympathize with how he feels. But it would be better if we asked—"

"We will not *ask* the Americans to help," Gustav said. "We will *demand* they get Grandfather out. We must act soon! Before any more time elapses! And that's why we will get the guns tonight!"

Phoebe could tell she'd startled Lars and Gustav when she went to get a cup of coffee and heard Gustav say they'd get the guns that night. She was dismayed by it, but she felt some satisfaction that she'd been right, after all. The Eklunds *were* gunrunners. They just hadn't bought the guns yet.

She didn't know how to ask people if they were terrorists and get an honest answer. But she had to say *something*. She took a deep breath.

"Guys. You remember me from the county building, right?"

They nodded, glancing at each other.

"Why do you need to get guns tonight?"

The Eklunds shuffled their feet and looked away.

"You said you wanted gun permits, but I know you're not hunters. I mean, you're *here*. You're not hunting."

Lars glanced at Gustav. "My girlfriend, Helga—she thinks America is a war zone," he said. "Guns on every street corner. She is afraid for our personal safety. I assured her that we would acquire protective handguns while we were here."

That idea seemed extreme but not out of the realm of possibility, especially if you lived abroad. If you lived in Sweden, you might think that America was a war zone. And it would be a huge relief if personal security was the only reason they wanted to buy guns.

"You have to be local residents to buy a gun legally," Phoebe said. "You won't try to buy guns illegally, will you? That might be dangerous. And if the police get involved, they might detain you, and that would complicate everything—your visit here, these investor meetings, possibly your ability to return to the States."

"Don't worry," Gustav said. "We were just trying to make Helga happy."

Phoebe narrowed her gaze. Gustav did not strike her as the kind of guy who lived to make his brother's girlfriend happy.

"Let me show you a photo of her!" Lars put down his coffee cup and took out his phone, tapping the photos into view. He scrolled through them quickly.

"Here she is," Lars said, beaming, handing Phoebe the phone. "She's the bookkeeper at our father's factory. Helga."

The blonde in the photo was stunning. But even more stunning were the photos of the Empire State Building Phoebe had caught a glimpse of.

"Helga is very attractive," Phoebe said. "You're a lucky guy. And I see you've been to New York." How did you ask people if they'd threatened that iconic building? "You went to the Empire State Building. When was that?"

"Before we came here," Lars said. "Check it out."

Phoebe swiped through the photos, looking for time stamps. She didn't see any, but the photos weren't exactly tourist shots—all the images captured the building's entrances and exits, security guards, elevators, doorways, and not much else. Not even the one iconic shot focusing straight up the tower.

"Did you see the police invasion there?" Phoebe asked. "That happened about two weeks ago."

"We heard about it," Lars said, glancing at Gustav.

"Only a little." Gustav glared at Lars. "It was all but over by the time we got there."

"Really?" Phoebe said. "You know, some people thought the threat came from North Koreans."

"Ridiculous," Gustav said.

"You didn't read anything about that in the Korean-language press?"

"No."

"Because you'd think those guys would be all over something like that." Phoebe knew for a fact that the Korean-language press had been all over it, because she'd read it there herself.

"We don't read the Korean-language press," Gustav said.

"Really," she said again. She didn't believe him for one English-speaking Swedish second. "Interesting photos you've got. You didn't go up into the observation tower?"

"We did, but I forgot to take photos." Lars took the phone back from her.

"Did you guys come in advance of the rest of the group? Or did you all go to New York together?"

"We wanted a vacation before we came out here."

Phoebe had run out of things to ask that weren't *Did you threaten the secretary of state at the Empire State Building*, and she knew Chase would want her to let this go. The coffee break was over anyway, and having pictures of the skyscraper—even pictures of all the doors and exits—wasn't evidence of a crime.

"Las Vegas doesn't have as much architectural interest as New York," she said. "But then, Las Vegas doesn't have as many terrorist threats, either."

And she was determined to keep it that way.

Kristin brought in lunch for everybody, and while Phoebe munched a ham and swiss on whole wheat—so much better than peanut butter—she thought about what the Eklunds had said. *We will get the guns tonight.* They couldn't buy them legally. So where could the brothers get guns without a permit?

A shady pawnshop maybe. An unscrupulous gun dealer. A military base was nearby. Had a rogue recruit offered to sell them military-grade weapons? Their story about personal security was marginally believable, and if so, fine, even if the purchase itself was illegal. She wouldn't ruin Chase's investment meetings over their personal reason. But if Lars and Gustav wanted to fill up that truck with high-grade weaponry, they'd have enough guns to take over a small country.

How could she stop it if that was their plan? She couldn't follow them on her bike.

Then she had an idea. It wasn't perfect, but it was *something*. She left the conference room and dashed down to the lobby and the receptionist's desk.

"Megan, do you have any tape—duct tape or something

heavy like that—that I could use for a second?"

"Sure." Megan rummaged around in her supply drawer and came up with a heavy roll of gray duct tape. "Will this do?"

"Perfect. Thanks. I'll bring it right back."

Phoebe flew out the front door and slipped to the side of the building, out of range of the security cameras. She pulled her plastic water bottle from her messenger bag and poured the water over the landscaping. Then she jerked out a length of the rubber aboveground irrigation tubing that kept the small plants alive.

The next part was trickier. The security cameras would catch her crossing the parking lot to get to Lars and Gustav's truck. Once she got there, though, the truck itself would block her from view.

She dashed to the truck and crouched down. Then she jammed one end of the irrigation tubing into the neck of the empty water bottle. She peeled off a strip of Megan's duct tape and taped the opening of the bottle to make it airtight and leak proof. Squeezing the empty bottle to force out the air, she shoved the other end of the tubing down into the gas tank and released the pressure on the bottle. Gas surged up the tubing and into the clear plastic bottle. She ripped off the tape and pulled the tubing out of the bottle, and the gas poured out of the tubing onto the parking lot.

Lars and Gustav wouldn't be driving anywhere tonight. Not on an empty gas tank, they wouldn't.

Sorry, Sierra Club, she thought as she watched the gas gush away on the concrete. She vowed to donate part of her check to a groundwater group.

By the time Lars and Gustav came out and discovered their truck wouldn't start, the gas would have evaporated, although there'd be a stain on the cement. They'd never know how they ran out of fuel.

In a couple of minutes, the flow of gas stopped. Phoebe pulled the tubing out of the gas tank and screwed the truck's gas cap back on. Now all she had to do was reinstall the irrigation tubing and toss the water bottle.

She was forcing the irrigation tubing back together, out of

sight of the security cameras, when Chase strode around the side of the building.

"What the *hell* are you doing?"

Phoebe's heart sank. *Busted.*

"Ah. Well—"

"Anytime now! Since I'm paying you to translate for my investors, not vandalize their vehicles."

Crap.

"Okay, here's the deal," Phoebe said. The irrigation tubing finally went together, and she stood up, brushing off her hands. "I don't want Gustav and Lars driving around in their own vehicle. I know you don't believe me, but they're up to something bad. Just now during the break they said they were going to buy guns tonight."

"*What?*"

"I have to prevent that. I want them out of their truck so they can't easily do whatever evil thing they have planned. I want them to have to stick with the crowd and come and go in that minibus you drive everybody else around in. So, I, ah—"

"Drained their gas tank."

Phoebe winced. "Yes, I know. Bad for the environment. And I took apart that bit of irrigation, but I think I got it back together okay."

"I can't believe this," Chase said, shaking his head. "What do I have to say to get through to you? If you think the Eklunds are breaking the law, *call the cops*. Otherwise, stick to your job and leave them *alone*."

"I *will* call the cops," Phoebe said, "just as soon as I have enough evidence." She stomped back into the lobby, riled up now, too. She wanted to stop the terrorists *and* keep this job. If only Chase could see that.

"Thanks for your help," she said, returning the duct tape to Megan.

"No problem." Megan smiled and dropped the tape into her bottom door. "It's here whenever you need it."

Phoebe grinned. Chase would probably come through in two minutes and tell Megan never to lend her another thing ever again.

Draining the Eklunds' gas tank wasn't a permanent solution, but at least Lars and Gustav couldn't drive anywhere tonight. She'd have to think of a way she could ruin their transportation alternatives altogether.

Chapter 4

By the end of the day, Chase was a lot calmer about Phoebe's stunt. He didn't approve of her tactics or her reasoning, but he had to admit that he also preferred that Gustav and Lars travel with the main group. He was responsible for the investors—their comfort and safety—and he didn't like two of them splintering off. If the brothers were forced to travel with the main group in the minivan, so much the better.

Today had been their first full day with the investors. It would be a good idea if he and Phoebe reviewed the time, maybe discuss what was coming in the days ahead and what they should accomplish. And while he was at it, maybe he could talk her out of those harebrained ideas she had.

The conference room had emptied, and she was gathering her things when he opened the door and checked inside.

"So, *cher*, you want to catch some dinner and talk about how things went today?"

"Talk?" Phoebe sounded wary, as well she might, since he'd yelled at her at lunchtime. But she didn't look like a nut job right now. She looked tired. Well, she'd worked hard all day.

"Yeah, about the investor discussions," he said. "I'd like to get your take on their reactions. And then we can decide what needs to get done, what's important, make a schedule. Think ahead. Strategize. You know—a chalk talk."

Phoebe looked blank. "Chalk talk?"

Now that the investors had taken off, she seemed to have run out of words. Or maybe she didn't know what a chalk talk was. In any language.

"There's a place a couple blocks from here," he said. "A diner. Nothing fancy, but the food's good. You must be hungry. And then I'll give you a ride home later. I know you're tired, but a person has to eat. And this might be the only time we get a chance to plan things out."

She nodded. "Okay," she said. "Sounds good."

When they got outside, Phoebe took a deep breath of the dry desert air, lightly scented by a mix of creosote, yucca, and diesel fumes. She stretched, standing on her toes, reaching for the sky, and then stretched down, putting her hands flat on the concrete sidewalk, and held that pose for an impossibly long time. Chase watched her fold herself in two, her shoulders straining against the stretch, her poodle skirt riding up, nearly baring all. He glanced away. *Employee*, his brain scolded. *You're an idiot*, every other part of him scoffed.

"It feels good to get outside," she said, finally standing up straight again and pushing her hair back behind her ears. "It's a long day indoors. No offense."

"None taken," Chase said, his mouth dry. Thank God she'd finally stood up. *Focus on her eyes.* Yeah, that was it. Not the butt and the skirt. The *eyes.* "Diner's this way."

The diner was small, and the parking lot was crowded. When he opened the door, a wave of tantalizing smells hit his nose with the force of a Category 5 hurricane. Everything he ate here reminded him of home.

"Mmmm, something smells wonderful," Phoebe said, entering the diner. "What's the special tonight?"

"Fried chicken." Darla, his favorite waitress, squeezed by with a tray loaded with steaming plates. She pointed them to a booth on the far wall where a busboy was wiping down the remains from the last diners. "Hey, Chase. Take that seat over there. I'll bring menus."

"I don't need a menu," Phoebe said. "I'm having the fried chicken."

"Hi, Darla," Chase said. "Make it two."

Darla nodded. "I'll place your orders."

He settled into the familiar booth and watched Phoebe while

she gazed around at the busy counter, the old movie posters, the blackboard advertising the specials.

"This place would fit right into my old Brooklyn neighborhood," she said after she turned back to him. "Sort of an old-fashioned type of diner. I like it."

"Old-fashioned diners must be universal," Chase said. "It reminds me of my favorite diner in Louisiana."

Darla brought out two huge plates of fried chicken. Phoebe sat up in anticipation, picking up her cutlery with enthusiasm. *She likes to eat*, he noted.

That was a change. All the women he dated—and most of the women he'd worked with—were expensively groomed, well dressed, and polished. They ate sparingly, in small bites, of low-calorie foods. They were aware of him at all times. Phoebe, on the other hand, was oblivious of anything right now but her meal.

"That looks delicious," she said, eying the food as Darla put the plates down. "And you brought it really quickly. Thank you."

"Chase Bonaventure is our special customer," Darla said, smiling. "What can I get you folks to drink?"

"Soft drink for me," Phoebe said. "Any brown cola is fine."

He ordered iced tea for himself, and the waitress hustled off to get the drinks.

Phoebe picked up a chicken leg and bit into it with all the gusto of a gator at an all-you-can-eat riverboat buffet.

"This is fantastic," she said, her mouth full. "You have no idea how hungry I am."

Phoebe closed her eyes as she chewed, trying not to moan. The chicken was beyond delicious. It was sweet and steaming hot, tender inside but coated with something crispy and spicy, and fried to juicy perfection. Phoebe had never in her life eaten chicken this good. She was conscious—barely—that Chase was pouring gravy on his mashed potatoes, but she couldn't talk while this chicken was here, waiting for her to devour it. *Eat me*, it begged. And she was happy to oblige.

"Tell me about this CIA thing, *cher*," he said.

Wasn't that annoying. He didn't believe her about the CIA. Why should she bother to explain? Besides, the drumstick demanded her full attention. She swallowed the last bite of her chicken leg, dropped the bone back onto her plate, and licked her fingers.

"The cook knows her way around a chicken," she said. "Why do you want to know about the CIA?"

"Make me a believer."

Phoebe sighed, trying to decide between the breast and the thigh. "You could just believe me. That would be simpler."

Chase smiled. "Satisfy my curiosity then, all right?"

Phoebe shrugged. He'd promised her a ride home. He was feeding her. And maybe she could convince him the Eklunds really did want to buy guns.

"What do you want to know?" she asked, picking up a thigh.

"All of it."

"I'm not letting my chicken get cold just because you're curious," she said, biting into the thigh.

"Understood."

Phoebe chewed and swallowed. "It started because I wanted to go to college." She reached for a biscuit. They looked good, too.

Chase smiled at her as he bit into his chicken. "The American dream."

Phoebe nodded, spreading a pat of butter on the hot biscuit. Chase was really handsome when he smiled. He should quit doing that.

"Mom didn't earn enough to pay for college, even if she thought that college is important, which she doesn't," she said. "And I didn't want to come out of university with a ton of debt. I looked around. The CIA has a loan program that pays for school and training if you work for them afterward. They want the languages I speak. I'd get a free ride plus living expenses if I kept my grades up. So I signed up."

Chase halted, his fork midair. "How many languages do you speak?"

Phoebe tore a piece of thigh meat off the bone, sandwiched it between biscuit halves, and took a bite. It was every bit as good as she'd thought it would be. The cook clearly knew her way around biscuit dough, too.

"Seven fluently," she said, her voice thick as she chewed.

"Korean, Arabic, Hindi, Spanish, Russian, Polish, and Mandarin. Some Hebrew. And English, of course. So I guess, eight and a half altogether."

"Are you *kidding* me? Nine languages? That's—how did you learn nine languages?"

Phoebe took a sip of her soft drink.

"We lived in Brooklyn. Every time Brenda got a new boyfriend and ran off with him for a while, she farmed me out with the neighbors. Our building had a lot of immigrant families. They spoke their language at home. Whatever it was, I learned it."

Chase speared some of the glazed carrots on his fork.

"So you went to college on the CIA's dime and now you have to work for them? For how long?"

"I don't *have* to work for them—I *want* to work for them. But my term is six years, four months. If I don't work for them that long, I have to pay them back for my education. That's about three hundred thousand dollars."

Chase put his fork down. "Three hundred *thousand*?" He whistled.

When he said it like that, it might as well be three hundred *million*. It was a fortune—more than she could ever repay. But she didn't want to repay it. She wanted to work it off. Six years and four months. And then she could do whatever she wanted after that, but she was pretty sure she wanted to stay at the CIA.

And in the meantime, she wanted to eat the mashed potatoes while they were still warm.

"I went to NYU," she said putting more butter on her potatoes. "Do you have any idea what that costs? And then after graduation, the agency sent me to language training. That's terribly expensive."

"So what happened? Why did they fire you?"

It always came back to that.

"I'm not fired. I'm *suspended*. But okay. I'm a language analyst. I thought there was a terrorist plan about to unfold in New York. I wrote a memo. Nobody said I was wrong. Everybody was all, great going, Phoebe. Good analysis, Phoebe." She took a long swallow of her soft drink.

"Wait—New York? Don't tell me."

She licked some mashed potatoes off her fork, trying to taste them, trying not to feel angry and defensive all over again. "Yeah. You got it."

Chase grinned. "The Empire State Building? SEALs rappelling down to the observation deck? SWAT in the buildings, soldiers at the corners, tanks in the street? All that? That boondoggle was *your* doing?"

Phoebe stabbed her fork into the carrots. "Now you sound like Brenda."

Chase put his head back and laughed.

It would be *so easy* to stab the fork into his chest. "It isn't funny!"

"*Cher*, it is. I'm sorry you lost your job, but no wonder they fired your ass. That's straight out of a movie. Jean-Claude Van Damme. Or maybe the Three Stooges. I'm not sure which."

"Still not funny. And I'm not *fired*."

"So there was a bloodbath at the CIA? The ranks were purged?"

"Just me. I took the fall."

"Shit runs downhill?"

Phoebe shrugged, feeling her stomach ache with the loss. "I guess."

Chase polished off the last of his chicken. "So why Happy Memories Wedding Chapel? I would think a person who speaks eight languages plus English would have a lot of job options."

"She does, theoretically. Tourism, insurance, international trade, banking, even law enforcement—probably lots of stuff. But the CIA would say I'd quit if I took full-time work that used my language skills, and then they'd stop their investigation of my actions at the Empire State Building. I wouldn't get my job back, and I'd never get cleared. I'd never get a security clearance again. And then the clock would start ticking on that loan, too. I'd owe them all the money for school, principal plus interest. I'd never get out from under that debt. And another thing—"

She took a deep breath. "I *want* that job. I worked hard to get it, ever since high school. I planned and studied like crazy, took all the advanced courses and got good grades. I never really thought about doing anything else. Brenda works hard and earns every penny she brings home, and she—okay, inadvertently—gave me the language tools for the CIA, which is beyond great. But I don't want to be a cocktail waitress. I want a *career*, that *CIA* career. I don't know how to do anything else."

Chase pushed his empty plate to the side and leaned back in the booth. "You think they'll ever take you back?"

"I sure hope so. They've invested a lot in me, plus, it—everything—wasn't totally my fault."

"How was a massive boondoggle at the Empire State Building not totally your fault?"

Phoebe scowled. "I followed all the procedures. And I'd been there only two months. All the senior people on the Korea desk were away somewhere—nobody would say where."

"An undisclosed location?"

Phoebe snorted. "I'd bet my life they were all in Korea, in those negotiations the North and South were having a couple of weeks ago that came to nothing. But nobody would tell me."

"But those negotiations were in the news!"

Phoebe shrugged. "Leave it to the CIA to deny and confuse. Anyway, I'm not abdicating responsibility. I read the material, I formed the conclusion, I wrote the report, I pushed for action. And all the bosses who were in the loop backed me up. But those people weren't Korea specialists. So—I don't know what happened. But I still think my analysis is correct. I think something's in the works."

She closed her eyes for a second, reliving those moments when she'd inadvertently and dramatically sent her career off the rails.

"Anyway, if the investigation finds that I acted 'competently,' whatever that means, they'll lift the suspension and I'll go back to work."

"And if not? If they fire you? What about the three hundred thousand then?"

"Yeah, still owe them."

Chase shook his head. "*Cher*, you got you some bad juju. So… why are you here in Las Vegas? Not that I'm not damn happy to have you translating, the way things turned out."

Phoebe shrugged. "CIA language analysts don't earn that

much, you'll be shocked to learn, and I'm fresh out of school. I don't have any savings. I couldn't afford DC while the CIA investigated, which could take months. Brenda had followed her last boyfriend out here and said I could sleep on her couch. I put the ticket on my credit card, and here I am."

"Huh." Chase fiddled with his fork. "That working out for you?"

"So far. It won't be for long, anyway. I *hope*. I'm worried about reinstatement, of course. The CIA is nothing if not capricious. And I don't know what they're focusing on or what they're thinking. So I'm doing all I can to get back."

"That's where my investors come in. *Cher*, don't make another Empire State Building mistake. Don't get so wrapped up in what you're imagining that you go off the rails again. That would be bad for all of us."

Phoebe rolled her eyes. She couldn't even get mad at him, not after he'd brought her to this wonderful diner.

But she'd still do everything she could to investigate what the Eklunds were up to. It was something—she felt it in her bones.

They left the diner, Phoebe bouncing down the steps. Chase had to grin. Funny how delicious fried chicken could improve a person's outlook.

"That place is my new favorite restaurant," she said. "Thank you for treating me."

Her high spirits were infectious, and now that she'd eaten, she had a little spring in her step, a little swing in her hips. A very *nice* swing in her hips. Not that he should be thinking about her hips.

"I'm glad you enjoyed it."

They strolled down the dark street toward the plant. They hadn't talked much about strategies for the investors, but Phoebe would do fine. She could think on her feet. Any problems that came up, they could solve.

"So now, you," Phoebe said. "Why did you take on this car company? Couldn't you get on TV doing sports? Announcing, or whatever? Or modeling underwear like David Beckham?"

Chase laughed. "I'd rather rappel down to the Empire State

54

Building from a helicopter than model underwear. Did you know that David Beckham is afraid of birds? He's got ornithophobia. Fact."

Phoebe halted and planted her hands on her hips, staring up at him. "No way! David *Beckham?*"

He nodded, enjoying her astonishment. "Yup. One time at a barbecue—Well, never mind. Not important."

"You've been to a barbecue with David *Beckham*? What was it like?"

"Do you have a crush on David Beckham? Because remind me not to invite him *and his family* over while you're here." He rolled his eyes.

She grabbed his arm. "You invite *David Beckham* to your *house?*"

"You do have a crush."

She sighed, releasing his arm. "Who wouldn't? Have you seen him in his underwear? He's gorgeous."

"I have not seen David Beckham in his underwear!"

"You should. It's a life-changing event. Even when it's just in a magazine."

"I doubt it," Chase said. "What's the deal with David Beckham? I mean, he's a friend of mine. I like him. But hey. I'm a sports hero, too. What about me?"

Phoebe stared at him with something that resembled pity. It couldn't be *pity*.

"Chase, come on. You played football for, what, ten years? Pretty good career. Fine. David Beckham played *twice* as long. He's an *icon*. His right foot is a *national treasure*. He models *underwear*. Case closed."

Now he'd had a "pretty good" career? This woman could deflate an ego faster than the Patriots could deflate a football.

"Anyway," Phoebe said, walking again, that spring in her step making her skirt swish around her legs. "Why build cars? Don't tell me you were compensating because"—she lowered her voice to a whisper—"your stats didn't measure up." She was grinning again.

"My stats are just fine, thank you. This conversation is very inappropriate."

"I'm sorry," she said, sounding contrite, but he swore her eyes were twinkling. "Did I make you uncomfortable? Comparing your stats to David Beckham's?"

Chase shook his head. "I'm not talking about stats anymore. At all. Moving on. Why did I take over the car business, you ask? Like you, *cher*, I needed a job. When I retired from the Rattlesnakes, nothing related to football opened up. All my job offers were public relations gigs for companies that wanted to capitalize on my name, such as it is. I didn't want to live on the coattails of my football career, where I have *record-breaking* stats, thank you very much."

"I thought we weren't talking about stats."

"We aren't. Anyway, a PR job doesn't interest me. I decided that even if this car business didn't work out, I'd know that I'd given it everything."

"You're prepared to lose the company?"

"Hell, no. I hate losing. Hated it when I was still playing, hate it now. But I won't lose. If Midnight Sun comes through, we'll be turning a profit in two years. Maybe less."

"And if Midnight Sun doesn't come through?"

"They will. Or I'll think of something else. I'm not losing the company." He'd keep his employees working, the factory producing—and show the world that he was more than a hunk of muscle who could throw a football.

He just had to convince Midnight Sun to come along for the ride.

Chapter 5

The next morning, Lars and Gustav, lugging a five-gallon red plastic jug, got out of the minivan with the other investors. As the others filed inside, they hauled the jug over to the disabled white truck in the visitors lot. Gustav unscrewed the gas cap on the truck, opened the jug, thrust the nozzle into the opening, and poured the gas into the truck's tank.

"The translator did this," Gustav said, balancing the jug on his hip as the gas flowed in. "She drained the gas tank. I know she did."

"Why would she do that?" Lars dug out his phone and fiddled with the tiny keyboard. "I wonder why Helga's not answering my emails? And I've texted her a million times."

"She's a pain in the ass, and I'm tired of her snooping around."

"*Helga?*"

"The *translator*," Gustav said. "Pay attention. Everything we do here is to get Grandfather out of the North."

"Not *everything*." Lars shook his head and put his phone back in his pocket. "Father did tell us that he wants us to learn as much as we can about American manufacturing methods. Among start-ups, this company stands alone in terms of maximizing return on investment."

Gustav shrugged. "That is not our mission. Our mission is freeing our grandfather in North Korea and making a home for him with us in Sweden. Tonight we will finally get the guns, and tomorrow we must investigate the hotel where they're holding the conference next weekend. We need to get all the information we can if we are to be successful."

"What if Phoebe follows us?" Lars asked, leaning against the side of the truck.

The last of the gas drained into the tank, and Gustav recapped the jug. "She can't follow us on that damn bicycle."

"She's done okay so far knowing where we'll be. And if she did drain the gas tank like you said, her strategy was brilliant. Last night she completely tied us down." Lars thumped the side of the truck for emphasis.

Gustav stowed the can inside the cab of the truck, and then they headed toward the plant.

"Then we'll have to completely tie *her* down," he said. "I've got an idea."

When Phoebe went outside at the lunch break to get a breath of fresh air, she was unsurprised to find that her bicycle had been stolen, the padlock cut and the bike gone. Gustav and Lars must have taken it when they went out during the morning break. She'd bet any money it was in the back of their truck, but she didn't see how she could ask them about it.

It was an old bike and she'd bought it used, but without it, she wouldn't be able to get to the factory. She tossed the useless padlock in the trash and went inside to find Chase.

"Can I get an advance on my salary?" she said when she'd tracked him down in his office.

He was eating one of the sandwiches that they'd brought in for the investors. It was a roast beef on rye, and it reminded her that she hadn't eaten yet. "That looks good."

"Sure. How much do you need?" He handed her the uneaten half of his sandwich, dusted off his hands, and dug a ledger out of a desk drawer.

"Maybe five hundred?" She bit into the roast beef. Delicious. "Or whatever you think. My bike's been stolen. It's my only transportation."

His hand halted midway through writing the check.

"*Stolen*? Who would come all the way out here to steal a bike?"

"Well, I think Gustav and Lars took it, so they didn't have to go all that far. I wish Daryl had stopped it, though. But they probably didn't look suspicious out there in the parking lot."

"I don't have to tell you that this is what comes of draining a gas tank."

"Right. You didn't have to tell me that."

He sighed, fiddled with the pen.

"What you need is a car," he said. "I'm all for physical fitness, but I need you on the premises, on time, every day for the next week. Totally on top of your game. Anything less won't get Midnight Sun to sign on the dotted line."

"I'm fine with a bike," Phoebe said. "If you'd just finish writing that check."

"We've got cars here," he said. "I'll give you one. A loaner, anyway. I don't know why I didn't think of it sooner."

"Thanks, but that's really not necessary."

"You live way over on the east side. That's too far for you to bike, and the buses don't come out this far."

"I bike that far all the time." She was annoyed now. Why didn't he *listen*? "It's not a big deal."

"I know you can bike that far, *cher*, but my interest is not in how far you can bike but how well you can translate. How well you can impress Midnight Sun."

"If you advance me the money for a new bike, I can get out here on time."

"Here's what we'll do. I'll lend you a car. That would save you a lot of time and aggravation."

"No," Phoebe said. "I can't—"

"It's no problem," he said. "We have some testers sitting around. You can have one right now. They're all bright yellow, but it's good advertising."

"But I can't—"

"It'll be a loaner. Just for when you're working for me."

"I can't drive!"

Chase blinked. "What?"

"I can't drive."

"You can't drive? *Cher*, everybody can drive."

"I can't. I understand the general principles. But I don't have a license."

"You speak eight languages but you can't drive a car? Driving is an important life skill. Why don't you have a license?"

Phoebe shrugged. "Grew up in New York, went to college in New York. People don't drive in the city, so why learn? Went to work in DC."

"People drive in DC."

She sighed. "Yeah, I probably would have learned to drive there. But I was at the CIA only two months before... you know."

Chase shook his head. "I've never met a nondriver. That I know of, anyway."

"It's not like it's a freak show," Phoebe said, rolling her eyes. What was with this guy? What bubble did he live in?

"How could somebody who worked for the CIA not drive? How could somebody who works for *Venture Automotive* not drive?"

"Call Guinness World Records," Phoebe said. "Now, if you'll just fill out that check. So I can get a *bike*."

He signed the check and handed it to her.

"How are you getting to work tomorrow? Since you won't have a bike and you can't drive. And the buses don't come out this far."

"You need that bike by this afternoon, Phoebs?" Kristin asked, joining them in Chase's office. "I can call the bike shops while you guys are working and get one delivered out here."

Phoebe whirled around, surprised and pleased. "You *can*?"

"Sure." Kristin grinned. "You have no idea how every business in town wants to do something for Chase Bonaventure. Or least meet him. But we live to disappoint on that front."

"If you can get a bike delivered this afternoon, that would be awesome. Thank you!"

"Consider it done. Ten-speed, right? Any color you like in particular?"

"Well, blue. If they have it. Then red. Then—"

"*Ladies*. Duty calls. Thank you, Kristin."

Chase stood up and Phoebe followed him, tossing the sandwich wrapper in the trash. This afternoon they were touring the assembly operations. She hoped she was ready.

They picked up the investors in the conference room where they'd been eating lunch, and then they all trooped down the stairs and across the lobby to a frosted-glass double door at the far end. Chase pulled open the doors, and they all filed into the manufacturing side of the building.

"You know this will be my weak spot in translating," she told Chase, adjusting her hard hat. "I won't know all these specific car parts. At least, I don't know them in Korean."

"You'd know them in English?" Chase sounded surprised.

"I'd know them in Arabic. Mr. Alfarsi ran a body shop, and I used to hang out there. I'm pretty good with parts of the car in Arabic."

"Good to know for next time."

They walked over to the first step of the assembly line. Phoebe examined what seemed to be a bent sheet of metal—or maybe it was plastic?—that sat on a conveyor belt. The room was full of robotic arms, but they weren't doing anything.

Chase coughed to get their attention. "This is a formed-floor chassis," he began when they all looked at him.

"Hold it right there," Phoebe said in English. "I don't know what that is in any language. Can't you keep it simple?"

"*Cher*, you have to give it a shot."

"I *am* giving it a shot! But you have to speak English. Not car talk. Or engineering talk. Or whatever talk you were talking." She glared at him. "*Chassis*. I bet Koreans don't even *have* a word for chassis."

"Koreans build Kias and Hyundais—of course they have a word for chassis. Not to mention the Swedes build Saabs and Volvos. *Everybody's* got a word for chassis."

"I wonder if Korean uses the English word for chassis?" She turned to the investors. "Do you know the word *chassis*?" She said it all in Korean except for *chassis*.

They stared at her blankly.

"You were right—they don't use the English word for chassis," she told Chase. "Okay."

She turned back to the group and patted the squarish piece that squatted on the assembly line. "This part is called a *chassis* in English. Can you tell me what the Korean word for it is?"

One of the men did. Then he said, "See that empty space there in the middle? I expect that's where the battery pack goes. See how low it is? That's the interesting part. That will lower the car's center of gravity, making it more stable. Ask Mr. Bonaventure, please, what size battery pack he proposes for his vehicles."

Phoebe beamed at him. These guys were the best. They weren't mad because she didn't know all the Korean terms, and they were asking questions. Chase would love that.

"Please excuse my forgetfulness," she said. "You are Thor Olafsson, correct?"

When the man nodded, she turned to Chase.

"Mr. Olafsson, Thor Olafsson, believes that the battery pack will go here." She patted the middle so Thor would know she was asking the right question. "He wants to know what size battery pack you expect to use."

"A seven-thousand-cell," Chase said, looking surprised and pleased. "We're experimenting with other sizes. Ask him about his experience with that size and what he thinks."

Phoebe translated and the investors all nodded and started talking about battery packs. With Phoebe interpreting, Chase replied and asked questions of his own. Finally the discussion wound down.

"Let's keep moving," Chase said, stepping down the assembly line. "This is the motor. The electric current flows into the stator—a group of copper coils—right here. This creates a rotating magnetic field that spins the rotor inside the stator by repelling a series of electrically conductive bars that run along the rotor's circumference. Tell me if I say too much or not enough."

"Mr. Bonaventure just described how the motor works," Phoebe said in Korean, pointing at it. "You probably know that already." She nodded at Chase. "Next?"

"I know you didn't say everything that I said."

"I translated the gist."

"*Cher*, please translate exactly what I said."

Phoebe turned to the investors. "Mr. Bonaventure wants me to translate exactly what he said about how the motor works, but it's very complicated. So, this piece is the motor, and this is how it works: *vroom, vroom*."

They laughed, and Chase shook his head, rolling his eyes.

"I don't know what you said, but I know it wasn't what *I* said. There is no *vroom, vroom* with electric cars. You can't rev an electric motor. When you step on the accelerator, you go faster. Not noisier."

"My mistake." She cleared her throat, and the investors turned to her. "Vroom, vroom, *vroom*," she whispered.

The group laughed harder. Even Gustav cracked a smile.

Chase stuck his hands in his pockets. "Really? This is how we're explaining my electric cars to them?"

Phoebe said something in Korean. All the investors laughed and nodded.

"What did you just say?"

"I told them no revving. And that one of the advantages of the electric car is that they're very silent, so they're good choices in urban environments as a way to lessen sound pollution as well as air pollution. Sorry about the revving. Now what?"

Chase eyed her suspiciously. "You didn't say that. What you said to me wouldn't make anyone laugh. And they laughed."

Phoebe tried not to grin. "You're right, Coach. I did tell them about the sound pollution. But I also said that you were correcting my Korean. They got a charge out of that."

Chase shook his head, but he was smiling. "I never realized how hair-raising working with translators could be. But you made them laugh. That's good. Smart. The personal connection is huge."

Phoebe felt a little tendril of pleasure unfurl in her chest. "Thank you," she said.

"All right. Next on the assembly line here. This is the motor controller."

"Keep it simple, Coach," Phoebe said, but she was smiling.

"Vroom, vroom," Chase said.

The investors laughed again, and Thor nudged another investor in the ribs. They had a sense of humor, Phoebe was happy to see.

By the end of the afternoon, her head was reeling with new vocabulary, substitute vocabulary, and made-up vocabulary. But she was pretty sure the investors were enthusiastic. They'd seemed to enjoy the tour, and she was having fun, too.

"Very interesting presentation," Thor said as they prepared to leave for the evening. "Will we be able to test-drive one of the models?"

Phoebe asked Chase. "I have an idea," she added. "We could have a race! Against gas-powered cars! We could make it a publicity stunt. Get newspapers here, or car magazines. Go big!"

"That's not a bad idea." Chase turned to Tony Minaya, his head software engineer, who'd been with them most of the day. "Tony, we've got nine investors. Can we build nine or ten cars in ten days?"

"It'd be faster if we had all the robots working instead of standing around like headstones at a software cemetery," Tony said. "But even without the robots, we can make ten cars."

Phoebe turned back to the Midnight Sun investor.

"You'll test-drive a model, yes," she said. "And we have a surprise for you at the end of next week. I can't tell you much about it, or I'll spoil it."

"That sounds exciting."

"We hope so." Phoebe smiled. "Midnight Sun is an interesting trade group. Tell me a little about your organization."

"Midnight Sun was formed to help Korean immigrants to Sweden succeed in business so our families could have better lives," Thor said, gathering his notebook and briefcase. "There are so few of us, we thought we could benefit from mutual help. We adopted Swedish names to show our commitment to our new country."

What Thor said made sense—and obviously they'd been very successful. But it didn't explain why the Eklunds wanted to buy guns.

Thor waved good night as Phoebe glanced around the emptying lobby. All the investors were drifting out to the minivan that would take them back to their hotel. All except the Eklunds, who were talking to each other and looking intense. Like maybe they were arguing. Or discussing how to buy guns.

She *had* to find out what they were up to. If she saw them buy guns, she could report them to Greg Peeling, her boss. That would help her case with the CIA.

Even better, if she could discover what the Eklunds wanted

to *do* with the guns, then she—and the CIA or FBI or Homeland or whoever—could stop it, could prevent one more bad thing from happening. And then Greg would offer her her job back, and she'd be on the next plane to DC and back to Langley, working off her humongous school debt and doing her bit to get bad guys off the streets. Chalk one up for Team Phoebe.

But she couldn't follow them, even on her new bike, because she'd never be able to keep up. That left her with only one option.

She pulled out her phone and called Sanjay.

"It is good to hear from you," Sanjay said. "I am just dropping off a passenger. Do you need a ride?" He lowered his voice. "For your sleuthing?"

"Yes, I do. Can you get to Venture Automotive quickly?"

"I'm in the area, loosely speaking. Give me ten minutes. I shall fly faster than the chariots of the gods."

"Thanks, Sanjay. I'll be outside." Phoebe disconnected and ducked into the restroom, knowing it could be a long evening. After she washed her hands, she tightened her ponytail and smoothed down her skirt. Her wardrobe was all but nonexistent, and she couldn't wear this poodle skirt uniform to the factory more than a day or two. She'd have to make time to go shopping. Maybe Kristin could advise her on some discount places.

"Hey, girlfriend," Kristin said, spotting her as she left the washroom. "How's it going?"

"Good, despite my efforts to screw up the parts of a car in Korean," Phoebe said, keeping one eye on the Eklunds. "Thanks for getting my new bike out here this afternoon. It's beautiful."

"No problem. The first shop I called was thrilled to deliver. Toss Coach's name around and doors open, so to speak."

"Good to know. And now, for my next retail trick, where can I do some clothes shopping? Someplace not too expensive that I can bike to."

Kristin perked up. "You want to go shopping? I'd *love* to take you shopping. Tonight?"

"I can't tonight," Phoebe said with real regret. "Those Koreans I'm worried about? I think they're planning to buy guns tonight. I have to follow them."

"*What?* Phoebe, are you sure? We should tell Coach."

"And he'll do what that I can't do? I'll just follow and watch. If they buy guns like they said they were, I'll call law enforcement and get out of there."

Kristin looked torn. "But Phoebe—Coach has an interest in these guys, too. If the investors bring guns to the plant, that's not good. Or if they get arrested, it might break up the group, and then we'd never get the investment. Besides, Coach has a lot of clout in this town. He could help you."

"Maybe," Phoebe said. "But he doesn't believe me about the guns. He isn't even sure that I work for the CIA."

Kristin bit the inside of her lip. "I could come with you. My boyfriend could come, too. That would be better than going alone."

Phoebe was touched by the offer. When had anybody offered to put themselves into danger for her? Not that she'd be in much danger.

"I appreciate that, but I'll be fine. A friend is driving me, and I won't try to stop the Eklunds. I just want to find out what they're up to."

Kristin still didn't seem happy. "I'm all for catching gunrunners, and of course public safety is the main thing. But I don't see—"

Over Kristin's shoulder, Phoebe saw the Eklunds head for the exit. She grabbed her new bike and pushed it toward the door.

"Gotta go! Sorry Kristin, they're on the move. Thanks again for my new bike! Don't worry! Everything will be fine!"

"Turn left in two hundred feet," the navigation system said in Swedish, but Lars was in the wrong lane and couldn't pull over. Las Vegas had so much traffic, and many drivers were very aggressive. Changing lanes at the last minute was usually impossible. He sped through the intersection.

"You missed the turn," Gustav said. He sounded impatient. Well, it was easy for him to be impatient. He wasn't driving. And he wasn't driving probably because he didn't want to be criticized for missing a left turn.

"Recalculating," the navigation system said. "Turn left in six hundred feet."

Lars angled left to be ready this time. "Where are we going?"

"A pawnshop. They should have what we need. Although it is widely understood that in America you can get guns on any street corner. Helga, I believe, is correct in this matter."

Lars put on his left-turn signal and glanced in the rearview mirror. Would any of these drivers let him in?

"Not the street corner by our hotel."

Gustav snorted. "Not obviously, anyway. This is why we're going to a pawnshop."

Lars nodded. "The pawnshops will sell us guns without asking questions?"

"Yes."

"Because we couldn't get gun permits at the county building." Lars tried to keep the challenge out of his voice.

"Pawnshops are different."

Lars nodded again, grinding the gears as he slowed down. Not having enough English to commit a crime effectively made him nervous. They'd checked in Sweden to find out what they had to do to buy a gun in Las Vegas. But the website was in English and the automatic translation feature hadn't worked that well, so he hadn't understood it and he'd been reluctant to ask Helga to translate. Then, when they arrived at the government building in Las Vegas, he couldn't get the permit, and he wasn't sure why. And the translator had seen them there, which sharpened his anxiety. Now they were flying in the dark about how to get a gun. They hadn't made a plan B. They hadn't thought they'd need one.

"Turn left," the navigation system told him, and this time he was in the correct lane and turned with the other traffic.

"Remember Grandfather," Gustav said. "Remember our commitment. Remember our family honor."

"Yeah, yeah," Lars said. "I remember."

As they drove, the streets changed from the glitzy neon Strip to grayer, shabbier neighborhoods. Tourist shops and malls gave way to liquor stores and convenience markets. Stores and houses had bars on the windows.

"We're getting close," Gustav said.

"It's a no-questions-asked neighborhood."

"There it is," Gustav said, pointing.

Lars slowed down, but a lot of the cars parked on the street seemed to be more or less permanent. They found a double space about a block down, so they parked, locked the truck, walked back, and entered the pawnshop. A short, heavy man with thinning hair sat in a barred, glass cage, reading the *Financial Times*.

He glanced up as they approached.

"Help you guys?" he asked.

Lars realized immediately the language problems they were about to have. Too bad they couldn't have borrowed the translator in the dog skirt for this errand. Of course, that would have been impossible. At least he'd had the foresight to look up a few words on his Swedish-to-English translation app.

"Guns," he said.

"You want to buy a gun?" The owner stood up and looked them over. "I need to see some ID first."

Gustav glanced at Lars. Lars felt panic set in. What had the man said?

"ID," the man said again. "Photo ID. Get it? Picture ID. Drivers license."

Now what? Lars had no idea what the man was saying.

Gustav shook his head.

"Jesus Christ on a stick." The man reached into his back pocket and pulled out a fat, creased wallet. He showed his drivers license to the two men.

"This is a Nevada drivers license," he said. "I need to see one of these."

Lars turned to Gustav in relief. "He needs identification," he said. "He wants to see our passports."

They reached into their pockets and pulled them out. Behind them, another customer entered the shop, and Lars glanced at him, his anxiety ramping up. They didn't want more witnesses than necessary to their gun purchase.

"Not a passport," the man said. "I need *Nevada state photo ID*. Do you have that? Because if you don't, I got enough trouble with the cops. I ain't selling you guys no handguns if you don't speak English and you don't have no Nevada state photo ID. *Capiche?*"

"Somehow the passport is inadequate," Lars said to Gustav.

"How can that be? It is the most legitimate identification."

"This must be what Phoebe was talking about," Lars said. "We have the wrong ID. He's not accepting our passports."

"Go on, get out of here." The man stepped out of the cage, took Gustav by the arm, and steered him toward the door. "I ain't selling you guys nothing. I don't even want you in here. Now get out."

He pushed them toward the door and they left, shaking their heads.

"Now what?" Lars asked when they were out on the street.

"We go to the next one, and if he doesn't sell us guns, we go to the next one," Gustav said. "We're bound to find somebody who will sell us some guns without whatever ID that guy wanted."

We can just go to any street corner, Lars thought, but didn't say it out loud. Clearly America was not quite the free-for-all gun smorgasbord that Gustav had read about in Sweden. Helga, at least, would be relieved to hear that.

They walked back to the truck and got in.

"Where to now?" Lars asked.

Gustav consulted his smartphone and then keyed an address into the navigation system. "The next pawnshop store is six blocks away."

"Drive north for fifteen hundred feet," the navigation system said.

"You heard her," Gustav said.

Lars put the truck in gear and edged away from the curb. After a few minutes, Gustav pointed to a small, dingy building. This store did not have a neon sign.

"Is that the place?" Lars asked. It didn't look like much.

"The address is correct."

"You have arrived at your destination," the navigation system said.

Parking was still bad, the curb crammed with cars that looked like they hadn't moved in ten years. Lars finally squeezed into a partial red zone at the corner.

This time a stocky young man with a beard glanced up from behind a barred, glass cage.

"Help you guys?" he asked.

"Guns," Lars said, more comfortable with the drill now.

"We got a nice selection."

Lars didn't know what the man said, but he hadn't sounded angry and disapproving, and he hadn't reached into his wallet to show them anything. So he pointed to two handguns behind the case.

"Yes," he said.

"Ah," the man said. "A Glock 26 subcompact featuring a dual recoil spring with a standard capacity of ten rounds. Nice choice. Three hundred. Each."

Lars held up two fingers and pointed to the handguns. The man grabbed an envelope from the counter, turned it over, picked up a stubby pencil, and wrote three hundred twice.

Gustav nodded, pulled out his wallet, and counted out the bills.

"You want some ammo to go with that?" the man asked.

Gustav halted, still counting out the money, and gazed at him. When the man reached below the counter, Lars and Gustav both tensed, but the man pulled out two boxes of bullets.

"Yes," Gustav said, nodding to the man.

"That's another fifty bucks." The man wrote it down on the envelope.

Gustav counted out another couple of bills.

"Receipt?"

Lars frowned at the man. What did he want now?

"No receipt," the man said, putting the guns and ammunition in a paper bag. "Nice doing business with you guys."

Lars and Gustav hesitated. The man waved goodbye, and they took the bag and left the shop.

"Now we are one step closer to saving Grandfather," Gustav said as they got into the truck. "When we get back to the hotel, we'll go over the plan again."

"Oh, good," Lars said. "The plan."

He hoped the plan didn't get them killed.

"There they are!" Phoebe leaned forward, straining to see through the windshield. "Do you see— Yes! They've got a paper bag. Right?"

Sanjay peered down the darkened street. "You are correct.

They are indeed carrying a bag."

"Do you think they bought handguns? I thought they'd want to fill up that big truck with big weapons. But maybe not. What would they want with handguns?"

"I could not say. To shoot something, perhaps."

"Unless there're no guns in the bag and they needed something else to do whatever they plan to do," Phoebe said, frowning in concentration. "But then, why go to a pawnshop and not a hardware store? I'm going in. I have to find out."

"Excuse me, miss, but they are getting away! Don't you wish to follow them?"

"You're right. We have to split up."

"Split up! We cannot do that!"

"I'll go into the pawnshop, and you follow them. Don't confront them, though! Just watch and see where they go."

"This plan seems very unwise. How long do I follow them? And in the meantime, what is to become of you?"

"If they go back to the hotel, fine, you're done. Go home. I'll take the bus from here. If they go someplace else, call me. We can figure out what's best to do then."

"The bus! No, really, miss, this plan is most unsafe. You should not be in this neighborhood alone after dark. Indeed, I'm not sure you should be alone in this neighborhood at *all*. We should *both* follow the truck. Tomorrow is soon enough to come back and inquire of the proprietor here what your suspects bought."

Phoebe scoped out the area. Dusk had settled in. The street was mixed commercial and residential. Houses had bars on the windows, and several businesses were boarded up. Trash littered the streets. Young men loitered on corners. She really didn't want to wait for a bus. If buses even came down this street.

"A cab, then, not the bus," she said. "I'll call a cab. We need all the information we can get on these guys. Splitting up is the only option."

"Very well," Sanjay said in resignation. "Then the most prudent course of action would be for me to provide you with a weapon."

Phoebe blinked. Sanjay didn't seem like the type of guy who carried weapons in his cab. He popped the trunk and got out while she glanced down the street. The Swedish-Koreans were walking to their truck, not looking around, so she got out, too. Sanjay rummaged around in a box of odds and ends and extracted a small folding umbrella in a pink floral print.

"Here," he said, handing it to her.

"What's this?"

"It's an umbrella. You can use it to strike any attackers."

"With *this*?" Phoebe pointed to the interior of the trunk. "Why can't I have the tire iron?"

"I need the tire iron. In case your terrorists attack my taxi. Or I have a flat tire."

"No one's going to attack your taxi, Sanjay."

"No one's going to attack you, either, miss."

Phoebe scowled. "What happened to 'it's not safe'? I swear you said that just a second ago."

"That was when I thought I could persuade you not to go in there."

"Fine," she said, taking the umbrella from him. "I guess it's better than nothing."

She glanced down the street again. Lars and Gustav were already in the truck. The engine roared to life, and the vehicle pulled away from the curb.

"You better get going, Sanjay," she said. "You don't want to lose them."

"Wait inside the pawnshop when you call the cab," Sanjay said. "Then call me. Do not take the bus. That is a plan so bad it is breathtaking in its badness."

"I *said* I won't take the bus," she said. "Now *hurry*."

She jogged across the street and took a deep breath when she got to the front of the shop. Then she pushed open the door and entered.

"Help you?" the man behind the bulletproof window said.

"Two Korean men came in here a few minutes ago and bought something," Phoebe said. "What was it?"

The man's eyes narrowed. "Who wants to know?"

Phoebe smiled—winsomely, she hoped. "I'm a tour guide leader," she said, waggling the umbrella. "I take those guys and thirty other people around on a bus all day to look at the sights.

Those two have been talking about the violence in Las Vegas. I'm afraid they bought guns here. And our company policy strictly prohibits guns on the bus."

"Yeah, I ain't saying what they bought here," the man said. "I gotta protect my clients' privacy."

"Really." Phoebe nodded, looking around the shop. It was cluttered and dusty, crowded with small appliances and household items. But the man behind the counter definitely sold guns. He had big guns behind a tall, locked case on the wall, and in the locked case in the front, a row of handguns filled the top shelf.

Which had a gap. A gap that would have accommodated about two handguns. A clean, shiny gap surrounded by a layer of dust, as though something—or two somethings—had recently been removed.

"I see they bought two handguns," she said. "Did you sell them any bullets?"

"Lars and Gustav bought two handguns and fifty rounds of ammunition," she told Sanjay as she peered out the window of the pawnshop, waiting for the taxi. "Where are you?"

"Just turning in to the back driveway of their hotel. Of course, this information that you have learned is interesting, but if you'll excuse my saying so, miss, knowing that doesn't seem to help us very much, if at all."

Phoebe sighed. Headlights were coming down the street. Maybe that was her cab.

"I suppose not," she said, lowering her voice. "I thought that when they talked about guns, they planned to fill that truck with them. If not, why didn't they rent a car? A truck is too noticeable. Besides, it uses more gas and costs more to rent. And it's harder to park."

"Perhaps they got the truck for something innocuous that you don't know about," Sanjay said. "Or perhaps their first choice of rental cars was not available. Have you called a taxi, and has it arrived yet?"

"Yes and yes," Phoebe said, waggling the pink umbrella at the owner as she pushed out of the pawnshop.

"Your investors have gone into the hotel," Sanjay said.

"What do you want me to do?"

Phoebe glanced at her watch. "Are you hungry? Should I pick up some takeout and bring it over to the hotel parking lot? We could watch for a bit and see if they go right out again. But I *hope* they're settling in and ordering room service, because I can't stay up all night waiting for them to do something. I have to work tomorrow."

"As do I," Sanjay said. "Takeout would be most welcome. I am eclectic in my tastes, except for beef. I don't eat beef."

A few minutes later Phoebe paid off her taxi and slid into the front seat of Sanjay's cab, carrying a bag of steaming fish and chips.

"They have not gone out," Sanjay said, tearing into the bag. "At least, not from this side."

They munched in silence for a few minutes, and then Phoebe tossed her used cutlery and empty coleslaw container into the bag for trash.

"All right." She wiped her mouth with her napkin. "I'll go check the odometer on the truck now and see what mileage they've got. And then tomorrow when they're at the factory, I'll check it again. How many miles between here and the factory?"

"I would estimate that distance to be about fifteen miles."

"Okay. So if there are a lot more than fifteen miles added by tomorrow, we'll know they went out during the night. It's not as good as watching all night, but it's just you and me. The two of us can't surveil them twenty-four seven."

She slid out of the taxi and walked swiftly to the white truck. But the window was too high and the dashboard at too inconvenient an angle. She couldn't see the odometer. She tried the door. Locked. Now what?

She glanced back at the taxi. Sanjay rustled under the seat and then got out and joined her.

"Stand close, miss." He reached inside his sleeve and drew out a long, thin steel blade and slid it down the window into the truck's door. He jerked it up, and the lock popped open.

"It's a jimmy," Sanjay said, sliding it back into his sleeve. "We have trouble with the cabs sometimes down at the garage."

Phoebe grinned. "Or trucks in the parking lot." She yanked

open the door and stepped up into the cab. "Twelve thousand, four hundred thirty-eight. Got that?"

She hopped out again, pushed the lock button down, and slammed the door.

"Got it," he said, leading the way back to the taxi. "And now I am most ready to abandon this surveillance for the evening."

Phoebe was bone tired, too. Following the two Swedish-Korean investors—trying to figure out what they were up to— was more challenging and more exhausting than she'd planned on. She couldn't watch them every minute of every day. She had to sleep. She had to go to work.

She couldn't go on like this. But she couldn't stop, either.

Not until she knew what they were after.

Chapter 6

The next morning Phoebe hit the snooze button too many times and then rushed around, getting ready for work. She put on her one pair of jeans, a white T-shirt, and a jacket from one of her CIA suits. Good to go. But she definitely needed more clothes. Today at lunch, she was hitting the outlet stores.

She ate a quick peanut butter sandwich, careful not to smear anything on her outfit, while she listened to the message her mother had left on the landline—"Bud and I are *keeping busy.* I'll call you later about the rent"—whatever that meant. Then she dashed out of the apartment. If she pushed, she'd get to Venture Automotive on time.

Phoebe hopped on her new bicycle and headed west to the plant. The sun, even at seven in the morning, was already warm, and a brisk breeze cooled her face. But by the time she got to the edge of town, the wind had kicked up. Sharp gusts blew across the desert, pushing her bike around on the road. Grit stung her skin and got in her eyes. At times like this, she wished she had her drivers license. Not to mention a car.

From a distance, she noticed a lump of brown fur limping along the shoulder of the road. At first she couldn't tell what it was. She slowed down and pulled out into the roadway to avoid it. Just what she didn't need was to be attacked by a rabid fox or whatever it was.

As she got closer, though, she saw it was a dog. She gave it a wide berth and glanced at it as she pedaled past. The dog, a medium-sized, shaggy, brownish mutt, watched her. Not a rabid or pathetic look. But more of a "how on earth did I get here, can you believe it?" look.

She slowed. Then stopped. And turned back to check out the dog, who was walking alone on the side of the road in the desert. She knew what *that* felt like.

"Hello," she said, and the dog tilted his head at her. "Are you lost?"

She was nuts, talking to a dog, but he acted like he was listening. This dog would believe she was in the CIA.

"I'm in the CIA," she said, testing it out.

The dog wagged its tail and grinned. Phoebe grinned back.

"Yeah, I know," she said. "That and a buck gets you a burger at Wendy's. Does your owner live around here?"

The dog whined a little, shifting on its paws. The pavement was probably hot on its feet.

Phoebe got off her bike and put down the kickstand. The dog whined again, wagging its tail but not coming closer.

"You seem like a smart dog." She knelt down and reached out her hand. "Come sniff me and see if we can be friends. I'll find your owner for you. They're probably worried."

Or not. The dog was too thin, his coat was matted, and his paw was bleeding. She shouldn't take him with her, but she couldn't leave him out here on the road to be hit by a truck.

The dog edged up to Phoebe and reached out to sniff her hand. It gave her a tentative lick on her palm, and Phoebe gazed into eyes that looked hopeful for the first time.

"I'll call Brenda," Phoebe said, scratching the mutt's ears and checking to see if he had a collar. "She'll take you to her apartment, and you can rest there until I get home. I hope you're house-trained."

The dog barked.

"Then that's our plan." Phoebe called her mother, praying Brenda would pick up. It was awfully early to be calling if her mom had worked a late shift, but Brenda was her best option.

Brenda answered, sounding half asleep. "Sweetie? Is there an emergency?"

"Sort of. Can you help me? I found a dog, and I was wondering if you could pick him up and take him to your apartment. I'll be home by six at the latest."

"A dog? Phoebe, you can't take a dog to my place. The land-lord doesn't allow pets. Sorry, honey." She disconnected.

Phoebe put her phone back in her pocket. So Brenda was out. That left her with exactly one option.

"You'll have to come with me," Phoebe said. "I have to go to work, but I'll get you some water and food there, and then after work we'll go to the vet and get your paw taken care of. And the vet will see if you're microchipped and we can find your owner that way. And if not, then I'll put up posters tomorrow. How does that sound?"

The dog barked once and wagged its tail.

Phoebe smiled. "Let's go, then," she said, standing up. "You'll have to ride on my bike with me. That won't be so easy. Promise you'll be good."

The dog barked again. He really did seem to understand everything.

Phoebe got up and walked over to her bike, and the dog limped behind. "My panniers will be a tight fit for you, and you can't wriggle around. Understand? Plus I need some ballast, because you're big enough that I'll tip over if I have you on one side and nothing on the other."

The dog grinned up at her.

"Okay, then. Sit. Stay." Phoebe looked at the dog doubtfully, but he wasn't going anywhere, so she stepped off the shoulder and gathered some stones. They were too small and wouldn't be enough, but she couldn't spend a lot of time searching for something better. She put them into one of the panniers.

"Let's just go," she said. "I hope you haven't cracked any ribs or anything. I don't want to hurt you. More than you already have been, I mean."

She picked up the dog, who struggled when she tried to put him in the pannier. The bike toppled over, scattering the rocks she'd stowed.

The dog looked at the fallen bike and then at her.

"Yeah, smarty-pants, I *said* this would be a problem. Let's try again."

Phoebe put the dog down, brought up the bike, scooped up

the ballast rocks that had scattered, and dropped them in the pannier. Holding the bike frame with one hand, she picked up the dog with the other and placed him feet first in the pannier. The dog did seem to understand what was required and didn't squirm this time, but it was a very tight fit. And the handlebars swung to the right and bonked her on the head.

"Ouch," Phoebe said. "I suppose it would have been too much to ask for you to be a Chihuahua."

The dog struggled in the pannier.

"I didn't mean it," she said. "Stay!" But she couldn't hold the dog in and keep the bike upright, too. To her relief, the dog stopped squirming once he'd maneuvered his front feet over the side of the pannier so they rested on the edge of the canvas sack.

Phoebe rolled her eyes at him. "If you're comfortable now, we can take off." The dog lolled its head at her, and Phoebe laughed and slung her leg over the seat. "Here's hoping."

But in less than one hundred yards, Phoebe saw that her plan wouldn't work. The bike was too unbalanced with the dog on one side. She couldn't ride it that way. She'd have to walk. She checked her watch. If she walked, she'd be late. Really late, that is. With a sigh, she got off the bike, helped the dog out of the pannier, dug her phone out of her pocket, and called the factory.

"Hi, Megan, it's Phoebe," she said to the receptionist. "Is Kristin there?"

"She's in the break room doing something for the Midnight Sun people. There's no phone in there. Want to leave her a voice mail?"

"I guess so. Wait. Listen, Megan, I'm out on the highway with my bike and a lost dog, and I need a ride in. That's what I wanted to ask her. Is somebody there who could come out and pick us up? Daryl? Anybody?"

"How far out are you?"

"Two miles. Maybe three."

"Okay, sit tight. I'll find somebody."

"Thank you," Phoebe said, but Megan had hung up already.

"Somebody's coming for us," Phoebe told the dog, scratching his ears and feeling the grit in his fur. "Don't overthink this, but you're looking a lot like I feel."

A few minutes later a bright yellow electric SUV sped down the highway. As it got closer, Phoebe saw that Chase was driving. He did a U-turn and parked in front of her.

Crap! It would have to be Chase. No way could she sneak in on time with a dog now.

"Thanks for coming," she said as Chase got out of the car. She leaned the bike against the fender. "I'm sorry I'm running late. I met a dog."

"So I see," Chase said, eying the dog with disfavor. "I wasn't sure if I should believe Megan when she told me. Although, why not? It's a much simpler story than 'I'm in the CIA and your investors are gun-toting terrorists.'"

Phoebe scowled. "He's a bit of a mess because he's lost or somebody abandoned him, but he's a nice dog. He won't cause any trouble."

"He's already causing trouble. And you need a car if you're going to be picking up dogs along the highway."

"Just the one dog."

"So far. Is he packing a gun?"

"Go ahead and laugh," Phoebe said, annoyed now.

"*Cher*, I'm not laughing. Believe me."

Phoebe gulped. "Are the investors impatient?"

"They're chowing down on breakfast." He raised the hatchback and stowed the bike in the back of the vehicle, but when he whistled for the dog to come, he didn't move. "Kristin decided they might like Korean food, and she's cooking some soupy rice thing in the employee kitchen. The crowd, as they used to say in football circles, is going wild."

"I bet she's making jook. It's sort of a comfort snack food in Korea. It's probably hard to get in Korean restaurants around here."

Chase nodded. "Jook. Right, that's what she called it. Where did you find this dog?"

"Right here, just walking along. I couldn't leave him." Phoebe opened the car door and patted her thigh. "Here, boy. This is our ride."

The dog gazed doubtfully at the bright yellow car plastered with dark green logos.

"I know, the color's enough to make you barf, but it's safe," Phoebe said encouragingly to the mutt. "At least I think so."

"You think the dog is questioning the vehicle?" Chase asked. "He's got a nerve. Since he's a mess. And probably has fleas."

"We can fix that." She smiled down at the dog, who was still sitting on the side of the road.

"Let's get moving, *cher*. Time's a-wastin', and we've got to make tracks if we're going to the pound."

"We're not going to the pound!" Phoebe stared at him in shock.

"Where then? You can't take him to the plant."

"Why not? He's a nice dog. We can maybe give him a quick bath, and then after work, I'll take him to the vet and get his paw treated and see if he's chipped so we can find his owner."

"*Cher*." Chase exhaled. "We—*you*—don't have time for that. You're working, remember? You should be working right now. We're not a hotel for lost dogs out there."

"Well, no, but I can't take him to the pound."

"*You can't take care of a dog*. And my staff is not taking care of him for you."

"Please. He's hurt. They'll euthanize him at the pound. He'll be good. Just for one day."

Chase shook his head, but his voice softened. "Phoebe, I'm sorry. We can't take care of an injured dog that might be sick, too. I have to focus on the Midnight Sun folks. Who could be waiting for us right this minute. We aren't taking the dog to the plant."

Phoebe felt sick. "Okay," she said, nodding. "Okay. You've got the investors. They're waiting. You're probably right about that."

"The dog will be fine at the pound," Chase said soothingly. "They'll take care of him. They'll—"

"I can't take him to the pound. I quit."

"*What?* No, you don't."

Phoebe held up her hands. "I'm sorry. I have to. I was working for you for only two weeks anyway. I'm just quitting early. It didn't work out."

"You can't quit!"

"I have to." She turned to the dog. "Sorry, dog. We have to

82

walk, after all. But I promise you, it'll get better after this."

Chase slammed down the hatchback with such force that the car jumped. Phoebe swallowed; he looked furious.

"This is your idea of commitment?" he said. "You agreed to work for me for *two weeks*. I am paying you an outrageous amount of money for that time. And now you're blackmailing me with this damn *dog*?"

Phoebe lifted her chin. "I'm not blackmailing you. I'm doing what I have to do. I'm sorry about the translating job, but you can find somebody else."

"I can't find somebody else! You were my last resort! You have to do your part! People depend on me!"

"This dog depends on *me*."

"He'll survive at the pound!"

"I'm not throwing away this dog!"

"The investors come first!"

"Not for me!"

They glared at each other.

The dog barked. They both looked down. He looked up anxiously from Phoebe to Chase and back.

Phoebe felt her heart hammer in her chest and realized how quickly she was breathing. She didn't want to quit; she liked the work and she needed the money. But she couldn't abandon the dog. He needed help, and he could die out here without it. And she wasn't taking him to the pound, where they might kill him even faster.

She glanced at Chase. His jaw was clenched and he was breathing fast, too. Okay, the investors were important to him. She got that.

"Just *one day*," she said more quietly. "I promise you, on my honor, he won't be any trouble. I'll work for free if he is."

"I don't want you to work for free," Chase said, his voice sounding tight and clipped. "I want to pay you for your best job, your focused job, the job that gets Midnight Sun to sign on to my company and my product."

"Well, I'd rather not work for free, either, if it comes to that." Phoebe bit her lip. "How about this? We take him to the plant and tie him up outside in the shade with food and water. I check on him once at lunch. And take him away at night. That's it. No fussing. One day. Never again. In exchange, I'll do you a favor, whatever you want. Anytime. *Please*. As a friend."

Chase looked from her face to the dog and back. His tight face gradually relaxed, and he sighed. "How come none of my other friends wants me to keep a mangy dog at the plant? Okay, *one day*. And he better not be any trouble."

Relief surged through her, and she threw her arms around him in a bear hug. "He won't be! You'll see. *Thank you.*"

Chase disengaged from her arms. "Let's get going then, *cher*. We got us some ground to cover."

"What do you think he eats? Could we stop and get some dog food for him?"

Chase rolled his eyes. "I *knew* it," he said. "*Already* we're fussing. All right. In for a penny, in for a pound, I guess. We'll stop at the fast-food joint on the way back, get him a hamburger. Mutt, get in the car right now—I don't care if you don't like it. Or else we're leaving you behind."

The dog grinned and jumped up onto the seat.

"See?" Phoebe said, climbing in after him. "He likes you already."

Kristin had promised to take Phoebe clothes shopping at lunchtime, and dog or no dog, Phoebe didn't plan to break that date. She really needed a couple of new outfits. She owned the jeans she had on, the poodle skirt, and her CIA suits. That was it. And she couldn't bike in the suits.

But while she waited outside for Kristin to join her, Phoebe had a couple of things to do. She filled her dog's water dish and glanced around the lot while he drank it. Sanjay had lent her a jimmy and taught her how to use it, but unlocking his taxi was a lot different than unlocking a truck in a parking lot that had surveillance cameras and people who actually watched them.

She strolled out between the cars and stopped on the side of the truck that faced away from the cameras. After a quick glance around, she took out the jimmy and slid it down the window the way Sanjay had shown her. It took her three nervous tries before the lock popped open, and then the dog barked.

"Not you, too!" she hissed. "Be quiet! I'm not stealing anything."

She opened the door a crack, stepped up on the running board, and leaned across the seat to read the odometer—12,454 miles. Gustav and Lars had driven sixteen miles from their hotel to the factory this morning, so they'd stayed at the hotel after buying the handguns.

What were they up to? It had to be *something*.

She pushed down the lock on the door, dropped to the ground, and shut the door as gently as she could.

"Let's eat our sandwich before Kristin comes," she said to the dog. "And before Chase comes out here and fires my butt. And takes you to the pound."

And Chase was more trouble in the making. When she'd thrown her arms around him this morning, she'd been so happy that he'd agreed to her bringing the dog to the plant that she hadn't given the hug a second thought.

Of course, hugging her boss was wildly inappropriate. And if he were truly her boss, she never would have done it. Had she ever been tempted to hug Greg Peeling at the CIA? No. Not in ten million years. But Chase would be her boss for only two weeks. Just until the investor meetings were over. So—not really a boss. No harm, no foul, right?

Except...those shoulders. Those cool, gray eyes. Those powerful thighs, so poorly concealed in dress slacks. Even with the bum knee, he was the image of a strong, graceful athlete. And, of course, running a start-up electric-car company that needed so many things, he had to be smart, too.

She hadn't been prepared for how she'd feel about having her arms around what had to be the hottest CEO in the business world. *She'd liked it.* For that second that she'd held him, the desert sand hadn't stung, the wind hadn't whipped, and the only heat she'd felt had been internal. Her heart had pounded faster, she'd been breathless, she'd *wanted* him. She wanted *more*.

That was so wrong on so many levels.

If the CIA exonerated her after it finished its investigation of her actions regarding the Empire State Building, she'd be back at Langley in a few weeks, back to her analyst job, doing what she wanted and needed to do, which was identifying terrorist threats. She'd be three thousand miles away from Chase Bonaventure, who wanted and needed to succeed at building a car company.

The animal attraction was there, sure, at least on her side. But one thing Phoebe was certain about—you couldn't trust animal attraction. Her mother trusted hers, and look what that got her—a lifetime of short-term affairs with men who wanted a good time and nothing more, plus a daughter she hadn't wanted, fathered by a man she didn't know.

Phoebe knew her mother loved her and had raised her the best she could. And her mother's long absences during her childhood had been the direct reason Phoebe had qualified for the CIA, so all good there.

But she didn't want to relive her mother's life, either. She wanted something different. She wanted to wear suits to work. She wanted health insurance and a retirement fund. When—*if*—she decided to stay with a guy, it wouldn't be because her heart pounded too fast when he said *it's bring your dog to work day*. No. When she hooked up with someone, it would be because they *knew* each other. Because they'd spent time together. Because they could count on each other.

Phoebe sighed, tearing her sandwich in half. She gave one piece to the dog and took a bite from the other.

She had to be realistic. Getting involved with Chase was off the table. She wouldn't be in Vegas long enough to build anything with him. And if she wanted to get back to the CIA sooner rather than later, she should tell Greg about the Swedish-Koreans and let him figure out what they were up to. He'd see how good she was, how committed. She'd get her job back. And then she'd be out of here.

She punched in Greg's number.

"Phoebe," he said when he picked up, disapproval strong in his voice. "What did I say about your calling? Are you on a secure line?"

"I'm not asking about the Empire State Building investigation," Phoebe said quickly. "I want to tell you about something else."

"What else could there possibly be?"

"I'm in Las Vegas, visiting my mom," Phoebe said. "I heard two guys, Korean speakers, talk about buying guns. They're pretending to be part of a Swedish trade delegation, but they have a truck. What do they need with a truck full of guns? That truck could even be a bomb."

He was silent.

"I think somebody should investigate." She plowed on. "Because Hoover Dam is right here. Right? Anything could happen."

"What else did they say?"

"That's all I heard. But when I pretended to call the cops, they drove out in a hurry."

Greg sighed. "That's not enough, Phoebe. You're seeing terrorists behind every tree. Two men, even if they speak Korean and talk about guns, don't present a national threat."

"If we wait, though, it could be too late. It couldn't hurt to check into it, could it?"

"You want to do something? Call the police. Local law enforcement is perfectly capable of handling this."

"But—"

"They're on the scene. They might even know these guys or who they're dealing with."

"The thing is, Greg—"

"You realize, Phoebe, don't you, that calling makes you look irresponsible, correct? These phone calls are information we add to the file we evaluate for your reinstatement."

"Okay, right, that's why I still think—"

"Call the cops. Goodbye, Phoebe."

The connection went dead, and she put her phone in her pocket. *That went well—not.*

The dog whined and put his head in her lap, and Phoebe scratched his ears. Maybe Greg had a point. Really, why *not* call the cops? What did she have to lose? They might be able to help. And if not, she wouldn't be any worse off than she was right now.

She checked for the police nonemergency number on her phone and tapped it out.

"Sixteenth precinct."

"Hi," Phoebe said. "I want to report a crime. At least, I think it's a crime. And also, I'm pretty sure a bigger crime is about to be committed."

"Is there a crime or not?"

"Yes," Phoebe said. "There's a crime. I observed someone, two people, actually, buy guns without a permit. That's a crime, right?"

"You saw this."

"No. Not exactly. I saw them come out of a pawnshop with a paper bag. But they'd said they wanted to buy guns, and they didn't have a permit, so I went to ask the pawnshop owner if they did buy the guns, and he said yes. So *he* saw it. Maybe he committed a crime, too. Is the crime the same if one person *sells* guns to someone without a permit and one person *buys* guns without a permit?"

"Do you know who these people are?"

Phoebe hesitated. If she gave the cops Lars and Gustav Eklund, they could be traced back to Venture Automotive. She didn't want Chase's business to be disrupted or embarrassed. She'd sort of promised Kristin. And Chase was trying to get his company off the ground, and he was paying her a lot for two weeks' work. She didn't want to do him a bad turn.

But those guys were on the brink of doing something bad. Foreign nationals didn't talk about guns and drive a truck around because they were interested in the flora and fauna of the American Southwest.

"Lars and Gustav Eklund," she said.

"Spell that," the cop on the phone said.

Phoebe did, then waited while she listened to clacking on a keyboard.

"And you are?"

"Phoebe Renfrew. R-E-N-F-R-E-W."

"What day and time was this, and where did the incident take place?"

Phoebe gave him the details.

"All right, Miz Renfrew, we'll check it out and be in touch. You want to find out what's happening, ask for case number— You ready for this?"

Phoebe scrambled for a pen while he read off a number.

"Any precinct can help you," he said. "Thank you. Goodbye."

Phoebe finished scribbling the numbers on the back of her hand and stared at the silent phone. This was what she could expect from the police? A vague half promise to investigate? On the other hand, she couldn't follow Lars and Gustav on her bicycle when they decided to do whatever they planned to do. So the cops were ahead on points in terms of transportation.

She checked her watch. Kristin would be out here any second. She'd done all she could for right now.

She fed the last bit of her sandwich to her new dog, who thumped his tail and looked at her, she thought, with heartfelt appreciation.

"You won't feel that way after I leave you for the afternoon." She ruffled his fur. "But at least you won't be wandering around on the highway, and Chase found you a nice water bowl. You have to be enjoying that."

The dog barked.

"I know you like him," she said, spotting Kristin coming out of the building. She stood up and brushed the crumbs off her lap. "But just forget about it, okay? I'm telling you, there's no future in it."

Chapter 7

By the time Phoebe got back to Brenda's apartment that evening, she thought she'd never had a longer day in her life,
even counting the day that she'd sworn that the secretary of state
would be killed or kidnapped by terrorists, thus causing Navy
SEALs to rappel down from helicopters onto the Empire State
Building observation deck in front of millions of people and
worldwide media outlets. Although that had been a very long day.

Kristin, she found out, had a sharp eye for fashion and the
energy of a whirlwind at the outlet mall. She had unerringly
pulled tops and bottoms from the racks at her favorite store and
thrust Phoebe into the fitting room to try them on. By the time the
lunch hour was over, Phoebe had added several cute outfits to her
wardrobe.

The dog had been more trouble than she'd assured Chase
that he would be, but the investors seemed to like him after an
initial hesitation and had even helped to give him a bath. Everyone had laughed and gotten wet and seemed to enjoy the break
from the conference room.

But she couldn't bike with the dog in her bicycle panniers, so
Chase had driven them to a vet, where she paid a small fortune to
get the dog patched up and learn that he wasn't chipped. And now
here Chase still was, driving her home.

She'd be lucky if she could hold on to this job until *tomorrow*, much less two weeks.

"Thank you for the ride," she said, opening the door almost
before Chase came to a full stop at her mother's apartment build-

ing. The dog, clean but still nameless, hopped out and looked back at Chase, wagging his tail.

"Yeah, I'm coming up with you," Chase said.

"That's not necessary. But thank you again." She reached down and snapped the new leash on her dog's new collar, thinking she should probably have done that before he jumped out of the car. She had a lot to learn about dog care.

"*Cher*. Dog's got stuff now. You've got a lot to carry. Plus the bicycle. It's no trouble."

Phoebe swallowed. She thought it probably was a lot of trouble. Chase had been right about that. But she'd worked hard today; the investors were satisfied. They'd been interested. They'd laughed. They'd stayed focused. So that was going well.

She'd be happier if Chase didn't have to see their apartment, but hey. She straightened her shoulders. Couldn't hurt the rich, former football star, now up-and-coming CEO, to see how the ninety-nine percent lived.

"Thank you," she said again.

Chase popped the hatchback and lifted out Phoebe's bicycle, and Phoebe grabbed the bag of dog food and other stuff she'd charged to her credit card. She didn't want to think of what she'd spent so far on the nameless mutt.

"This way," she said.

The dog trotted alongside her as she turned in to the U-shaped courtyard and headed up the outside concrete steps to the second floor. For the first time she noticed the rusty iron railings, the peeling paint, the bent aluminum windows. She wondered what Chase was thinking about her digs. *Probably that he could have paid me a lot less*.

"I'm staying with my mom for now," she said. "She's probably not at home, though." *She's probably with Bud Corvallis. Somewhere.*

"I'm sorry I won't have a chance to meet her."

"You don't have to be so polite," she said. "It makes me nervous."

Chase laughed. "Too bad, *cher*. My mom would smack me upside the head if I weren't polite to a lady. Or at least a female person."

Phoebe grinned appreciatively. "And I bet your mom taught you the difference."

She walked down the long outside corridor, but when she got to their door, it was padlocked with a heavy chain. She stared at it in incomprehension.

"What's the matter?" Chase asked. He lifted the bicycle from his shoulder and leaned it against the second-floor railing. She wouldn't have believed it if she hadn't seen it, but the movement caused the shirt to strain against his chest and arms, and his muscles *rippled*. He was just too damn good-looking.

"Um," Phoebe said, distracted. "Ah, there's a padlock on the door. Why would that be?"

"Your mom wouldn't have put it on for some reason?"

"I don't see why."

"*Hey!* You!" A short, middle-aged man seemed to be bellowing at her from the courtyard. He ran toward the stairs. "Don't go anywhere!" he yelled.

"Where would I go?" Phoebe said to Chase. "I live here. Temporarily, at least."

"Who are you?" the middle-aged man demanded as he huffed toward them. "I never seen you before."

"Who wants to know?" Chase seemed to uncoil from his slouch against the wall and now towered over the shorter man, all six-foot-whatever of prime athletic muscle against a shorter, squatter guy in a damp shirt.

"Wait. Aren't you—"

"Yes," Chase said. "And you are?"

"Barry Spinalsky. I'm the landlord. I can't believe I'm standing here with Chase Bonaventure! I'm a big fan."

"Thank you, Barry," Chase said. "Why is there a padlock on—" He glanced at Phoebe.

"Brenda Renfrew," Phoebe said.

"—Brenda Renfrew's door?"

"Tenant complained," the landlord said. "Renfrew's got an illegal roommate, some chick. That would be you, I suppose. That's the final straw. She hasn't paid her rent in months. She owes me three thousand dollars. She's not answering her phone. I sent her notices. Now I'm done. She's out."

"What?" said Phoebe. "That can't be right! She works! She has a job!" Then she remembered the giggly message Brenda had left on her phone the other day. Something about the rent. What had her mother meant? Maybe that she owed Barry three thousand dollars.

"Job or no job, she ain't paying her rent," Barry said. "Tell you what. For three thousand bucks, you can have the place. Assuming you pass the background check."

"I'm Brenda's daughter," Phoebe said. "I'm just staying here for a few weeks."

"Same deal," Barry said. "Three thousand or out you go." He glanced at the dog. "No pets allowed."

Chase turned to her. "What do you want to do?"

A familiar blend of resignation, disappointment, loss, and fury rolled through her. *This was just like her mother.* Taking off with some guy for who knows how long, leaving no forwarding address. Leaving Phoebe to fend for herself with no notice, no help, no advice, not even a farewell.

She took a deep breath and exhaled. On the other hand, she hadn't learned Korean and Chinese and Arabic and five other languages because her mom stayed home and sewed curtains and made mac and cheese for her. And she was an adult now. She had options. Not many, but some.

She sighed. "I don't have the money," she said.

"Do you want me to pay you in advance?"

Phoebe scowled. She had to stay *somewhere,* but she didn't want to pay three thousand dollars for her mother's back rent on this crummy apartment. And she didn't want Chase to pay her for work she hadn't even done yet. And she had her dog to consider. Barry didn't take pets.

"No," she said. "I don't want to pay mom's back rent. And I still have the dog."

Chase nodded and turned to Barry Spinalsky. "Can Phoebe go in to get her stuff?"

"I don't have much," Phoebe said, seizing the chance. "One suitcase. It won't take long. Five minutes."

Barry looked from Chase to Phoebe. "All right," he said finally. "Seeing as you're a friend of Chase Bonaventure. Five minutes only, though. Brenda Renfrew's stuff stays."

"No problem." Phoebe looped the dog's leash around the railing while Barry unlocked the padlock and shoved open the door. She charged into the apartment and dragged her suitcase out from under the sofa. She didn't have much to pack. She'd never taken her CIA suits out of the roller bag, the only place in her mother's apartment where she could store her things.

"Is anything in the kitchen yours?" Chase asked, watching her fly around the living room as she plucked clothes off the curtain rods and lampshades.

"No. But can you grab those books from the top shelf there? Those are mine."

"Here's a box," Barry said helpfully.

"I'll get the bathroom stuff," Phoebe said. But first she watched while Chase stretched up to reach the books. *Crap*. Guys who had muscles like that should be illegal.

"I think that's it," Chase said, putting the books in the box and dusting off his hands.

"Could you double-check? Just to make sure you have them all."

Phoebe watched Chase stretch again and feel around for any possible books that might have missed his reach. She sighed.

"Nope, that's it." Chase leaned down and closed the box. "Do you have everything?"

"Bathroom stuff." She zipped into the cramped space, tossed her toothbrush and toiletries in a plastic bag, then dropped it in her suitcase and closed the lid. Done.

She looked at Chase standing in the middle of the shabby apartment, holding the carton of books, her most valuable possessions after her laptop. This kind of uncertainty, the endless shortage of money—this was the life she'd wanted to get away from when she joined the CIA. And yet, here she was still.

"I'm ready to go," she said.

She led the way out of the apartment, and when she got to the front door, she saw her dog quivering with anxiety. A small puddle decorated the outdoor corridor by the apartment door. Evidently Dog had not been able to contain himself. Or perhaps he was expressing an opinion of Barry Spinalsky and his apartment-management skills.

She had to laugh. Chase, next out, caught her eye and grinned.

Barry did not think it was funny. "This is why we do not allow pets at the White Sands Suites," he said.

"Pets are the least of your problems, Barry," Phoebe said. She turned back to grab the roll of paper towels from the kitchen and went outside, where Dog greeted her with heartfelt relief that she hadn't abandoned him.

"Don't worry," she told the dog as she wiped up the mess and fended off his enthusiastic gestures of affection. "I'd have done the same in your shoes."

Task completed, she stuffed the soiled sheets into the outside trash, wiped her hands with a clean towel, and tossed the roll back into the apartment.

"Thanks for letting us come in," Chase said to Barry. He shifted the books to his hip, took the dog's leash, and turned to Phoebe. "Ready? Onward."

Phoebe led the way back down the hallway, dragging her roller bag. "And upward."

Chase stowed Phoebe's bike, carton of books, and suitcase in the back of the yellow Venture Automotive SUV and slammed down the cargo door. He didn't know what to say. This was a woman with no place to live and almost nothing to her name. In his entire life, he'd never possessed so little or not known where he'd be sleeping.

Phoebe opened the hatchback and the dog hopped in. Then she closed the door and came to stand with him where he leaned against the passenger door.

"Well, *cher*, what now? Where would you like to go?"

"Babette and Harry might put me up for a couple of days," she said. "Or maybe Kristin. What would be best is a hotel. I'd ask you to recommend a cheap one, but you probably don't know any cheap ones."

"You're right, I don't know any cheap ones," Chase said. "That won't work, anyway. You've got a bicycle and a dog. No self-respecting fleabag hotel will take you with that kind of baggage."

"Hey," Phoebe said. "I've got a suitcase, too."

"It's not the suitcase that'll upset them." He frowned, thinking about the worn roller bag. "Although that one might. Kristin isn't an option. Did you know that she lives with her boyfriend? Nick's allergic to dogs. Actually, I think he's allergic to everything."

"Oh. I didn't know. That won't work, then."

Chase wanted to invite her to stay at his place. It was huge, and he had more than enough room. The problem with that idea was the hug she'd given him this morning out on the highway. He remembered how he'd felt when her arms—those strong arms—had gone around him. This woman could squeeze. And he'd had an immediate image of her naked in his bed, soft but strong, squeezing him just like that.

And the thing that had turned him on was that she'd hugged him simply because he'd said she could bring her mangy dog to the plant. That was all. He did her a favor, and she hugged him for it. Except for hugs from his family, that might be the first time in years that a woman had hugged him because he'd done her a favor. Not because he was a football player, or rich, or famous, or because they wanted to get up close and personal, or whatever screwy reasons women had for coming on to him.

Not that those weren't legitimate reasons, and not that he hadn't dated any of those women, because he had. But football stuff was a shell, trappings of what he used to be. And Phoebe didn't seem to care about that stuff. Hell, she didn't seem to care about football at all. And that, he realized in shock, was a big turn-on.

But he didn't date employees. Never had, never would. If it wasn't illegal for a CEO to date an employee, it should be. The risk just wasn't worth it.

Not that Phoebe was an employee, exactly. She'd be working for him for only two weeks. When Midnight Sun left, so would she.

Not that he should pay any attention to *that* brain.

Not that he planned on asking her out on a date. But he couldn't let her think she didn't have any options, or friends, right now. He couldn't let her go to some cheap, nasty hotel in a shitty part of town where she could be mugged or worse. If he invited Phoebe to stay at his place, he could keep it platonic.

He took a deep breath. "Listen, *cher*, you could stay at my place. I've got plenty of room. No strings attached."

"Oh, thank you, but I couldn't. It's nice of you to offer, but we don't know each other very well, and I've got the pooch here, and… I'll call Babette and Harry."

"What do you mean, we don't know each other very well? You and I have known each other exactly one day less than you've known Babette and Harry. The exact same amount of time you've known Kristin. And you were willing to stay with her."

Phoebe laughed a little too ruefully. "Still. I'm calling Babette and Harry first. If they say no, we'll talk more."

That was probably for the best, even though he felt a stab of disappointment. He'd have liked to have had her close, but he supposed anywhere but a fleabag hotel would be acceptable. Phoebe dug out her phone and keyed in a number.

"Hi, Babette," Phoebe said. "It's Phoebe. Listen, I need to ask a huge favor. I just got to my mom's place, and the landlord's locked us out. Can I sleep on your sofa for a couple of nights? I'll make another arrangement as soon as I can."

Chase looked away while Phoebe listened.

"The other thing, Babette, is I have a dog now," Phoebe said. "He's a good dog, though. He can sleep outside in the courtyard. I promise you he won't be any trouble."

The dog whined.

"Thank you! We'll be right over." She disconnected and dropped the phone in her bag with a sigh of relief.

"That dog knows his name," Chase said. "Trouble. He follows you wherever you go."

Phoebe rolled her eyes, but Trouble barked. They grinned at each other.

"Damn you for naming my dog," Phoebe said, smiling. "Trouble it is."

"I'm a man of many talents. Are you all set with Babette and Harry?"

Phoebe nodded. "They live behind the Happy Memories

chapel."

"I know where the place is."

They got to the wedding chapel in less than fifteen minutes, and Babette and Harry were waiting outside for them when they pulled into the driveway.

"Chase Bonaventure, it's a pleasure to finally meet you!" Harry said, shaking hands with Chase. "I'm Harry O'Shea."

"Thank you so much for taking us in," Phoebe told them. "You're a lifesaver."

Babette wrapped Phoebe in a hug. "Phoebe, honey, we're glad to have you," she said. "The couch in the living room pulls out. You won't have much privacy, and Harry gets up pretty early, but you're more than welcome."

Chase didn't much like the sound of that. The O'Sheas seemed like good people, but how well would Phoebe sleep on a pull-out couch in the living room? That bit about Harry getting up early sounded ominous. He didn't want to be selfish, but he needed to sign those investors. Every day was game day until that happened as far as he was concerned. Right now Phoebe was probably the key player on the Venture Automotive team. Would she get enough rest here to do a good job translating?

But if Harry was a fan of his, they'd do more for Phoebe. He had to count on that.

"Chase Bonaventure," Chase said, turning from Harry to shake hands with Babette. "You must be Babette. Forgive my calling you by your first name, ma'am. Phoebe talks about you so often I feel like I know you already."

"And Harry talks about you so much that I feel the same," Babette said, smiling. "Although now I understand that it will be some other quarterback that I'll lose my husband to on Sundays."

"That's true enough," Chase said, smiling back. "You won't be able to lay that at my door anymore."

"The Rattlesnakes won't be the same without you," Harry said. "What do you think the chances are for another Super Bowl?"

"The players and coaches are working hard."

He went to the back of the SUV, clipped on Trouble's leash, and lifted out Phoebe's bicycle. The dog jumped to the ground.

"This is Trouble," Chase said. "The dog, I mean. And I've got the rest of Phoebe's stuff here." He handed the bicycle to Phoebe and took out her books and suitcase.

"That's it?" Babette asked.

"That's it," Chase said.

"Would you like to come in for a drink?" Harry asked. "I've got some fine beer cooling in the fridge."

Chase glanced at Phoebe, who looked tired. "Thank you, but another time. Phoebe, what about work tomorrow? Can you make it in on your own?"

She frowned a little, her hand lightly scratching Trouble's ears. *That damn dog.* He knew when he'd first seen it that it would give him nothing but grief. And now here she was, wondering how she could go to work with the mutt.

"Your dog can stay here," Babette said. "He'll be fine, and I'll enjoy the company."

Phoebe brightened. "Are you sure? That would be fantastic, Babette. Then I guess I'm all set. I'll bike in tomorrow, as usual, Chase. And thank you for moving me."

"No worries, *cher.* All moves should be this easy."

He didn't like leaving her. She was too pale, she was dead on her feet, and he didn't see how crashing on the O'Sheas' sofa would be very restful. But as long as she got to work on time and did a good job, that was all that really mattered.

He just needed to keep reminding himself of that.

Chapter 8

Phoebe was so tired that she slept soundly that night, even though the pull-out sofa had a protruding support bar right smack in the middle. But the uncomfortable sofa bed seemed like a luxury when Harry got up at six to do his vocal exercises.

"La-la-la-la-la-la-la-la-laaaaaa," Harry warbled from the kitchen, just one thin wall away.

Phoebe lay stunned, not believing what she heard.

"La-la-la-la-la-la-la-la-laaaaaa," Harry trilled again.

What was he *thinking?* She got up and stumbled into the kitchen.

"Harry, whatcha doin'?" she asked, rubbing her eyes.

"Practicing my scales," Harry said. "La-la-la-la-la-la-la-la-laaaaaa." He sounded like a walrus in heat. Not that she was a connoisseur of Elvis impersonators doing scales at six in the morning.

"Aren't you afraid you'll wake up Babette?" *Not to mention the neighborhood.*

"Nah," Harry said. "We got her some powerful earplugs. Plus, that woman could sleep through a nuclear attack, I swear. La-la-la-la-la-la-la-la-laaaaaa."

"How long do you practice your scales?"

"About an hour. Until I'm warmed up. La-la-la-la-la-la-la-la-laaaaaa."

An *hour.* And what happened when he was warmed up? Would he sing something worse?

She'd never get back to sleep. She liked Harry, but if she had to listen to him belting out scales for one more minute, she might have to kill him. And she wasn't trained for *that*.

"Carry on," she said. "I'll get out of your hair."

Harry nodded, waving vaguely. "La-la-la-la-la-la-la-la-laaaaaa."

Phoebe staggered back to the living room, pulled her suitcase out from under the coffee table, and examined her clothing purchases. What to put on? She'd worn her jeans yesterday, so she slipped into her cute new swingy skirt and floaty top and went out to the courtyard, where Trouble greeted her with all the exuberance of a welcome committee embracing an explorer recently returned from a two-year expedition to the south pole.

"Hey," Phoebe said, kneeling down and staggering as the dog barreled into her. "I'm not leaving you, you know. We're good here."

Trouble licked her face, making happy noises, and Phoebe grinned in spite of herself. "Yeah, yeah, you're glad to see me. Gotcha. Let's go for a walk, and then I'll get you some breakfast. Babette's taking care of you today, but I'll be back later."

She clipped the leash to Trouble's collar and they started out. The dog still limped, and Phoebe didn't want to overdo it. When she got back to the apartment, Harry had moved his vocal warmup to the back patio, and Babette had taken over the kitchen.

"Coffee's ready, honey," Babette said, glancing up from her newspaper, her own cup at her elbow.

"It smells great." Phoebe filled Trouble's water bowl and poured out some dry food for him. Then she poured her own coffee and, at Babette's nod, filled her cup, too.

"La-la-la-la-la-la-la-la-laaaaaa," Harry sang, his voice somewhat muted now that he was outside. Phoebe glanced out the window from him to Babette, who seemed not even to notice that a man with a voice like a mating walrus was serenading the neighborhood.

Phoebe sat down at the table, cradling her coffee. "Babette, can I ask you something personal?"

Babette looked up from the paper, her gaze over her rhinestone drugstore readers sharp and focused. "You can ask. I don't promise to answer, though."

"You and Harry—how long have you been married?"

Babette laughed. "Phoebe, honey, that's not personal. That's a matter of public record."

"But how long?"

"Thirty-five years." Babette folded the paper and stacked it on the table. "Why do you ask?"

"I was wondering how you knew that Harry was the right guy." Phoebe watched out the window as Harry bawled his scales to the birds, the bees, and the city of Las Vegas.

"I'm not sure I *did* know," Babette said, taking a sip of her coffee. "It's a leap of faith, isn't it? Harry was terribly handsome, and I'm a sucker for a gorgeous guy. And he had more charms than a jeweler's bracelet. When we were dating, we always had a great time. It seemed like we'd keep having a great time if we got married. So one day, we did."

That was it? Babette thought Harry was handsome and charming? How did anyone stay married for thirty-five years on that basis? She'd be divorced in five minutes if she had to listen to Harry sing scales every morning.

"Okay," Phoebe said. "You got married, but time goes on, right? And then—what? How—why—do you stay together? What's the secret? Your magic formula?"

Babette laughed. "I wish there was a magic formula," she said. "Everybody's formula is different, but I think the most important thing for me? Harry makes me laugh. A sense of humor is important in marriage. At least, to my marriage. You have to have a sense of humor if your guy dresses up like Elvis and caterwauls to the county at the crack of dawn."

Phoebe laughed, and Babette grinned across the table at her.

"What's all this about? Are you thinking about tying the knot with somebody?"

"I was thinking about my mom," Phoebe said. Her mom, who at that very moment was AWOL with her latest great hope for a wedding ring. "She's been, I guess you could say, a serial monogamist ever since she started dating, but she never married."

"Marriage isn't for everybody," said Babette. "Best if you understand that about yourself early in life. Now, you need more than coffee for breakfast if you're riding your bicycle all the way out to that factory. How about eggs and toast? Harry will stop singing and come in when he smells food, I promise you."

Kristin got to the factory early and lugged her grocery bags into the company break room. After that first day when the Midnight Sun group barely touched the breakfast pastries, she'd wondered what they might prefer instead, so she'd searched the internet and found a recipe for jook, a soft rice dish that a cook could augment as desired. Yesterday she'd tried barbecued pork and green onions, and every last bit got eaten. Score! Today she was going with salmon and ginger.

She started the rice and then went up to her desk on the mezzanine. Ten minutes later Chase strode through the lobby, looking like he was still charging on the football field. All the women in the company had a big crush on him, and he was, she had to admit, very attractive in a muscly sort of way. She went in more for nerds. Her boyfriend, Nick, was an IT guy. He was skinny and short, and he wore heavy glasses with dark frames—pretty much a nerd cliché. But he was hers and she was his, and they were right for each other.

"Coach," she said as he came up the stairs.

"Morning, Kristin."

"Coffee's brewing, and I started the jook for the Midnight Sun people. But there's also cereal for those who are very afraid."

"Speaking as one of the very afraid, thank you. Although I've had breakfast, so I won't have to appear cowardly in front of the investors."

Kristin grinned. "Smart game plan, Coach. So, other than that, what do you need from me today?"

"Do you have all the financials pulled? Their accountants want to start looking at that stuff on Monday."

"Financials and sales projections," Kristin said. "One-, three-, and five-year rollouts all done. Paper copies on your desk."

"Supplier commitments?"

"Included with manufacturing costs."

"Sales partnership contracts?"

"Attached to the sales projections."

"Marketing plans?"

"Paper copies will be ready after lunch."

"Commemorative football jerseys?"

Kristin rolled her eyes. "Should arrive tomorrow. Don't forget you have to autograph them. And have your picture taken with each person wearing one."

Chase groaned. "I will bet you any money that in a week I'll see those shirts on eBay."

"You think so? Let's print up a few thousand and sell 'em ourselves. We'll make a killing."

Chase laughed. "Oversupply will lower the value. All right, I guess that's it, then. Good job, Kristin. And for figuring out the rice thing, too. It was a huge hit. And it shows the investors that we can adapt, understand a market, go the extra mile. Now let's hope the accountants can impress them with the financials."

Kristin hoped so, too. Among other things, if the company got this investment—and if she proved to Chase that she was worth it—she hoped she'd get a raise, maybe even a promotion.

"How are things going so far?" she asked. "Phoebe's translating, right? She'll make it entertaining."

"I hope so." Chase ran his hand through his hair. "They do seem to like her."

Kristin laughed. "Well, Coach, come on. Of course, they like her. She's a *trained operative*."

Chase snorted. "You can't think she's really CIA. She says she speaks a lot of languages, but we only know for sure that she speaks Korean. But if she's CIA, then I'm— I don't know. Captain Kangaroo."

"You do have awfully deep pockets," Kristin said, her eyes dancing. "But I think Phoebe's telling us the truth, don't you? That poodle skirt is a master disguise. After you see it, you don't see anything else."

I see something else, he thought. Even though she probably wouldn't be wearing that poodle skirt anymore. She'd abandon her old uniform now that she had those new clothes he'd seen her tuck into her roller bag.

Conversation trickled up from the lobby and he looked over the edge of the mezzanine to check it out. Phoebe had come in and was chatting with Megan. Right behind her, the investors drifted in. The engineers came out of the production area and were saying hello. They were leading the aerodynamics demonstration today.

Time for work.

Technically, he didn't have to tag along to this presentation. Aerodynamics was the specialty of his engineering team. They could handle it far better than he could, and he wanted the investors to see that his engineers were top-notch. He could stay up here and do some paperwork, prepare for upcoming discussions.

But maybe the Midnight Sun folks would have questions for him. And he'd rather see how things went with the investors than do paperwork.

He headed downstairs, and when he got closer to the test lab, he heard laughter. Phoebe was charming the investors again. She might be nuts, but if she could get these guys to see the value in Venture Automotive so they'd open their checkbooks, she'd be worth the trouble she caused.

He walked into the test lab in time to see the wind fans for the aerodynamic tests blow Phoebe's short skirt up. She grabbed it, laughing, looking just like the iconic Marilyn Monroe photograph. Only better. A lot better.

She grabbed bunches of the swirly fabric in one hand and her hard hat in the other. She said something in Korean, and everyone in the group laughed, too.

He gulped. Phoebe Renfrew might act like a fruitcake, cost him too much time and money, and bug the crap out of at least two of the Midnight Sun folks. But right now, he didn't care very much about any of that. He didn't care that she was an employee and he didn't date employees. The only thing he could think about was how he could get her to laugh like that with him.

He was so screwed.

That night on her way back to Harry and Babette's, Phoebe stopped at the police station to see what the detectives might have learned about Lars and Gustav buying illegal handguns from the pawnshop. Maybe they'd made some progress. She locked her bike to a nearby No Parking sign and went inside.

"I'm here to ask about a report I made," she told the duty officer. She gave him the case number, and the cop typed it in.

"Detective Greenaway is handling that. I'll see if he's in."

He picked up a phone and hit the extension. "Someone to see you about a case," he said. He listened a moment and hung up the phone.

"Through the door to your left," he said. "You'll find him."

Phoebe pushed open the door and entered a large, noisy room that was crowded with cops and desks. She turned left, looking for a guy who seemed like he might be expecting her. About four desks in, a tall, barrel-chested African-American man with tired, assessing eyes and graying hair stood up and watched her approach.

"Miz Renfrew? I'm Detective Dave Greenaway. Tell me about this case." He gestured to a chair by his desk, and Phoebe sat down.

"Well, that's why I'm here." Phoebe crossed her legs, smoothing down her new swirly skirt. It was a little short, and it had almost embarrassed her today in the testing lab. She didn't want to embarrass herself in front of the cops, too. "I'm wondering what you found out, if anything, about that gun buy."

Greenaway tilted his head, eying her. "Yeah, I'm wondering how you came to be in that area of town just when these guys were out buying guns. Did you know they'd be there?"

The question put her on the defensive. *Was this about her now?*

"I followed them," she said. "I'd heard them talking about buying guns. They're Swedish nationals, so they can't get a permit, and any gun buy they make would be illegal. Right?"

"Right. You better explain this to me."

"It's complicated."

"I can probably understand it."

"Sorry," she said. "I didn't mean that the way it sounded. It's *convoluted*. It all started because I'm in the CIA."

Greenaway laughed. "Good one," he said. "Try again."

"I *am* with the CIA," Phoebe said, irritated. "But okay, suspended."

Greenaway raised his eyebrows. "Really. You're telling me

this is official for the CIA?"

"No! No. Not at all. I *wish*." Phoebe took a deep breath. "Like I said, I'm suspended. I was at the courthouse—the Clark County courthouse downtown—and I heard these guys talking about buying guns. They were speaking Korean, and—"

"Hold on," Greenaway said. "I thought you said they were Swedish."

"Right," Phoebe nodded. "They are. Swedish-Koreans. Swedish nationals, ethnic Koreans, speaking Korean."

"Really?" Greenaway said. "How many Swedish citizens are ethnic Koreans speaking Korean, do you know?"

"About four-tenths of one percent," Phoebe said. "Forty-six hundred people. What are the odds, right? So I was worried about their talking about guns, because remember? That Empire State Building threat a few weeks ago had Korean origins. So—"

"Hold on," Greenaway said. "You mean there really was a threat in New York? Not just drama? And you're saying these guys were connected to that?"

"Yes. No. I think so, but I haven't proved it yet. But that's why I was worried. So I followed them to—" Then she remembered that Kristin had asked her to keep Venture Automotive out of the public eye, if possible.

"What?" Greenaway said. "You followed them to where?"

Phoebe sighed. "I'd rather not say, if I don't have to. But the upshot is that these Swedish-Koreans are part of an investor group, and I'm doing the translating there now, and I heard them talk about guns at the... the start-up, too. I followed them after work, and they did buy guns, and can we keep the start-up's name out of it until something breaks? Because they're working to build something here, and it would be a shame if—"

Greenaway held up his hand.

"So I hoped you might be able to do something," she finished. "Figure it out. Whatever it is."

Greenaway shook his head. "There's not a lot we can do," he said. "We know about that pawnshop you reported—it makes illegal gun sales if the price is right. If it's any comfort to you, your Swedish-Korean guys probably paid too much for what they bought."

"It's not much comfort."

"We sent a patrol car over there to check the books, just to jerk the owner's chain a little bit. Looked for a gun sale on that date, and we found one, too."

"And?" Phoebe asked, trying not to sound eager.

"No names that matched those you gave us."

"Probably fake," Phoebe said.

"Probably. The IDs are probably also fake. And our Asian task force, our theft and burglaries unit—none of our departments has any intel that something is going down with Koreans. Or Swedish guys who speak Korean. So we're pretty much at a dead end on our side."

"You can't do anything?"

"We'll do something after they commit a crime with those guns. You have my promise on that. Maybe we can call on the CIA for help."

Phoebe sighed. "I don't know why I have so much trouble convincing people I'm with the CIA."

Greenaway laughed. "You're not wearing a black suit and sunglasses. Or a trench coat with sunglasses. Does that skirt you have on say CIA to you?"

"I blame the movies," Phoebe said. "Damn stereotypes. I'm CIA, or I was, anyway. I will be again. I hope. As soon as I catch these guys. I know something is fishy there."

Greenaway shook his head, still grinning. "When you catch those fishes committing a crime, give me a call. Until next month, when I'll be retired and somebody else has to make sense of this. Until then, I'll be here with my net to reel them in."

Phoebe left the police station and went out to her bike. Now what? Greg Peeling at the CIA wouldn't help her, the cops couldn't help her, Chase didn't believe her, and she needed a place to stay. She didn't want to inconvenience Harry and Babette any longer than she had to. She'd promised them it would be for only a couple of nights. And here it was, after five o'clock, and she'd done nothing about finding another place.

And she felt guilty that Babette was minding her dog.

Maybe she could go to back to her mother's. Maybe Brenda

had paid the back rent. And if not, maybe she could talk her into it. She could give it a shot, anyway.

Phoebe sat down on the retaining wall, took out her phone, and punched in the number.

"Phoebe!" Brenda said. Phoebe could hear the clink of glassware, indecipherable conversation, some clanking and shouts. Her mother was at work.

"Hey, Mom," Phoebe said. "I'm checking in. Did you get my message about your apartment? Your landlord's locked you out."

"I did hear that, sweetie. I'm so sorry for you! What a shock that must have been!"

"Yeah, it kind of was. Do you have a plan? Are you going back there? Maybe you should pay Barry. He won't let you get your stuff if you don't."

"That's the thing. I'm not sure that I want to pay him."

"What? Why not?"

Brenda lowered her voice. "I've been staying with Bud. We're having the best time! I just *know* he's going to pop the question. And Phoebe, he's loaded. I won't need any of my old stuff—I won't *want* any of it—when he does. It's not worth three thousand dollars."

"Really? What about your clothes? And don't you have some jewelry?"

"Cheap stuff." Brenda sniffed. "Besides, I have a few outfits. Otherwise, I don't need much, you know what I'm saying?"

Phoebe wished she didn't. "Okay, Mom. Well, I just wanted to let you know that I'm staying at the O'Sheas for now."

"Oh, that's nice! The way you described them, they seem like wonderful people."

"Yeah, they are." Wonderful enough to take her in when her own mother bailed on her. She cleared her throat. "Stay in touch, Mom, all right?"

"Of course! Listen, sweetie, I gotta go. Customers coming. Love you! Bye!"

"Bye," Phoebe said to the silent air. She put the phone away. She hoped this wouldn't be her future—sleeping on the sofas of unsuspecting but kindly folk. *My life is a space alien movie script,*

110

she thought. Homeless creatures from the CIA invade living rooms across the country!

She smiled to herself, but her shoulders sagged. Crashing at people's houses was an unpleasant reminder of her childhood—the part of her life that she thought she'd put behind her for good. How wrong she'd been.

Maybe someday she'd have a permanent home of her own. With a husband or even a steady boyfriend who would just be there for her.

As if. The way things were going, that would never happen.

She picked up some Indian food—the best in the city, according to Sanjay—and took it back to the O'Sheas' apartment, where Babette gave her the bad news.

"We're sorry, honey," she said sympathetically. "We'd be happy to have you stay here forever. But our son—he's a contractor—called. He's been planning to build our extension for almost a year, when things slowed down a little for him. And that's now. He's coming Saturday, and he'll be staying here while he works. Of course, you can stay here until he gets here. But with the noise and the dust and the crowding—a place of your own will be best for you. Since Chase wants you tip-top for his job."

Phoebe nodded, looking as cheerful as she could. "Sure thing! And thanks for everything, you guys. You'll love that new extension."

When dinner was over, she checked the ads and called apartments for rent. None of them took dogs. After she'd run through the list, she clipped on Trouble's leash for a walk.

"Take him down to the Stars Rising chapel," Harry said as she headed for the door. "Might as well let him pee on the competition's bushes."

"Will do, Harry," she said, grinning.

The night was warm, and she let Trouble out on his retractable leash and thought about how she could get more information about Lars and Gustav—and fast. Who could help? She'd tried the cops. And the CIA—Greg—wouldn't do anything. But maybe someone else at the CIA would. Nattie had gone to advanced training with her and then sat next to her in the office. And Nattie owed her big time for that data breach problem she'd caused back during their training days that Phoebe had fixed, no one the wiser. Maybe she'd help.

She led Trouble down a quieter street and then pulled out her phone and called. Her luck was in. The time was already ten o'clock in DC, but Nattie was still working. She must be on to something important.

"Natasha Wilkinson."

"Nattie," Phoebe said. "It's Phoebe Renfrew."

"Phoebe!" Nattie said. "How are you? *Where* are you?"

"I'm in Vegas, visiting my mom for the time being," Phoebe said. That was stretching the truth, which was that she couldn't afford the rent on her DC apartment when she wasn't getting paid, but Nattie didn't have to know *everything*. "I'm fine, doing a little work, even. Listen, can you do me a favor? A big favor."

"I'm sorry, Phoebe, I can't. Greg put out a memo saying we can't even *talk* to you while the investigation is ongoing."

"I'm not surprised. But I'm working on something that could get me reinstated, and I need your help with some information."

"Phoebe, really, I could lose my job. Or my clearance."

"It's important, Nattie."

"I *can't*. But Greg really is investigating what happened at the Empire State Building. You'll be cleared, and then you can come back. Everything will be fine. You'll see. You won't have to work on anything. No favors required."

"I didn't do anything wrong, but I might not be cleared." Phoebe felt a lump in her throat as she said it. "Greg might not want to clear me. But I'm on to something that—depending on how it plays out—could make them take me back."

"Phoebe, *don't*. Whatever you're up to, it sounds like it could just get you into more trouble."

"I didn't want to bring this up, Nattie, but you owe me." Phoebe waited for several seconds, holding her breath.

Then Nattie came back, sounding resigned. "What kind of favor?"

"It's like this," Phoebe said, more cheerful now. "While I kick my heels in Vegas, I got a great job translating"—*for two weeks*—"at this start-up that's building electric cars. And get this—the CEO's a retired football player, so—"

"You're working for *Chase Bonaventure*?"

Phoebe hadn't known Nattie was a football fan. Maybe she should have led with that fact. Maybe Nattie wouldn't hate her for forcing her to help.

"Yeah, that's right," she said, regrouping. "Chase Bonaventure. You know him?"

"Omigod," Nattie said. "Chase Bonaventure! Of course I don't *know* him, but I know *about* him. I can't believe it! Listen, I've got some vacation time coming. Why don't you invite me out? I'd do anything to meet Chase Bonaventure. I mean, the guy is walking temptation. Are you"—she lowered her voice—"having a fling?"

Phoebe wanted to lie; she really, really did. Thinking about that chest—watching him reach for her books—made her feel like Jell-O. Really hot Jell-O. But she couldn't lie.

"Nope, just friends," she said, stretching the truth about the concept of "friendship" until she thought she heard it shriek in shock and horror. "I'll see what his schedule is and let you know. Now, about this favor."

"Phoebe, is this, ah, government work? Are you on a secure channel?"

Phoebe paused, and Nattie took a deep breath. *Asked and answered.*

"An invitation to meet Chase Bonaventure is nonnegotiable, then," Nattie said. "What do you need?"

"I've run into two foreign nationals supposedly here in Vegas with an investment group. But they've made an illegal weapons purchase, and I wondered if we're tracking them."

"At least that shouldn't take long. Names?"

Phoebe could already hear clacking in the background. *Great.* Nattie was bringing up the database.

"Lars and Gustav Eklund. They're naturalized Swedish citizens, emigrated from North Korea."

Nattie tapped and then there was silence.

"Well, there's *something*," she said eventually. "But it's not clear what. There's a Gustav Eklund, Swedish—you're right there—originally from North Korea. There's a watch but not a hold on him. Same for a Sven Eklund, also originally from North

Korea. Does that make sense to you?"

"Yeah," Phoebe said. "Sven is the father of Gustav and Lars."

"There's nothing on a Lars Eklund," Nattie said. "They're good to travel here, but—I can't figure this entry out. Why we're watching them, I mean. Maybe just because two of them are originally from North Korea."

"Can you dig deeper?"

"I could, but not without raising a lot of red flags that will get us both fired. Are you okay with it if I ask Greg?"

Phoebe didn't want to tell her that she'd asked Greg first. "I guess I'd rather you didn't. Unless you absolutely have to for some reason."

"Okay. If I can discover anything else without alarming the watchdogs, I'll let you know. And Phoebe? Find out when I can come out for a visit."

"Thanks, Nattie. I'm sort of in transitional housing right now, but it'd be great to see you, and I'll check Chase's schedule. I'll talk to you soon, right? These guys are here only for two weeks."

"We never sleep. You know that."

Phoebe disconnected. Nattie would help as much as she could. And the agent had told her one important thing.

The CIA thought Gustav and Sven were worth watching.

Chapter 9

Early the next morning, Chase had just finished up some paperwork for his second bank loan when Phoebe came up the stairs to the mezzanine. He'd become accustomed to her routine—she'd drop by to find out what the investors would see that day, and then she'd join them in the conference room for the jook breakfast that Kristin had made earlier. Today, though, she waved to him through the open door and then plunked down in Kristin's guest chair. He didn't intend to eavesdrop, but you couldn't avoid it when his admin was right there and there wasn't a door to close.

"Phoebs," Kristin said. "What's up?"

"I'm losing my bunk at the O'Sheas."

He knew it. He'd thought that the O'Sheas wouldn't work out. What would she do now?

"Oh, no," Kristin said. "Can I help?"

"I was wondering if you knew of a place—if you have a friend looking for a roommate, or you know of any space in a dog-friendly building."

"Not offhand," Kristin said. "Everybody I know is pretty settled."

"I hate to ask it, but—do you think I could stay with you a few nights? I know Nick is allergic, but I can keep Trouble tied up outside."

He stifled a sigh. He was paying this woman a ton of money to translate, and she couldn't find housing. The thought drove him nuts.

"I'm sorry, Phoebs," Kristin said, real regret in her voice. "If it was just me—but Nick would have a fit, and you *know* something would happen to bring him in contact with Trouble. I'll make some calls today, though, okay? Maybe I can find something."

He had heard enough. He stood up and beckoned her into his office. "Phoebe, come in here, please."

She got up, looking both reluctant and wary, which just about took the cake, as far as he was concerned. She—*they*—needed to get this settled. She didn't have a place to stay, and he needed her stable and functioning and, most of all, *on her game*.

"Housing trouble?" He motioned her to the sofa in the small discussion area at the edge of his office, and more importantly, out of sight of Kristin's desk.

"As of tomorrow," she said, taking a seat on the couch. "The O'Sheas' son is coming, and he needs the sofa bed."

"Stay at my place for now," he said, sitting next to her. "I've got plenty of room. It's simplest."

It wasn't a great solution. For one thing, he was attracted to her. Not that that had to get in the way. He'd just have to remember his no-dating-employees rule.

"Oh, thanks, but I can't. You're my boss, and—"

"You don't have a place to live," he said ruthlessly. "You're *homeless*. You can't be at your best when you're tired and worried, and I need you at your best. Besides, you asked Babette and Harry, your other bosses, for a place to stay, but you can't stay with me? I'm hurt."

That was a lie. He wasn't hurt. Exasperated, yes. But he also felt sorry for her. Her mother was a piece of work. If she'd shown one iota of interest in her daughter—or even if she'd shown enough self-interest to hang on to her apartment—but it was too late for all that. He just felt bad for people who, when they turned to their folks for help, their folks turned away.

Not that he'd ever tell her that. She'd revolt at a sign of pity, and she didn't even easily accept sympathy.

"It's different with Babette and Harry," she said. "I don't know anything about you. I can't—I don't even know for sure if you're—"

"What?" Chase said. "What are you talking about?"

"If you're married," Phoebe said.

"Oh," Chase said, surprised. What did that have to do with anything? Unless she was interested in him. And wasn't *that* an intriguing thought? "Right. Not married. Was once, not anymore. No children. No pets. And, let me add, really big house."

"Thank you. For the information. And it's nice of you to offer. But I still can't stay with you."

"Why not? Of course you'd rather have your own place. I get that. But the short-term rental market tends not to welcome dogs. And you don't have any other place to stay."

Her chin came up.

"*What*?" he said, exasperated again. "Just tell me what the problem is here?"

Her chin came down again. She sighed. "I don't want to take any favors from you."

"How are you taking any favors? You're not even *at* my place yet. If you're still there in a couple of years, *then* we'll talk how you're overdoing it."

She snorted.

He picked up her hand, which she had fisted on her thigh, and uncurled her fingers. Her skin so soft, her will so strong. Her independence, such a pain in the ass.

"This is a one-time, short-term, no-strings offer that I'm begging you to take," he said, willing her to give in. "It's the best— the smartest—solution. Everything's gonna work out, you'll see. As long as Trouble is housebroken. If he isn't, I'm feeding him to the gators."

Phoebe laughed. And that was the problem. She liked Chase too much. She didn't have a problem with accepting a favor when she needed it, because everybody needed a hand now and then. What she couldn't do was repeat her mother's life. She couldn't move in with a guy she liked after she'd known him for only five days. That way was disaster, on top of her other already existing disasters.

But Chase was paying her an outrageous amount of money to do a good job, and she owed him that, at the very least. And in the short run, if she stayed at his place, she wouldn't have to spend time looking for an apartment. She'd get more sleep at Chase's place, as well, and he'd probably drive her to work, too.

And she wanted to stay at his place. Not that she could afford to factor that into her decision.

Maybe it could work. She was pretty sure that Chase liked her, but he probably dated beautiful, high-maintenance types. Models. Professional cheerleaders. Like that. She could stay at his place—for a short time, anyway—and not get hurt or tangled up. Or destroyed.

"How much space do you have, anyway?"

"You can have your own room, if that's what you're asking. Even your own bathroom."

Her own room. Her own *bathroom.* And she was so tired. Phoebe sighed.

"Just say yes," he said, stroking her hand.

It would be so easy to give in.

"All right," she said, nodding. "Thank you. For one night. Until I find something more permanent."

"For longer than that," he said. "At least until Midnight Sun leaves."

Her own bathroom at least for a week. She could be bought after all.

"Okay. Let me tell Harry and Babette." She pulled out her phone and tapped the number.

"Babette? Good news. Well, mixed news, I guess. I'll be staying with Chase for a while."

"That's not good news, Phoebe, we loved having you."

"Thank you for letting me stay. And for taking care of Trouble."

"Anytime. I mean that, Phoebe. If we weren't expanding the wedding chapel right now, you'd still be more than welcome to stay for as long as you liked."

Phoebe felt her throat close up a little. Babette was being nicer to her than own mother.

"Is Chase there? Let me talk to him for a minute," Babette said, and Phoebe handed him the phone.

"Babette wants to talk to you," she said.

Chase took the phone with a question in his eyes.

"She's a special girl," Phoebe was close enough to hear Babette say when he got on the line. "You mind how you go. I expect you to take good care of her."

"Yes, ma'am, I intend to," Chase said. "We'll be over after work to pick up her things."

That night it took no time to pick up Phoebe's books, her suitcase, and Trouble, and a short while later, Chase pulled into a circular drive and stopped in front of what appeared to be a decent-sized hotel. Outside lights were on over the portico, and another dim light shone through the lobby, but otherwise the three-story place was dark. Pretty quiet for a hotel.

"Where are we?" Phoebe asked.

"My place."

"Get out. You *live* here? By *yourself?*" Phoebe jerked her head to see Chase's rueful grin. "I mean, you said you had plenty of room, but this is something else."

"Yeah. Now you can see why you won't crowd me."

"No kidding." Phoebe turned back to gaze at the house. "I mean, holy crap. Look at this place."

She got out of the car and stared up at the building. It was huge. Gorgeous. Flawlessly landscaped. A fountain burbled. Night jasmine bloomed. The gleaming white structure seemed to be half a city block long—except that the neighborhood they were in didn't seem to have city blocks.

"Where is this place, anyway?"

Chase went to the back of the SUV and opened the door. "We're still in the city, if that's what you mean. The back of the house borders a golf course and park. No neighbors back there."

Phoebe took a deep breath, smelling the dry desert air mixed with the florals. "Jeez. It's a freaking mansion. Or bigger than that. A castle. Why did you get this place?"

He took out her suitcase and books. "I used to live in a regular house. This place was another investment, like the car company. I always meant to turn it into a hotel, but I didn't get around to it. Then my ex-wife got the house we lived in, I had to live somewhere, the Snakes were in the postseason, and I didn't have time to house hunt. So I moved in here. I like it, but I don't need fifteen bedrooms."

Phoebe halted in her tracks. "*Fifteen* bedrooms?"

Chase grinned. "And nine bathrooms. Full baths. Six half baths."

"Six half baths," Phoebe repeated. She felt faint. Nobody she'd ever met could afford a place like this—or even a place half this size. Fifteen bedrooms!

"Perfect for a small hotel, right? The first floor even has a bar with a view of the pool. Of course, I'd need to add some bathrooms. Or expand the small ones. But small change."

"Small change," Phoebe said. "To add bathrooms. To the nine you've already got? Now you're teasing me."

He grinned, hoisting up the box of books with one hand and the suitcase with the other. "Come on. I'll show you around."

"That'll take a *week*," Phoebe said. "We'll get lost, and we'll starve to death looking for the kitchen. Our bones will be found by archeologists living one hundred years from now."

"Don't exaggerate." Chase unlocked the front door and pushed it open. "It's not that big. And it's a simple layout. The archeologists will find us in fifty years. If not sooner."

"Oh, good," Phoebe said. "That's so comforting."

"Come on, Trouble," Chase called, and Phoebe's dog gave up sniffing the shrubbery and trotted inside.

Phoebe blinked when Chase turned on the lights. "Okay, I'm beyond shock and awe. Seriously, did someone build this place to be a house? Because it looks like a hotel. A really nice, expensive hotel."

"That's what I thought, too," Chase said, setting the carton of books on the entryway table. "Like I said, that's why I bought it, to be a hotel. But someone did build it to be a house."

"They must have had a lot of kids."

"They had too much money, *cher*. That's what they had. So, I'll give you the quick tour and you can settle in."

"Can I pick my own bedroom?"

"Why would I have fourteen available bedrooms if you couldn't pick the one you like?"

Phoebe grinned suddenly. This was like living a fairy tale. "Okay, let's check it out."

"Kitchen's that way," Chase began, pointing down the hallway to the left. "Also pantries, dining rooms, and solarium. Down this hallway..."

Thirty minutes later, dizzy from choice, she picked the bedroom she'd seen first.

"It's fantastic," she said, drinking in the room's decor. "It's got all those palms out the window, but I can see the stars, and the doors open right onto the patio, and the pool is right there!"

"And one of the nine full bathrooms is attached."

"A major selling point." Phoebe grinned and then she couldn't help it, she twirled around in the middle of the most beautiful bedroom she'd ever seen. It was a soothing shade of pale aqua, and the drapes were light and fluffy in aqua and white. She had a dull orangish and aqua rug on the hardwood floor, and the walk-in closet was about as big as her mom's former apartment. And the bathroom! She could soak in the tub all day. Or stand under those giant, rainy-type showerheads in the separate shower. She'd never seen such luxury.

"I'll just let you, ah, dance around or whatever." Chase edged away. "Do you remember where the kitchen is? I go to the office fairly early, but it's Saturday tomorrow—you should sleep as late as you like. There's plenty of stuff for breakfast in the morning. Help yourself to anything you see."

"Okay." She sat down quickly on the bed, feeling overwhelmed. "Thank you again."

"No trouble, *cher.* Just ask me if you can't find something. Sleep well."

Phoebe blinked. "Wait. How do I locate you if I can't find something? I need flares or an emergency warning system or something."

Chase nodded and walked over to the bed, holding out his hand. "Give me your phone."

"My phone?"

"So you can call me if you need something."

Phoebe, embarrassed, felt her face get warm. "I was kidding."

"I'm not. Phone."

Phoebe handed it over, and Chase keyed in his number for her.

"There," he said, handing it back. "Call me now, so I'll have your number."

Phoebe tapped the Call icon, watching him as his phone rang.

"Hi," he said into it, smiling at her.

"Hi," she said, feeling a little breathless.

"Call if you need me." Chase headed for the door. "Flares are hell on the carpets."

The next morning when Phoebe woke up, she didn't know at first where she was. Dappled sun broke through the blinds, creating a cool pattern on the bamboo floor. Crisp sheets covered a very comfortable bed, not a sofa. Then she remembered.

Chase's house-or-hotel. The place with fifteen bedrooms.

She stretched, feeling like a princess, the cool silkiness of the sheets stroking her skin. Then Trouble whined, and the princess feeling evaporated.

"I bet you wish you had your own bathroom," she said to the dog. "Although I suppose in the dog universe, the world is your bathroom." She slipped on an oversized tee and opened the door to the patio.

Trouble streaked outside and promptly watered a towering palm.

"You have to pick up after him," Chase said. "Because I sure as hell am not."

Phoebe shrieked.

"Sorry, *cher*. Didn't mean to scare you. How are you this morning? Ready for breakfast?"

He was lounging in the shade at a poolside table that was set for breakfast. The long lap pool was still now, the water as smooth as aquamarine glass, but damp patches along the edge showed that Chase had gone for a morning swim. He wore a white terry robe and his hair was wet. Next to him, Phoebe felt terribly underdressed. She wasn't wearing anything under her T-shirt—her oversized but still much-too-short T-shirt. She didn't know where to look.

"I need to get dressed first," she said.

He shrugged. "Wear my robe, if that makes you more comfortable." He took it off and held it out to her.

122

Like that was better? Now there he was, sitting there all bare-chested and rippled muscles again. She *still* didn't know where to look.

"Sit down," he invited, his mouth twitching. "You're probably ready for coffee."

In fact, the poolside table was covered in dishes, and the plate in front of Chase showed evidence of a breakfast partly consumed. A coffeepot was plugged into an outlet in one of the columns that supported a trellis. Outlets by the pool! Incredibly convenient, and a miracle nobody got electrocuted.

Her nose twitched at the coffee aroma. It would be a shame to waste it.

"Thanks," she said, putting on his robe and rolling up the sleeves. It was soft and way too big for her, but it was damp, just enough to feel good in the dry air, and slightly warm from his body. It smelled like sandalwood. Phoebe shivered.

She slid into the chair opposite him and poured herself a cup of coffee. "Delicious," she said, taking a sip. "Do you always get up early and make breakfast?"

"You have to thank Marta for breakfast. She comes in two days a week, and she usually makes some cold stuff for the weekend. There's ham, boiled eggs, fruit. Unless you want something hot."

Phoebe eyed him over her cup. "You've got staff."

"Of course, I've got staff. The place is too big for just me."

Phoebe rolled her eyes, but she grinned. "There's one thing about all this I don't get," she said, taking a hard-boiled egg from a bowl that Chase passed her.

"Only one?"

Phoebe smacked the egg on the mosaic-tiled table and rolled it around to crack the shell.

"You're stinking rich," she said, peeling it. "Plus, you've got stinking-rich friends. Why do you need Midnight Sun? Not that I'm not happy to be cashing in."

Chase almost choked on his toast. Then he shook his head, clearing his throat.

"I need the Midnight Sun money, at least to get off the ground," he said when he got his breath back. "When I first took over this company, I put everything I had into it. Every cent. That was about fifty million, which was not nearly enough. Think of the car companies in Detroit. They're multi*billion*-dollar global operations. That's what I want for Venture Automotive. So I need a lot more money than what I personally have, or what my friends have."

"It's incredible that in some circles, fifty million is chump change," Phoebe said, biting into her egg.

Chase grinned. "I wouldn't call it chump change, exactly. But I also want to partner with Midnight Sun because they have a lot of experience in car manufacture, including cars that run on alternative fuels. I want to know if they think this operation is sound. If so, we're in business. If not, I have a very expensive hobby. That's not what I want. If my company isn't feasible as it is, then I'll either fix it or get rid of it. But I think it's feasible. Just undercapitalized."

"Oh." Phoebe swallowed some egg. "Okay. Makes sense."

Chase grinned. "Too much soapbox?"

"Not too much," she said, her voice muffled around the egg. "I've never discussed world domination over breakfast before. It's stimulating. We overtake GM by lunchtime, right?"

"Game on."

Phoebe finished the egg and swallowed some coffee. "Is that fruit salad over there? And bagels?"

Chase handed her the dishes. "And if we're overtaking GM by lunchtime, I have to get to the office. Do you need anything before I go?"

"Nope. What do you need me to do?"

"Swim. Nap. Read. Watch movies. Some of the investors are going to Hoover Dam today, so—"

"*Hoover Dam?*" Phoebe choked on a grape. "Are the Eklunds going?" *What if they had a bomb in that truck?*

Chase shook his head. "Just the engineers. They wanted a behind-the-scenes tour, but the Hoover Dam people said no. So they're going as tourists with one of those headset audio tours that has Korean on it. That's why I didn't ask you to go with them. You're not planning to do anything to the Eklunds, are you?"

"What could I do to the Eklunds?" Phoebe said, evading the question. At least they wouldn't be blowing up Hoover Dam today. That was good news.

Chace watched her for a second while Phoebe averted her eyes, popping a sliced bagel into the toaster.

"Anyway, there's nothing for you to do at the plant," he said finally. "Will you be all right out here?"

"Do you have internet access?"

"Of course I have internet access. Do you think I live like a savage?"

Phoebe laughed, glancing at the pool, the landscaping, the beautiful house curving white against the cloudless blue sky. *Savage* was not exactly the word she'd have used.

"Just checking. In that case, I have plenty to keep me occupied."

"I thought tonight we—I—could cook something. Nothing fancy. Steaks on the grill. Does that work for you?"

Phoebe nodded. "Sounds terrific. But I'm putting you to a lot of trouble."

Chase shrugged. "I have to eat whether you're here or not." He stood, his wet swim trunks clinging to powerful thighs.

And then Phoebe saw a white scar that snaked around Chase's kneecap and down his leg. Her stomach churned at the sight of it.

"What happened to your knee?"

Chase looked surprised. "Blew it out in a game. That's why I'm not playing anymore. I thought you knew."

"It must hurt."

He grinned ruefully. "It hurt more at the time, believe me, *cher*," he said. "Now it's just all rehab. So, I'm gonna go. Make yourself at home. Call if you need something. And leave the Eklunds alone."

She felt a flare of irritation. Chase's offer to put her up had been generous, and she was happy to be living, however temporarily, in the lap of luxury. But she couldn't afford to get too comfortable. Not in the house. And certainly not with Chase.

Especially because she couldn't leave the Eklunds alone.

Saturday morning dawned, another bright day in Las Vegas—did the Las Vegans never tire of this weather?—and Lars sat in the hotel restaurant and picked at his plate of bacon, french toast, and scrambled eggs with cheese. The food was too heavy, and there was too much of it. He'd tried to make his preferences known to the waitress with the help of the translation app, with little success. At least the menu had pictures. That helped.

They all had trouble ordering in restaurants because of the language barrier, but he'd been born and raised in Sweden and had Swedish tastes. Gustav, older than he by fourteen years, hadn't arrived in Stockholm until he was twelve, and their father hadn't escaped North Korea until he was middle-aged. Gustav ate Swedish food without complaint but without relish; Sven had never fully acculturated to the West, and for him, the food choices were mostly unpalatable. Right now he pondered his damp tea bag and untouched, congealing oatmeal.

Gustav finished his coffee and cleared his throat. "Father, let's go over our plans for today."

"Our appointment with the hospitality representative at the conference venue is at ten o'clock," Sven said.

Lars nodded. "We probably shouldn't count on her telling us very much about the conference."

Sven pursed his lips into a thin line. "We can see the layout and check out the security," he said. "We'll ask how they set up their conferences. That will be informative."

"Of course. You're right, Father," Gustav said.

He's such a toady. Gustav always went along with their father and his *Masters of the Universe* fantasy. Lars could only hope that it didn't get them all killed.

"It's almost nine," Gustav said now. "Are we ready?"

Lars swallowed the last of his coffee and grimaced. While they were out, he wanted to get Helga a present, and he'd also check out the nearest Starbucks. This hotel coffee managed to be both weak and bitter, which should be a crime, considering what they charged for it.

"Ready," he said, signaling for the waiter.

Gustav signed the check.

"Okay," he said. "Let's go see about a kidnapping."

Chase left for the office and Phoebe finished her breakfast. Hoover Dam was safe from Swedish-Korean terrorists—for today, anyway. She'd been checking the odometer on the truck every morning, and the Eklunds weren't driving anywhere at night. But what did Lars, Gustav, and Sven have up their sleeve?

She took a shower and put on her new red skinny jeans—*thank you, Kristin, for the shopping trip*—with her sleeveless striped top. She felt like a new woman. Who was staying in a fancy hotel. With a celebrity. What would Nattie do if she could see her now? She'd be green with envy. For the first time, she felt almost cheerful about being suspended without pay.

She dug out her phone and called Sanjay. "Sanjay. It's me, Phoebe. What are you doing?"

"Doing?" He sounded a little groggy. "What should I be doing at eight thirty in the morning except sleeping after working last night until the wee hour of three o'clock? Of course, I am not sleeping anymore. Now I suppose I am awake. That is what I'm doing."

"Oh, I'm sorry! Never mind. Go back to sleep. We'll talk later."

"Your optimism is ever refreshing, but it is much too late for that." Sanjay sighed, and Phoebe heard some rustling and thumping in the background.

"There," he said. "Now I am sitting up and can take whatever bad news you have to tell me. Why have you called at this unconscionable hour of the morning? Even the birds are not yet awake."

"I hate to tell you, the birds are awake," Phoebe said. "They're out catching worms. But today's Saturday. Nobody's at the factory except Chase. I wondered if you wanted to trail Lars and Gustav with me?"

"Right now?"

"Well, yeah. It's the weekend. They're out there, unsupervised. I want to know what they're doing."

"My best guess for their activity right now is that they're sleeping in."

"You can't possibly know that. That's why we have to go on a stakeout."

"Is it so impossible that you go by yourself?"

"Don't you remember how, a few days ago, you said I could

call you anytime to go sleuthing? Besides, it's too hard to follow them on my bike."

"Seriously? It hasn't occurred to you that Mr. Bonaventure, for whom you are working, if I am not mistaken, is the owner of an electric-car manufacturing concern? Are you attempting to persuade me that you cannot ask him for the loan of an automobile for one week? He must have more cars lying about than our own taxi service does."

"His cars are all bright yellow," Phoebe said, annoyed. For a person who just woke up, Sanjay was being awfully argumentative. "Yellow's not exactly a subtle color if you don't want to be noticed. Now, do you want to come with me, or not?"

"The taxi is yellow," Sanjay said. "And orange. And pink. That color palette is hardly subtle, either."

"*It's a taxi*," Phoebe said. "Nobody notices taxis. They're everywhere. The Eklunds have been looking at Chase's yellow electrics all week. We'd be spotted."

Phoebe heard a long sigh on the other end of the phone.

"Very well," Sanjay said. "I'll pick you up in—Where are you?"

"At Chase's," Phoebe said with a rush of relief. "Thanks, Sanjay. I owe you."

"You are *where*? At *Mr. Bonaventure's?*"

"Right. Do you have the address? It's—"

"You're staying at the home of Chase Bonaventure?"

"Well, yes," Phoebe said. "For a little while. Like maybe a week."

"At the actual home."

"*Yes.* I'll make sure you meet him before I move out. When can you get here?"

"I do not wish to obtrude myself on Mr. Bonaventure."

"He isn't here right now. He went to the office. So, no opportunity to obtrude."

Sanjay grunted.

"But it wouldn't be an obtrusion if you did want to meet him. He wouldn't mind."

"In that case, I would be delighted to meet him," Sanjay said. "It would be a very great honor."

"I'll see what I can do," Phoebe said, holding on to her patience with effort. "Now—when do you think you can get here?"

"Perhaps thirty minutes."

"Thank you, Sanjay. I appreciate your help. And I'm sorry I woke you."

"Do not worry about waking me. I do not need any sleep. I might be so tired today that I injure myself on the road, but I'm sure the local hospitals are well-equipped for emergencies and especially amputations."

"Don't be grouchy," Phoebe said. "I'll make a thermos of tea for you. We'll keep the radio on. You can take a catnap if there's a stakeout. It'll be fun."

"Make it milky tea," Sanjay said. "As I said several days ago, call anytime. Perhaps again early tomorrow morning."

"That can be arranged," Phoebe said, grinning. "Because I know you don't want to miss anything."

Phoebe put Trouble in the fenced, grassy terrace by the kitchen—*really, it was exactly as if Chase had* planned *to get a dog*—and made a sack lunch for herself and Sanjay, just in case. The tea was a little harder. When she was ready and everything was packed into her messenger bag, she went outside to wait.

Phoebe strolled around the front of the house, checking out what she hadn't been able to see the night before when they'd driven up in the dark. The place was huge but graceful with simple, soaring lines. The garage bay had five doors—*who owned five cars? The people who needed fifteen bedrooms*—but only one vehicle sat in the space, a large black SUV. She looked longingly at it. It would be nice—and certainly more convenient for following the Eklunds—if she could drive. She wished she had time to learn.

Besides the car, the garage housed only some aluminum shelving holding sports equipment and a few plastic bins. Chase really didn't need all this space.

Sanjay arrived inside the promised thirty minutes, and when they got to the hotel where the investors were staying, the white truck was still in the parking lot. Sanjay pulled into a space, turned off the ignition, and poured some tea into the thermos cap.

"What now?" he asked. "Do you propose that we just sit here

and wait for them to emerge?"

"And follow them when they go somewhere. Assuming that wherever they go, they'll drive the truck. What if they decide to take a taxi and leave by the front? I hope I didn't guess wrong about this."

But she hadn't guessed wrong. Shortly after nine, Lars, Gustav, and Sven came out the rear entrance of the hotel, got into the truck, and drove out of the lot. Sanjay gulped the last of his tea and handed her the empty cup, fired up the taxi, and followed them out onto the street.

"We are on the hunt," he said, sounding excited, edging the taxi into the left-turn lane after them. "We will follow these miscreants and discover their wrongdoing! I apologize for my earlier skepticism. I'm not a morning person."

"No worries, Sanjay," Phoebe said, her eyes glued to the white truck. "I'm glad you're here. Now let's figure out what these guys are up to."

Chapter 10

ustav drove the white truck, forcing Lars and Sven to cram into the remaining seat.

"It's not far," Gustav said. "It won't take long, even though the streets are such a maze."

Lars scowled at Gustav, who could afford to be smug about their discomfort. Wasn't that just like him, pointing out the softness of others while pretending he was making the difficult choice?

Traffic was light at this time of day, and they reached the Desert Dunes Resort and Casino with fifteen minutes to spare. The place was enormous, with its own convention center that was attached to the resort hotel by a long glass concourse, simplifying accommodations for conference attendees. Quiet today, the convention center would be bustling in a week when the next conference came to town.

"Nice place." Lars looked around at the decorative fountains and colorful tile embellishments of the resort/ casino's massive lobby.

"We are not here to book a stay," Sven said.

"I *know*." Honestly, did his father never lighten up? "We're here to kidnap the secretary of state. As if I didn't know. *Jeez*."

"Will you shut up?" Gustav said. "Somebody will hear you."

"*Relax*. Nobody's paying any attention. Plus, nobody here speaks Korean."

"Except for the person we're meeting," Sven said.

Lars sighed and looked for someone who could help them. Tucked away by a smaller side entrance was the concierge desk and bell captain's station, cordoned off by red velvet ropes.

"The concierge is over there," he said. "Why don't we ask him where the hospitality person is?"

He powered up the Swedish-to-English translation app on his phone as he led the way to the corner desk. This language problem was getting old. Why couldn't Sven have sent him and Gustav to regular Swedish public school? That way they'd have been learning English since forever, and they'd be fluent in it. Maybe if they had English, they could have just written a nice note to the U.S. secretary of state and asked for help, and they wouldn't have to go through this kidnapping joke, which he'd always been against.

But no. His father had wanted them to learn Korean ways, so they had been privately tutored at home and only in Korean. It was a miracle he and Gustav had even learned Swedish. Thank heaven the Swedish government didn't allow homeschooling anymore. Now kids had to go to school, where they learned English.

Lucky them.

"Can I help you gentlemen?" the concierge asked in English.

"We have a ten o'clock appointment with the hospitality captain," he said in Swedish into the phone, and then he held the phone out to the concierge.

"We-have-an-a-point-ment… with the hospital leader," the computer voice jerked out in English.

"The hospital leader?" the concierge said. "Are you sick? Do you need a doctor? Or an ambulance?"

The guy seemed confused. What had that stupid translation app said that wasn't right? This was one more example of why attending public school in Sweden would have been a good idea. Want to kidnap the U.S. secretary of state? *Learn English first.* When this was over, he was going to write a book.

"Do you speak Swedish?" Lars asked the concierge directly. "Or Korean?"

The concierge shook his head no. Okay.

Then Lars saw an advertising brochure for a guided tour to Hoover Dam. Maybe that word would work. He spoke into the phone.

"We have an appointment to tour the hotel," he said and held the phone out to the concierge.

"We-have-an-a-point-ment-to…make-a…tour-of-the-hotel," the translation app said.

"Oh, a *tour*!" the concierge said, clearly relieved. "You want the hospitality captain."

Lars felt himself smiling at the concierge. International communication, one translation app at a time.

Seconds later, a beaming middle-aged woman wearing a navy suit that seemed to be the hotel staff uniform came out of a back office, stepped around the red velvet rope stand that marked the bell captain's area, and shook everyone's hand.

"I'm Mrs. Chu," she said in Korean, addressing Sven. "You're the folks who made the appointment to tour our hotel and convention center."

"Yes," Sven said. "My sons and I are members of a Swedish investment group, and we hope to hold a trade conference here. We wanted to tour your facility in person before we commit."

"How wonderful!" Mrs. Chu said. "How many people would you expect to attend?"

"We can't be sure," Sven said. "If it is not too much trouble, we'd like to see what facilities you have for up to several thousand."

That was the size of the conference that the secretary of state was attending next week.

"We can accommodate that easily," Mrs. Chu said. "In fact, we're hosting a conference of about that size this upcoming weekend. You can see our arrangements. Please come this way."

"There they are!" Phoebe said as Sanjay pulled into the Desert Dunes parking lot. "They're just going into the hotel."

"Going from one hotel to another," Sanjay asked. "I am not fully comprehending this itinerary. Perhaps they are up to no shenanigans. Perhaps they are having a relaxing day only, enjoying a meal or the spa services, or visiting the casino. Perhaps there is a special event here?"

"If we wait out here in this sweltering parking lot, we'll never know," Phoebe said, opening the taxi's door.

"If they spot you, they'll know that you're following them."

Phoebe turned back. "That's okay," she said. "I'd stick to them like glue if it meant they couldn't do anything bad." Anyway, she didn't have to be all trench-coaty about it. She didn't have to lurk. She could give them a reason she was in the hotel. She might not discover what they were up to, but she might learn *something*.

The inside of the resort hotel was wonderfully cool and calming. Phoebe strolled through the impressive lobby and within seconds spotted the Eklunds over by the concierge desk, talking to a hotel employee.

"There they are," she said, nudging Sanjay. She pasted a big smile on her face as she approached. "Sven! Gustav and Lars! What a surprise running into you here!"

Surprise was not the word she would have used to describe how they looked at seeing her. *Horrified* was more like it.

Three heads whipped around. Gustav did a double take. Lars dropped his phone. Sven jumped, backpedaling so fast that he tripped on the stand that anchored the red velvet rope. Losing his balance, arms windmilling wildly, he pitched back, falling against the bell captain's podium. His head cracked sharply against the corner, and he dropped to the floor, smacking his head again against the tile floor. Blood spurted from a cut on his temple.

He lay still.

Phoebe stared in shock. She hadn't meant for *that* to happen.

"See what you've done!" Gustav shouted, pointing his finger at her. "You've killed my father!"

Heads turned at the crash and shouting.

"No!" Phoebe said in Korean. "He can't be dead! I just wanted to—"

"We need an ambulance!" The concierge leaped out from behind the desk and knelt down, reaching for Sven's pulse.

Mrs. Chu reached for the concierge phone, but Sanjay already had his phone out. He dialed 911 as the concierge whipped off his jacket and propped it under Sven's feet. Phoebe dug out a packet of tissues from her bag and dabbed at the blood on Sven's head.

"A man has had a most terrible fall at the Desert Dunes hotel," Sanjay said. "Please make all possible haste!"

"You'll be sorry!" Gustav snarled at Phoebe.

"I didn't mean to startle him!" Phoebe said.

"It was an accident." Lars handed a bottle of water to Phoebe, who used it to dampen the tissues she held.

"You tried to kill him!" Gustav said. "He will never recover!"

"Let's see what the EMTs say," Phoebe said. "You know I didn't try to hurt him. I just said hello!"

Within minutes, the ambulance arrived and paramedics rushed into the main entrance. Phoebe jumped to her feet and waved her arms wildly.

"Over here!" she shouted, and the EMTs dashed over.

By now they'd attracted quite a crowd, but Mrs. Chu had reorganized the red velvet ropes to keep the curious away. The EMTs started to work on Sven. One of them, a tall African-American with ED stitched on his pocket, turned to Gustav and Lars.

"Are you with this guy?"

"They are," Phoebe said, stepping up. "They're his sons. The three of them speak Korean and Swedish. No English. I know them. I speak Korean."

"You should probably come with us, then," Ed said, "at least until he's admitted. They might have somebody who speaks Korean or Swedish at the hospital. Tell them."

"Okay." Phoebe turned to Lars and Gustav.

Gustav glowered. Lars looked anxious.

"We're all going to the hospital." She told them what the EMT had said. "I'm sorry this happened," she added. "But they don't seem to think his injuries are life-threatening."

The EMTs stood up and buckled Sven onto the gurney.

"We're going to Mercy Hospital on Hollywood Street," Ed told her. "The sons can go in the ambulance, or they can follow us in their own vehicle. You have a way to get there?"

Phoebe glanced at Sanjay.

"Of course," he said.

Phoebe gave Lars and Gustav the information.

"We'll find it," Gustav said.

"I'll meet you in the emergency room," Phoebe said.

Gustav and Lars followed the EMTs out of the hotel lobby,

and Phoebe turned to Sanjay.

"Sorry about this, Sanjay," she said.

"No worries," Sanjay said. "I'll call my taxi dispatch and tell them. If we are not sleuthing any more today, my cousin Amir might want me in the garage after I drop you at the hospital."

"I'll go out and see if anyone needs any translating before they take off."

She hurried outside. The EMTs slid the gurney into the ambulance, and then Ed jumped in the back. Gustav and Lars were already in the white truck, waiting to follow them.

Sick with worry, she glanced back at Sanjay, who was talking on the phone and walking through the lobby toward her. What if Sven needed extensive care? Chase would be furious about all of it. The accident might derail his plans. He'd warned her not to jeopardize the meetings. And just this morning, he'd told her not to bother the Eklunds.

She'd better call him. She dug through her bag for her phone. Just as her fingers closed around the device, she glanced up to see the white truck barreling down the driveway, heading straight at her.

"I'll kill her!" yelled Gustav. That woman! That interfering busybody! Why couldn't she leave them alone? He revved the engine and bore down on the accelerator, steering wildly around pedestrians. "She tried to kill our father! She is destroying our plan!"

"She isn't! She didn't!" Lars shouted. "It was an accident! Slow down!"

"I'll put an end to this!"

He yanked the wheel to the left, steering the truck straight at Phoebe, who was searching in her bag for something, not watching traffic. He stamped on the accelerator, and the truck leaped forward.

"Gustav! No!" shrieked Lars, grabbing for the steering wheel. He and Gustav struggled to control the weaving truck. As it roared down on Phoebe, Lars jerked the wheel one last, desperate time. The truck veered to the right, away from the curb, missing the translator by mere inches, and barreled instead toward a traffic median landscaped with palm trees and other desert plants.

Lars didn't care. He hung on to the wheel for dear life, fighting with Gustav for control. As long as Gustav didn't kill anyone, smacking into a palm tree would merely be an up-close visit with local vegetation. Gustav cursed as the van jumped the curb. The door scraped against some landscaping cacti, the metal shrieking as spines scratched the paint. Then Gustav wrenched the wheel over, out of Lars's hands, and straightened out, swinging the truck back into the traffic lane.

"Phoebe!" Lars said, twisting in his seat, trying to see out the side. "Did you hit her? Is she all right?"

"I don't know and I don't care!" Gustav snarled, but he'd gotten himself under control. He was still driving too fast, but he was following the ambulance, which had streaked out of the parking lot. Gustav turned left onto the major thoroughfare without squealing the tires.

Lars heaved a sigh of relief and settled back into the seat. He hadn't seen any bodies in the road. Gustav hadn't smashed the truck or themselves, and the police hadn't arrested them, either. So far, so good.

For an instant as the truck bore down on her, Phoebe was frozen to the spot in shock. And then it was on her. The protruding side mirror smacked her in the shoulder, and as she stumbled, the vehicle grazed her hip. The force flung her into a concrete column, and she bounced hard to the sidewalk, sprawling on the gritty surface. The scrape sent a white-hot shot of pain to her knee, her hands burned, and her elbow felt numb. As her heart hammered in her chest, she tried to assess if whether anything was broken. She didn't think so. Her hip ached and her scrapes stung, but her wrists and knee moved freely. Probably none of her injuries was serious.

The doorman and Sanjay reached her at the same time.

"Phoebe! Speak! Tell me you're alive!" Sanjay said, leaning over her, his face creased in concern.

"Miss! Miss! Are you all right?" the doorman asked.

"I'm fine," Phoebe said, struggling to sit up. "I think."

Her new red jeans had certainly taken a beating. The fabric

was abraded down one side where she'd skidded across the concrete, and the knee was torn out. Through the tear, Phoebe saw a bloody gash. Her arm was scraped up, too. Maybe something was wrong with her wrist after all.

"You do not appear to be fine," Sanjay said, looking at her knee.

"My jeans took the worst of it," Phoebe said. "Although I'm not too sure about my wrist. Help me up, will you?"

"That driver should be arrested!" the doorman said. "Did anyone get the license plate?"

"It'll be on the security camera," one of the valet parking attendants offered.

"You don't need to do that," Phoebe said, leaning on Sanjay's arm as she got slowly to her feet. "I know who's driving the vehicle."

The doorman blinked. "Not very nice friends you have."

"No," Phoebe said. "You're right about that."

"Why don't you go inside and rest for a minute, miss?" the doorman said. "Ask the bartender for a brandy or some coffee or anything on the house, tell him I sent you. You don't want to be driving right away."

"I'm driving her," Sanjay said. "Phoebe, what would you like to do? Should we be going to the emergency room?"

"I think I'm okay," Phoebe said. "Let's just go to your cab." She nodded to the doorman. "Thank you for your help."

She hobbled across the driveway and into the parking lot with Sanjay. When she got in the taxi, she leaned back with a sigh of relief.

"The rat bastards tried to run me over!" she said. "And now I'm mad and everything hurts and my new pants are ruined and I don't want to go to the hospital to help them. Even if I could help them, which I might not be in any shape to do."

"If you are thinking that you owe them anything, you must be suffering from concussion," Sanjay said. "Are you absolutely certain that you don't wish to go the hospital yourself? An MRI or even an X-ray could answer any pressing medical questions."

As quickly as her anger had come, it was gone, leaving her exhausted and shaky. The effects of an adrenaline rush, she supposed.

"My head is about the only thing that doesn't hurt, but I want to get some ice on this wrist. Take me home. To Chase's home, I mean."

"Very well," Sanjay said, turning the key in the ignition. When they got to Chase's, he helped her inside, made up an ice pack for her wrist, admired the living room and kitchen, and declined a self-guided tour. Phoebe called the hospital, where an emergency room nurse told her that Sven had a translator, was undergoing tests, and would be admitted to the hospital overnight for observation.

"He's going to be fine," Phoebe, hugely relieved, told Sanjay.

"I am not caring all that much about how any of those murderous miscreants are faring," Sanjay said.

Phoebe appreciated Sanjay's loyalty, but she was worried about Sven—for himself, and for how his injury could damage Chase's work with Midnight Sun.

"I could go to the hospital tomorrow when they discharge him. He'll have papers to sign, and they won't be able to read them."

Sanjay shook his head. "Don't go. I've seen those discharge papers. The English-speaking patients don't read them, either."

Phoebe laughed, feeling her ribs ache. "I'll see how I feel. Thanks for all your help, Sanjay."

"It is of no moment," Sanjay said as he headed for the door. "Take it easy tonight."

"I will," she promised.

But she didn't see how she could take it easy. She had to tell Chase what had happened. And that would be a very difficult conversation.

Juggling two grocery bags and a briefcase, Chase let himself into the house late that afternoon. Usually he stayed later, but Phoebe was waiting. She'd been home alone all day, and he'd had trouble concentrating on what he should be doing. He'd finally given up, gone to the store, and gone home.

And here she was, greeting him at the front door in her fluffy skirt with her wrist wrapped in an elastic bandage, clutching a sheaf of paper and looking sick. And that was before he saw the scrapes. And a huge gauze bandage on her knee.

Trouble sat next to her and leaned against her leg. If a dog could look worried, he did.

A stab of fear made his voice sharper than he intended. "*Cher*, what happened to you?"

She flinched. "I was in an accident."

At least she wasn't in the hospital. He dropped the grocery bags on the entry table.

"What kind of accident? Where? Tell me what happened." He bent to examine her knee. Her leg was red with abrasions— she couldn't have been wearing that skirt when it happened or her skin would be in much worse shape—but he saw some bruises coming up. She probably had bruising he couldn't see, too. A little blood had soaked through the gauze pad. She sucked in a breath when he put some pressure on the wrist joint.

"That hurts?" He straightened and took the papers out of her bandaged hand, then dropped them on the entry table, noting that her skin was too cool. He warmed her hand briefly in both of his and then gently rotated it. She tensed, but she didn't gasp. Sprained for sure.

"Did you see a doctor?"

"It didn't seem serious enough. I took some painkillers and I've been lying down with ice packs."

"Your wrist doesn't seem broken." He manipulated her fingers, pressing down on the back of her hand. She closed her eyes and exhaled, her breath coming out in a shaky sigh.

He felt a surge of sympathy. He knew how it felt to be on the business end of a big thump.

"Am I hurting you? When I press here, do you feel any pain?"

"No, it's okay. My hip is probably the sorest. I sort of feel… delicate. Tender all over."

"You got banged up, *cher*. Did you mix it up with some asshat? Why don't you lie down and you can tell me what happened."

"I'll just stiffen up. I have to say, that bathtub with the jets is a miracle worker."

"If you're up to it, then, come into the kitchen with me. I

140

want to put the frozen stuff away."

He picked up the bags and she followed him into the kitchen, Trouble nudging her leg.

"Want some of this?" he asked, taking out a carton of ice cream. "Chocolate chocolate chip. Unless you'd like something stronger."

Phoebe brightened. "I've already had something stronger. Ice cream, please."

He grinned, took down a bowl, and scooped some ice cream into it.

"Or I could just eat it out of the carton," she said.

He laughed outright. His sisters always ate ice cream out of the carton, too, when they were upset. He pushed the bowl and a spoon across to her and put the carton in the freezer.

"You'll want some again later," he said. "So tell me."

Phoebe took a bite of the ice cream and let it melt on her tongue.

"You won't like it," she began, her voice muffled.

Why wouldn't he like it? She was hurt. She was his employee. She was here in his house. And she was bleeding. He was already mad on her behalf.

"Why not?" He dug out a bag of dog treats and tossed one to Trouble, who jumped and caught it.

"It's about the investors," Phoebe said, watching the dog, scooping up more ice cream.

"I'm listening," he said, but he felt his sympathy ooze away. To occupy himself, he took the steaks out of the refrigerator and drained off the marinade.

"You can cook," Phoebe said. She was stalling, so it must be bad.

"I can make about five things that won't poison people," he said, taking some potatoes and onions out of the bin. "And most of them are things I put on the grill. I won't be upset. Tell me how you hurt yourself, *cher*, and how the investors are involved."

Haltingly, she told him what she'd done.

He'd lied when he said he wouldn't be upset. Chase's frustration built with every addition to the story. Was she *trying* to ruin him?

"And then Gustav tried to run me down," she finished up. "He drove straight at me. The truck grazed me, and I landed on the concrete sidewalk. I slid a little. That's how I got hurt."

Chase put down the knife he'd been using to peel the onions. She didn't need to think he would kill her with it if he started waving it around.

"Are you sure Gustav tried to run you down?" he asked, keeping his voice calm and even. "Are you sure he wasn't just in a big hurry to follow the ambulance that was taking his father to the hospital? So he was upset and driving erratically?"

"He steered straight at me." Phoebe finished her ice cream and pushed the bowl away. "I'm sure. That's what Sanjay and the doorman saw, too."

He didn't think she was lying, but he couldn't believe that the Eklunds would do something that would jeopardize their goals—even if their goal was gunrunning, which he didn't believe for a second.

"I'm real sorry you're hurt, *cher*, but I'm not convinced Gustav tried to kill you," he said. She could hang on to a harebrained idea tighter than a tick to a coonhound. Take the mutt now staring at him, hoping for another treat. First she'd blackmailed him with Trouble, and now the damn dog was living *in his house*. He glared at the mutt, who whined softly, and tossed the dog a second treat.

"Sven hurt—this is a problem," he said, focusing on Phoebe again. "He's key to this group, and I need Midnight Sun—*all* of them—to sign on the dotted line. That's why you're here. To help them do that. So I need you to *let it alone*. Leave my *investors* alone."

"What if your investors are criminals? International gunrunners? What then?"

He couldn't fire Phoebe, because he didn't have another translator. But maybe that could still be arranged.

He leaned forward over the counter. "Let the police do their job. And you do yours. I thought I'd made it clear. Don't go off on some wild-goose chase looking for trouble."

Trouble woofed, recognizing his name or asking for another treat, he wasn't sure which.

142

"It wasn't a wild-goose chase," Phoebe objected, her eyes narrowed.

"You think it's okay to frighten, injure, and alienate these people on their day off? Phoebe, you're missing the point here."

"The fact that they were so horrified to see me should tell you that I'm on the right track," Phoebe said. "I didn't *plan* for Sven to trip and fall. I didn't *push* him."

"I should hope not." Chase brushed some oil on the potatoes and onions. So far, the investors liked Phoebe, but an injury to one of their own could ruin the dynamics of the entire group. "Here's what's going to happen."

He wrapped the vegetables in foil and set them aside. Phoebe's jaw was set as she watched him wash and dry his hands. She was mad at *him*? She could kill this deal. And then the factory and the livelihoods of more than one hundred people would be destroyed. Not to mention the time, money, and dreams wasted. For *nothing*.

He folded the towel and placed it on the counter.

"I'll say it again, and this time I hope I'm making it crystal clear: *you leave the Midnight Sun investors alone*. You want me to believe you work for the CIA, fine. You think those guys are, I don't know, gunrunners, fine. You can do anything you want, follow them all you want, after next week, *when their visit is over and we have a signed agreement*. Up until then, your time belongs to me, am I clear?"

"I hear you, but—"

"No buts! You leave them alone."

She was silent, but she looked mulish. He didn't care. He had to drop the hammer or she'd keep pushing until the deal went sour. Eventually she'd get over her snit. The main thing was that she did what he said.

"You will go to work, you will translate, and that is *it*. Do you understand?"

Now she was mad, too.

"What do you think I've been doing all week?" she said, planting her hands on her hips. She might as well have added "asshole" to that question, it was so clear on her face. "Sven fell down because he's scared of me for some *reason*. Gustav tried to run me over for a *reason*! And their reasons—their *goals*—have nothing to do with your timetable!"

Time to make his point. *Again.*

He came around the counter and got in her face. "Phoebe, are we clear? *Do not* interfere with my investors. They have not committed any crimes. If they do commit a crime, the police will handle it. Not you. No more amateur detective work. *Let it go.*"

"What about running me down?" she asked, thrusting out her chin. "Isn't *that* a crime? What about *that?*" She glared up at him, not backing down or backing up by even one inch.

Tough. He could not let her ruin his deal. That was the bottom line.

"I don't know if it's a crime. What did the cops say?"

She blinked.

Just as he'd thought.

"So you didn't call the cops. Phoebe—if you didn't call the cops, there's no crime."

Her jaw clenched and she nodded several times, thinking. He could practically hear the wheels turning in her head.

"I want my check," she said finally. "Everything you owe me for the first week. Ten thousand dollars."

He felt a new kind of sizzling anger flow through him, heating his blood.

"*That's* how you want to play this? You're mad now and you want your money so you can quit on me?"

"Did I earn it or not? Just give me the money."

He felt his fury settle, hot and throbbing, behind his eyes. "Fine. Wait here."

He strode to his office and wrote out the check. When he got back to the kitchen, she was still standing where he'd left her.

"Take it."

She grabbed the check, looked at it—*who the hell was she that she didn't trust* him?—and nodded.

"Okay," she said. "I'm going now. You have my number." She turned and limped out of the kitchen, Trouble nosing her hand anxiously.

He wadded up the towel threw it into the sink. *Dammit*! He had no idea if he'd made any impression on her whatsoever. For all he knew, she'd be chasing after those guys with an ice pick next.

And with that ten thousand dollars, she could buy a lot of ice picks.

When Phoebe got back to her room, she flopped down on the beautiful queen-sized bed—the nicest bed she'd ever slept in. Trouble jumped up beside her and pushed his head against her arm, whining a little.

"Now what, Trouble?" she asked, stroking his ears as tears threatened below the surface. She didn't want to leave. Chase's house was beautiful, and Trouble had a good home with a fenced yard and room to run and a guy who bought him treats. She even had a ride to work. She was selfish and shallow even to think that that kind of stuff mattered, but she had to face facts.

And okay—her injuries weren't life-threatening. But did Chase even *care* that Gustav had tried to run her down? *No*. Well, maybe a little. But mostly he was worried about his investors.

And, okay—Sven was in the hospital, and that wasn't good. But still—she couldn't do what Chase wanted. She couldn't stop trying to find out what the Eklunds had planned, and not only because she wanted to get her job back at the CIA. If they were organizing some kind of attack, she had to find out what it was and stop them if she could.

If she couldn't live by Chase's rules, she couldn't stay at his house. That was a lesson she'd learned long ago. On the up side, she had a lot more options now. She had ten thousand dollars.

She couldn't stay with Kristin even if she'd said yes, because she'd put her new friend in a difficult situation with their mutual boss. So that was out. And she couldn't go back to Babette and Harry.

She didn't know where her mother was. *Like usual*.

She called Sanjay.

"Listen," she said when he picked up. "I'm sorry to put you on the spot, but I need to find another place to stay. I have to leave here right away, tonight. Do you know of a hotel or motel or someplace where I can stay with my dog? Chase paid me for the first week, so I've got money."

"What has gone wrong between you and Mr. Bonaventure?"

"I just need my own place, Sanjay. Can you help me?"

"You weren't rude, were you? You are a guest in his home, and you were rude, and he kicked you out."

"I wasn't rude! We had a disagreement, and I can't stay here. Can you help me or not?

"Most assuredly. Let me make a few calls. I'll swing by within the hour."

"Thank you, Sanjay. I'll be waiting."

She disconnected, slid the phone in her pocket, and scratched Trouble's ears.

"So that's that," she told the dog. "We're moving out. I'll get our stuff together and then Sanjay will be here."

She dragged her suitcase out of the closet and packed all the new clothes she'd just hung up last night. Well, all except her red jeans. Those were ruined, and she'd already put them in the trash.

Packing took five minutes. Then she sat down to write Chase a note, which took twenty. She took the note and her box of books to the bedroom door.

"Stay here," she told Trouble. "Enjoy the room while you can. Jump on the bed or something. I'll be right back."

She lugged the books to the front door. From down the hall she heard the muted sounds of the television—that might be the home gym where Chase worked on rehabbing his knee. The place was so big that he wouldn't hear her move around. He probably wouldn't even hear the taxi drive up.

She carried the books out to the front portico, then went into the kitchen, dropped the note on the table, and found a folded-up grocery bag underneath the sink to stash Trouble's dishes in. Then she went back for her suitcase and dog.

Five minutes later, she was outside waiting, Trouble straining at his leash. And five minutes after that, Sanjay drove up the driveway and parked, popping the trunk as he got out.

"Mr. Bonaventure is such an extraordinary person, and his home is so beautiful," he said, carrying her books to the taxi. "And he is so generous to let you share it. I can't believe you want to leave."

I don't want *to leave. I* have *to leave.*

146

"It didn't work out," she said.

Trouble jumped into the back seat, and Phoebe got into the front. Sanjay put the taxi in gear, and they drove down the driveway and out into the street.

"Thank you for helping me, Sanjay."

"I am happy to oblige," Sanjay said. "Also, you are paying me for the ride. Where do you wish to go?"

"I don't know," Phoebe said. "I thought you were finding me a place."

"I *am* finding you a place," Sanjay said. "My uncle Boo-Boo is a real estate agent, and he manages many, many buildings. I left him a voicemail telling him of your emergency. I am sure that he will have a place for you. Perhaps tomorrow. Or at the latest, the next day. However, today he is at the wedding of his second cousin's niece, so tonight he cannot help you." He glanced at her, frowning. "What did you say to Mr. Bonaventure that he threw you out?"

"He didn't throw me out!" Phoebe said. "I walked out!"

"That was your best idea? That house is so large that you wouldn't even have to see Mr. Bonaventure if you didn't want to. Although that I do not understand—not wanting to engage Mr. Bonaventure in conversation."

She wasn't sure she understood it, either. "I just can't stay there anymore, okay, Sanjay?"

Sanjay sighed. "There is a problem in the short-term housing market," he said. "Everything is booked. Every place that is safe for you and that takes dogs. There's a big conference next weekend at the Desert Dunes and two more at lesser venues. The hotels are all full."

Phoebe's heart sank. "Every place can't be full. We'll have to stop and work the phones. There hasn't been enough time to check places."

"I am a taxi driver," Sanjay said. "The best taxi driver. This is what I know: the big hotels won't take a dog. I have already tried the well-known places that do take dogs. They are full. The smaller places, still no. To unsuitable places I am not taking you. You would not like these places, and you would not be safe. And Mr. Bonaventure would not like it if you stayed in such places, either."

Phoebe slumped back against the cushions. She felt Trouble's hot breath on her cheek. The poor pup was leaning forward, his nose just inches from her ear, straining from anxiety. She reached back and scratched his ears. Where, indeed, could they go?

"I thought of inviting you to stay at my house for one evening," he said. "My mother is most hospitable. However, afterward she would expect us to marry, and my mother is most forceful when she has her mind set on something. As much as I enjoy our sleuthing outings, I do not wish to marry you. Intending no offense."

"None taken," Phoebe said, a little startled. "I certainly don't want to give your mother any ideas. Okay. I'll call Harry and Babette. They might take me in again for one night, since it's an emergency. Even though their son is there."

"There is one other option," Sanjay said. "Not the best one. But I have tried everywhere, and there are no other options. Therefore, it is the best option."

"Anything would be fine. Believe me, I've stayed in some bad places."

"This motel is not fancy, but it's clean and secure. With complimentary Wi-Fi. It is run by my aunt Aminda. It, too, is full."

"How does that help me?"

"She will let you sleep on the sofa in the lobby if you do not lie down until midnight and you are gone by five in the morning. She does not wish her other guests to see a hobo in the lobby."

"I'm not a hobo! I have money!"

"But she has no free rooms. The lobby, though, you can have. If you desire it. Are you sure you do not wish to go back to Mr. Bonaventure's lovely home?"

Phoebe gritted her teeth. "I'm sure. And your uncle will be back from the wedding tomorrow? And he can get me a place?"

"I am positive," Sanjay said, doing a U-turn. "Almost."

Sanjay drove her to the Taj Mahal Motel, where Aunt Aminda greeted Phoebe with polite reserve.

"My nephew Sanjay has told me a story," She looked Phoebe over with a critical eye. "I hope it is true."

"I've been in Las Vegas for only a couple of weeks," Phoebe

said. "I'd been staying with my mother, but she lost her apartment. Last night I stayed with my employer, but that's not a good idea any longer. So I'm in a bit of an emergency."

"Hanky-panky?" Aunt Aminda asked, brightening up a little.

I wish. "No, nothing like that," Phoebe said. She and Chase were so far from hanky-panky, it was laughable. Not that she hadn't thought about it, but she had to get all hanky-pankyish thoughts out of her head. They were doing her no good.

"One night only," Aunt Aminda said. "Tonight you come in at midnight. Your dog can stay with you. You sleep on the sofa. I will give you sheets. Tomorrow I wake you at five and you are gone. Is that suitable?"

"That's wonderful. Thank you very much."

Phoebe walked Sanjay out to the taxi.

"Keep your toothbrush with you in your messenger bag," Sanjay said. "I'll keep your suitcase and books in the trunk of the taxi. They'll be safe. And do not worry. The tongue of my aunt Aminda is as sour as a pickle, but she will not let harm befall you."

Phoebe nodded. "I'm happy she'll let me stay here. Do you have any ideas where I can spend the next few hours that are within walking distance?"

"Indeed, yes. Three blocks from here there is a restaurant similar to a Denny's but not a Denny's that is open all night. The waitresses will not mind if you spend quite a lot of time there."

"Sounds perfect. Thanks, Sanjay. We'll talk tomorrow."

"Please. Not too early. Have a leisurely breakfast at the restaurant before you call. And then also a leisurely lunch."

Chapter 11

Phoebe woke the next morning to the brisk prodding of a determined Aunt Aminda.

"It is fifteen minutes to five," she said. "Wash up, and then you must go."

Phoebe nodded, her eyes scratchy, her head thick. After spending almost four hours last night in the restaurant that wasn't a Denny's, she'd surprised herself by falling asleep instantly on the Taj Mahal's surprisingly comfortable lobby sofa. But four hours of sleep just wasn't very much.

Phoebe sat up, dropped her feet to the floor, and rubbed her eyes. "I'll be quick, and then I'll get out of your hair."

She staggered over to the rest room off the lobby, washed her face and brushed her teeth, then finger-combed her hair. Not a particularly good look, but the best she could do under the circumstances. Then, feeling a little better, she went back to the lobby.

Aunt Aminda held out a large paper cup. "Coffee."

"Thank you." Phoebe took it gratefully. She took a sip. Strong, milky, and sweet. Usually she preferred her coffee black, but this was just what she needed.

"Perfect," she said. She dug into her pocket and pulled out a twenty-dollar bill, handing it to her hostess. "Thank you again. You saved me last night."

Aunt Aminda waved away the money. "Tell that Sanjay nephew of mine to come for dinner on Sunday."

Phoebe laughed. "I sure will."

She clipped Trouble's leash to his collar, waved goodbye to Aunt Aminda, and headed out to the dark streets of Las Vegas, where Trouble promptly watered a street-sweeping sign.

"That's telling 'em, dog," she said and headed back to the restaurant for breakfast.

At nine o'clock the waitress who'd served her coffee since five told her she had to go, that people were waiting to eat and her manager was talking about escorting her out. That didn't fool Phoebe, because she could see several empty tables and no one at the door, but she knew better than to tangle with managers. And who could blame them? She *was* homeless. She *did* look ratty and tired.

She went outside and untied Trouble from the street sign, then uncapped the bottle of water she'd bought for him.

"Have some water, sweetie," she said, tilting it toward him.

He got it immediately and lapped furiously, his tail wagging just as fast.

"You are the best," she said when he seemed finished. She opened the takeout container of meatloaf and mashed potatoes she'd ordered and set it down for him. "See how you like this."

The dog gobbled the food and then sat down, grinning at her.

"Yeah, you lead a dog's life." She picked up the container and tossed it into a nearby trash container.

She checked her watch. Nine fifteen—too early to call Sanjay. She could check up on Sven. If she went to the hospital, Gustav and Lars wouldn't try to hurt her there in front of witnesses, right? And if they did hurt her, she'd be in the hospital already. Silver lining right there.

She called the Vegas Fun Fare main number for a cab.

"I have a dog," she told the dispatcher. "And I'm a friend of Sanjay Agarwal."

"He isn't working until this afternoon," the dispatcher said.

"I know," Phoebe said. "I just said that so you'd take my dog."

"As long as the animal doesn't pee on the upholstery, we're fine with pets. If it pees, you pay."

"That should be your motto."

"It is our motto," the dispatcher said. "Or at least a rule."

"I'll be waiting." Phoebe disconnected and looked at Trouble.

"We got a ride," she told him. "If you have to pee, do it now."

Fifteen minutes later when they arrived at the hospital, Phoebe tied Trouble to a tiny landscaped tree, gave him more water, and went inside. She took the elevator up to Sven's floor, and as she walked down the hallway, Lars pounced on her, seeming almost happy to see her.

"Hello! How are you?" he said. "I was afraid—" He flushed.

"I came to see how you were doing with the discharge paperwork," Phoebe said. At least Lars didn't want her dead.

"Yes, well, this invoice is incorrect," he said, handing her a bill. "Can you fix it? We don't know what to do about it."

Phoebe glanced at the bill and gasped. She'd never been to the hospital as a patient in her life, but of course the news was full of stories about the high cost of health care. But—nine thousand dollars? For one night? You could buy a lot of Band-Aids for that.

"I'll check it out," she said.

She took the elevator back down to the accounting department and stood in line to talk to a soft-spoken woman sitting behind a window in the smallest cubicle Phoebe had ever seen. Taking up valuable real estate on the clerk's tiny desk was a nameplate that said M. GRACE.

"Is this bill correct?" Phoebe asked, handing her the invoice. "It's a lot of money for less than twenty-four hours. And no surgery."

M. Grace glanced at the bill and shrugged. "It looks ballpark," she said. "Let me find out."

She leaned forward and tapped on her keyboard, checking the invoice as she did so. Then she sat back.

"Sven Eklund," she said. "Are you Phoebe Renfrew?"

"How did you know that?" Phoebe asked, surprised.

"You're on the form here. Yeah, that's the bill. Do you have his insurance information? We didn't get it at admission."

"Probably because there's a language problem. He's from Sweden, but he only speaks Korean."

The clerk blinked. "That's probably it, then. Well, that's the correct total for his charges. Bring in his insurance info and we'll file the claim for him. Insurance should cover most of it. One

153

thing you should know—if Mr. Eklund doesn't have insurance and doesn't pay, the bill collectors will come after you, because you're listed in the system as his guardian."

"Guardian! I'm not his guardian! I'm his translator!"

M. Grace shrugged. "I'm just the messenger."

"Crap." Phoebe stared at the bill. "How do I get off the system as his guardian?"

"Beyond my pay grade," the clerk said. "You'll have to talk to my supervisor. Who is off today, because it's Sunday."

"Of course," Phoebe said. "Okay. Thanks for your help. I'll deliver the bad news."

When she got upstairs, Lars was waiting outside in the hall for her.

"What did they say?" he asked.

"This really is what the hospital is charging you for the stay." She handed the invoice back to him. "They need your insurance information, and then they'll file the claim for you. I'll go down with you."

Lars stared at her blankly. "Insurance? What insurance? In Sweden, we go to the hospital and give them our ID card. And then afterward, they send us a bill for the daily charge. Which is"—he peered up at the ceiling while he did the math—"about twelve dollars."

"Twelve dollars?" Phoebe asked. "That can't be right. You're doing the currency conversion wrong."

Lars thought again and then shook his head. "Yeah, a little less. One hundred Swedish kronor per day, that's the cost. That comes to about eleven dollars and fifty cents. Say, twelve dollars. Unless, of course, your stay is a long one. In that case, the rate is less."

"Less?"

"Yeah, about"—he did some math again—"ten dollars a day."

"*Ten dollars a day?*" She hadn't even really believed the twelve-dollar part. She stared at the invoice in Lars's hand. *Nine thousand dollars*. For one day. And no surgery.

The discharge nurse bustled in. "How are you feeling this morning?" she asked, smiling at Sven. She took his pulse and temperature, then checked his chart.

Phoebe translated and Sven shrugged. "I'm fine," he said.

"He says he's fine," Phoebe said.

"*You're* not looking so hot, though." The nurse eyed the elastic bandage on Phoebe's wrist and the stained gauze on her knee. "Were you in the same accident he was?"

"I'm fine," Phoebe said.

"Ooookay," the nurse said, doubt radiating from every pore. "Well, Mr. Eklund's vitals are normal, and he's set to go. He just needs to take it easy for a bit." Then she saw what Lars held in his hand.

"That bill is probably giving them a heart attack right about now," she said. "If you take the insurance information downstairs, they'll make the adjustment."

"Already talked to accounting," Phoebe said, feeling numb. "The Eklunds don't have insurance. There's no insurance in Sweden. If you get sick, the hospital rates are twelve dollars a day."

"Get out." The nurse stared at Phoebe. "No insurance? That can't be right."

"And if you're sick for a while, the rate goes down to ten dollars."

"They don't have insurance, and the hospital rates are *twelve dollars* a day?"

Phoebe shrugged. "Yeah, or ten. Depending."

"Unbelievable. I guess at that rate, you don't need insurance."

"I guess not." Phoebe looked again at Lars holding the bill.

"Sit tight," the nurse said, heading for the door. "I'll send in a wheelchair for him and he can go."

"Hey, Dr. Melchik!" she said to a passing doctor. "We got a guy here, says the hospital rates in Sweden are ten bucks a day! Can you believe that? We can't even get Starbucks for that."

"Ten bucks! He should have gotten sick in Sweden, poor guy. Bad planning there."

Phoebe heard the nurse's footsteps recede down the hallway as she called out, "Agnes! You won't believe what I just heard about Sweden!"

Phoebe sighed. She couldn't ask the Eklunds to pay the bill. Even if they had the money, they were Chase's guests. He wouldn't want the money to come out of their pocket.

She couldn't ask Chase to pay the bill, either. The accident had nothing to do with him, and he was furious with her for being part of it. Asking him to pay would be adding insult to injury.

She hadn't made Sven fall, and she didn't owe the Eklunds anything—especially not after Gustav tried to run her over. She didn't *want* to pay the bill. But she could. She had the money. She still had the check Chase had given her.

If she paid the bill, she'd be broke again. Of course, she already owed the CIA three hundred thousand dollars, so paying nine thousand for Sven's hospital stay was… not even icing on the cake. More like sprinkles.

And then the Eklunds might not make a big fuss about the accident with the other investors, who therefore might still invest in Chase's company. As for Chase—well, she didn't care what Chase thought.

She took the invoice from Lars's hand. "Don't worry about this," she said.

"They made a mistake?" Lars nodded. "I thought so."

"I have to go down to the accounting department and talk to them again. But then it'll be fixed."

"Thank you," he said.

Sven's wheelchair arrived, and everybody rode down in the elevator together. When they got to the first floor, Phoebe said goodbye.

"I go this way," she said, pointing down the hallway. "Feel better, Sven. And no more crazy driving, eh, Gustav?"

Gustav's hot, angry eyes met hers for the first time, but Lars just snickered. Then the orderly pushed Sven toward the hospital entrance, the sons followed, and Phoebe went to pay the bill. Giving almost her entire paycheck to guys whom she was sure were gunrunners and out to commit a horrible crime was demoralizing and maybe even idiotic. But sticking the Eklunds with the bill wouldn't help Chase. And next week, if Chase didn't fire her in the meantime, she'd get another ten thousand. She was fine.

She hoped the same could be said for anyone the Eklunds might be targeting.

Phoebe called Sanjay when she left the hospital, hoping that he'd reached his uncle and that there was an apartment for her.

She'd like to be settled and secure in her own place before she had to go back to the factory and translate again. Face the Eklunds again.

Face Chase again.

"You are in luck," Sanjay said. "Uncle Boo-Boo does not approve of the second niece's third cousin on her mother's side, who did not tip the valet sufficiently generously and then also drank too much at the reception and made a fool of himself. Uncle came back early and was in a receptive frame of mind when I explained your situation and the high ideals you had about not remaining a guest in Mr. Bonaventure's home after you rescued the injured dog, since he is allergic to animals."

"What? Chase isn't allergic to animals," Phoebe said, confused.

"Of course, he is not," Sanjay said, sounding patient. "I couldn't think of what reason I could give Uncle Boo-Boo as to why you had moved out that he would believe."

"We had an argument," Phoebe said. "I can't live by his rules. That's the truth."

"Yes, but we needed something better than the truth," Sanjay said, "because the truth is stupid and you are being foolish. Who would not follow Mr. Bonaventure's rules? They are eminently fair."

"Sanjay," Phoebe said, at the end of her rope. "Do you have an apartment for me or not?"

"I do. A furnished apartment on a month-to-month lease. That would be suitable, correct? You need to run a few errands first."

"You found me a place? You really did? That's fantastic! Yes, let's go to the bank so I can deposit this check. Where's the apartment?"

"Not far from Venture Automotive," Sanjay said, "and the dog is welcome with a security deposit. If this place does not suit, Uncle can show you others. He would also deeply appreciate an introduction to Mr. Bonaventure."

Phoebe closed her eyes. "Really, Sanjay, I don't think—"

"It is fine if you cannot arrange it," Sanjay said. "But he would appreciate it."

"Your uncle Boo-Boo knows I'm working for Chase only for another week, right? Unless he fires me. But I'll do my best."

"That is all anyone can ask. In the meantime, Uncle Boo-Boo wishes to remind you that you will need sheets and towels. While the property is furnished, my uncle's generosity does not extend to supplying linens, even for a potential introduction to Mr. Bonaventure. Also, the apartment has no food. So perhaps you want to go to the grocery, as well as a home-furnishings store before we meet him over there. I could pick you up now. Where are you?"

Phoebe told him and sat down on the bench at the bus stop in front of the hospital to wait. Trouble lay in the shade at her feet.

"This is it, Trouble," Phoebe told him. "Things are looking up for us."

Trouble woofed and put his head on her foot.

Phoebe laughed. "At least you believe in me," she said, rubbing his head.

When they finally got to the apartment, purchases made, it *was* perfect. The tiny one-bedroom was on the top floor of an older, three-story walkup; it had large windows, fresh paint, and a dishwasher—a first in Phoebe's experience. Chase had a dishwasher, but she'd never had a chance to use it. The furnishings were few, basic, and a little banged up, but on the whole, Phoebe was ecstatic. Renting an apartment sight unseen from Sanjay's unknown uncle could have been a disaster.

"Do not let your dog poop in the courtyard," Uncle Boo-Boo said, giving her the keys.

"Absolutely not," Phoebe said, handing him a check.

"If he bothers the other tenants with excessive barking and such, you will have to go."

"He won't," Phoebe said. "He's a very good dog."

"Trash collection is on Monday, recycling is in the back, laundry facilities are on the first floor behind the office, rent is due the first of the month. What do you think the possibilities are of introducing me to Mr. Bonaventure, with whom I understand you are intimately acquainted?"

Phoebe raised her eyebrows at Sanjay. "Chase and I aren't dating," she said. "I work for him is all. But Venture Automotive is having a car race on Saturday that's open to the public. We're showing off the cars and what they can do. Maybe you've seen some of the publicity. Why don't you come? I'll have a better chance of introducing you there. Until then, he's pretty busy with investor meetings."

She hoped to high heaven that Kristin had started planning that race.

"Send me the details!" Uncle Boo-Boo said as he headed for the door. "I'll put it on my social networking sites!"

After he left, Sanjay helped Phoebe put away her groceries.

"I've got all this food here, but I'm too hungry to cook," she said, sliding a box of cereal into a cupboard. "Do you want to go get something to eat? My treat."

"I know a place that has the best chicken tikka masala," Sanjay said. "The cooks are all using my mother's recipe."

"I love Indian food. How did a restaurant get your mother's recipe?"

Sanjay grinned. "It's my mother's restaurant. All the customers love her chicken tikka masala. She's got plans to expand."

"Sounds great."

Phoebe filled Trouble's food and water dishes and put them down on some newspaper on the floor. "Make yourself at home, Trouble," she told the dog, rubbing his ears, "but no barking. I'll be back in a little while." She grabbed her purse and took a quick look around the small apartment.

It wasn't much, but it was all hers. She had her own bed. She didn't have to depend on anyone any longer for a place to sleep. Not her mom. Not the O'Sheas. Not even, she thought with a pang, Chase.

She picked up the shiny new key.

"I'm ready," she said. "Let's go."

Early Sunday afternoon, Chase went into his kitchen and discovered Phoebe's note, which annoyed him. And then he came out to his living room and discovered a bunch of papers on the foyer's entry table. That had to be Phoebe's crap about gunrunners, the papers she'd been holding when he got home yesterday.

That was the limit. He was fed up with her whacked-out theories about the investors as gunrunners. And he was pissed off about her taking off, moving out, basically without telling him. They couldn't have a difference of opinion without her running away? And where the hell was she, anyway?

He yanked his phone out of his pocket and called her.

"Coach," she said when she picked up. Her voice was cool.

She was mad? What could *she* be mad about?

"Phoebe. Where are you? I've been worried."

"You don't sound worried. You sound angry."

Chase blinked. *What?* Of course, he'd been worried.

"And it's after one o'clock," she said. "You just noticed now that I'm not there?"

"I just found your note," he said. "I thought you were sleeping in. Or that you'd gone out for brunch. You don't have to tell me where you go. Hell, the place has fifteen bedrooms. How am I supposed to know where you are?" Why was he feeling defensive?

"Whatever," she said. "I'm fine. Better than fine. You don't have to *worry* about me anymore."

She sure sounded mad. Well, he couldn't focus on her emotions. She was an employee. They weren't—and couldn't be—friends.

"Where did you go? You agreed to stay at my place. And then when you took off without telling me—"

"I *did* tell you. I said, 'I'm going.'"

"You said, 'I'm going now.' I thought you meant going back to your *room*."

"That's not what I meant."

"So I found out."

"Not my problem. I told you I was going, and I left. You're my boss. You don't owe me anything except my paycheck. Thank you for putting me up. I'm *fine*."

Were they arguing again? It sure felt like it.

"Phoebe—"

She sighed. "No, okay. I'm tired of arguing. I wanted to get out."

"Apology accepted."

Phoebe snorted. "I'm not apologizing! You were overbearing

and all, my way or the highway. The hell with that."

"You apologized. I accept. I was overbearing?"

"Yes. You're worried that Sven's injury could botch things up for you. I get it. But I don't have to put up with your garbage."

Chase blinked again. In all his football days, no one had ever called him overbearing. Or said he was full of garbage. He wondered what his other employees said about him.

"Where are you?" he asked. "And why don't you come back here? You can poke me if I get overbearing again."

"An attractive offer, but no, thank you," she said. "I have my own place now."

"You do? Where?"

"I'm in this apartment building not too far from the plant. It's called the Hollywood Arms. Go figure."

"I know the place." The complex was large and fairly well maintained. Phoebe *would* be fine there. She wouldn't have a reason to come back. The thought was depressing.

"So, what's up?" she asked. "You planning to badger me about the Eklunds again?"

"I wanted to talk to you about the rest of the week. We have to work out the schedule for the R&D tour and the finance side."

"Right," she said, her argumentativeness dissolving completely at the mention of work. "I have a few things to do this afternoon. Are you going to the plant? I could stop by in an hour or two, if that's okay?"

Even better. Maybe he could talk her into dinner.

"That works," he said. "See you then."

He tucked the phone back in his pocket and picked up the papers she'd left behind, shoving them into order. Her whole gun-running theory was ridiculous, but he might as well give the pages back to her. And then he wondered—had she proved anything yet?

The first page was called Indiegogo Campaign. What was that?

As he read, chagrin settled over him. Sometime—evidently on Saturday when he'd been at the plant and she'd been lying injured on his couch—Phoebe had planned a marketing campaign for Venture Automotive. And she'd made notes. Pages and pages of notes. Goals for completion. Plans for publicity. Prizes. The whole nine yards. To help him.

She'd also drawn up plans for the road race he'd promised Thor Olafsson, the investor who wanted a test drive. She'd put a lot of work into that one, too. He didn't know who she thought could execute those plans, but she'd put a lot of work into them.

He shoved the pages into his briefcase and headed outside to his car. Maybe she wasn't totally focused on his so-called gun-running, pistol-packing investors. Maybe sometimes she did think about his company's welfare.

But what did she think about him?

Chapter 12

C hase had always loved working at the plant on the weekend when the place was dim and silent and no one else was there, but he was happy when Phoebe came in at midafternoon, sweaty from a ride on her new bicycle, ridiculously sexy in her stretchy shorts. He poured a glass of water for her and watched her chug it down, the water running all over, including down the front of her T-shirt.

Employee. Employee. She's an employee. He had to remember that.

But it was easy to forget, possibly because none of his other employees looked like she did. Or told him he was overbearing. Or worked out Indiegogo campaigns for him.

"When you're ready, *cher*, tell me about what you've been working on," he said, pulling out the pages and laying them on the desk.

Phoebe put down the empty glass with a satisfied sigh.

"You looked at that stuff? What do you think? I made some lists. Well, I made some calls, too. Do you have anything to eat in here?"

He took a jar of mixed nuts from his bottom desk drawer and handed it over.

"That's it for food," he said, "unless you want to see if there's anything getting stale in the breakroom."

Phoebe grinned, opening the can. "No, thanks. The nuts will hold me for now. Yum, cashews." She picked out some cashews and then flipped open her messenger bag and pulled out her laptop. "Let me show you what I did." She plunked the laptop in the center of his desk and dragged her chair around it to sit close to him.

He exhaled. She was practically on top of him, her leg nudging his. When she leaned forward, her arm grazed his. Her skin was moist and rosy from the exercise. Her hair was tangled, and a damp strand clung to her neck. He wanted to touch that strand, curl it around his fingers, nudge her back—

Employee. She was an *employee*. He took a deep breath. Grabbed the edge of his desk instead.

"Sorry," she said, glancing at him. "I probably stink."

"You ever been in a locker room with a bunch of football players who've been sweating their asses off for a few hours in ninety-degree heat wearing fifteen or twenty pounds of gear? I've smelled worse."

Phoebe grinned. "I won't worry then. Okay, where do you want to start?"

"Show me the road race, because that's something we actually have to do by the end of the week."

Phoebe nodded. "Kristin already got started with this, so I added what I could. For starters, publicity. We've got the media covered, local newspaper, TV, radio, all that, and national automotive magazines."

"National?"

Phoebe nodded. "The outlets that are coming to cover the rally are in this column," she said, pointing.

He leaned forward, staring at the page. "Seriously."

Phoebe nodded again, grinning, sharing his disbelief. "Seriously. I know. Let me tell you, the things I've learned in the past week, you would not believe. Okay. Continuing. Social media."

"We're doing social media for this thing?"

"Absolutely. All the usual suspects, with one wild card."

"Which is?"

"Uncle Boo-Boo."

"Uncle Boo-Boo? What's that?"

"It's a he." Phoebe glanced at him, still grinning. When she looked like that, all enthusiastic and excited, he felt like he could just give her the keys to the company or anything else she wanted.

"Uncle Boo-Boo is Sanjay's uncle," Phoebe said. "He manages my apartment building. He's also a big Rattlesnakes fan in general and a fan of yours in particular. I said I'd introduce you at the race."

"You bribed Uncle Boo-Boo to get an apartment?"

"Mostly Sanjay did. Kristin told me last week how much clout you have in this town, and, okay, back then I was naive. I didn't understand the full extent of the power I had at my fingertips. But since I've been working on this stuff, let me tell you, my eyes have been opened. Mention Chase Bonaventure, and boom, whatever you want, you get. Your name is *magic*. It's better than abracadabra."

She was laughing now at the absurdity of it.

"Oh, my God. I'm afraid to ask. You put my name out—"

"Everywhere," Phoebe said, chortling like a five-year-old. "I put your name out *everywhere*. We bought radio and TV spots and internet ads. We're working a charity angle. This thing is gonna be big."

"A charity angle. TV spots. Really?" Chase didn't know if he should be ecstatic or scared shitless. Lots of people could be good. Lots of people could be a disaster, too, if the event or crowd management didn't go well.

"Yes. Think big. Super big."

"Can we handle that?" he asked. "What about, I don't know, security, food, water, crowd control. Porta-potties."

"We've got enough porta-potties to stretch to the moon," Phoebe said. "*Deluxe* porta-potties. The porta-potty people were delighted to help. They're only charging us the regular porta-potty rate for the super-duper porta-potties. And it's all been like that. The people at city hall have been tremendous. We've got everything covered. Permits, off-duty cops for crowd control. Bleachers, prizes, first aid tent."

"First aid?"

"The permits are pretty clear. But about Uncle Boo-Boo." Phoebe swallowed, looking self-conscious. "Um, he thinks you and I are an item. Not my idea," she added hastily.

"I don't mind," Chase said. *An item would be good.*

Phoebe glanced at him suspiciously. "It's what Sanjay told

him so he'd rent to me. Just so you know. In case he says something. And the other thing—"

"There's more?" Chase couldn't believe how much he was enjoying this.

"About social media. I told him—Uncle Boo-Boo—to put the race on his social media network, which I think must be vast. Sanjay's family—or connections, whatever—seems to go on forever. I think you'll be shaking more hands on Saturday than the queen at the annual garden party."

"Oh, good," Chase said. "I've always wanted blisters on my fingers."

"You play quarterback, right?" Phoebe said. "You throw the ball. You already have blisters on your fingers."

"I want to renegotiate my contract," Chase said. "I have to call my agent."

Phoebe rolled her eyes, but she laughed. "Listen up, Coach. *I'm* your agent until we're done with this thing."

He wanted to kiss her.

"What's the actual plan?" He cleared his throat and kept his hands to himself.

"We have a course set up in the parking lot for spectators to test drive the sedans. Tony will have cars available. And the sales guys will be out there with contracts."

"The race is in the parking lot?"

"No. What happens in the parking lot is a sales opportunity. The *rally* starts at eight in the morning—enough time for the media people to make their deadlines in the afternoon and before it gets too hot. The race is fifty miles over city streets and then county roads and back. Click here"—she tapped the touchpad on the laptop—"and you get the route. We're providing refreshments for the rally participants. We've got food trucks for the crowd."

"Las Vegas has food trucks?"

"Everybody has food trucks," Phoebe said, "and let me tell you—a car rally run by Chase Bonaventure? *Everybody* wants in. All the food truck people want to be there. Because it's all about—you know—*you*."

"I might be overbearing, but you're downright rude." Chase laughed and shook his head. "Get used to it, *cher*. I'm a hero.

166

What's wrong with you? People love their football. It's the national pastime."

Phoebe glanced up from her laptop and grinned at him. She was so close, her nose was just inches from his shoulder. All he had to do was lean in a little—

No, no, *no*. She was an *employee*. He had a rule about employees. And that rule was *never*. Never get involved with an employee.

"You're wrong about that," she said, and he got confused for a minute, not sure where they were in the conversation. "You're thinking of baseball. *That's* the national pastime." She looked dreamily off to the horizon, whatever horizon she could see from his office. "I love baseball. You eat peanuts and crackerjack. You don't care if you ever get back. You root, root, root for the home team. That's the American pastime."

"You know squat about sports. Tell me about the food trucks."

Phoebe snapped her eyes back, grinning again. "We've got ten food trucks lined up. We've got a waiting list of food trucks who want to sell food at this rally."

"Why can't they all come and sell food?"

"Not enough parking spaces on the route. The city's limiting us."

"Damn bureaucrats," Chase said. "After all I do to bribe them. Anything else?"

"Oh, yes," Phoebe said. "The big thing. Photo opportunities."

"Photo opportunities."

If anything, Phoebe's grin got wider. "Oh, yeah. Publicity, dude. That's what we're going for here. Get the word out, right? So, lots of pictures. Of you. You with the participants. You with the winners. You standing next to the cars. You in front of the factory. And of course, you and all the little people. Because you're their hero and all."

"Hey—"

"*All* the little people," Phoebe said, laughing now. "Each and every one. We'll have hookups in the media tent—"

"We have to get a media tent?"

"And prizes. Local merchants who donate prizes get an advertising consideration in the program."

"We're printing programs?"

"Yes," Phoebe said. "If the printer gets the info by Wednesday, he swears we'll get the programs by Friday. Kristin's renting the truck to pick them up."

"Christ. A truck."

"Well, if Lars and Gustav are still driving around in *their* truck, maybe we could borrow that one," Phoebe said. "That would be cheaper and more flexible, too. And it would keep them from putting guns in it. An unexpected upside."

Chase decided he would let that one slide. "We need a truck to pick up the programs? How many programs are we printing?"

"Twenty-five thousand. That won't be enough, but we don't get another price break until we order fifty thousand, and I don't know if we want to recycle that much paper. But I bet we get that many people."

Twenty-five thousand people, or maybe fifty thousand. Here he'd been thinking it would be only him and the employees and Midnight Sun out in the back lot.

"Do I have to shake hands with twenty-five thousand people?"

"If they want to. Don't tell me you can't handle it. We already talked about this. You're the quarterback. You've got magic hands."

Chase watched as sudden color bloomed in her cheeks. And wasn't that interesting?

She cleared her throat. "However, it's not *quite* all about you."

"It isn't? You've got some washed-up baseball player coming, too?"

Phoebe's eyes sparkled again. "What a good idea! No. Here's your list of confirmed interviews." She leaned forward and pointed on the screen to the television, radio, and print interviews next to his name.

When she leaned forward, her hair swung over her cheek, brushing her shoulders. Her breasts strained against her T-shirt. She was so close—

It didn't matter how close she was. She was an *employee*.

"That's ten interviews." He closed his eyes and strived to

corral his wayward thoughts.

"Yes. Some of it on the day, but some of this stuff is much longer term—way past what we'll do for Saturday's rally. And Matt, Tony, and the R&D guys have their own interviews with other outlets that better match their skill sets."

Chase leaned forward to look at the spreadsheet. Phoebe had more than just interviews lined up. She had conferences they could speak at, booths at conferences they should rent, festivals they should attend, races they could sponsor. For God's sake, drivers-ed classes they could teach.

"Ummm...there's one thing you should know." Phoebe glanced at him sideways. "About the prizes. The grand prize, I mean."

"I can tell I won't like this." When had his translator taken over his company? On the other hand, having Phoebe and Kristin take over this promotional stunt for the investors was keeping Phoebe out of trouble, and it looked like it could be huge. If it didn't crash and burn. Either way, he mused with fatalism, the publicity probably couldn't hurt.

"Don't worry," Phoebe said soothingly. "You won't even notice. It's just...the grand prize?"

"I won't notice what?"

"The grand prize winner gets a barbecue at your house," she said in a rush. "With you."

"What?"

"And ten of their friends. We had to think of something big. And, um, something that didn't cost anything."

"That's big, all right." He wasn't sure he could face making nice to ten—make that *eleven*—strangers in his own house. Maybe if Phoebe came and helped him out.

"So that's it for the race," Phoebe said, rushing on. "Here's the Indiegogo campaign. It's a long-term publicity campaign for the company. Not a stunt for the Midnight Sun investors."

Chase thought he'd feel mad or trapped or something, but mostly he was just amused. Maybe he should turn his house into a hotel now. Now would definitely be a good time, while she was bursting with ideas.

"I'm nervous to find out what that entails," he said.

She tapped a few keys on the laptop, and a second spreadsheet opened. "The Indiegogo campaign."

It was a $15 million marketing campaign. She had plans for promotions to professional athletes and celebrities. Publicity campaigns again. He saw that prizes included an awful lot of his autographs, photographs, test drives, factory tours, even—good grief—the opportunity to name a car model. He was surprised she hadn't included nights at his house.

"At least you didn't pimp me out for a big enough donation," he said.

"Um…"

Wait a second. There it was. SPEND A WEEKEND AT CHASE BONAVENTURE'S LUXURY HOME! The donor would also get to go on a factory tour, name a car, and take possession of a vehicle. But for that he or she would have to kick in a million bucks.

"Oh, I see. You did pimp me out." He shrugged. "Well, at least it's for a big donation. For a million, I'd do it. Nobody says I have to be at home when the winners stay here. And if we get fifteen million-dollar donors, we could pay for all the promo in one weekend."

"That's what I thought," Phoebe said, clearly relieved, "although we might need to have some flexibility there."

Chase sat back and tapped his fingers on the arm of his chair. "Is this worth your time, Phoebe? How much money can we realistically raise?"

Phoebe swiveled in her chair to face him.

"Honestly, I don't know." She shoved some stray hair behind her ear. "But you said everybody loves football. So it's worth a shot, right? Because you need to build more cars, and you need investment money to do it."

He nodded, thinking. His first priority was the Swedish-Korean investors, and he didn't want Phoebe spending her time on something like this when she should focus on translating. But if Midnight Sun decided not to invest, or not to the level he needed, here was Phoebe, telling him he had options. Pointing out ways to do it. Hell, even a million bucks would complete the renovations to the factory building that he needed.

"It's a good idea," he said. "And we don't have to start it tomorrow. We can wait until after the week's over and we see what Midnight Sun decides to do."

"I know, right? Plus, the money doesn't have any strings like with the investors. Except, um."

"Yeah, got it. If it works, I have to host half the state of Nevada at my house for a weekend."

She laughed. "I got the idea from a friend at the CIA. She's got, ah, sort of a celebrity crush on you. She wants me to invite her out for a visit. After she said that, it occurred to me that people would pay to stay at your house."

"You can invite a friend to stay at my place if you're there, too," Chase said promptly. "But if you're not, I don't want to give anyone any ideas about my availability." *I have my own ideas.*

"*Are* you available?" Phoebe's question so paralleled Chase's thought that he blinked. And then that delicious color bloomed across her cheeks again.

"Sorry!" she said, flustered. "I didn't mean—"

"I have a few ideas."

She glanced at him quickly, pinker than ever, and looked away again even faster.

He leaned forward. "Phoebe."

She looked back him. She was so close. He could all but hear her heartbeat throb against her temple and that delicate spot on her neck. Her skin was so clear, and now that delicate peach blush stained her light tan. He heard her breath hitch.

"What?" she whispered.

The factory was quiet. It was just the two of them.

He leaned into her. He shouldn't want to kiss her so badly, but he did. She wasn't exactly an employee. Really, she was a contractor. Not the same as an employee. And only for one more week. It wasn't like—

Her eyes were huge, a deep blue-gray, as she gazed at him. She leaned into him. Her lips were parted, and when she licked the lower one, he felt his blood surge.

He leaned farther. He was drawn to her like a magnet, helpless against her. He wanted to be part of her, taste her, feel her against him, taste her skin, hold that initiative, drive, passion in his arms. He wanted *her*.

The air between them hummed with a vibrant energy. The space shimmered with desire. She wanted him, too. He could feel it, see it in her eyes. She wanted him.

He would let her have him.

Only a couple of inches separated them now, and exhaling in surrender, Chase touched his lips to hers.

Phoebe didn't know when they'd stopped working and sort of kidding around. But she'd been having fun, and okay, maybe they'd been flirting a little bit, and then all of a sudden the air was thick and she couldn't breathe and she couldn't tear her eyes away from Chase's. He was listening to her and giving her credit, and then he was sitting so close she could feel his skin whisper when his arm brushed against hers, making her blood run hot, and she felt dizzy from wanting him. She wanted him to kiss her, wanted it more than she'd wanted anything in her life, wanted it with a terrible, frightening urgency that rooted her to her seat and left her unable to move.

She would die if he didn't kiss her.

And then he did.

It was like all her secret desires were met in that one second. Everything she'd ever wanted, everything she'd ever known to be true, merged in that one second when his lips touched hers, melded to hers, moved under hers.

The stars met and clashed and aligned, and a deep-pitched harmony swept through her, starting behind her eyes and running down her arms and legs before shooting out through her fingers and the ends of her hair until she felt the vibration in her breathing.

And then he broke away, but not far, leaning his forehead against hers. His breathing was a little ragged, or maybe that was her own breathing.

Her thoughts were tangled. He was so strong, so powerful, so graceful in his loose-limbed walk, and she'd wanted to touch him for as long as she could remember, but she was going back to the CIA and he wasn't for her. She didn't know what to think. She couldn't think.

But that kiss was one thing she didn't have to think about. She wanted more of that, a lot more.

"Again," she whispered.

Chase leaned down a little to look at her more closely, and she saw something hot and urgent flash in his eyes. And then he kissed her again, a lot harder this time. She opened her mouth under his and their tongues tangled, and then he had his arms around her and she scrambled to get closer to him, to feel his heat, that powerful back beneath her fingers. The only problem was that the damn office chairs were in the way. She was mostly in his lap, but she didn't have enough room to move and she couldn't reach anything she wanted to reach—

With a low growl, Chase wrapped his arms around her and stood up, carrying her to the sofa by the conference table. That woke her up.

"Chase! Your knee! Put me down!"

And then she was on the couch and he was next to her, lying next to her, and she was pressed against him on the narrow space. He was warm and vibrant, and his mouth and hands were on her, everyplace that felt great.

When she reached up and licked his ear, he laughed and slid his hands underneath her T-shirt. When she kissed his cheekbone, he unhooked her bra. When she kissed him on the mouth again, he rolled her on top of him, sliding his hands from her hips to her breasts and then pulling off first her shirt and then her bra.

"My knee's good," he said, his hand hot on her breast. "How's your knee?"

"Good," she said, but she was almost out of breath.

She could feel the hard edge of his erection through her shorts, and with his hands—magic hands, she'd been right about that—she was flying, soaring through space. He felt solid, grounded beneath her. He was pulling at her clothes, at his clothes, but she was too far gone to care about that. Clothes on or off, she couldn't stop now, rocking against his hips, enjoying the friction as the tension increased, wanting more, feeling him pull her down, his hot mouth against her cool skin, her breasts full, her hunger increasing.

His breath rasped in her ear as she bucked against him.

"More," he said, and then she hovered at the brink, at an edge so sharp and bright she was dazzled.

He tensed and pushed, and then she was over, cascading through layers of soft, hard, edge, bright, and then soft again as she relaxed into his chest and he pulled her close and wrapped his arms around her.

Phoebe closed her eyes and felt cocooned by him, wanted never to move.

She heard him chuckle, felt the rumble in his chest.

"Sorry," he said. "I haven't done that since high school."

She lifted her head. "You haven't had sex since high school?"

"I haven't had sex with clothes on since high school."

She put her head back on his chest. "Don't you dare apologize."

"Who's apologizing?" He kissed her forehead. "I swore I'd never date an employee, and see where that got me."

Ouch. "What's that supposed to mean?"

Chase tilted her head back and kissed her on the cheek. "It means, *cher*, that I couldn't resist you. That's what it means."

"Oh." Phoebe kissed him back. "If it makes you feel any better, technically we're not dating now, either. I mean, we haven't been on a date."

"Excuse me. I think we can call sex a date."

"Sex is not a date. It's—" *Fantastic*. This moment, lying with Chase, feeling him touching her everywhere, was wonderful.

"Fine. We'll go on a date. It's practically dinnertime. We'll go for dinner. If you insist on changing, which I don't necessarily advise, wear that short skirt."

"I have to change. I'm a mess. No one would let me in looking like this. Not even that nice diner."

"You'll be with me," Chase said, and Phoebe heard the laughter in his voice. "My name is magic, right? That's what you said. As long as you're with me, you can get in anywhere."

"Bragging is not an attractive quality. Especially from someone who doesn't know what the national sport is. When do you want to go?"

"Soon. First, I need a little more therapy for my knee."

Chapter 13

Detective Dave Greenaway sat at his desk in the relative quiet of a Monday morning before the shift change. He, like most of the other detectives, was doing paperwork. But the other detectives were filling out their case reports. He was checking out his retirement options. He couldn't believe how many decisions and choices had to be made and documents signed and notarized before they could be filed. No wonder they said to allow six months to get everything settled.

He was ready to get out of policing, ready for a change. He'd put in his twenty-five, so he'd get his full pension, and he was only forty-seven. He wouldn't stop working yet, though, not right away. His wife couldn't retire for another five years at the earliest, so he'd decided he'd open a PI firm. He could pick and choose his cases, and with the pension, he wouldn't have to sweat it if he didn't like what came in or he didn't get a full caseload right away. He and Cora had been looking at offices, she'd made up a nice business card for him, he'd gotten his license. He even had a website. He was all set. Except for the paperwork.

He'd just finished filling out his insurance options when the door to the squad room was flung open and three guys in dark suits and short hair strode into the squad room, each armed with a briefcase.

Feds.

And shit, they were heading his way. Now what the hell was going on in his jurisdiction that had put a cramp in the feds' collective behind?

The feds stopped in front of his desk. He stifled a sigh.

"Detective Greenaway?" The white guy taking point was the most medium guy he'd ever seen. Maybe five foot ten or eleven, brown hair buzz cut, eyes of indeterminate light color. Medium build. Dark gray suit, white shirt, conservative tie. He'd never stand out in a crowd. Good look for surveillance. Or if he decided to turn to a life of crime. Or politics. Same thing, really.

He nodded to the agent. "That's me. And you are?"

"Aaron Picone, FBI," the point guy said, flipping open his badge wallet. "This is Agent Robert Zilesky and Agent Charles Pratt." The other two guys, one taller, one thinner, the skinny guy also a brother, nodded and flipped opened their badge wallets.

Men in Black. Sometimes the movies got it right.

He nodded again. "How can I help you?"

"We have a situation." Picone glanced at the one visitor's chair that flanked Greenaway's desk. Clearly the three of them couldn't all sit on it. "Is there someplace we can talk?"

"A situation," Greenaway said. "What kind of situation?"

"We'd rather take this more private. Is your captain in?"

The feds could see for themselves if the captain, who would occupy the glass box in the corner of the room, was in. But Greenaway stared at Picone a moment and then stood up and glanced over to the captain's office. Nope, still too early. Cap probably wouldn't get in until the shift change.

"Looks like no," he said, turning back to the agents. "You can wait in his office."

"Not necessary. We should talk now. So—where would that be?"

Picone's voice had an edge to it, and Greenaway decided he might as well get it over with, whatever they wanted.

"We got a conference room," he said. "This way."

He led the procession through the alleys of desks to the conference room, heads turning their way as they passed. When they got to the conference room, Greenaway entered first. It might be the FBI's meeting, but he damn well would sit at the head of the table.

He took the one chair that still swiveled, and the feds arranged themselves around the table. "What's up?" he asked.

Picone whapped his briefcase up on the metal table. He snapped open the catches, lifted the lid, and took out a paper file. He closed the briefcase and put it on the floor again, opened the file folder, and took out several photographs, passing them across the table to Greenaway.

"Ever seen these men?" Picone asked.

The photos were street shots, taken in some urban area. In the first two, he couldn't tell what city. The third photo he was pretty sure was New York. Three men—one maybe in his seventies, one just a kid, one maybe in his late twenties or early thirties—all with Asian features, were in each photo. They were standing around, walking, talking to each other. One or the other of the younger men always carried a backpack.

"No." Greenaway handed the photos back.

"We have reason to believe they're in Las Vegas."

"Okay," Greenaway said. "Have they committed a crime? A federal crime? That I should be interested in?"

Picone took another photo and passed it across to him. "This woman? Have you seen her before?"

Greenaway took the photo. It was a small, cheap photo, like for a driver's license or an employee ID, one of those things where they lined you up in front of a white screen and blasted you with light. It was a crummy likeness. The woman's features were washed out. But he knew who it was.

"Phoebe Renfrew." He passed the photo back.

"How did your paths cross?"

Greenaway shrugged. "She was in here following up on a police report."

"What about?"

"She reported an illegal gun purchase. You guys going to tell me what this is about?"

"We're following up on an investigation," Picone said.

"The one where she wants to get her job back at the CIA? She'll be glad to know you guys are on the job."

Picone's expression didn't change, but his eyelids flickered.

"How do you know she worked at the CIA?" he said. "If she did."

"She told me. What's this about?"

177

"Tell us about the gun purchase."

Greenaway felt his irritation level ratchet up a notch. "It's in the police report. You guys probably read it already. Why don't you just ask me what you want to know?"

Picone's expression still didn't change. Guy could have been a model for Mount Rushmore if he'd been important enough.

"Why did Renfrew follow these individuals?"

Greenaway resisted rolling his eyes. The spirit of multijurisdictional cooperation could only go so far. "Maybe you should ask her."

"We will," Picone said. "Right now, I'm asking you."

Greenaway gazed at Picone for a count of ten, thinking about how mad he wanted to get at these FBI assholes when he was only a couple of months from his retirement. Then counted to ten again. "She overhead something," he said. "She decided to follow the guys who said whatever they said. End of story, until you guys showed up. Now, how does that interest the FBI? And me?"

"What names did she give these men?"

"I'd have to look up the report. Maybe you have it there in your briefcase." He really didn't remember.

"Lars, Sven, and Gustav Eklund," Picone said, pointing at faces on one of the photos.

"That sounds about right," Greenaway said.

"What's the connection between the Eklunds and Renfrew?"

"She's translating for some outfit looking for investors, and they're part of the investor group."

"Did she talk to you about their trip to New York?" Picone asked. "Did she say she knew them from before?"

"No," Greenaway said. "What are you getting at? She reported a crime. Here. In Vegas. *Like I said.*"

"We'll be in touch." Picone picked up the briefcase, snapped the locks open, dropped his file inside, snapped the locks closed, and stood up. "Thank you for your time."

Phoebe was getting ready to go to work when her phone rang.

"Detective Greenaway," she said, surprised.

"Miz Renfrew. I'm calling to see if you can shed any light on what happened down here at the station this morning."

"I don't know," Phoebe said. "What happened?"

"The FBI paid me a visit," Greenaway said, his voice rising. "And let me tell you, Miz Renfrew, there are much better ways to start the day than having the FBI stomp all over you in their shiny wing tips."

"I can imagine." Phoebe wasn't sure what a wing tip was, but she knew she wouldn't want the FBI stomping all over her in them. "What did they want?"

"They wanted to know about your interest in your guys. Those Koreans. Clearly they know something I don't. And let me tell you, Miz Renfrew, lying to the police is a bad idea for many reasons. Give me one why I shouldn't arrest you for obstructing a criminal investigation."

"I'm not obstructing. I *wanted* a criminal investigation! *Is* there a criminal investigation?" She wasn't sure what answer she wanted to hear. An investigation could get her reinstated to the CIA, although any arrest of the Eklunds might wreck Chase's investment plans. As much as she wanted the cops to figure out what the Eklunds were up to, she didn't want anything bad to happen to Chase's company. "Did you find out something about Lars and Gustav?"

"No! And the FBI isn't telling me anything, either!"

"Oh. Because— Well. If there's going to be an arrest, do you think you could wait for a week or so?"

"No, Miz Renfrew, I could not. When we get the evidence we need—if there's any evidence to get—we'll make the arrest."

"Because here's the thing. That start-up that I mentioned in our interview? Lars and Gustav are part of a group that might invest heavily. It's a local business, kind of a big deal. I don't want that to go south."

"You're talking about Venture Automotive."

Phoebe was startled. "How did you know that?"

"The FBI is good for some stuff."

"Oh. Well, if you know that, then you know how hard Chase and everybody are working to make the company succeed. So if you could just hold off for a little while, everybody would be happy."

"See, it's that kind of statement that makes me think you know more than you're letting on. It's time to come clean, Miz Renfrew."

"I told you everything I know at the station," Phoebe said. "But there have been a few small developments since then." She told him how Nattie had said there was a federal fly watch out for the Eklunds and how she'd followed them to the Desert Dunes, where Sven had taken a dive to the floor and hurt himself after spotting her in the lobby. She didn't think that information would jeopardize Venture Automotive.

"Does that help?" she asked when she finished.

"No. Not really. I got no freaking clue what those feds want."

"I'm *telling* you," Phoebe said, "Lars and Gustav are gunrunners."

"I'm pretty sure they're not."

"Why do you think that?" Phoebe asked, but Greenaway had already hung up.

Now who wasn't telling the truth? But the only answer she got was the dial tone.

Phoebe was worried about going to the factory. What if the investors blamed her for Sven's injury? And took it out on Chase? Even if she wasn't exactly directly responsible for Sven's accident, Chase would still pay the price if Midnight Sun didn't invest.

And now Greenaway's call had made her nervous. If the feds had hinted dark secrets to the detective, and it sounded like they had, those same agents would be pounding on her door any second. She had to figure out everything she could, as soon as possible, because… Well, the feds pounding on your door was far from pleasant, and she'd had enough unpleasantness from the feds to last a lifetime. *Two* lifetimes.

Besides, she didn't want to jeopardize Chase's business. She especially didn't want the feds to come pounding on Chase's door when they were looking for her.

Her heart beat faster just thinking about him, but that had to stop. She was going back to Langley and the CIA. And they'd only known each other for a week. She *couldn't* have feelings for him this soon.

Still, she couldn't pretend that nothing had happened on that couch. It wasn't sex according to Bill Clinton, but it was pretty darn close. It had sure felt like sex to her. To him, too.

Last night after they'd done what they'd done on his office sofa, they had an early meal at the diner and he'd asked her to spend the night with him. She'd turned him down with regret, but staying over at his place signaled an involvement she wasn't ready to get into so quickly. And he probably dated a lot. Probably he was dating someone else right now. Maybe *two* someones. Or even more. Because who in her right mind wouldn't want to spend time with him?

So Chase drove her home. And while Trouble's obvious delight in seeing her again was rewarding on its own merits, it didn't quite measure up to six-plus incredible feet of magic.

Between Chase and the Eklunds and the CIA investigation of the Empire State Building fiasco and the FBI lurking around, her life was pretty nerve-wracking.

Kristin wasn't at her desk when she ran up the mezzanine steps, and Chase was on the phone, his back to her. She watched him for a second, felt her throat tighten as she gazed at his broad shoulders, his right hand twirling a pen while he talked. *Magic hands.* She knocked lightly on the doorframe and he spun around, a smile brightening his face when he saw her. She felt breathless just watching him smile. That smile should be illegal. That smile made her want to do unthinkable things. That smile made her want to go over there, heave that phone out the window, climb in his lap, and devour him. Which, considering the size of the average NFL quarterback, could take a while.

Yum.

But they were at work, and his office didn't even have a door. And he'd probably moved on. With a *cheerleader*. Except he didn't seem like he'd moved on, exactly. He was smiling that lazy, knowing, hot smile that went with the determined look in his eye. And as much as every cell of her being urged her to march in there and have her way with him, she smiled back, waved briefly like a dork, closed her eyes to fight the lust, and turned to go.

Kristin entered the mezzanine and turned on her computer. "Hey, girlfriend," she said, leaning down and dropping her purse in her desk drawer. "Happy Monday. Have any fun over the weekend?"

Phoebe started and her face got hot.

Kristin straightened up from her desk and glanced at her. "Oh my God. You *did* have fun." She followed Phoebe's glance into Chase's office. "*Oh, my God.*"

"Quiet!" Phoebe hissed. "It's not what you think."

"I think it's *exactly* what I think," Kristin said, grinning. "And may I say, congratulations!"

Phoebe squeezed her eyes shut. "Kristin, don't say anything to anybody, okay? Chase has this thing about not dating employees, and—"

"Oh, sweetie, I know all about that."

"Yes, I suppose so. And it would be awkward, and I don't think it's going anywhere, and—"

"I know where it's going," Kristin said, her eyes dancing. "Highway to heaven, that's where it's going."

"Shhhh!" Phoebe said. "He's *right there.*"

"So close and yet so far," Kristin said. "Listen, if you want to go for a nooner—"

"Kristin, *stop it,*" Phoebe said. "It's not—We're not—We only—"

"It's only nine, so I suppose a nooner *is* a little early. Although it's noon somewhere."

"*Kristin.*"

Kristin laughed. "I'm sorry, I couldn't resist. This is *great*! I'm happy for you."

"Don't be anything. It was one date, that's all. I don't even know if there's going to be another."

"Of course, there'll be another. You had a good time, right? And he did, too. Everybody made everybody happy." Kristin wiggled her eyebrows.

"Kristin," Phoebe said, exasperated. "Stop. It's probably just a one-time thing, okay?"

"Even a one-time thing has details. Not that I think it's a one-time thing."

"Promise me you won't tell anybody."

Kristin tilted her head like she was thinking about it and tapped her finger against her cheek. Phoebe gave up. Kristin was probably just yanking her chain. She *hoped*.

"Listen, I have to go. The investors are waiting for me. And the accountants."

"Sure, right when it gets interesting. Listen, we're having lunch, and you're spilling. Unless you go for a nooner."

"No, I'm not. Not that, and I'm not spilling, either. But we do have to talk soon. Sooner than lunch if I can break away."

Kristin looked more serious now. "About?"

Phoebe patted her laptop. "I worked on the race over the weekend, and we still have calls to make. One thing you're right about—mention Chase's name, and the honey flows. I bet the president himself doesn't get this much attention."

"Told you." Kristin sat down and spun to face her computer. "Okay, Phoebe. You can run, but you can't hide. When you're done with the investors, we'll finish setting up the race. And then you're telling me *everything*."

So not doing that, Phoebe thought, but she couldn't resist glancing into Chase's office once more. He was off the phone, watching her, his eyes still hot, a lazy grin on his face. She felt a glow spread through her and then Kristin cackled, and she took off down the hallway to find the investors.

When Phoebe got to the conference room, the Koreans were sipping tea and snacking on soy crackers and fruit, and Chase's accountants were sipping coffee and snacking on Danish pastries and fruit. Between them on the wide table sat a stack of folders.

Phoebe already knew that Chase used an outside accounting firm rather than hire his own accounting staff. Some of the Midnight Sun group were also accountants and, theoretically at least, little translation would be needed, because numbers and accounting methodology were more or less the same the world over. But she was here in case anyone wanted to ask questions.

Chase's accountants, two men of late middle age, stood when Phoebe came in.

"Douglas Chen." The one nearest her held out his hand.

"Steve Leatham," the second one said.

"Phoebe Renfrew," she said, shaking their hands.

The Koreans stood and bowed, the accountants bowed, and then the formalities seemed to be over. Everyone sat.

"Tell me what you'd like me to tell them," Phoebe said to Chase's accountants. "I understand you might not need me here the whole time."

"I think just to get started," Douglas said. "After that, if you have other things to do, we can probably call you if we run into a snag."

"Sounds good," Phoebe said.

"Okay." Steve glanced around the table. "We've got the certified records of Venture Automotive's financials that we agreed to provide." He patted the folders, looking at the Midnight Sun accountants, who all watched him expectantly. "Before we begin, they have to sign a standard confidentiality agreement."

"Okay." Phoebe translated what the accountants had said, and then she translated, more slowly, the nondisclosure agreement.

She was happy to see that Sven's color had improved and he seemed stronger—although he was still wearing the bandage that the hospital had wound around his head. He was getting the sympathy vote from the other investors.

In a few minutes the room was quiet, the investors poring over the pages, the accountants peering into their laptop screens. Phoebe watched them for a second. They didn't need her, at least not this minute.

"I'm stepping out for a few minutes," she told the accountants. "Here's my number. Call me if you need me."

They both tapped her number into their phones. A couple of the investors glanced up, and she repeated what she'd said in Korean. She stood, looked at the silent room, then slipped out the door, letting it close quietly behind her.

She kept thinking about the feds. Why had they talked to Greenaway? He said he didn't know what they wanted, but he probably had an idea. It had to be about the Eklunds. Maybe her call to Nattie had stirred something up.

And maybe Nattie had something for her by now. She went down the hall away from Kristin's and Chase's offices, down the stairs, out the side exit, and sat in the shade on the concrete steps by the employee parking lot. She dialed the familiar number at the CIA.

"Nattie? It's me, Phoebe. Do you have anything for me?"

"Hi, Mom!" Nattie said. "You really shouldn't call here during work hours. Or at all. Didn't we talk about this?"

"Sorry, Nat. What do you have?"

"Todd is trying to concentrate here. Let me just get out into the hallway so we don't disturb him with talk about that stupid wedding present."

Phoebe knew Todd, a pointy-collared, by-the-book kind of guy, so she was happy to wait while Nattie went wherever she was going to get away from him. In a few seconds, she came back on the line, slightly breathless.

"Okay," she said. "Here's what I could get. Sven escaped to Sweden from North Korea when he was about forty-five, most likely with help from his father, who at the time was some big shot in the North Korean government, but probably even then on his way out."

"He must have been desperate to get out," Phoebe said. "Sven, I mean. Forty-five."

"Maybe he thought—or found out—that the family was targeted for a purge. Or even execution. It happens. Anyway. Sven's wife was dead, but he had a son. He left that kid behind."

"Yikes."

"Yeah. Sven married a Swedish woman five years after he got to Sweden, and *they* had a son, whom they named Lars. Around that time, they smuggled out Sven's older son, who took the name Gustav when he got to Sweden. Two years after that, Sven's second wife died."

"Sven has bad luck with wives."

"He sure does." Nattie said hello to someone, and Phoebe waited for her to get back to the call.

"Sven and the two sons have been trying to get Sven's father out of North Korea. So far, no luck. The father was disgraced and booted from his job. They don't know where he is, and anything's possible—prison, a work camp, you name it. Between you and me, he's probably dead. He'd be ninety by now. Or close to it."

"Bad."

"Yeah. The Eklunds asked the Swedish government to locate him and get him out, but nothing happened. Either they tried and didn't make any progress, or they didn't try that hard. The Swedes were a little vague about it."

"Trying hard to free a guy who might be dead would not be the way the Swedish government would want to expend a lot of political capital." Phoebe frowned as she turned over the information.

"No kidding. Anyway, the Eklunds exhausted Swedish diplomatic efforts to get Mr. Kang—his full name is Kang Ji-hoon, Kang being the original family name—out of North Korea. Then they tried extra-diplomatic channels."

"The Eklunds tried to bribe officials?"

"They sure did. Swedish and North Korean alike."

"I take it that didn't work."

"The Swedes said they had done everything they could and turned down the money. Can't know for sure about the North Koreans, but it's more likely they took the money and didn't do anything."

"Did anyone else get involved? Middlemen? Spies? Brokers? Shady underworld figures?"

Nattie laughed. "You left out Russian gangsters."

"Seriously?"

"Maybe. The Swedes aren't sure, but they think all of that. When even the underground couldn't shake Mr. Kang loose, the Eklunds went back to the Swedish government and sent threatening letters to their prime minister. I think that activity, combined with their origin of birth, put them on our watch list, because we don't have any records of them doing anything here."

"They made threats? And the Swedes have records of it?"

"Yup. The Swedes and Interpol both."

"The Eklunds want him out bad."

"They do. Well, family loyalties are strong in Korea. As far as we know, Kang Ji-hoon got out everybody in the family who was still alive. And now he's sitting there, can't get out on his own, and nobody can figure out a way to free him."

Phoebe thought about the force of family ties. Her own

mother hadn't been nurturing, but she was the only family Phoebe had. What would she do if Brenda were sick or imprisoned? Probably not go to the extent of threatening a prime minister, but still.

"So that's all I know," Nattie said. "And even more than Sven wants Mr. Kang out of North Korea, I want to come out to Las Vegas. Am I invited?"

"Of course! Whenever you like. I have my own place now, too, and it's small, but you're welcome. And I'll introduce you to Chase. We can do dinner or something."

"Phoebe, are we done now? I could get fired for telling you this stuff. You don't even have a secure channel."

"We're done. Don't worry, Nattie. Nothing will come back to you. And I'll owe you."

"Forever. You will owe me *forever*. Which you can start to pay off by introducing me to that hunka hunka burning love, Chase Bonaventure. I'm requesting my vacation days right now. How does the weekend work for you?"

After Phoebe hung up with Nattie, she thought about what she'd learned. It didn't add up. Even bribing North Korean bureaucrats or threatening Swedish diplomats didn't point to Lars and Gustav running guns in Las Vegas. Even if they wanted massive guns to get their father out of prison in North Korea, guns in Vegas couldn't bring that about. And how did the secretary of state fit in? If she did. It didn't make sense.

She stood up, dusted off her skirt, and went inside. She was glad to have Nattie's information, although she didn't see how the pieces fit together. But she'd keep working at it. The connection was there.

She just had to find it before something bad happened.

Chapter 14

Late that afternoon as Phoebe and Kristin sat in Kristin's mezzanine office, making calls and finalizing Saturday's rally, Phoebe's phone rang.

"It's Brenda," she told Kristin, feeling resigned to whatever her mother's latest tragedy would turn out to be. She jumped up and walked down the hallway, putting the phone to her ear.

"Mom? What's up?"

"Bud broke up with me!"

Bud. Who was Bud again? Oh, right, the rancher. He had a city for a last name… *Corvallis*, that was it. Bud Corvallis. The latest person Brenda thought was The One.

"He said he'd had a good time but it wouldn't work out, and then he took off! He just packed his bags and cleared out, and—" Brenda sniffed. "I thought he was the one."

"Mom, I'm sorry." Phoebe glanced at her watch. She and Kristin had a lot to do, and here was her mom, the great dreamer, derailed yet again by another man who didn't deserve her. Would Brenda never learn? This scenario had replayed so often in Phoebe's life, she didn't think it could get any older.

"—and now I have to go to work, and—"

Phoebe realized she hadn't been paying close attention to her mother's tale of woe, and now those words struck a cold knife in her heart.

"You still have your car, don't you?" she asked, realizing her voice was too sharp. But if Brenda had sold her vehicle because of that worthless bum and, worse yet, expected Phoebe to supply transportation, that would be the straw that broke the camel's back.

"Of course, I still have my car! I'm *hurting*, Phoebe, that's what I'm saying."

"Right. Sorry." Phoebe looked at her watch again. "Well, sure, Mom. Of course, you're hurting. So, listen—"

"And now I don't have anywhere to stay, because Bud's gone and Barry padlocked my apartment, and you said you were living with Chase Bonaventure, right? He must have a big place. How about I bunk with you for a bit? Meet the man who's keeping company with my daughter."

Phoebe jerked upright. "No, Mom, you can't. First off, I'm not 'living with' him." Phoebe drew quotation marks in the air before she realized her mother couldn't see her. "We're not even dating. I stayed there exactly one night, and I have my own place now. It's small."

Brenda sniffed again. "Smaller than my old place?"

Crap. Phoebe could hear "when I let you stay with me" as loudly as if Brenda had said it with a megaphone.

"You can stay at my place." Phoebe tried not to sigh. "I was just letting you know that it's not Chase Bonaventure's mansion."

Brenda got off work late and would get in at three in the morning, and she'd wake Phoebe up trying to be quiet, and then she'd never get back to sleep, and she'd be a lousy translator the next day as well as being a lousy CIA agent. But what could she do about it? The bottom line was, her mom needed a place to stay. Whether Phoebe liked it or not.

"I just need a place to lay my head," Brenda said. "Of course, it would have been great to see Chase Bonaventure's place. I bet it's something! But it'll be fun to stay with you in your cozy little apartment. We can hang out like girlfriends."

"You can stay with me," Phoebe said again, "but don't you just want to pay Barry the three thousand you owe him and get your own place back? That way you'd have your stuff, too."

"Tried that," Brenda said, an edge to her voice. "Barry already sold my stuff, the creep."

"If you gave him the money, you could probably get your apartment back, at least."

"*Phoebe!* I'm not giving that ingrate a penny more than I've already paid him! That apartment wasn't exactly the Ritz, you know."

Yeah, she knew, all right.

"Okay," Phoebe said. "It was just a thought. I'll leave sheets"— *I have to buy more sheets*—"and a pillow"—*get a pillow, too*— "on the sofa. Don't wake Trouble. If he barks, we'll all be kicked out."

"I never make trouble." Brenda sounded confused. "Who barks?"

"Trouble. He's my dog."

"You've got a dog?"

"Yes. His name is Trouble. And my rental agreement stipulates a quiet dog. I'll tell him you're coming, but hey. He's a dog."

"I can't believe my little girl has a *pet*," Brenda said. "You've got *Trouble!*"

"Yeah," Phoebe said. "Think of that."

Phoebe disconnected the call and walked back to join Kristin, who looked up when Phoebe pulled out her chair.

"Everything all right?" she asked.

Phoebe nodded. "Sure. It was my mom. Same old. Are we about done here for today?"

"For now. I'm waiting on some callbacks. I think we should talk again tonight. We can go over the spreadsheets and see what we're still missing." Then Kristin's eyes sparkled. "I'm sure you're impatient to go because your *boyfriend* wants to see you," she said in a low, theatrical voice, clasping her hands over her heart and grinning.

"Kristin. I get enough of that from my mom. He's not my boyfriend. Stop, already."

But when Kristin only laughed, Phoebe stomped into Chase's office.

Chase frowned when Phoebe glowered at him. "What's wrong?"

Phoebe dropped into his guest chair and scowled. "Kristin's teasing me. And my mom's moving in with me. So now I have to buy more sheets and a pillow."

"Your mom is moving in with you?"

She clunked her head against the back of the chair. "Yes. Because she was staying with, ah, Bud Corvallis when she got locked out, remember? And now he's gone, she can't get back in her apartment, and she has no other place to go. So she'll be staying with me."

Chase leaned back, frowning. "She's works late nights, right?" he asked. "She's a cocktail waitress. And you're going to put her up. In that one-bedroom apartment. With Trouble."

Phoebe closed her eyes. She'd been thinking the same thing, but she didn't like hearing him say it. It sounded so... crowded. And tiring. And annoying. "Yes."

"Phoebe, come sit with me on the couch."

Her eyes flew open. "I don't think that's such a good idea, Coach. The last time we sat on that couch—"

"I know, I had the best time of my life, but I can be strong," Chase said. "I won't let you seduce me this time."

From outside the office, Kristin snorted.

"Can you keep your voice down?" Phoebe whispered. "Unless you want everybody to know." But... *the best time of his life?* It had been the best time of *her* life, but Phoebe wasn't sure Chase could mean that.

"I want to talk to you, and not across this desk," Chase said. "I want to talk to you as a friend. In a comfortable setting. The way they teach you in business management school."

"Oh, well, if it's about business management, then." Phoebe got up and let him lead her to the conversation area.

They sat down and Chase stretched his arm along the back of the couch, his fingers barely touching Phoebe's shoulder. She wanted to lean into him.

She was so weak.

"This doesn't seem very businesslike," she said, feeling a little breathless.

"That's reassuring." Chase was fooling with her sleeve a little, and his fingers felt warm through the fabric of her blouse. "But we do have important things to discuss. I'm worried about how you're going to meet your commitments."

"You think that I can't be sharp if my mom moves in with me," Phoebe said, finding it hard to concentrate. "I know. To tell you the truth, I'm a little worried about that, too. But I have to give her a place to stay."

"I understand. That's your decision. And that being the case, you need to stay at my place, at least until Midnight Sun makes a decision."

Phoebe jerked back, startled. "We tried that once, remember? It didn't work out. Plus, I need my own place."

"You can have your own place next week." Chase shook his head. "Next week you can move you and your mom and Sanjay and Trouble and Uncle Boo-Boo and anybody else you can think of into a studio apartment and start a youth soccer league or a tuba band or whatever you want in there, I don't care. But right now, you owe me."

"What?"

"I need your best work, Phoebe. You got mad at me the last time we tried sleeping under the same roof, but we cleared the air. Now we're in the home stretch here. Everything hinges on what Midnight Sun decides. I can't afford to have you not as effective as you could be. We're a team here. We all work together. Everybody who works here is counting on you to do your share."

Phoebe blinked. *Kristin*, she realized. If Midnight Sun didn't invest and the company went broke, Kristin would be out of a job. And Megan at reception. Daryl in security. Tony, Matt, and Rinsho in production. Margo and Bill in R&D. Everybody—more than one hundred people—would lose their jobs.

Chase needed her to be on top of her game. And he was paying her a ton of money to do her best job. He was right—she did owe him.

Chase's fingers were playing with the ends of her hair. And if…if she stayed at his place, if something else happened between them, would that be so bad? Even if he was her boss. If she got involved, though, and then she had to go back to DC—that would be hard. Beyond hard. But how involved could she get in a week? Just thinking about the possibilities of staying with him again made a shiver of anticipation run down her spine.

Chase smiled. Know-it-all bastard. Still, he had a point. She was still tired from her long night and short sleep on Aunt Aminda's motel lobby sofa.

She nodded. "Okay. You're right. Brenda *is* a bit of a trial. I'll stay at your place."

Chase pulled her into his arms, holding her close and burying his face in her neck. "Nothing makes me hotter than when you agree with me," he said, his voice muffled. "Well, that and the short skirt."

Phoebe laughed, losing her breath and feeling the heat of him through to her bones, turning her insides to mush.

"Really? Because—"

A knock sounded on the doorframe. "Ah, guys?"

Kristin. Phoebe thanked her friend's discretion for not looking in. She scrambled out of Chase's arms and sat up, straightening her blouse.

"Listen, I'm going home," Kristin said from outside the door. "Phoebs, call me later, okay? Like we said."

"Are you working on the race?" Chase asked, his hand still warm on Phoebe's back. "Kristin, get in here. Why don't you come over to our place? Work there. Update me."

"Oooh, *your* place," Kristin said, sticking her head around the corner. "As in the both of you. Sweet. Wild horses couldn't keep me away."

"Make her stop." Phoebe rolled her eyes.

Chase grinned. "Seven thirty."

Chase drove Phoebe to her apartment, where an ecstatic Trouble threw himself at them both.

"Why don't I take him out real quick while you pack your stuff," he said, scratching the dog's ears. "He can run around at my place."

Phoebe nodded, pointing to her unpacked box of books. "Might as well take these out with you. As long as you're going."

"I'm getting too damn familiar with this box," Chase said, but he clipped Trouble's leash on and shouldered the box.

Phoebe sighed as she watched the muscles in his back ripple. A vision like that never got old.

Chase took the box and Trouble outside, and Phoebe packed

her clothes in record time. Then she sat down to write a quick note to her mother.

STAYING AT CHASE'S TONIGHT. MAKE YOURSELF COMFORTABLE. TALK TO YOU SOON. PHOEBE.

That should do it. Her mother would apply her own brand of thinking to Phoebe's situation and assume that she and Chase would be getting married any hour now. Well, Brenda could think what she wanted. She'd just be wrong about it.

The security buzzer sounded, and Phoebe let Chase in.

"I'm ready," Phoebe said, pulling out the handle of her roller bag.

"You sure travel light." Chase grabbed the bag of dog paraphernalia. "Except for that box of books."

"Yeah," Phoebe said, taking Trouble's leash. "Lots of practice."

They headed to Chase's bright yellow SUV, which had already attracted a small crowd outside Phoebe's apartment building.

"Hi, folks." Chase smiled, moving steadily through the crowd toward the car. "How y'all doing?"

"We miss you on the field, Chase!" a middle-aged woman wearing a scandalously bright floral-print scarf wrapped around her head called out. "What are the Snakes' chances for the Super Bowl this year?"

"Coach and players are working hard," Chase said, opening the car doors. "The team appreciates your support. Let's go, Phoebe."

"Don't forget to come to the rally on Saturday!" Phoebe stood on the running board and called out to the crowd. "We're testing Venture Automotive electric vehicles against gas guzzlers—even a 1957 baby-blue Cadillac! Chase is signing autographs! Check the website for details!"

Chase reached out and tugged on her skirt. "Jesus. *Get in the car.*"

Phoebe dropped into the seat. "Might as well make use of your celebrity," she said, buckling her seat belt. "We want people to come out to the rally. Good thing you've got this yellow car everybody notices."

"I've been thinking about changing the logo's colors," Chase said as he started the ignition. "I took the advice of a professional marketer on the yellow, but maybe we need to go with more conventional colors."

"Not until after the rally."

"Listen to you."

Phoebe glanced at him as he pulled away from the curb, but Chase grinned. "I was planning on making spaghetti for dinner," he said. "That work for you?"

"I love spaghetti," Phoebe said. "But I love almost everything. I'm a United Nations of food preferences. Sorry, but I have to call Harry real fast. He's driving against your luxury line, that SUV model. I don't think he realizes yet that he's going to lose."

She tapped the Call icon, and then Harry came on the line. "Harry, it's Phoebe. Listen, I'm with Chase now—you're on speaker—and I wanted to finalize your schedule for the rally on Saturday morning. Eight o'clock. Does that still work for you?"

"The race is fifty miles, right?" Harry said. "Two hours from start to finish? That's all I can do, because I've got that big performance Saturday at the Desert Dunes and I have rehearsal beforehand. I can't be late—it's a solo. But I can't wait to get out on the track and show Chase Bonaventure what a road-grabbing V-8 monster can do when it's running full throttle."

Phoebe shook her head at Chase. *Won't happen*, she mouthed to him.

"You wish," Chase said into the phone, keeping his voice stern but mouthing *What?* to Phoebe. "Come Saturday, you'll be eating my dust. You and that overdecorated hunk of scrap metal you're so proud of."

"Ooo*kay*, great. Thanks, Harry," Phoebe said. "Yes, you'll be done by ten o'clock. Get to Venture Automotive at seven. We'll get you registered, photos taken, all that. Rally starts at eight sharp."

"I'm gonna want one of those photos to take to rehearsal and show the guys."

"No problem. Hey, can you get me in to see the show, Harry? I'd love to see you guys perform."

"I'll try. Security'll be a bitch. Okay, gotta go. See you Saturday, Chase. Prepare to put second prize in your trophy case."

"Crap," Phoebe said when he disconnected. "Kristin and I forgot to order you a trophy case. I better do that before I forget." She dug into her messenger bag for her laptop.

"Yeah, about that, Phoebe," Chase said, braking at a red light. "How many races are you planning, and how many do you realistically expect Venture Automotive to win?"

Phoebe cracked open her laptop and powered it on.

"Don't worry," she said. "We'll win them all."

"How is Venture Automotive winning all the races?" Chase asked later that evening after Kristin had arrived.

He'd broken out a bottle of wine, and they were all sitting around the kitchen table, peering at laptops. The table, he reflected, that was practically larger than Phoebe's current living room. He refused to think how she and her mom and Trouble would all have fit in that tiny apartment.

"Easy-peasy," Kristin said blithely, beaming at him.

He felt his heart sink. "Really? Because I don't want to be a spoilsport, but I can't cheat. My reputation would never recover."

"Oh, you won't have to cheat." Phoebe squinted at her laptop. "Matt and Tony and I have it all worked out."

"My electrical and software guys are in on this? What exactly did you work out?"

"We're not running a *race*," Phoebe said. "We're running a *rally*."

Kristin nodded. "It's cool. It's a bunch of challenges. So, like from point A to point B is one challenge and then point B to point C is another. And whoever wins the most challenges overall wins the *rally*."

"Not a race," Phoebe said. "Getting from point A to B in the least amount of time isn't the goal."

"Seriously?" Chase asked. How could a race not be about time? "You're running a contest where I come in last every time but still win? That won't look like cheating, I'm sure."

"You won't come in last." Phoebe seemed too damn smug.

"I take it you think Venture Automotive will win the most challenges."

"Sure," said Phoebe. "We rigged it."

He groaned. "I said, *no cheating*." He wanted to win the races, but he'd rather lose than cheat. He wanted Midnight Sun—and the spectators—to see a level playing field.

"First challenge," Kristin said, ticking off her fingers, "which car—gas or electric—makes the least noise driving past the hospital."

The light dawned.

"I'm guessing that would be the Venture Automotive vehicles." Chase grinned.

"You'd be right," Kristin said. "We've already measured. Well, Rinsho measured."

"My foreman? He's out there rigging car races for me, too?"

"*Rallies*," Phoebe said. "Yes. He is. But it's not rigging the races. We're"—she paused, looking for words—"issuing challenges that play to the strengths of Venture Automotive's vehicles. The strengths that will sell cars for you now and into the future."

"You sound like an advertising campaign now."

"Exactly!" Phoebe beamed. "You have to think long-term."

"Take fuel economy," Kristin said. "We've got everybody beat there."

Phoebe nodded. "In the second challenge, all the cars start out empty, put in two dollars' worth of fuel, and drive until they run out of fuel or get to the finish line, whichever comes first."

"That one's easy," Chase said. "Venture Automotive comes in first again."

"Bingo." Kristin typed something into her laptop.

"Then we'll capture emissions and measure those," Phoebe said. "Winner, Venture Automotive."

"We're working on something where the final leg requires an emergency generator at the finish line, and we can use the Venture Automotive car battery for that," Kristin said. "That would be so cool."

"I bet we could blow something up," Phoebe said. "That would be dramatic. Except that since I'm worried that the Eklunds might have a bomb in their truck, demonstrating how to blow something up is probably not my best idea. Let's talk to Tony about it tomorrow. He'll have an idea. He's been a tremendous resource."

"Speaking of the finish line." Kristin stood up and carried her glass to the sink. "I have to get going. Tonight's a school night."

"I'll walk you to the door." Phoebe stood up, too.

"Yeah, you have to, because I won't be able to find my way out of here. Place is like a hotel."

Chase rolled his eyes and carried the glasses to the dishwasher. "*Good night*, Kristin."

When Kristin got to the door, she pulled Phoebe outside. "Honestly, Phoebs, the two of you should totally go for it. You're great together."

Phoebe shook her head. "It won't work. If all goes according to plan, I'll be going back to DC. He doesn't date employees. It's a no-win situation. But—"

"You want to."

Phoebe sighed. "I do."

Kristin shrugged. "You're not exactly an employee," she said. "And, okay, DC is a problem, but there's weekends and holidays. Cross-country jet travel. You could work things out."

If she was tired now, imagine weekly or even monthly cross-country flights. And for how long?

She wanted to go for it, she really did. She thought of his strength, his heat, his smile. She wanted that. But she just didn't see how any long-term relationship would work out. A short-term fling was one thing—that would be fun, for sure. Maybe even romantic.

But long ago, Phoebe had sworn to herself that she'd never be like her mother. Brenda fell for "perfect" guys all the time, always after too brief an acquaintance, moving in with men who never stuck for the long haul.

With any luck, she'd have to leave soon for the CIA. And if she moved in with Chase, a guy she'd had an instant attraction for, could maybe even fall in love with—but who couldn't possibly work out—she'd repeat her mother's pattern.

And that was something she simply couldn't afford to do.

Chapter 15

The next morning Phoebe woke early, the cool, thin light of dawn dappling the pale aqua walls of her room in Chase's house. The sheets were crisp and fresh, and a warm arm held her loosely against a strong, muscled chest.

A girl could get used to this.

She listened to Chase breathe, felt the slow rise and fall of his chest against her back. Outside, a bird chirped.

She'd love to lie here most of the morning, make love again, find out if Chase was as thorough and tireless an athlete in the morning as he was in the evening.

But she still had a lot of work to do to make sure that everything was in place for the rally on Saturday. And she needed to focus whatever time she could on the Eklunds' involvement in gunrunning. She was worried that they hadn't yet made their move—and that she hadn't yet figured out what that move would be.

She turned her head slightly and kissed Chase's arm, then carefully slid out from under it. His robe lay flung over the lounge chair and she put it on, inhaling the soft sandalwood scent. Then she picked up her laptop and tiptoed out of the room.

She put on a pot of coffee, let Trouble out, and powered up her computer. While the coffee brewed, she checked out Harry's conference. The Las Vegas All-Elvis Revue was the Saturday entertainment for the military security conference, a gathering of several thousand generals, politicians, and business types. Why generals, politicians, and industry tycoons wanted an all-Elvis revue for entertainment, she couldn't guess. But this was Vegas. Nothing made sense here.

She clicked through the conference program. Harry had said security would be tight, and she could see why—big names were everywhere. He probably wouldn't be able to get her in. It looked like attendees had had to apply for a security clearance months ago.

And then she got to the page that announced the keynote speaker.

The secretary of state.

Phoebe stared at her screen, frozen in shock. Whatever she'd miscalculated in her Empire State Building analysis, Phoebe believed that she'd been correct in the essentials: The secretary was the target, not the president, and not the building. In which case, the threat against the secretary could still be real.

The secretary was here in Vegas, and the Swedish-Koreans were here. Just a couple of weeks ago, the secretary had been at the Empire State Building. At some point the Eklunds had been at the Empire State Building, too, because Lars had that photo of it in his phone.

And the Eklunds wanted guns.

Of course, it wasn't conclusive. It was barely *suggestive*. But CIA analysts were trained to connect the dots. And she knew dots when they jumped off the page and waved their arms in her face.

Nattie could help. And—she checked the wall clock—she'd be in the office by now.

"Nattie," she said, when her friend picked up. "It's Phoebe. Listen."

"Phoebe! What's up? I'm coming out in a couple of days. Did you get my email?"

"I must have," Phoebe said. "I've been busy. Listen, this is important. Have you picked up anything that the secretary of state is in danger out here at this military-industrial conference thing she's attending?"

"Phoebe." Nattie's voice carried a warning.

"Please tell me what you've got," Phoebe said. "I'm worried. Should I call the cops? I know somebody on the force."

"That conference has more security than Fort Knox," Nattie

said. "You don't have to call the cops to add more. Everybody federal is going to be there. Even the Secret Service."

"The president's coming?" Phoebe asked, startled.

"No. That conference is of national security, according to Homeland. Hence, Secret Service."

"Those useless twerps," Phoebe said. "They're probably in cahoots with Homeland to have fun at a junket. They're probably out getting drunk with hookers right now."

Nattie laughed. "At nine in the morning?"

"It's five o'clock somewhere, right? Please, Nattie. Is there a threat against the secretary?"

Nattie sighed. "There's no specific threat we can identify," she said, her voice lowered. "But there's a heightened alert."

"Of course. That's why the Secret Service is involved, too, then," Phoebe said. "Can you do me a favor? Can you tell me when the Eklunds entered the United States and what their port of entry was?"

"Phoebe."

"*Please.*"

"You are so lucky that you know Chase Bonaventure." Phoebe heard keys clacking in the background.

"Sven, Gustav, and Lars Eklund entered the United States at New York two weeks ago," Nattie said. "Is that what you wanted to hear?"

It wasn't what she wanted to hear. But that time frame completely fit her Empire State Building miscalculation. Maybe she'd been wrong about the gunrunning. Maybe the Eklunds really wanted to get to the secretary of state for some reason. Was *that* why they were here? They wanted to hurt the secretary, wherever she was? Maybe now they planned an attack on this conference?

"Do you have anything else?"

"No," Nattie said. "That's all I can tell you. You're welcome."

"That's great, Nattie, I mean it. Just one more thing. For comparison. When did Thor Olafsson arrive?"

More tapping. "One week ago, through Chicago. Who's he?"

"Another investor. Thanks."

"Don't forget I'm coming in a couple of days," Nattie said.

"I want to meet your boss."

"We'll be here. Looking forward to seeing you."

When they disconnected, she called Greenaway.

"Detective?" she said when she got through. "It's Phoebe Renfrew. Sorry I'm calling so early." She glanced at the clock and winced. Six thirty. Yeah, a little early. "Is there anything more on the feds and the Eklunds?"

"Why are you asking, Miz Renfrew?"

"I, ah, conferred with a colleague at the CIA, and it turns out that the Eklunds entered the country a full week before the other Midnight Sun investors. That's the week of the Empire State Building bomb scare. And there's a heightened security alert for that big conference this weekend at the Desert Dunes, where the secretary of state will be speaking. So I'm curious. And a little worried."

"How heightened?"

Phoebe shrugged. "I don't know. It would be heightened just because of who's attending, but it's more heightened than normal heightening."

"For supposedly being the country's big spy team, you all don't seem to be that good at nailing down the details," Greenaway said. "No offense."

"None taken," Phoebe said. "That's just how it works, and that's why it can go wrong if you're not careful. I'm the poster child for that one."

"So it seems."

"Yeah. So…have the feds been back in touch? You know anything more?"

"No and no," Greenaway said. "But since we're in the spirit of sharing here, I think I'll have a quick, informal chat with the Eklunds."

"You can't do that!" Phoebe said. "We don't have any solid evidence! And Chase—It would ruin the investor meetings."

"This is a case of national security," Greenaway said, his voice sympathetic but unwavering. "And this is my city. And so far, it doesn't look to me like the feds are doing that great a job at figuring out what the threat is here."

Greenaway disconnected, and Phoebe sat back, thinking.

What could she do now? If the Eklunds wanted to hurt the secretary of state, they couldn't do a better job than blow up the conference where she was speaking. She had to make that harder for them to do.

She had to get them out of that truck.

And then she had an idea so brilliant in its simplicity, she couldn't believe she hadn't thought of it before.

She'd searched the truck the day she'd followed the Eklunds out to Venture Automotive. She'd found the rental agreement. Now she called the rental company.

"Sunshine Rentals," the clerk said. "Darren speaking. How can I help you?"

"Hi, Darren. This is Phoebe Renfrew, personal assistant to Chase Bonaventure at Venture Automotive."

"*The* Chase Bonaventure?" the clerk said. "The *quarterback*? Jeez, I'm a big Rattlesnakes fan. We're going to miss him next year."

"Coaches and players are working hard," Phoebe said. "The team thanks you for your support, and it personally means a lot to Chase. Listen, he needs your help with something."

"Sure, anything I can do for Mr. Bonaventure."

"He's got a couple of foreign clients visiting for a few days. They're staying at the Silver Moon, and they rented a truck from you guys, which it turns out they don't need. They're not even that secure driving it in Las Vegas, you know? And they're in client meetings all day, so I was wondering if you could come to the hotel this morning and pick it up."

"Sure!" Darren said. "We can get there by five this afternoon."

Phoebe glanced at her watch. It was six forty-five. She wanted that truck out of the hotel parking lot before the Swedish-Koreans were likely to head to Venture Automotive, which would be around nine. She didn't want to give them another second to drive around in that thing.

"Well, that's great, Darren, but I really wanted that truck out of the parking lot by eight thirty, if at all possible. The hotel is getting edgy that it's taking up too much room, and the guys aren't driving that well. We think they're going to hit somebody, and then it would be a big mess. A big mess with bad publicity."

"Gotcha," Darren said. "Listen. We're not far from there. I can put the answering machine on and dash over there myself. No problem. I'll just charge the card for time so far—is that okay? And then we can skip the signature."

"*Thank you*, Darren. That's awesome. Give me your address. I'll get an autographed commemorative jersey out to you today."

Phoebe took down his contact information and disconnected. *There*. That problem solved. She didn't even care what the Eklunds might say to her about it or how the other investors might respond when they found out. It was more important to prevent a potential attack on the secretary. And the Eklunds didn't need that stupid truck anyway.

She turned when she heard a sound behind her.

"There you are." Chase, wearing only his boxers and a smile, entered the kitchen and joined her at the table. His walk was as loose-limbed as a panther's, all coiled athletic grace. A knot rose in her throat.

"Hey," she said, her throat dry. How on earth did she think she'd ever be able to walk away from him when the CIA reinstated her? He probably knew it, too, the rat bastard.

"Good morning, *cher*." He pulled out a chair and sat down, his knees bracketing her thighs. His hands slid up her arms to her face, and he pulled her in for a kiss. Phoebe's heart lurched. When he released her, he stroked her palm.

"Working already? I'd hoped to have a little more time with you this morning."

He was so beautiful. His dark hair was rumpled, his gray eyes the color of fresh rain, and his body—she shivered.

"I want everything to go well with this rally," she said. "But also—"

She hesitated. How to tell him?

Chase laced his fingers with hers. "Also what? Something troubling you?"

Phoebe nodded. "I don't know. I don't have very good information. But I'm afraid something could go wrong at Harry's conference this weekend."

"What could go wrong? Forty Elvis impersonators could get

out of step?"

Phoebe smiled, but her heart wasn't in it. "The secretary of state is the keynote speaker. I think there could be a threat against her, but I'm not sure what. And I have to tell you"—she took a deep breath, not wanting to look at him, not able to tear her eyes away—"I think it could be from the Eklunds."

"Phoebe, please don't go there with this crap." His voice was soft with an edge of steel. But at least he didn't let go of her hand.

"You're right—I don't have solid intel." Phoebe nodded quickly, not wanting him to let go. "I talked to my friend Nattie at the CIA, the one who's coming to visit in a couple of days. She checked something for me."

"What was that?" His grip was a little strong.

"I asked her to find out when the Eklunds entered the country. She said they got to New York in time for the Empire State Building mess, a week before the rest of the Midnight Sun group. That's why I think they might be the threat. Although I don't know what their agenda might be."

"Didn't we talk about this last night?"

"I know how important these investors are to you," Phoebe said, covering his hand with her own. "And I would never do anything to jeopardize these meetings."

"But you *are* jeopardizing them." He squeezed her hand and let go, and her heart sank. But she had to follow up on what she believed. If she wasn't confident in her analysis, she wasn't worth anything to the CIA. Or anyone else.

She watched him stalk to the window and stare out. A caged panther this time.

"Chase, if there's a threat to the secretary of state, I have to act on it. You know I do. And you'd act, too. Don't tell me you wouldn't."

He turned around and leaned against the sink, frowning down at her. "Yes, if there really was a threat. But you're just guessing. And maybe wishful thinking. So you have a clear shot to get back to the CIA."

Was that true? She didn't think so. She sure hoped her thinking wasn't clouded by any personal circumstance.

"There's more to it than that." She shoved her hair back.

207

"Detective Greenaway from the local police said that the FBI came and asked him about the Eklunds. He didn't know anything about them, but what are the feds looking at? Sven and Gustav are on a federal watch list. But it could still mean nothing. It's not like the feds never make a mistake."

"And you're sure proof of that."

Phoebe felt her mouth go dry again, and not in a good way.

He pushed away from the sink, his jaw tight. "I have an appointment at the bank this morning, so I won't be going straight in to the plant. Maybe Sanjay can drive you in. I'll see you later, I'm sure."

"Okay." Phoebe watched him walk out of the kitchen, feeling anything but sure.

The appointment with the loan officer wasn't until eleven. Until then, Chase worked on his rehab with a ferocity that left his knee throbbing and his anger unabated. He got up from the machine that was torturing him and hurled his workout towel into the laundry bin. *Enough.* He needed to focus on what was important. He needed to talk to his bankers and get that second loan approved. He stepped into the shower, hoping it would cool him off.

He'd tried to cut her some slack. But *damn it*. That woman could try the patience of a saint. Which he was far from being.

More than an hour later, still annoyed, he dressed in a tie and jacket and headed for the foyer. And now that they'd had another argument, she'd probably head back to that stupid, teeny apartment with her mother and her dog and God knows whatever other stray she could pick up. And speaking of Trouble, the dog was sitting right there at the door, looking at him.

"You better come with me," he said. "The place is too big for just one dog. And—" And the simple truth was that Trouble reminded him of Phoebe. And he liked having Phoebe around.

Trouble barked, and Chase bent to scratch his ears.

"She's killing me here," he told the dog. "You're my witness."

Trouble barked again and went to the door, and Chase laughed at the eager dog. But when he stepped out onto the portico, he saw what Trouble had been barking at. A nondescript gray sedan had pulled into his drive, and three men in dark suits got out.

Men in Black, Chase thought.

"Chase Bonaventure?" one of the men—the most nondescript one—asked. He reached into his jacket pocket and pulled out a badge wallet and showed it to him.

Crap. FBI. Phoebe would flip. Either these were the guys investigating her for her CIA reinstatement, or there really could be something to this Eklund-family, gunrunning, secretary of state thing she kept going on about.

Chase nodded. "And you are?"

"Aaron Picone," the first man said. "My colleagues, Robert Zilesky and Charles Pratt."

The other two men nodded.

"We're looking for Phoebe Renfrew. We understand she's living here."

"What is this in connection to?"

"We'll discuss that with her. Is she in?"

"I think so. Wait here."

He snapped his fingers at Trouble, who'd been sniffing around Picone's shoes, and reentered the house. Whatever Phoebe had done or not done, she needed a little warning if the FBI was on her tail.

He walked back to her room and knocked on her closed door. "Phoebe! FBI's here!"

She didn't answer. But she had to be in there. He could see both the living room and the pool area from the front door, and she hadn't been out there. The house had a lot of rooms, but not many places Phoebe hung out in.

He knocked again and entered the room. It was tidy—hell, she didn't *own* anything—although some clothes were strewn about. The shower was running.

He went to the bathroom door and knocked again. "*Phoebe!*" he yelled. "The FBI's here!"

"*What?*" The water shut off, and seconds later she emerged, wearing only a towel. Her wet hair hung in dripping strands around her face.

"Yeah, three guys."

"*Crap*," she said. "Greenaway—the police detective—told me they'd come by to see him, and I guess they're making the rounds. Unless they're here following up on my CIA reinstatement. Which at this point I think is unlikely."

"Do you want me to stay while you talk to them? Assuming they let me. I could say I was your legal counsel."

She smiled wanly. "Not necessary. Believe me, I'm used to the FBI giving me the third degree. Not that I relish it much. Thanks, though."

"Are you sure?"

Phoebe shrugged. "I'll be fine. In fact, you should head out to your appointment. Don't get connected with whatever mess this is. I'll move out of here this afternoon. I can stay in a hotel for a few days. I can afford it now, and you don't want to be associated with persons who are targets of FBI investigations, believe me. Their light, whether deserved or not, shines very hot. Very, very hot."

"Don't start with that moving-out crap again. We agreed it's best if you stay here for now. So if you're sure, I'll take off, but let me know right away what happens."

"Okay."

"And I'm going to leave them standing in the driveway until you're ready."

Phoebe grinned. "Maybe you can make Trouble pee on their shoes."

"He thought about it. But he didn't like the smell."

She laughed outright. "Okay, go. I have to get dressed and meet my agents of doom."

He gave her a quick kiss on the cheek, which brought a little color to her face. He didn't want to leave her alone with the feds, but he was willing to let her handle things her own way.

For now.

Chapter 16

After an unpleasant meeting with the FBI, Phoebe called Sanjay, who dropped her at the Venture Automotive plant. She was relieved to learn that the Midnight Sun investors were still busy examining the company's financial statements. They were so *quiet*. Only the tapping of computer keys and the occasional rustling of pages disturbed the silence. Every so often the investors asked Phoebe a question in Korean, and she'd relay it to the accountants. That was it.

Then her phone vibrated. Kristin had sent her a text. *Get out here*.

It must be something about the rally, she thought, and slipped out of the conference room to see what she wanted.

Kristin ran up and grabbed her arm as she came down the hallway.

"Something bad is happening," Kristin hissed at her. "Coach isn't here, and he isn't picking up. I don't know what to do."

Phoebe halted. "Do about what?"

She heard raised voices from the lobby and looked over the mezzanine. Megan and Daryl were trying to keep out a posse of Las Vegas's finest. Led by Detective Dave Greenaway.

"Oh, no," Phoebe moaned. "I begged him not to do this."

"Do what? Phoebe, do you know those cops?"

"I know Detective Greenaway." She started down the stairs. "I'll talk to him. Try calling Chase again."

Kristin shot over to her desk, and Phoebe ran downstairs.

"Detective Greenaway!" she called. "Can I help you?"

The detective looked past a determined Daryl. "Miz Renfrew. Always a pleasure."

"What are you doing here, Detective?"

"You know what I'm doing here, Miz Renfrew. I'm here to question Sven, Gustav, and Lars Eklund about their activities while they've been in Las Vegas. And how those might tie into any activities they engaged in while they were in New York."

Fear and anger surged through her. Why had Greenaway picked this moment to barge in here? What had the FBI done to trigger it? And, most important, what could she do to stop it? If the Eklunds were a threat, and they might be, *of course* she wanted Detective Greenaway to take them in. But doing that would kill Chase's hopes of any investment help from this group. And that would just about kill *her*.

"You know what the cops want, Phoebe?" Daryl's face full of suspicion.

Megan stared at her, wide-eyed. Kristin had come down the stairs, her phone to her ear, but she put it away when she got to the lobby.

Phoebe sighed. "Do you have a warrant, Detective?"

Greenaway rolled his eyes. "I'm not searching the plant, and I'm not arresting the Eklunds. I'm bringing them in for questioning, that's all. If they cooperate, they'll be back by lunchtime. If they don't want to come in, I'll get a warrant, I'll be back by two o'clock to pick them up, and you won't see them for forty-eight hours. At a minimum."

That didn't give them too many options. "They don't speak English," she said.

"Then you'll have to come with us."

"I can't leave the investors who are working here."

"Miz Renfrew. You can come with us or not. I don't care. The Eklunds are coming with me now. If we have to search out a Korean translator, fine. When we're done, I bring 'em back here."

"It's not that easy to find a Korean translator on short notice," Kristin said. "Believe me, we tried. No offense, Phoebe."

"I'm talking to the Eklunds, whether you translate or no," Greenaway said. "You want me to get a warrant? Or you want to do this the easy way?"

Phoebe felt trapped. "Okay. I'll get them. Wait here."

"Like hell I will."

Kristin led the way across the lobby. "I've been expecting Coach anytime now, but he still isn't picking up," she said to Phoebe, keeping her voice down. "He won't like this."

"I know. I'll do my best to get them back here as fast as I can. Do you know any defense lawyers? We might need one."

"I'll find one. Why do the cops want to talk to them? I suppose it's in connection to why the FBI wanted to talk to you."

Phoebe lowered her voice. "As far as I know, all that Greenaway knows is that the Eklunds bought handguns illegally. But the FBI did talk to him down at the police station. I don't know what they said."

Kristin stared at her. "Oh my God."

Phoebe nodded. "It's not good. None of it."

"*Miz Renfrew*," Greenaway said. "Let's *go*."

Kristin went to her desk, and Phoebe led the way to the conference room.

"I'll go in and get them," she said.

"No, you won't," Greenaway said. "You'll come in with me and tell them what I say. There's no point in trying to be discreet. You won't be keeping any secrets from anyone in the plant, anyway."

Phoebe sighed. "Okay."

She followed Greenaway into the conference room. He went straight over to Sven.

Phoebe watched in alarm. How did Greenaway know which person was Sven? He'd never seen Sven.

As far as she knew.

"Sven Eklund?" Greenaway asked, and Sven nodded. "Please come with me. We want to ask you some questions."

Phoebe translated, and then Greenaway picked out Gustav and Lars. That was just scary weird.

The small cavalcade left the conference room and headed down the stairs. As they crossed the lobby, Chase stormed through the front door.

"What the hell is going on here?" he demanded.

"I'm taking these men in for questioning," Greenaway said.

"What for?"

"We're looking into weapons possession. They are not under arrest. I'm conducting no searches of their person or vehicle or this business."

Chase turned on Phoebe. "Did you know about this?"

"Sort of. Greenaway told me that he wanted to talk to them. But—"

"And you didn't think to warn me? I swear to God—" Chase ran his hand through his hair and a muscle in his jaw tensed.

"I told you the authorities were interested!" Phoebe said. "I didn't know what Detective Greenaway was planning."

"As if I'd tell a civilian," Greenaway said, taking Sven by the arm. "Let's go."

He led the men out the door.

"If I go with them, I can get them back sooner," Phoebe said, following them to the door. "Kristin is calling defense attorneys."

"Just go, Phoebe," Chase said, turning away from her. "Get the hell out of here."

They drove to the police station. Greenaway and the other cops ushered them into the building and separated the Eklunds into separate interview rooms.

"How am I supposed to translate for them now?" Phoebe asked. "They're in three rooms."

"One at a time," Greenaway said, heading to his desk. "Take a seat. Be with you in a minute."

Separate interviews meant that the Eklunds would be at the station longer—which wasn't good for them, for her, or for the rest of the investors back at the plant who couldn't talk to anyone there, ask questions, or just go about their business without her. Phoebe felt her anger mounting at Greenaway, who, last she'd heard, didn't have any more information on the Swedish-Koreans than she did. So why was he bringing them in now?

Her phone buzzed, and she looked at the text message.

Nattie. Oh, no. She'd totally forgotten about Nattie's arrival. If she ever knew it. Not that she'd been checking her personal email much lately.

In LV airpt, Phoebe read. *Where R U?*

Sending cab, Phoebe texted back. *Name is LV Fun Fares, Sanjay driver*. Then she called Sanjay.

"I need a favor," she said when he picked up. She tried to lower her voice, but the radio on his side blared a hip-hop rhythm. Several of the cops glanced her way.

"Can you pick up my friend Nattie Wilkinson from the airport? She's my height, short blond hair, glasses. I gave her your cab and name."

"Normally I would be most happy to pick up a friend or, indeed, any paying customer." Sanjay lowered the volume on his radio. "However, at this precise moment, I have been previously booked with two fares."

"I'm at the jail."

"You're in *jail*?"

Phoebe lowered her voice. "*At* the jail. I'm with Sven, Gustav, and Lars. The police are questioning them about the pawn-shop buy, and I have to stay to translate for them. I can't leave. Chase is furious."

Sanjay sighed, which directly in her ear was louder than the hip-hop.

"Okay," he said. "I'll ask Ranjeet to take my fares. He should be more than happy to oblige, and I'll get your friend for you. Think nothing of it."

"Nattie," Phoebe said. "Her name is Nattie. Thank you, Sanjay. I owe you."

"Most assuredly, you do," Sanjay said. "Although I am unwilling to keep track of favors on which I am unlikely ever to collect."

"What do you mean, you'll never collect? I'm renting an apartment from your uncle that would otherwise be empty. And I'm paying a premium for my dog."

"I'll speak to him about a kickback. And if I am not mistaken, your mother is staying in the apartment. And she is not exactly a reliable tenant."

"*Hey*—" Phoebe said, but Sanjay had disconnected.

Everybody's a critic today. Phoebe rolled her shoulders, trying to untense her neck, and called Kristin.

"Is there any word about a defense lawyer?" Phoebe asked,

keeping her voice low. "I'm worried over here."

"I don't have anybody lined up yet," Kristin said. "What's going on?"

"Nothing so far. We're waiting. The cops are sitting around. I think they're trying to make us nervous. Speaking for myself, it's working."

"I'll push. Do you want to talk to Coach?"

Phoebe thought about what he'd looked like and what he'd said when he'd turned away from her, the first time he'd ever done that.

"I'll wait until I have something to report," she said. "Or when we get out of here."

She disconnected and glanced around. Greenaway was at his desk, gazing at his monitor. What was he doing over there? She got up and joined him, sitting in his visitor chair.

"Detective Greenaway," she said, trying not to let her irritation show. "Tell me, will you, what's your plan for us? We seem to be cooling our heels here."

The detective didn't even glance up from his screen.

"If that's what it seems like, then that's probably what it is," he said. "Sometimes a cigar is just a cigar."

So much for hiding her irritation.

"This stalling around that you're doing is affecting potential investment, jobs growth, and economic opportunity here in the greater Las Vegas area," she said. "We'd appreciate it a lot if you could get your interviews underway so we could get back to work."

"You mean Chase Bonaventure can't get his investors to sign on the bottom line? Too bad. I have to think about all the citizens of Las Vegas, not just one ex-football player. I'll get to your guys all in good time."

Phoebe went back to the hallway, pacing to the end and then back. She glared at Greenaway's back. What could she do to move this along? Locking up the Eklunds would not be good for Chase's business. Of course, if they wanted to blow something up, that would be bad for Las Vegas. It wasn't like she didn't see the cop's point of view. She felt the same, in fact.

Maybe she could just ask the Eklunds what they wanted.

She stopped, startled by the idea. It seemed too obvious, but why not? What did she have to lose? The cops sure weren't doing anything.

She'd seen the cops put the investors in rooms all along this hallway—the first room was Sven, the second was Gustav, and the third was Lars. She decided to go with Sven, who might be the ringleader. She was a little afraid of Gustav, not that she thought he'd try to kill her right there at the police station. But you never knew.

She went into Sven's interview room. He frowned at her as she closed the door behind her.

"What's going on?" he asked. "Why are we here?"

"I don't know," Phoebe said. "I asked the detective who's in charge, and he won't tell me. I called the factory, and they're sending over a lawyer for you guys." She cleared her throat.

"I know what the cops said they want to talk to you about. It's about those guns that Gustav and Lars bought at the pawn-shop. I know about that, and the cops do, too. What do you want those guns for?"

Sven glowered. "It's none of your business."

Phoebe waggled her hand back and forth. "See, it sort of is. And if you don't have a reason that makes the cops happy, you'll be here a lot longer than you want to be. I'm just trying to get you out of here faster."

"I've done nothing wrong!"

"Do you *plan* to do something wrong, though?"

"That's a stupid question!"

Phoebe sighed. "I suppose it is. I know you don't believe me, but I'm not out to hurt you or even stop you, unless you're plan-ning a crime. I want to go back to the factory with you and trans-late for everybody. I hope that Midnight Sun will invest in the plant. It would mean a lot to Chase and the people who work there, and I think it would bring in business for you, too. I hope you all get rich from the cars Venture Automotive builds. But none of that will happen if we don't get out of here, and that won't happen until you tell me or the cops what you guys want. I don't think that the gun purchases are why you're here. Is there something you're not telling anyone?"

"I'm not talking to you!"

Phoebe sighed. "Fine. Then you'll be talking to the cops. And I have to warn you—I think everything will get a lot more complicated before it gets simpler."

Her phone rang and she checked the display. *Sanjay.*

"Sanjay, what's up?" she asked, shaking her head at Sven and leaving the interview room.

"Where do you prefer that I bring your most delightful friend Nattie?" Sanjay asked. "To the factory or to your apartment? Or to Mr. Bonaventure's house?"

"Oh, my gosh, I don't know," Phoebe said. "My mom's in my apartment, and I'm at the police station with Detective Greenaway. I don't think—"

"That will be fine. I will be bringing her to the police station."

"No, Sanjay! Wait!" But he'd already disconnected.

Well, why not? The day had already gone south. She might as well have the CIA running around the police station, too. How bad could it get?

She sat down on the unforgiving plastic chair in the hallway. Fifteen minutes later, Nattie walked in, wearing a black suit and white blouse and pearls, dragging a roller bag and carrying a suit bag, makeup case, and purse.

Just how long did Nattie intend to stay?

Phoebe jumped up and went to give her friend a hug. "Nattie! You got here. I'm sorry I couldn't pick you up. What are you doing with all this luggage?"

Nattie sniffed. "You're the only person I know who can get by for months at a time on three suits and a pair of jeans. A girl has to dress."

Phoebe grinned. "And you met Sanjay. Did he make you pay? I told him I'd pay the fare."

Nattie grinned back. "He said *double* the fare."

Phoebe rolled her eyes. "He used to say he wanted to help with my sleuthing. But now it's all, for double the fare."

Nattie looked around the police station. "So, Phoebe, not that it's not nice to see you, but what are you doing here in the cop shop?"

"My investors are here. The Swedish-Koreans I asked you about."

"They're here? Oh my God, what have they done?"

"Nothing. Not yet, anyway. Not that I know of. That's why I'd like to know what's going on. But Detective Greenaway is not speaking to this matter."

"I'll go ask him. I do not intend for my fabulous, five-day weekend in Vegas to be spent here at the police station. Are you dating Chase Bonaventure?"

Phoebe stopped in her tracks. "*What?* No. Except, um—"

Nattie eyed her with a grin. "You lucky dog. He is one prime piece of manhood."

"As soon as I'm out of here, you'll meet him, of course," Phoebe said. "Probably. And stay at his house, too. He's mad at me, though, so predicting events is a little tricky."

"That'd be nice," Nattie said, "since I came all this way. You're a fast worker. How long have you been out here? A week?"

"Almost two."

"A long-term relationship then."

"Shut up," Phoebe said. "It's not like that."

Nattie grinned.

Just then Detective Greenaway, carrying a file and a laptop, strode down the hallway toward them. He stopped when he saw Nattie.

"And who are you?" he asked.

"Detective Greenaway, this is Nattie Wilkinson," Phoebe said. "She's with the CIA."

"Seriously? We got more CIA here?" The detective gazed at her critically. "At least you *look* CIA. Not like your friend Phoebe here. Not that I need any more feds running around."

"You've got other feds here?" Phoebe asked.

"No," Greenaway said, sounding harassed. "Like I said. Come on, let's go. Hey—" He turned back to Nattie. "Do you speak Korean?"

Nattie's eyes danced. "I wish I could say yes, but I don't. Urdu, Hindi, Spanish, French, Arabic. Phoebe's the Korean speaker."

"Damn. Okay, Miz Renfrew, get the lead out."

"*I've* been waiting for *you*," Phoebe pointed out, but Green-away was already opening the door to Lars's interview room.

"I don't think Lars is the ringleader," Phoebe said as they entered the room.

"I know he's not," Greenaway said. "I'm letting the other guys stew a while longer."

Phoebe sighed.

"You think you got problems?" Greenaway slapped the folder down on the table. "Two months before my retirement, this is what falls in my lap. Don't talk to me about problems. Here, sit down. No, not next to him, next to me. Let's get this show on the road."

They sat down. Greenaway opened his laptop.

"Lars Eklund?" he said.

"Can I call my girlfriend?" Lars asked. Phoebe translated. Greenaway shrugged.

"Five minutes," he said, handing him his phone.

"You took his phone?" Phoebe asked. "Is that procedure?"

"Sure," Greenaway said.

"I don't think it is." Phoebe raised a brow. "Not if he's not under arrest."

Greenaway shrugged again.

Lars called and spoke animatedly into the phone.

Greenaway leaned over and whispered directly in Phoebe's ear. "What's he saying?"

"I don't know," she said. "He's speaking Swedish."

"You don't speak Swedish? You speak every other damn thing."

"Not Swedish," Phoebe said. "There are no native Swedish speakers in Brooklyn."

"Sez you."

"If there were and they did babysitting, I promise you, my mother would have found them and I'd be able to speak Swedish," Phoebe said. "But there aren't and they didn't, so she couldn't and I don't."

Greenaway shook his head as Lars disconnected the call.

"Thank you," he said, handing back the phone. "That was

Helga. My girlfriend. She's very upset."

"I'm sorry to hear that," Greenaway said after he heard Phoebe's translation. "We just have a few questions."

"She thought we'd need the guns," Lars said.

Greenaway looked at Phoebe for a translation.

Phoebe beamed at him. "Lars said he's happy to help, and he hopes this doesn't take too long."

Chapter 17

Greenaway dug in. Everything he asked was routine. What was he trying to get at?

Minutes ticked by. After a half hour of establishing time frames and investor meetings and whereabouts, Greenaway opened the folder sitting in front of him.

Whatever's in that folder is why we're here, Phoebe realized. Everything else was just a smokescreen.

Greenaway took out a photograph and slid it across the table to Lars. "Tell me what this is."

Phoebe snatched the photo away. She knew in her heart that the Eklunds were up to something, maybe—probably—something to do with the secretary of state. She didn't know what, and she—they—needed to figure that out to keep everyone safe.

But whatever Greenaway was doing, it was wrong. He was fishing, trying to get Lars to incriminate himself, his brother, and his father, without any evidence of misconduct. If the Eklunds had committed a crime, she'd be first in line to make an arrest. But until they had something solid, she wouldn't let Greenaway corner Lars, who didn't understand American law or procedure and whose court-authorized translator hadn't arrived yet. Much less his lawyer.

And she owed Chase something, too. Maybe the investors didn't want to blow anything up. Maybe they were about corporate espionage or something else she hadn't thought of. She didn't want the Eklunds falsely accused just to satisfy overenthusiastic FBI wannabe hotshots. She'd had plenty of firsthand experience with how overenthusiastic the FBI could be.

"What the hell are you doing?" Greenaway asked, trying to take the photo away from her.

Phoebe held on to it. "Wait."

"Lars, before you say anything else, you should ask for a lawyer," she said in Korean. "Chase is hiring one for you. As soon as you ask for a lawyer, the cops have to stop questioning you until your lawyer is present. You don't know how something you say can harm you. And the police can use whatever you say now against you in court."

"What are you saying?" Greenaway asked, sounding irate.

"I'm cautioning him," Phoebe said. "He doesn't have a law-yer."

"He doesn't need one! He's not under arrest!"

"Not yet, maybe, but he does need a lawyer."

"Whose side are you on, anyway?"

"I'm on everybody's side!"

Greenaway slammed his hand on the table. "Give the suspect the photograph!"

Phoebe held the photo as far away from the detective as she could. "Now he's a suspect?"

"Of course, he's a suspect! He's always been a suspect! *You* made him a suspect!"

Phoebe shook her head. "The only crime I could accuse him of is buying a handgun without a permit. Something else is going on here."

"Yes, it is. And if you show Mr. Eklund the photograph, perhaps he can clear it up for us."

Phoebe looked at the cop and then at Lars, shaking her head.

"Lars, ask for the lawyer," she said in Korean. "It won't be much longer now before someone gets here."

"I have nothing to hide," Lars said. "Show me the photo."

"I don't know how, but somehow it could incriminate you in a crime," Phoebe said. "Or maybe incriminate Gustav or your father."

Lars shrugged. "I've done nothing wrong. I don't believe they have, either. I don't mind looking at the photo."

"Show him the photo, Phoebe," Greenaway said, his mouth a

tight line.

"He doesn't mind looking at it," Phoebe said. "He says none of them has done anything wrong. But if you're sandbagging me or them, I'll be pissed off, Greenaway."

"Are you trying to *threaten* me? I could arrest you right now for obstructing an investigation."

Phoebe sat up straighter. "Right now I'm Mr. Eklund's only representation, so *back off.*"

Greenaway stared at her, and Phoebe watched his face go from fury to resignation.

"Jesus," he said. "You come in here wearing that ruffly skirt. You sure as hell had me fooled."

"Do you want to take a break for a minute? I'd like to see if Mr. Eklund's attorney of record is on his or her way."

"Sure, let's take a break. Why not."

"Should I look at the photo?" Lars asked Phoebe in Korean.

"Not yet. I want to get your attorney here for this."

She started to hand the photo back to Greenaway, glancing at it as she did. Then she took a closer look, trying to school her face into what she hoped was an expression of calm. Because what she saw in the photo scared her.

It was a grainy, black-and-white capture from a security camera. The picture showed an intersection of streets. The side-walk was jammed with pedestrians, who were held back by security barricades. Gustav and Sven were in the foreground. Lars walked a little bit behind, peering at the phone in his hand. Phoebe didn't exactly recognize any of the buildings, but she would have bet her last nickel that the shiny deco facade of the building that the camera had captured in close-up was the Empire State Building. And she'd also bet that the crowds were there for the U.S. secretary of state.

"That photo say something to you?" Greenaway asked.

Phoebe handed the photo back to him, willing herself to remain expressionless.

A knock sounded on the door, and a young cop stuck her head in the door.

"Attorney for the Eklunds is here." She admitted a tall, lean, young man wearing a rumpled suit and carrying a bulging briefcase. A shorter, older, tired-looking woman stood behind him.

"Dean Alvarez," he said. "Chase Bonaventure called me for the Eklunds. This is Annika Eriksson, court-certified Swedish translator. I see we've arrived just in time."

Phoebe heaved a sigh of relief. "I'm Phoebe Renfrew, the Korean translator, and am I ever glad to see you." She reached over the table to shake hands with both of them. "I take it you don't speak Korean."

"Miz Renfrew," Alvarez said. "They said I'd find you here. Nope, no Korean. Not much call for that here in Vegas. I do English and Spanish only."

"That's why I'm here," Eriksson said. "They speak Swedish, right? I'm translating from the Swedish for Mr. Alvarez."

"Two of them speak Swedish. The father does not. I can translate Korean to English, but I'm not court certified."

"Okay," Alvarez said. "Why don't you tell me what's going on here."

"Detective Greenaway was about to show your client a photo, but he decided to wait until you arrived."

"Decided, my ass," Greenaway said. "Obstructing justice, that's what Miz Renfrew was doing." At least the detective didn't sound angry anymore. He closed the folder with the photo inside.

Dean glanced at her sharply, and Phoebe shrugged.

"I thought we should wait for you," she said.

"You'll want a few minutes with your client." Greenaway stood and headed for the door.

As he reached it, however, it swung open, and FBI Agent Aaron Picone blocked the way.

It's getting crowded in here, Phoebe thought. *How many cops does it take to change a light bulb?*

"Agent Picone, FBI." He flashed his badge to Alvarez and Eriksson. "Come with me please, Miss Renfrew. We'd like to ask you a few questions."

"*Me*? What about?" Phoebe eyed the one-way glass in the interview room. Had the FBI been there the whole time?

"Routine. This way."

Nattie stuck her head in the door. "Phoebe? What's going on here?"

"The FBI is here," Phoebe said. "This is agent Aaron Picone. They want to talk to me for some reason."

"At least it's not the Secret Service," Nattie said. "Then we *would* be in the soup." She turned to Picone. "In the interests of interagency cooperation, what do you want with Phoebe?" She flashed her CIA badge.

"Not that it's any of the CIA's business, but we are about to determine her connection to the Eklunds, the planned attack at the Empire State Building, and why she's here in Las Vegas."

"So there was a plan!" Phoebe wanted to whoop she was so relieved and thrilled. "I *knew* I was right!"

"Phoebe, I'm thinking maybe you want to have a lawyer here," Nattie said, frowning. "You know how the FBI is."

"*What do you mean*, how the FBI is?" Picone asked.

"I don't need a lawyer," Phoebe said. "They found a plan! I'm cleared!"

"The FBI is not part of your reinstatement investigation," Picone said. "This is about another matter."

"What other matter?" Phoebe asked. "There is no other matter that's about me. I'm the translator for the Eklunds. Ask anybody. Ask the *Eklunds*, for crying out loud."

"We will," Picone said, taking her arm. "Let's go."

"Wait a second." Phoebe yanked her arm away, looking at Greenaway. "Detective, what's going on here? What kind of investigation is this?"

Greenaway glared at her. "What do you think? Once the FBI gets here, it's their investigation, whatever it is."

Picone grabbed Phoebe's arm again and steered her into an interrogation room. "It's an interagency operation," he snarled as he slammed the door.

"Don't say anything, Phoebe!" Nattie yelled. She turned and pointed to Alvarez. "You better go with Phoebe. She's the one who's in the biggest trouble here. Also, evidently, she's the smart one."

"*Hey*," Greenaway said.

"I can't," Alvarez said. "I'm representing the Eklunds. I can't represent them both."

227

"*Crap*," Nattie said. "I have to get Phoebe a lawyer. Give me Chase Bonaventure's phone number."

"I'm not sure I should do that." Alvarez shook his head.

"Of course, you should. She's living at his house. You think he doesn't want to know if she's in trouble? *Which you know she is*. So give it to me!"

"They're living together?"

"We can gossip later. Please. Give me the number."

Alvarez brought up the number and held his phone out to Nattie. She tapped the number into her phone, praying that the ex-football star and CEO would pick up, even though he wouldn't recognize her number. And then he did.

"Oh, thank God." Nattie breathed a sigh of relief. "Hi, Chase Bonaventure? Listen, we haven't met, but I'm Nattie Wilkinson, I work for the CIA, I'm friends with Phoebe, I came for a visit, we're at the police station, and she's in trouble."

"Of course, she's in trouble," Chase said. "When isn't she? And now, the CIA to the rescue, just what I need. What kind of trouble?"

Inside the interrogation room, Picone pointed Phoebe to a chair. He sat down opposite her, opened his briefcase, and took out a folder.

I have a folder now? Phoebe felt a surge of fear and anger roll through her. *What is this really about?*

"Tell us about the Eklunds." Picone leveled his gaze at her.

"What am I suspected of?"

"I'm asking the questions here."

"You said, 'Tell us about the Eklunds.' First of all, there is no 'us' in this room, so I suppose your two sock puppets are behind the glass over there. Second, 'tell us about the Eklunds' is not a question."

"You're in a world of hurt here, Renfrew, so don't mouth off. I asked you nice, but I can arrest your ass, and then you can kiss the CIA or any other federal job goodbye. Tell us what the fuck we want to know."

Phoebe had practiced keeping a poker face during her training, and she was pretty sure that she hadn't let Picone see how scared she was by what he'd said. He was right—if he arrested her, she'd never get her CIA job back, and then all this would have been for nothing.

But she couldn't let the FBI push her around, either. The CIA might have suspended her, but until they finally and forever fired her, she still counted as a fully qualified, duly employed CIA officer. And the CIA trumped the FBI any day of the week.

"If you arrest me on specious grounds, the CIA will come down on your butt so hard you won't be able to sit for a year," she said. "Nattie out there is proof of that. Why do you think she came? You try arresting me, you'll never see your pension. So *don't threaten me*. You want interagency cooperation, right? I'm cooperating."

"You sure as hell don't act like you're cooperating."

"You're threatening me without telling me what you want to know. Ask me something specific."

"Jesus fucking Christ. *Tell me what you know about the Eklunds*. Consider that a question."

"There's nothing to tell. I'm translating temporarily at Venture Automotive while the Midnight Sun investor group is visiting. The Eklunds are part of the evaluation team."

"We've been following the Eklunds." Picone flipped open the file. "It seems that you were, too. And we turned up something interesting."

How did the FBI know that she'd followed the Eklunds?

"I wasn't really following them," Phoebe said. "Tailing people is harder than it seems."

"So we subpoenaed your phone and bank records."

"You did *what?*"

"And here's what we found. You got a big deposit from Venture Automotive, and then you paid off Sven Eklund's hospital bill. I'm thinking that's a lot of money changing hands. And you've called Nattie Wilkinson at the CIA. More than once. Trying to get her to tell you about the Eklunds' movements. Now—you want to tell me what that's all about?"

"How did you know that?"

Picone snorted. "CIA. Think they know everything."

Phoebe frowned. Whatever the FBI thought she'd done, they

wouldn't be able to make it stick. She hadn't committed any crimes. Whatever they thought they saw, whatever evidence they thought they had, they weren't seeing the big picture.

That didn't mean she should try to explain. If she'd learned anything from the Empire State debacle, it was not to go into small, closed rooms with trained interrogators who wanted to blame someone for something.

"There's a few options here," Picone said. "Option one: Venture Automotive bribed the Eklunds through you for something—say, better terms on the deal. Maybe something else."

Phoebe stared at him. "What? That deposit was my paycheck. Sven needed medical care. Have you looked at what it costs these days? Seriously. This is what you want to talk to me about? My *paycheck*?"

"Another option: you conspired with the Eklunds to create a false emergency at the Empire State Building, thus improving your own chances for promotions and raises at the CIA, or—"

"Cripes. That's *nuts*. Even for the FBI."

"Or you conspired with the Eklunds to murder the secretary of state."

That was going too far. Too terrifyingly far. And she worked for the CIA. She knew what happened to people who got caught in treasonous conspiracy plots.

"I want a lawyer," Phoebe said.

Chase closed his eyes and took a deep breath as he listened to Nattie Wilkinson.

"The FBI is questioning her in connection with the Eklunds and their planned attack on the Empire State Building," she said. "And you know how the FBI is."

"I'm happy to say I have no idea how the FBI is. So there really was a plan for an attack?"

"Oh yeah. The FBI guy I've seen—but there's got to be more than one—claims that Phoebe had something to do with it. And generally speaking, the FBI, they're not always right, and when they put their minds to something like that, it's not good. They tend to shoot first and ask questions later. On the upside, at least they're not the Secret Service. Al-though the Secret Service would probably shoot and miss."

"*Shoot?*"

"Just a metaphor. I don't see what the FBI could have on Phoebe, but they must have something."

"I know what it is," Chase said. "She paid Sven Eklund's medical bill with a check. The hospital called to verify her employment. Unbelievable."

"That would do it. She's in an interrogation room now, so she needs a lawyer right away."

"Didn't I already send a lawyer?"

"Yes, and he's here, but he represents the Eklunds, so he can't represent Phoebe, too. Phoebe might not talk until a lawyer comes, but she says she's innocent, and you know how that goes. Innocent people tend to talk."

Alvarez nodded.

"And that's never good," Nattie said, and Alvarez shook his head. "Will you send somebody?"

"Hell, yeah, I'll get somebody over there," Chase said. "Try to keep the FBI from shooting anybody, will you?"

"Do my best," Nattie said.

After Nattie disconnected, Chase sat for a minute with his eyes closed. Phoebe had been right all along. Whatever the Eklunds were doing in Las Vegas, they'd planned that attack on the Empire State Building. And now they'd used his investor meetings as a cover to do something here.

He'd been wrong about the attack. He'd bullied her and yelled at her, and he'd been wrong.

Whatever the FBI thought was going on here and now, of course she had nothing to do with it. Hadn't she spent every spare moment trying to prove there had been an attack? Didn't she want more than anything to get back to the CIA?

The CIA was her life. Finding terrorists was her calling. The FBI was wrong, plain and simple.

As he tasted the fear that came with knowing the FBI was interrogating her, he realized how much he'd come to rely on her— her good judgment, her good humor, her loyal commitment. To him. And his company. How she'd come through for him time and time again when he'd needed her.

And now she was in trouble. And she needed him.

Chase looked at the phone in his hand. When had his life become one mad swirl of international intrigue and clandestine spy craft? Just a couple of weeks ago, all he'd had to worry about was getting a few robots installed and making the payments on a second bank loan.

Those were the good old days.

"Kristin!" he called.

"Coach?"

"We need a criminal defense lawyer down at the police station right away."

"We got one down there." Kristin came into his office.

"Yes, but he represents the Eklunds. We need somebody for Phoebe."

"Phoebe?"

"I know. She spends all her time trying to get someone to listen to her about that spy crap, and when finally someone does, they blame her for it. Let's hurry, all right? We need to get her out of there."

"I just called the defender's office. You have to call this time, Coach. They'll think I'm punking them."

He reached for the phone. "What are those cops thinking? It's *Phoebe*, for Christ's sake. She worked for the CIA. She doesn't want to bomb anything."

Then his call connected, and he explained to the receptionist what he wanted.

"You're certainly having a bad day at the office, Mr. Bonaventure," she said. "Let me see who's available now."

In a moment, a woman's smooth contralto voice came on the line.

"Tiffany Bailor," she said. "Am I really speaking to Chase Bonaventure?"

"You are," he said. *Tiffany?* He'd dated professional cheerleaders named Tiffany. If they were anything to go by, a lawyer named Tiffany would be smart enough and tough enough to get Phoebe out of jail. He filled her in.

"I'll get right over there," she said. "If they invoke the Patriot Act…Well, let's not waste any time. It's tough getting out from under that."

"I'll meet you there." He felt better about Tiffany already.

"Not necessary, but a show of support can sometimes help."

"She'll have that," Chase said and disconnected.

When Chase burst into the police station, Kristin right behind him, he didn't see anyone who could be FBI, CIA, Secret Service, police detective, or for that matter, dogcatcher.

"Mr. Bonaventure, it's an honor to meet you," the desk officer said. "We sure are sorry you had to take early retirement. What do you think the chances are for the team this year?"

"Players. And. Coaches. Are. Working. Hard," Chase said through clenched teeth. "Where can I find the detective in charge?"

"I'll call Detective Greenaway." The desk officer reached for the phone, and Kristin dug Chase in the ribs.

"I think the lawyer might be here." She nodded back toward the door.

Chase whipped around and saw a woman, about forty-five, carrying an extra twenty pounds and looking good with it. Her blond hair was pulled back in a severe style, she toted a briefcase, and she wore a dark suit and white blouse. Thank you, federal public defender. She looked extremely competent, although he knew by long experience that looks could be deceiving.

"Chase Bonaventure." The woman came up to him and stuck out her hand. "Tiffany Bailor."

"Miz Bailor," Chase said, shaking her hand. "Thanks for coming."

"It's my job. Let me find my client and get her out of here."

"I'd appreciate that."

"And after I do, you can tell me why on earth the Snakes don't go with a shotgun formation more often, when that idiot Coach Seaquist must know on average it gives you more yardage than plays under center."

Chase grinned. A fan. And smart. Phoebe had a good lawyer. "I'm not sure I can answer that. But Coach is working hard."

Bailor sniffed. "Not hard enough. But first things first. Let's hope the FBI sent somebody with an IQ above dull normal. If not, we'll never get anywhere."

Chapter 18

When Tiffany Bailor led Phoebe from the interview room hours later, the first person she saw was Chase, his feet planted in the hallway, his eyes trained on the door. And when he saw her, his face relaxed and he broke into a smile.

The tension that had been holding her together for the past couple of hours cracked and fell away, and relief rushed in and tears threatened to leak out. She walked toward him and then she ran.

Chase grabbed her in a bear hug. "Are you okay?"

"I'm fine." She sniffed and closed her eyes, squeezing her tears back, holding him close, drinking in his warmth and the steady beat of his heart. "Thank you for sending Tiffany. She is the *best*."

"No problem." He was holding her super tight, molding her to his strong chest, so that she couldn't even wiggle. Not that she wanted to. He lifted his head.

"Did they beat you with rubber hoses?"

"Yes, and we're going to sue their asses. For—How much do you need for the plant again?"

Chase laughed and kissed her, and then Kristin, Nattie, and Sanjay surrounded her, all of them beaming and patting her on her back.

She basked in the attention for a moment, and then she remembered. She released Chase and turned around, spotting her defense attorney smiling at her a few steps away.

"Thank you for coming," she said to Tiffany, going over to shake her hand. "I can't tell you how grateful I am."

"Think nothing of it. Can't let those FBI nutjobs think they own the world. At least it wasn't the Secret Service, or we'd still be twiddling our thumbs in there."

"Do you think they're done with me?"

"Hard to tell. Call if you get into trouble. Here's my card."

Phoebe pocketed the card and turned back to Chase. "What about the Eklunds?"

"They're still with—" Chase started.

Just then, though, another door opened and Gustav emerged with Dean Alvarez. The lawyer's tie was askew, and his suit was even more rumpled, if that was possible. Gustav looked belligerent, although he was quiet as they came down the hall.

"We're okay for now," Dean said, shaking hands with Chase. "The Eklunds aren't in custody, but the feds have their passports while they continue their investigation. Your investors aren't going anywhere."

Annika Eriksson emerged from the interview room, looking exhausted, waved weakly to the assembled group, and lurched down the hallway in the opposite direction.

Chase turned to Phoebe. "Why didn't you tell me you paid Sven's hospital bill?"

"How on earth did you find out?"

"Kristin told me. The hospital called to verify your employment. She said I had to cut you another salary check for that week."

"You don't have to do that. I didn't tell you because I knew you'd be mad that Sven fell when he saw me." Phoebe glanced at Gustav, who slumped sullenly, glowering at her.

"What angle is the FBI pursuing with the Eklunds?" she asked, grateful now that they didn't speak English. "I saw a photo, and I wondered—"

"Let's get out of here before we talk about that," Dean said.

Everyone made murmurs of agreement, but Phoebe shook her head. "We can't leave them here without transportation."

"I have my cab," Sanjay said, shrugging. "I can take them back to their hotel, but I must confess that I would be sorely disappointed if I were to miss hearing the summary of today's events. Are you all planning to convene somewhere? Perhaps I can meet up with you in a short while?"

"My place," Chase said. "We'll order out, it'll be more comfortable."

"And no one will be able to overhear us," Nattie said.

"Plus, wait till you see his house," Phoebe said. "It's enormous. You won't believe it. It's like a hotel."

Chase sighed, and Phoebe grinned at him.

"Are we all ready?" he asked. "Miz Bailor, can you join us?"

"Wouldn't miss it," she said. "Call me Tiffany."

"I'll explain it to Gustav," Phoebe said. She turned to him.

"Gustav," she said in Korean. "You're all free to go. My friend Sanjay here drives a cab, and he'll take you and Lars and Sven back to the hotel when you're ready."

"This police harassment is your fault," Gustav snarled.

"I'm sorry, but it isn't," Phoebe said. "You bought guns illegally, remember? You broke the law. And even so, *you're free to go*. Chase sent a lawyer, and he made sure you got out. That's your good fortune."

Gustav snorted and walked away.

Phoebe sighed, watching him leave. This situation couldn't be good for Chase. And why had the police and feds dragged in the Eklunds and then released them? It didn't make sense. But Alvarez would update them once they got to Chase's.

"Looks like the Eklunds are ready to go to their hotel," she said. "I guess we can leave, too. Thanks for driving them, Sanjay."

An hour later they were all sitting around Chase's dining room table, eating Chinese takeout from colorful ceramic plates.

Phoebe helped herself to the moo shu pork and passed it to Kristin. "Dean, were you able to figure out from their questioning what the FBI thinks is going on with the Eklunds?"

Dean swallowed his dumpling and nodded. "Some." He passed the Mongolian beef to Nattie. "The feds got involved because Greenaway dug into the Eklunds about that handgun purchase. He went into national databases. That triggered both the CIA and the FBI, because the Eklunds—Sven, anyway—has written letters to North Koreans officials, Swedish officials, and maybe U.S. officials about getting his father out of North Korea."

"We knew that," Nattie said, sounding smug.

"Would that alone trigger this kind of questioning, though?" Phoebe asked. "Seems extreme."

"Yes," Dean said. "But for some reason, someone somewhere examined the Empire State Building incident."

"Somebody connected the dots." Chase glanced at Phoebe.

"Right," Dean said. "The FBI has been analyzing surveillance photos of the area, and they ran facial recognition software against the images. That turned up the Eklunds."

"And then they had to let them go because even though the Eklunds had written letters to diplomats, the cops couldn't prove that the Eklunds had planned a threat on the Empire State Building," Phoebe said.

"It looks that way." Dean scooped up the last bit of rice on his plate. "But they'll probably keep digging. They'll want to figure out their involvement."

"I don't want to be all clingy and selfish here," Phoebe said. "But I was in a very unpleasant interview for a long time, too. What about me?"

"I'm pretty sure you're off the hook," Tiffany said. "The way I read it, the FBI was on a fishing expedition with you."

"Not that that's ever stopped them if they want to go after someone," Phoebe said.

"No. But in this case, what with all the press coverage of the, ah, misstep at the Empire State Building, and your obvious and traceable efforts to clear it up, I think they'll let it drop. Also, the CIA is doing its own investigation, and the feebs are unlikely to pursue something the CIA is willing to drop."

Phoebe let out a breath. "Good."

"So what does this mean for the investor meetings?" Kristin asked.

Chase shrugged. "We've got two more days to make our case, and then the rally's on Saturday, and that's it. The group is supposed to decide within a week after that. Of course, they might let me know tomorrow."

Phoebe glanced at him. He wouldn't say anything to these people, who'd all worked hard for him today, but she could see his tight jaw and the bleak look in his eyes. He thought the investors were sure to bow out now. Because of what she'd brought down on him.

She touched his hand. "I'll try really hard tomorrow. I'll explain everything clearly. I'll apologize."

His smile didn't reach his eyes. "You work hard every day, Phoebe," he said. "It was bad luck. Not your fault. Nobody wins them all."

"Indeed," Sanjay said. "No one could have predicted that the Midnight Sun investor group would be concealing three armed and desperate terrorists."

There was that.

"What happened at the plant today?" Phoebe asked to change the subject.

"Megan said the accountants just kept working," Kristin said. "They were unflappable."

Someone's cell rang, and everyone looked at their phone.

"Mine," Sanjay said. "I must get back to the garage. The evening has been most enjoyable. Phoebe, congratulations on surviving your harrowing afternoon. Next time, Mr. Bonaventure, for a change but also a taste delight, I know a place that delivers the most delicious chicken tikka masala."

Everyone helped to clean up and then they took off, leaving Nattie and Phoebe with Chase in the kitchen.

"Let's find a room for Nattie," Chase said. "You two probably have a lot to talk about, but Phoebe, find me afterward. I want to talk to you before we all go to bed."

Phoebe nodded, her heart sinking. She couldn't have stopped what had happened this afternoon. But whatever Chase wanted to talk about couldn't be good.

"Where would you like to sleep?" Phoebe asked Nattie as she grabbed her friend's roller bag. "Pool view, garden view, upstairs, or ground floor?"

Nattie's eyes widened. "How many bedrooms are there?"

Chase sighed, and Phoebe grinned.

"Fifteen," she said. "Two on the ground floor are currently occupied."

"Fifteen bedrooms."

"Yup. Although you'll want one with a full private bath, so that narrows your options a bit. To seven."

"Seven."

"There's a nice suite on the second floor. Should I show you that one? You have your own sitting room, too."

"Sure," Nattie said, sounding bemused. "Show me that one."

They went up the deep-carpeted stairs.

"This could be a hotel," Nattie said, gazing around.

"It *will* be a hotel," Phoebe said, hauling the roller bag with some difficulty over the thick carpet and up the steps. "But first there has to be an elevator. And all the half baths have to be converted to full baths. But that should be about it. Chase seems to think that won't be much of a problem. I tend to agree. It's unbelievable how you just have to mention his name in this town and doors open."

"Not so much if any of this domestic terrorism stuff blows back on him."

"No. In that case, probably not." Phoebe stopped at the landing and looked at her friend, feeling the knot of fear in her stomach. "I don't want him to be hurt in all this."

"If the Eklunds are dangerous, they have to be stopped," Nattie said. "The investigation will determine that."

"I hope so," Phoebe said, heading down the hall. "I hope it's not another one of those FBI rush-to-judgment things."

"They can get carried away sometimes. At least—"

"It's not the Secret Service," Phoebe finished for her, and they broke out into a laugh. "Here we are," Phoebe added with a flourish, throwing open the door. "The suite."

The suite was painted in warm tones of gold and white and held a king-sized bed.

"This house is beautiful," Nattie said, taking in the room, "and that bed is the best thing I've seen since I left DC. Even including Chase Bonaventure."

"The bath's through that door, the towels are in here, and the sitting room's over there," Phoebe said, pointing. "I do want to catch up, but maybe tomorrow? You're probably tired, I know I'm tired, and Chase wants to talk." Probably he wanted to yell at her again, but she might as well get it over with.

Nattie nodded, yawning. "It has been a long day."

"Chase and I go to the office around seven thirty, but you don't have to get up then. Help yourself to anything in the kitchen. Call me when you're up."

"Sounds good." Nattie zipped open her roller bag. "Get out of here, Renfrew. Chase Bonaventure is waiting. And if I had that piece of chiseled gorgeousness waiting for me, I wouldn't hang around. Go and leave me to my fantasies."

Phoebe laughed. She didn't want to tell Nattie that they were her fantasies, too.

Phoebe found Chase in the gym, running on the treadmill. He turned the machine off when he saw her come in.

"Should I come back later?" she asked, approaching. "If you want some time—"

He jumped off the machine and enveloped her in his arms.

Surprised and breathless, she hugged him back. This was a much better response than she'd hoped for.

"I'm sorry I doubted you," he said, his voice muffled against her hair. "I'm sorry I didn't believe you. Or support you."

"That's okay," she said, burrowing into his chest. "I know it was a crazy story. And I was wearing that poodle skirt a bunch of the time. Who could take me seriously?"

"I should have." He pulled back and looked at her. "Those FBI jerk-offs—"

"Yeah, they can do some serious damage if they put their minds to it. But you got me a lawyer. I'm okay. And it seems like maybe they're done suspecting me."

He led her to a bench and pulled her down next to him. "I sure as hell hope so. Those idiots couldn't find a bad guy in a crowd if his picture was up on the jumbotron."

He'd been worried about her.

Not just worried because she was his translator and he needed her to interest the investors. He'd been worried about *her*, Phoebe Renfrew. Because he liked her.

A warm glow washed through her. She knew this thing that they had wouldn't last forever, but for right now, it was pretty perfect. She sighed and leaned into his arm.

"What's a jumbotron?"

Chapter 19

Saturday morning dawned bright and clear, perfect weather for a car rally. Phoebe looked down from the window of Chase's office to the employee parking lot below. The lot, which they were using as the staging area for the day's events, was filled with cars, drivers, employees with clipboards, equipment she didn't know the purpose of, and a refreshments table. She was happy to see the rally taking shape. She and Kristin had worked hard, and it had paid off.

But the rally also meant that her work at Venture Automotive was complete. When today ended, she'd be back at Happy Memories Wedding Chapel, handing out brochures on the courthouse steps. And Chase... Well, her time with Chase was probably over, too. She'd move out of his house tomorrow at the latest, maybe even tonight, back to her own apartment. It would be crowded there with her mom and Trouble, but the sooner she got back to reality, the better. The CIA would make its decision about her soon, and then she'd be back at Langley.

Which was what she wanted.

But that didn't mean she wouldn't miss Chase or her other friends here in Vegas.

She still didn't know what the Eklunds were up to, although she'd connected them to the secretary of state in New York and now, because the secretary was speaking at that big conference, in Vegas. But she hadn't been able to go any further with it on her own. And she hadn't heard from law enforcement. The FBI probably wouldn't tell her anything, anyway.

But even without developments on that front, the CIA would have to find that she'd acted responsibly in the Empire State Building fiasco. And then she'd be back at her desk job at the agency.

Which was where she belonged.

Chase put his arm around her, warming her and claiming her attention. "You're pretty quiet, *cher*. Everything okay?"

"Sure."

"Are you happy with how everything shaped up? Looks like you'll get a big crowd." He smiled down at her. "Maybe even bigger than the Super Bowl."

Phoebe leaned back to see his face. "Any word on how the investors are leaning?" All this would be for nothing if the investors didn't commit. The meetings had concluded yesterday. She'd shaken everyone's hand. They'd thanked her and gone back to their hotel. And that had been that.

"Not yet. But they're all here and signed up to drive."

"That has to be good, right? They'll see your cars outperforming gasoline-powered vehicles. That'll convince them."

Chase grinned. "I have every confidence that my cars will do great, since you've given them no other option."

"The other investors didn't seem too upset about the Eklunds. Thor Olafsson told me that Sven has always been too intense, and Lars doesn't have any interest in business. I want Midnight Sun to come through for you."

"I know, *cher*. We all did the best we could. Especially you."

Phoebe tried to shake off her depression. She still had a job to do. The rally was starting. It needed to go off without a hitch. She watched as a Mexican-themed food truck drove up and pulled into its designated parking spot. Just seeing it made her stomach growl. And she wanted to be out there doing something, not in here, alone with Chase, feeling sorry for herself for no good reason.

"Can I buy you a breakfast burrito?" she asked. "Your check is burning a hole in my pocket. And I'm starving."

"Big spender."

"Stick with me—I do things right." She smiled at him. "Come on. Last one downstairs is a rotten egg."

"Wait, *cher*. I won't see you all day. I need a little sugar first."

He pulled her closer, bent his head, and kissed her.

Phoebe felt that whoosh of rightness, that flash of lightning zoom through her blood like it always did when Chase touched her. The room receded and the noise of the rally below faded away. She kissed him back, trembling against his lips, feeling the loss of him as strongly as she felt his presence, his protective arms, his strength, his heat, and his passion. They might break up tonight or tomorrow, and she might never make love with him again or even kiss him again. His departure would be heart-wrenching.

"*Cher?*" Chase said, looking at her sharply, but he pulled back when another voice broke in from the doorway.

"You guys should get a room."

Phoebe's eyes had brimmed with tears, and she blinked rapidly to hide them from Chase and Kristin, who now stood in the doorway.

"Oh, wait," Kristin said. "You've got a room. Fifteen rooms to be exact." She grinned wickedly. "Come on. We have to run a rally and save our sorry butts."

"Way to ruin a romantic moment," Chase said. "We'll be right there."

"Don't be long. Your fans await." Kristin clattered down the stairs.

Then his arms were around her again, and Chase drew her back against his chest. Phoebe squeezed her eyes shut.

"Tell me what's wrong," he said. "Why are you crying? I thought you'd be excited today."

"I'm not crying," Phoebe said, sniffing. "I'm excited."

"*Cher.* I've got sisters. Don't lie to me."

Phoebe sniffed again. "Just, everything's wrapping up. I'm tired, that's all."

"No wonder. You've been working like a dog. One more day and then you're done. Tomorrow you sleep late. Take Monday off. That's an order."

Tomorrow she'd be back in her own apartment, and Monday she'd be back at Happy Memories. But she wouldn't think about that now.

"Sounds good," she said, although she wouldn't be having

those lazy days.

"Come on, then, or Kristin will have my hide for tanning. And you said you'd buy me breakfast."

When they got to the lobby, Chase gave her a swift kiss. "We'll have a quiet night tonight at my place when this is over. Unless you want to go out and paint the town red."

Phoebe smiled, trying to look cheerful. The job was over, and she needed to get back to her own apartment—the sooner the better. This wasn't the time or place to discuss it, but she didn't want to get too used to the comforts that Chase's mansion provided.

Chase had a company to run, and—she hoped—she had a job at the CIA to get back to. They weren't each other's destiny. That was the kind of thing her mother believed in. And she wouldn't follow her mother into a lifetime of short-term relationships that had no hope of working out.

She followed Chase out the lobby door to the parking lot, where they were assaulted by early-morning heat and immediate demands on their attention. Chase, as planned, started to mingle, shaking hands and welcoming people. Kristin would be in the employee parking lot at the rear of the building, coordinating the drivers. Phoebe's job was back there, too, to translate any problems that might come up for the Korean speakers. But if she didn't get that breakfast burrito, she wouldn't last more than an hour.

She ordered one for herself and one for Chase, and then as she went to find him, she bumped into Harry O'Shea. He already wore the bright yellow vest that indicated he was a driver in the event.

"Great to see you, Harry! Are you all set to go?"

"I'm ready to drown that tree-hugging, eco-nut, ex-football champeen in a pool of glorious motor oil, if that's what you mean." Harry grinned at her as he chomped into his egg-stuffed burrito.

Phoebe laughed. "Don't trash talk until you win, Harry. Pride goeth before a fall."

Harry swallowed. "The only falling that's happening is Chase Bonaventure off that pedestal you've put him on."

"Oh, I don't think he's on a pedestal." Phoebe watched

246

Chase work the crowd, handsome and charming, surrounded by groupies, standing a full head taller than most of them, the sun glinting off his sunglasses, dark hair, and bronzed skin.

Okay, he looked a little bit like he was on a pedestal.

Harry snorted.

"Listen, I gotta go," she said. "You know where you have to be, right? I'm following in the support car, so I'll see you in the lineup in about a half hour."

"I'll be there," Harry said, his voice muffled through his breakfast.

Phoebe carried Chase's burrito over to the crowd and then realized she'd never get through to him in the crush. As she wondered how she could get his attention, she saw a buxom brunette put her hand on his arm and lean into him. A flare of—what? Fury? Surely not jealousy—shot through her, and she realized that she might not be at her diplomatic best. Perhaps she should let Chase worry about his own breakfast.

A young guy with thick glasses and bushy hair, wearing a yellow Venture Automotive T-shirt, walked by, muttering into a walkie-talkie.

Phoebe stopped him. "Hi. I'm Phoebe. I have your breakfast burrito."

"Hi, what?"

Phoebe beamed, thrusting the burrito into his hands. "Bon appétit."

"Um, okay." The kid stared at the burrito for a few seconds and then bit into it, moving on, still talking into the walkie-talkie.

She felt a little bit bad for Chase missing breakfast. But if he was that that hungry, one of those vultures hanging on his every word could get him something. She had too much to do to think about buxom brunettes. Or buxom anybody.

Tony and Matt were out back, checking out the cars and positioning them for the start, and Phoebe saw Harry's baby-blue Caddy lined up next to the Venture Automotive SUV it was competing against. Four other vehicles, all of them sporting the bright yellow magnetic door signs and numbered roof cones that marked them as contestants in the rally, also stood ready, their drivers lounging against their fenders.

Thor, the Swedish-Korean investor who was driving the electric vehicle in this challenge, looked excited and nervous, and Phoebe went over to see him.

"You ready to stomp all over these gas guzzlers?" she asked him as she approached.

"This is thrilling," he said. "I can't believe you organized all this just for us."

"It was your idea," she said, smiling. "And now lots of people get to enjoy the race, too."

"Your company is very inspirational. Young and energetic, with experienced people in key positions. I like that, and I like the cars. I hope to do your vehicle justice."

"You'll do great," she said. "It's mostly about showing everybody what the cars are capable of. The course is marked, so you can't miss it. I'll be following in a support vehicle, so if you run into any problems, I'll be there. Good luck and have fun."

"Oh, I will!"

She saw Harry and waved. Too bad he had to lose. That vintage car was a collector's dream come true. Those fins! Huge and impressive in their own gas-guzzling way.

Matt and Tony took away the traffic cones that had blocked entry to the parking lot.

"Are we all set?" she asked.

This challenge, the one that demonstrated fuel economy, required that each vehicle start with two dollars' worth of "fuel." That would be a killer for the gas-powered cars, who couldn't pump even one full gallon for two bucks and would travel at most twenty miles on that. The electric vehicle would have a full charge and would easily finish the fifty-mile leg.

"Yup," Tony confirmed. "Ready to go."

"Nobody's figured out our strategy yet?"

"I think they've figured out that they're unlikely to win, even if they're not exactly sure how or why," Tony said. "Nobody seems to care that much. They're having fun, and—let's face it—you're probably underestimating how much people want to get close to Coach."

Not me, Phoebe thought. *I totally get it.* "I'm beginning to appreciate that."

"It's time," Matt said. He lifted the bullhorn to his mouth. "Drivers ready," he called out.

The drivers of the five gas-powered vehicles in this event jumped into their cars and fastened their seat belts. Thor saw the other drivers getting in their cars and did likewise. Phoebe went over to his car to translate while Matt gave the final instructions.

"Remember, it's not primarily about speed," Matt said to the drivers. "The main objective is to finish the course."

Phoebe finished her translation. "Do you understand everything?"

"Oh, yes," Thor said, buckling his seat belt. "It is just as you said. I'm ready."

Tony got behind the wheel of the electric SUV that would be the support car, and Phoebe hopped into the passenger seat.

Matt raised a white flag and all the engines roared to life. Then Matt dropped the flag, and the cars sped out of the back lot, onto the frontage road, past the crowds mobbing the front of the plant, and out onto the road back to town. Phoebe heard a yell from the crowd as their support vehicle followed.

"We're off to the races," Tony said, following the lead cars.

"The faster they go, the sooner they run out of gas," Phoebe said.

"We warned them about speed." Tony kept his eyes locked on the road and the cars ahead of them.

"They'll lose no matter how slowly they drive."

"That's the beauty of it," Tony said, and Phoebe laughed.

The miles sped by. The fifty-mile leg was scheduled to take an hour, but the first gas guzzler stalled in fifteen minutes. Harry's beautiful baby-blue Caddy was the third car to give out.

"What did I tell you about bragging, Harry?" Phoebe asked, jumping out of the support car and pulling a gas can out of the back.

"I should have known," Harry said, looking disgusted.

"You should have." Tony grinned, checking Harry's mileage and making a note on a clipboard.

"This was fun, but I gotta head out," Harry said. "I got that rehearsal at the Desert Dunes. Phoebe, invite me out to Chase's for barbecue. You owe me."

"No promises. But I'll see what I can do." She finished pouring in the gas, enough to get him to the nearest gas station. "Okay, that's it. You're good to go."

He grinned, patting the Caddy's door. "I'm never giving up this baby, but if I ever get a new car for the occasions when I don't care what vehicle I'm driving, I'll give one of those electric can openers a shot. Assuming the price is right."

"I can put in a good word for you." Phoebe tossed the can back into the SUV. "I know the owner."

"Come on, Phoebe," Tony said. "Let's go. We've got other last-century cars to save."

"Gotta dash, Harry," Phoebe said. "But I'll see you at work on Monday."

"Really?" Harry got into the car and slammed the door. "Well, sure, if that's what you want."

It's not what I want, Phoebe thought as she climbed back into the support car. *It's what I have to do.*

Chapter 20

By one o'clock, Phoebe needed lunch, but she and Kristin had neglected to schedule that for themselves. She grabbed a plate of shrimp rolls from the Ginger Palace food truck, a restaurant she'd been wanting to try, before she and Tony started on the last challenge. Now they were attempting to eat as they sped after the contestants in the sports car rally. And all three Eklunds were driving in this challenge. Maybe they were trying to outrun her. Or something.

"I see you guys had to get three sports cars finished for this one," she said to Tony, swishing a shrimp roll in its ginger sauce. She closed her eyes as she bit into it and the tanginess hit her tongue. Unbelievably good.

"Mmpfh," Tony agreed, biting into his hamburger. He held the burger with one hand and steered with the other.

Phoebe hoped he wouldn't drive them off the road. She polished off the last shrimp roll, licked her fingers, and wiped them on her paper napkin.

"As long they don't smash the cars and nobody gets hurt, that's all I care about." She stashed the sticky paper plate in the trash bag they kept on the console. "Well, and that we win. I care about that, too."

So far, as planned, the electric vehicles from Venture Automotive had dusted the gas-powered vehicles in all the challenges.

As they approached a T intersection, the lead electric car—was that Gustav?—turned left instead of right, plowing over the orange traffic cones that had blocked access to the wrong way.

"What the—" Tony stomped on the brakes, which pitched them both forward, and he cursed as the remains of his sandwich flew to the floor. All the gas-powered cars careened right, following the race markers, while the two electric cars driven by Sven and Lars turned left, following Gustav, and sped down a city street clogged with traffic.

"Go left!" Phoebe said. "Follow the electrics!"

"Are you sure? We're supposed to follow the route."

"Our cars are the electrics, and my job is to translate for the Korean speakers. And—" *I'm afraid of what the Eklunds might do or where they might go.* "Just turn left. Please. I'll call Chase."

His phone rolled over to voicemail though, so she left him a message.

"I don't know why they left the track," she said into the phone, "but I don't like it. I'm following them."

"What do you mean, you don't like it?" Tony asked when she disconnected.

"They've been questioned by the police and the FBI," Phoebe said. "I think they're planning something bad—like newspaper-headline bad—but I don't know what it is. I think something involving the secretary of state."

"*What?*" Tony had taken the left turn, but he slammed on the brakes again.

Phoebe stuck out her hand to stop herself from pitching forward. "You're driving like you've never seen a clutch. What's the matter with you? Step on it!"

"What's the matter with *you*?" Tony said. "If they're dangerous, call the cops! We're not taking on dangerous people. I've got kids. And this car doesn't *have* a clutch. Which you should know!"

"*Keep following them,*" Phoebe said. "I'll call the cops, but we can't tell the cops where to go if we don't know where they are. So *don't lose them.*"

"Dammit!" Tony said, but he stomped on the accelerator. By now the electric cars were mere dots in the distance, but Phoebe could see the bright yellow racing cones on the car roofs, which made them more visible than they'd probably expected.

Wishing she had his cell phone number, she called Greena-

252

way's direct line at the office. He didn't pick up. No surprise there. He might be providing security for this race. Today might even be his day off. She left a voicemail.

"It's 1:07 p.m. I'm on Charleston at, ah, just passing Tenth, heading west, following the Eklunds, who have broken away from the rally route. Whatever they're planning, I think this could be it. I'm betting any money they're heading to the Desert Dunes, because that's where the secretary of state is. Would appreciate some backup."

"Nobody was home at the *police*?" Tony leaned forward in the seat, his eyes glued to the road, and his knuckles were white with the pressure of his grip on the steering wheel.

"I've been talking to one particular detective," Phoebe said. "He's the one who's up to speed. I guess I'll call the FBI. I don't much like those guys, though. And Agent Picone is a pill. He wants to tie me into it."

"Jerk-off. Still, don't let me stop you. Call the FBI, by all means. Call *somebody*."

"CIA first." Phoebe smacked into the doorframe as Tony yanked the steering wheel sharply to the left. Tires squealed as the car heeled over and righted itself in the wrong lane of a city street full of automobiles.

"Ah, careful!" Her heart hammered in her chest as she called Nattie.

"Nat," she said, still breathless when her friend finally picked up. "The Eklunds left the route. I think this is it. They're driving crosstown really fast. We're following them."

"I'll come after you. Where are you?"

Phoebe gave her the current direction. "If you see him, tell Chase. I've called the cops. I think we're headed to the Desert Dunes. The secretary of state is speaking there."

"I'll call Agent Picone," Nattie said.

"He might actually believe you. I'll call Greg. Maybe he can help."

"You'd think our boss could make something happen, but I don't have heaps of confidence."

"Worth a try. Okay, now we're heading due south on Maryland Parkway. If we hang a right on Sahara, we'll be about at the

Desert Dunes. We're maybe ten minutes out."

"On my way. Keep me posted."

"You heard what I said, right?" she asked Tony. "Let's just go right to the Desert Dunes. I think the Eklunds must have something planned."

"Christ," Tony said, pressing down on the accelerator. "Call security there, why don't you?"

"Oh, good idea." Phoebe searched for the number and called the convention center. Then she had to wait precious minutes for the manager to come on the line. "Hello," she said, knowing this was not the time for tedious background details. "This is Phoebe Renfrew of the CIA. Three suspected terrorists are on their way to your venue right now in what we believe will be an attack on the secretary of state. The FBI and local police have been informed, and the CIA is monitoring the situation. Please alert your own security team."

"Is this a hoax?" the manager asked. "Give me a number where I can call you back."

Phoebe sighed. She should have called Greg first, even if he thought she was crying wolf on this one. He at least had a CIA phone number.

"This is not a hoax," she said. "Please alert the secretary!"

"I don't believe you," the manager said. "If you're the CIA, why don't you alert the secretary?"

Good point.

"Thank you, I will," Phoebe said. "You might do the same. And if you don't, and the secretary is killed or kidnapped, we'll see you in court. And next year, when we're planning this conference? We won't be coming to the Desert Dunes." She disconnected, wishing she could slam down the receiver like the old-fashioned landlines. Sometimes technology was very unsatisfying.

"That'll show him," Tony said. "Not having the conference there next year."

"He didn't believe me. I hate it when that happens." Phoebe frowned at her phone and braced herself as Tony took a hard right too fast. "I have to call the secretary of state."

"Do you have her number?"

"Of course not. Maybe I can find it." She scrolled through

her government contacts and pulled up a number that she thought would work. "Here's something," she said. She tapped in the number and waited way too long.

"Hello," she said when someone picked up. "Please connect me to the secretary of state or her security detail. This is Phoebe Renfrew at the CIA. It's a matter of life and death."

Seconds later she dropped the phone and turned to Tony. "They hung up on me. Stupid Secret Service. How much farther to the Desert Dunes?"

"Five minutes out."

Her phone rang, and she glanced at the ID screen. *Sanjay*. At least somebody was talking to her.

"Phoebe!" he said when she picked up. "What is happening? What is your planned destination?"

"We're chasing the Eklunds. I think they're heading to the Desert Dunes. But I don't know what their plan is."

"We're right behind you! Alert the convention center!"

"Done, not that it helped. Be careful!" She disconnected and turned to Tony. "Sanjay's following us."

"Does he have a gun?" Tony asked. "I've been thinking about weapons. None of us seems to have any weapons."

"Sanjay gave me a pink umbrella once for a weapon, so he's got that. If he's in his taxi, he's got a tire iron, too."

"That would be better than nothing."

Phoebe nodded, punching in the number for Greg. *He* could bring in some weapons and call the secretary, as well, while he was at it.

"Greg, hi, it's Phoebe," she said when he picked up.

"Phoebe, I've *told* you—"

"Yeah, yeah, I know. Listen. Here's the deal. The Eklunds—those guys you have on photographs at the Empire State Building, you know about that, right? The FBI kept you in the loop?"

When he didn't say anything, Phoebe felt a small thrill of triumph. Greg knew she'd been right about the threat at the Empire State Building, so that had to be good for her evaluation. Not that this was time to gloat while the secretary was still in danger.

"Okay," she continued. "The Eklunds are heading to the Desert Dunes, where the secretary of state is scheduled to speak in"—she glanced at her watch—"holy cats, about thirty minutes. I think they're planning to try something there. The convention manager didn't believe me, so they won't notify her. Please call her. Or her security detail. The Secret Service hung up on me."

Greg uttered an oath not suitable for family television. "If you're wrong, Phoebe—"

"I'm not. It all makes sense."

"I'll call," Greg said. "*Dammit*. What's in place for law enforcement?"

"I called the local police detective who's working the case and left a message. I don't know what they're sending. If anything. Nattie Wilkinson is here. She called the local FBI. Guy's name is Aaron Picone."

"Is there anything else I should know?"

"Not a thing! Thank you!" Phoebe heaved a sigh of relief and disconnected. "My boss is doing something," she told Tony.

"Coach?" Tony sounded confused.

"No. My boss at the CIA." Her phone trilled and she checked the display. Greenaway. "Detective Greenaway, thanks for calling back."

"Where are you headed?"

"The Desert Dunes. Tony and I could use some backup."

"You got it," he said. "The FBI is here too. SWAT's on alert. What the hell. We'll all come."

"Great. Thank you." But he'd already hung up.

A few seconds later, Tony braked sharply and turned left into a driveway that had a huge sign for the Desert Dunes. "Right," he said. "Here we are."

Phoebe's heart suddenly clogged her throat. *This was it*.

"Check the parking lot," Tony said. "I'm pretty sure this is where they turned in. Where are their cars?"

Phoebe searched the lot, pursing her lips, her eyes narrowed on the spaces. Bright yellow cars with cones on the roof couldn't be that hard to spot.

"There!" she said, pointing.

"Let's go!" Tony parked in the red curb area next to valet parking.

"Hey!" a guy in livery said. "You can't park here!"

Phoebe jumped out of the car, flashing her Venture Automotive ID badge for less than a second before shoving it in her pocket.

"CIA!" she said, heading for the entrance.

"CIA!" Tony flashed his own employee badge and followed her.

"CIA? Wait!" the valet yelled, but he didn't tackle them, so they dashed for the revolving door.

"That worked," Phoebe said, running through the doors, checking the lobby, looking for the Eklunds. "One for the good guys. Now let's go save us a secretary of state."

When the Eklunds broke away from the race and sped across town, Brenda Renfrew turned from the orange-and-blue, paisley-painted, Indian-themed food truck and stared as the small cavalcade—the three electric sports cars driven by the investors and then the electric support vehicle—bashed their way through the traffic cones that marked the route and peeled off in the wrong direction.

"That's weird," she said to Uncle Boo-Boo, who had taken her to his sister's food truck start-up and introduced her to the tasty miracle that was chicken tikka masala. "Why are those cars going off the track? Why is Phoebe following them?"

"Perhaps it is secret CIA business!" Uncle Boo-Boo said, beaming.

"What is that about which you are speaking?" Sanjay stuck his head out of the food truck's order window. "CIA business? Is Phoebe in danger again?"

"We don't know!" Brenda frowned after the cars. "It's very odd."

"I think it's secret CIA business!" Uncle Boo-Boo said.

"Perhaps we should follow them," Sanjay said. "Phoebe has exhibited a most distressing habit of taking risks. Perhaps she could use our help."

"An excellent suggestion!" Uncle Boo-boo said. "Let's go!" He unhooked the chalkboard menu that hung from the side of the truck and stashed it on the counter.

Sanjay disappeared inside, and in seconds, a cloud of black smoke erupted from the tailpipe as the truck roared to life.

"We're chasing them in the food truck?" Brenda didn't think they could catch them in the clumsy vehicle. Or even keep them in sight, no matter how bright those ghastly yellow cars were and how tall the cones stood out on the vehicles' roofs.

"With what else do we have to chase them? By all means, in the food truck!" Uncle Boo-Boo finished clipping the menu securely to the counter and then nudged her toward a small door in the side of the truck. "You do not see any other vehicles here, do you? The food truck is what we have. The food truck is what we'll take."

Brenda heard a shout from inside the truck, and a skinny teenaged boy started slamming down the window covers. In seconds, the truck was secured and ready to go.

"No time to lose!" Uncle Boo-Boo beamed and opened the side door.

In for a penny, Brenda thought and tripped up the steps in her killer heels. At the top she bumped into the teenager. "Oh, sorry!"

"This is the nephew of my nephew Sanjay," Uncle Boo-Boo said. "Justin."

"Justin?"

The teenager, a beautiful younger replica of Sanjay with dark brown eyes, dark hair, and pants at least four sizes too big, shrugged.

"Better sit!" Sanjay yelled from the driver's seat. He ground the gears into first and stepped on the gas.

The truck was heavy and slow, but even so, the lurch sent Brenda flying into Uncle Boo-Boo.

"Here, we have seats in the back," he said, holding on to her firmly. "With belts. Better than an airplane."

They staggered to the back of the truck, where Uncle Boo-Boo pulled down a jump seat for the two of them, and Justin braced himself in a crevice between two built-in cupboards.

"Hang on!" Uncle Boo-Boo called gaily as Sanjay ground the gears into second and the truck lurched again. Uncle Boo-Boo grabbed Brenda's leg for emphasis, which was a lot less irritating than she thought it would be.

She looked into his twinkling eyes and smiled. "Where are we going?" she asked. "Can we still see them?"

"If we make all possible haste, I believe that we have every chance of overtaking them," Sanjay called, glaring into the traffic, his eyes focused on the road. "They will not get away." With one hand on the wheel, he dug his phone out of his pocket and hit the speed dial.

"Phoebe!" he said. "What is happening? What is your planned destination?"

He listened for a minute, swerving around traffic with one hand, leaning on the horn when he had to.

"We're right behind you! Alert the convention center!" He disconnected and shoved the phone back in his pocket. "The Swedish-Korean terrorists are making their move! It is go time!"

"Terrorists?" Brenda said. "What terrorists? I never heard anything about terrorists!" She'd never even been positive that Phoebe worked for the CIA. Her daughter seemed to have a boring desk job at some gray agency in Washington where she sat all day and pushed paper around. She was a spy? When did that happen? Although there was that thing with the SEALs at the Empire State Building. That had been big.

"The Swedish-Koreans! Phoebe has been following them most diligently for some time! They are most dangerous! We must stop them!" Sanjay stomped on the accelerator.

Hungry pedestrians, seeing the food truck barreling down the street, tried to flag him down, but he gestured wildly to get them to move out of the way. Then he turned on the truck's exterior speakers and hit a button. Music from a Bollywood film blared out into the Las Vegas desert.

"Ah," Uncle Boo-Boo said. "That is 'Lat Lag Gayee.' Very nice tune."

"What?" Brenda said, hanging on to Uncle Boo-Boo for dear life as Sanjay careened around a corner.

"From the film *Race 2*," Uncle Boo-Boo said, holding Brenda firmly. "Not my favorite film, but I do like the music. Don't you?"

"Ah, sure."

The truck sped down the street, music streaming out to the public. Several other vehicles honked. Sanjay honked back. From her position on the jump seat, Brenda could see only a tiny sliver of the front-facing windshield. Buildings sped by, but she had a hard time orienting herself to where they were. And then Sanjay slammed on the brakes, and they all lurched forward.

"We're here!" Sanjay threw open the driver-side door and leaped out of the truck.

Uncle Boo-Boo helped Brenda to her feet and she, feeling unexpectedly hampered by her stilettos, followed him out the side door, gratefully taking his hand. Justin jumped down and hiked up his pants with one hand after he landed. Brenda gazed up at the imposing facade of the Desert Dunes casino. What was Phoebe doing here? What was happening?

"Hey!" the liveried valet parking guy said. "You can't park here!"

"CIA!" Sanjay flashed his food vendor's permit for less than a second.

The valet grabbed Uncle Boo-Boo's arm. "Stop right there!"

"They're with me," Sanjay said. "National security!"

"At least turn off that music!"

"CIA!" Uncle Boo-Boo said, shaking his arm loose and flashing his Realtor's license. "It is most urgent."

"I'm the cocktail waitress," Brenda said, wondering if the valet parking guy might actually hold her back. That might be a good idea. He was kind of cute, and her feet were killing her. When she'd accepted the date with Uncle Boo-Boo to see the rally, she hadn't expected to do so much running.

"Hey! Wait!" the valet guy said, but Sanjay dashed to the revolving doors without looking back.

Uncle Boo-Boo towed Brenda, who tripped along as fast as she could, and Justin slouched behind.

"We're in," Sanjay said as he entered the lobby. "Now let us find the secretary of state before disaster befalls the nation."

Chapter 21

Detective Dave Greenaway was monitoring traffic and surveillance cameras with FBI Special Agent Aaron Picone and a bunch of other FBI types who were wearing clothes too hot for the weather in a command center set up in an undisclosed location. He was both bored and annoyed. While the photos of the Eklunds at the Empire State Building had mostly convinced him that the Swedish-Koreans had planned for something to happen there, the fact was that nothing had happened in New York. And probably nothing would happen again today, even though Phoebe Renfrew thought otherwise. Plus, the FBI guys were being snotty about how few traffic cameras Las Vegas had operational. Shitheads could pay for them if they thought they were so damn important.

His phone rang and he took the call, walking across the room, glad to be away from the feds for five minutes.

"Greenaway."

"Detective, this is Officer Wade Heimermann," a young and nervous-sounding cop said. "I'm sorry if I'm interrupting you, but you said you wanted to be informed if anything suspicious happened out here because of the potential of a terrorist threat and all? I don't know if this is suspicious, but—"

Jeez. He'd be ready for retirement before the rookie got his speech out.

"Fewer words, Heimermann."

"Yes, sir! I mean, a couple of the cars broke away from the race, crashed through the cones, and just took off down the street.

And the support vehicle followed. Is that the kind of thing you want to know?"

Hell, yes.

"What direction were they headed?"

"West. At a pretty good clip."

"Good work, Heimermann. All right. Stand by for a possible terrorist threat. Be ready to move."

"Yes, *sir*!"

Greenaway called Phoebe. He had a pretty good idea of their destination, but it wouldn't hurt to check in with those in pursuit.

"Where are you headed?" he said when she picked up.

"The Desert Dunes. Tony and I could use some backup."

"You got it," he said. "The FBI is here, too. SWAT's on alert. What the hell. We'll all come."

He disconnected and turned back to the FBI, who weren't scowling at the monitors anymore but were huddled in a tight knot, talking in low voices.

"Detective," Picone said, glancing up. "You need to activate your SWAT team now. Our chief has had a message from the assistant second deputy department director, Greg Peeling, at the CIA. The Eklunds are on the move."

"Yeah, I know," Greenaway said, feeling a childish wave of satisfaction that he could one-up the FBI. "They're headed to the Desert Dunes. Let's roll."

Nattie finished her phone call with Phoebe and looked around for Chase or Kristin. Now that the rally itself was in its last leg, thousands of interested spectators had streamed back to the plant, wanting test drives or autographs or food trucks. The early-afternoon crowd was at least twice as large as the early-morning bunch, and she couldn't see either of them through so many bodies.

She had Chase's number, anyway. She'd call. Maybe he'd pick up.

She tapped the Call icon and got sent to voicemail, so she pressed Redial and looked around for somebody on staff. *Some-one* would know where he was. A yellow-shirted employee with a clipboard went by.

"I saw him in the back about an hour ago," he said, and she jogged off in that direction. Nothing.

She hit Redial again, saw another employee. Asked for Chase or Kristin. Nothing. She tried to stay cool, but time was passing. She needed to find them *now*. Or she needed to go without them to the Desert Dunes. She wasn't sure how she could help Phoebe, but she would have to try. She hit Redial. Maybe they were inside.

Running into the plant, she saw a small group of men and one woman standing in a small knot with Chase. They were well-dressed and evenly tanned.

They had to be potential investors. Or at least potential purchasers of vehicles. How could she get him away without damaging his chances of signing those folks up?

"Excuse me, Mr. Bonaventure," she said, striding up to him. "Hello." She nodded to the potential investors, ridiculously glad that she was wearing a suit. Right now she needed the credibility. "Natalie Wilkinson, CIA. Mr. Bonaventure, I have the president on line one for you in your office. He wants to talk to you about his plans for a task force involving tax credits for alternative fuels. Please come with me immediately."

Chase blinked in astonishment, but he didn't argue. "Very well." He turned to his guests and smiled. "Evidently the president is holding. Please excuse me."

"Of course!" They all beamed.

Nattie smiled. They were all happy they were brushing shoulders with the man who brushed shoulders with the president. They better invest big.

"What's Phoebe up to?" Chase asked softly as they walked away. "Because I know the president sure as hell does not want to talk to me about alternative fuels or task forces or anything else."

"The Eklunds broke away from the race and are on the way to the Desert Dunes, if they aren't there already. The secretary of state is speaking at a conference there."

The sudden tension rolled off him like a tsunami. He changed direction, heading for a side door. "Phoebe's chasing them."

She nodded. "I called our boss at the CIA, and he's calling the FBI. Phoebe called the local cops."

Chase nodded, pulling out his phone. "Missed messages." He punched in numbers. "Phoebe. And this number I don't know—that was you?"

Nattie nodded.

Chase tapped in a number. "Kristin," he said into the phone. "I have to leave right now and leave quietly. It's Phoebe. Hold the fort here." He listened for a second. "All right, but come right now."

He'd barely shoved the phone back in his pocket when Kristin burst into the lobby from the front entrance, Trouble at her heels.

"It's the Eklunds, right?" she said, running up to them. "Phoebe was right. What are we waiting for? Let's go!"

They charged outside again into the crowd. Spectators recognized Chase and moved toward him.

"We have to keep moving," Kristin said. "Like sharks. Or these nice people will trap us here and we'll die."

Across the parking lot, Chase saw Matt directing one of the returning electric vehicles to a parking space.

"Over there." Nodding and smiling but not stopping, he charged through the crowd. The eager spectators fell away like outstripped defenders on the football field.

Kristin, Nattie, and Trouble followed close in his wake.

"Nice seeing you," he said as he bulled his way through the crowd. "Thanks for coming. Glad you could make it."

"Touchdown!" Kristin whispered to Nattie.

"Matt!" he said when he reached the parking area. "Keys!"

Matt tossed them over and Chase caught them and yanked open the driver-side door in one smooth motion. Kristin and Nattie scrambled into the back seat and fastened their seat belts, and Trouble took a flying leap and landed splat on their laps. Kristin slammed the door shut and put her arms around the dog.

"We're going to go fast, sweetie," she told the happy mutt. "I don't want you to slide around."

Chase hit speed dial on his phone as he fired up the car.

"Phoebe, where are you? What's happening?" He steered the car out of the lot with one hand.

He navigated around race goers with reckless speed, scattering loiterers like pins in a bowling alley. He hoped that all the off-duty cops providing security were gone or doing something else.

"I know all that." He turned sharply onto the road that led to downtown and stepped on the accelerator. "Can't you wait for the cops?"

He listened again.

"*Cher*. Don't do anything that'll get you killed, okay? I'm coming. Just... be careful."

Chase disconnected and glanced in the rearview mirror. "Everybody buckled up? We're finally gonna see how fast this thing can go."

Backstage at the Desert Dunes conference center auditorium, Harry O'Shea stood in costume with the forty other Elvis impersonators of the Las Vegas All-Elvis Revue, waiting for their cue. The air conditioning wasn't doing its job back here, and all of them were moist from the encroaching afternoon heat. *Lord, please don't let my makeup sag or my costume wilt.* Fred Propson over there—the heaviest of the Revue Elvises and the best representative of the Las Vegas glitter period—had already lost the battle with his shirt, which clung damply to his chest.

While this gig paid well and of course it was prestigious, so far it was something of a bust. Instead of dressing rooms, they'd had to make do with a curtained-off area—a *hot*, curtained-off area—in the loading dock. They'd all shared one small mirror, so the makeup on most of them was hit or miss. They hadn't gotten the refreshments they'd asked for, either, and no one had had any water for more than an hour. Who knew what their voices would sound like when they finally got on the stage?

Harry dug a finger underneath his wig to scratch his scalp and waited for their cue. He liked performing, liked the adrenaline, but he wasn't convinced this crowd was their core audience. The sooner the show started, the sooner it would be over, and he could go home, take a shower, have a cold brew, and watch the ball game.

Lars wasn't happy. They'd adjusted the plan on the fly, which didn't seem like a good idea to him. The original strategy had been to drive the white truck to the convention center, grab the secretary, and drive away. They could talk to the secretary in the truck and keep her there until she agreed to help.

But then the plan fell apart.

First the truck disappeared. Sven and Gustav were sure that the translator had had it towed, but Lars thought that somebody stole it. Crime was terrible in the States—everybody knew that.

Whatever. They didn't have the truck.

Then Sven decided that they could use the opportunity of this car rally to commandeer vehicles for their kidnapping plan. Driving—expropriating—bright yellow electric cars with cones on the roofs didn't seem smart to him, but he'd been overruled.

And now—when they got the secretary—*if* they got her— what could they do with her? They'd outfitted the truck with a couch and chairs, even a cooler with snacks and beverages, to make her as comfortable as possible for however long they needed to persuade her. That truck had been perfect—hideaway and getaway at the same time. But now, the electric cars exposed them too much. And it wasn't like they could grab her and then go back to the bar and have a friendly chat over aquavit cocktails. Everything could go badly wrong. Those federal security agents had guns.

They'd walked into the lobby at a good clip but not running, not wanting to draw attention to themselves. The secretary was speaking in the auditorium at two, and there weren't that many hallways that led to the auditorium stage. They would reconnoiter to see what was roped off. That's where she'd be. And then they'd wait until she showed up.

"Father," he said as they crossed the lobby, working their way through the crowd that loitered in front of the auditorium doors. "Maybe we should postpone our plans today. We don't have the truck. We can't make a getaway. How will we be able to speak with the secretary?"

"We're not canceling," Sven and Gustav said at the same time.

"We canceled at the Empire State Building because our timing was bad," Sven added. "We are not canceling again here. The timing will never be perfect. We must get our ancestor out of

North Korea. Today we make a stand."

"The secretary will help us," Gustav said. "Do not be such a coward."

"I'm not a coward," Lars said. "I'm *practical*. I'm just asking if our plan is achievable today. And if it isn't, we can live to fight another day."

"We will succeed today." Sven scowled.

"Tell me how, then," Lars said. "I want to understand. And I want to know my part."

"The plan is the same," Sven said. "We take the secretary. She goes with us."

"In the yellow car?" Lars asked. "The one with all the windows that has the cone on the roof? We put her in the back seat all nice and cozy where everyone can see her? That's the part that I think won't work."

Sven glared at him. "It will work, or we'll die trying."

Lars shook his head. "I don't want to die. I want to have a plan that works."

"Our plan will work," Sven said. "You'll see. Now we must hurry. She will be coming this way any minute. Let's find the stage entrances."

They slipped through a service door and entered the long, bare hallway that ran behind the stage. Lars tried to imagine them surviving an outright attack on the secretary. He'd been an idiot, he realized. He hadn't taken any of his father's plans seriously enough. Now that they were here, he saw what a monumental screwup this would be.

Gustav yanked open the first door, which led to a short stairway that was jammed with dozens of men, all of them with dark, thick hair and wearing the same costume—black pants and black-and-white striped T-shirts. Who were these people? One of them said something that sounded faintly hostile, and Gustav slammed the door. But not before Lars saw that the stairs led to the stage.

The three of them rushed down the hall to the next stage entrance, but they never reached it. Several big men stood in the corridor and looked threatening. Hotel security? Secret Service? Lars couldn't tell. All those uniforms looked alike. For all he knew, they were parking attendants.

They stopped, and one of the men said something to them. You didn't have to know any English to know that he'd said: "Get out of here." Lars was all for that. Gustav and Sven were waiting for him to say or do something, but what was he supposed to do? He knew a few words of English, like "okay" and "please" and "thank you," and none of it had been all that useful so far on this trip. But it didn't take a rocket scientist to know that this guy wanted them to go away.

The man said it again, louder this time, and waved his arms. Lars tried to figure out the words, but it was hopeless. When he got back—*if* he got back—he was signing up for English night classes. A person couldn't live like this.

The man grabbed Sven's arm and marched him toward the exit that would lead them back to the lobby. Sven didn't put up a struggle—he was no match for the guard, and what could they do, anyway? They couldn't pull their guns yet. It was much too soon. The secretary was nowhere in sight.

Once they'd been dumped back in the lobby, they straightened their clothes and looked around.

"What's the plan now?" Lars couldn't help saying, but Gustav wasn't paying any attention to him. Lars blinked as Gustav's face turned almost purple with rage.

"I can't believe it!" he said. "Look over there! That damn translator followed us! Now what? We have to get rid of them!"

Lars glanced over Gustav's shoulder and saw Phoebe and a factory employee dash into the lobby. One thing Gustav had right: they were bound to interfere with the plan, such as it was, to kidnap the secretary. At this point, that wouldn't be a bad thing.

The translator hadn't seen them yet, largely because the lobby was crammed with hundreds—even thousands—of conference attendees, most of them men, some in uniform and some in regular clothes, who were milling about before the keynote began. And then the auditorium doors opened, and many—dozens at a time—streamed through.

Lars saw with shock that metal detectors blocked all the doors, and more burly men in uniform were examining briefcases and occasionally patting down some of the spectators. "The

268

doors," he said. "Check it out."

"I've *seen* them!" Gustav said. "I *told* you!"

"Not the translator," Lars hissed. "*Security at the doors.*"

Gustav whirled around. "Shit."

"We should have guessed," Lars said. "Well, that's it."

"What's wrong?" Sven said, turning around. "Oh. Security."

"Yeah." Lars shook his head. "We'll never get the guns through those metal detectors."

"We must," Sven said.

Their father was delusional.

"Not through," Gustav said. "Around. This way."

"Where to?" Lars asked.

"We'll go in the back way," Gustav said. "Where all those guys in the striped shirts waited. There weren't any metal detectors back there."

"But the big security men stopped us," Lars said. "We'll never get through."

"They'll be gone by now," Sven said confidently. "They're working the doors. And if they aren't gone, one of you will have to create a diversion."

A diversion? And how were they supposed to do that? Lars followed them, feeling skeptical. But anything to get his illegal-gun-toting brother and father out of the lobby with all the thousands of trained military personnel.

They got nowhere. This other side of the auditorium was laid out differently, and it was confusing. Gustav yanked open several doors that led only to service hallways, supply closets, or smaller meeting rooms. No matter where they turned, they couldn't seem to find their way back to the rear of the auditorium.

"Let's go back and turn the other way." Sven sounded frantic and harassed. "Probably the translator is gone by now."

"No!" Gustav pulled open another door.

Inside a narrow hallway staging area, waiters wearing white coats guarded a line of catering carts heaped high with food. They all turned around and stared at Gustav when he opened the door.

Lars glanced at the cart nearest him. Huge mounds of steak tartare, bowls of onions and gherkins, and piles of rye bread crowded this table. On the next cart, he could see platters of meat balls, chicken wings, and spare ribs. His stomach growled.

The waiter nearest him made a shooing gesture and then turned back to face forward, straightening his tie.

"Let's walk in with these guys," Lars said. "This food has to be going to the military conference, right? I think this is the kitchen over here, and the auditorium is on the other side of that door at the end."

The door to the left burst open, and a man wearing a black coat instead of a white one came out with a clipboard. He yelled when he saw the Eklunds, waved his arms, and pointed to the exit. Lars didn't understand the English, but comprehending what he meant wasn't difficult. Choices included "Who are you?" and "What do you want?" and "Get out of here, you dumbasses!"

Whatever it was, Lars knew that it was time to go. He turned to his father.

"We should—" he started.

A second line of wheeled catering carts nudged through the kitchen door on the left. Waiters jumped to attention, maneuvering the carts through the door, past the carts already taking up most of the space in the staging area.

No one was looking at them.

Without hesitation, Sven whipped out his gun and thrust it into the pile of steak tartare on the table nearest him. Gustav did the same. Lars, grimacing in disgust, was terrified that one of the waiters had seen or heard something.

Someone had.

"Hey!" the waiter yelled.

Lars could understand that, at least. The rest of what he said, Lars had no clue about. Even so, the waiter's intent was unmistakable, although maybe all he saw was three hungry visitors patting the globs of chopped pink beef with slices of rye bread.

"Let's go," Lars said, happy in a grim way that they'd managed to cover up the guns.

"Now we must hurry through security to retrieve the guns," Sven said. They dashed down the back hallways of the convention center and joined the dozens of military personnel still going through security at the front of the auditorium.

Lars went through first and headed to the side, where the catering carts were just entering the auditorium. In seconds Gustav and Sven had joined him.

"There," Gustav said. "The last one."

Lars nodded. Even from many yards away, he could see that the mound of steak tartare was misshapen. Evidently the food was intended for later, or possibly a break in the program, because the lights dimmed as the waiters lined up the tables and checked the alignment of the platters. Then they all hustled out.

"Now," Gustav said.

They dashed forward, Lars intent on getting to that last table before anyone else did. He glanced around. The audience had seen the catering tables, and a small trickle of interested persons, gaining numbers by the second, headed to the wheeled carts.

"Grab the guns fast," Lars hissed to Gustav and, taking his father by the arm, stood so they blocked access to the meat on the last table. Gustav plunged both hands deep into the glistening beef, the muscles clenching in his forearms as he grabbed the weapons and pulled them out of the pile. Chunks of fatty meat fell to the table and floor. Gustav stuffed the guns into his pockets.

"Excuse me!" said a tall, impatient man as he pushed them aside to get to the table.

Lars got the gist and pulled Gustav away from the catering cart.

"Now what?" he whispered. "Will the guns even fire now that they're coated in beef fat?"

"I don't see why not," Gustav said. "The fat didn't have a chance to penetrate anything."

As the lights dimmed to full dark and the lights on the stage came up, Sven led the way up the side aisle.

"Let's take a seat up front," he said, positioning them near a short flight of stairs that led up to the stage. "This spot is perfect. When the secretary comes out to speak, we go up the stairs and kidnap her from there."

Lars stared at his father. He wanted to kidnap the secretary of state right in front of everyone?

Father was deranged. He had to be. It was the only explanation.

"Father," Lars said. "There are too many people here, all of

271

them trained military. We can't possibly succeed here. Out in the open like this."

"We will," Sven said. "Or die trying. We will not shame our ancestors."

Lars didn't see how dying on the stage of a Las Vegas convention center auditorium in front of the army and a band of Elvis impersonators would bring honor to the ancestors, either. Maybe he could talk some sense into Gustav.

"You have to see this won't work," he whispered in Swedish, a language their father even now wasn't fluent in.

"It is Father's decision," Gustav said. "If he says it will work, it will work."

Lars shook his head. In a pig's ear, it would work. But he'd let this go for so long, and Father and Gustav were so determined. What could he do now?

Maybe the translator could help somehow. She could call the cops and explain everything, at least.

He glanced around, trying to find her in the crowd, but didn't see her. You'd think a woman would stand out, especially one who wore a blue skirt with a dog on it or bright red slacks, but no.

"Excuse me," he said to Sven. "I have to use the rest room."

Sven stared at his son in astonishment. "*Now?*"

"Yes, now." He stood up and sped back down the aisle. Maybe it wasn't too late to stop this madness.

But once out in the lobby, he didn't see her. Would the hotel's hospitality captain, the woman who spoke Korean, be able to help? The hotel that adjoined the convention center was probably a full city block away, given the size of these buildings. Was it worth running down there to find out?

Lars stood for a moment in the center of the lobby, torn by indecision. And then from inside the auditorium, someone pulled the doors shut and he heard the strains of an old Elvis tune drift through.

The program was starting. That meant that the secretary was probably backstage now, or on her way.

He wouldn't have time to run down to the hotel to find the Korean-speaking hospitality captain.

Should he call the cops himself? Alert hotel security? Talk to the guys at the security checkpoint at the doors? What could he say to any of them that they would understand?

If the secretary was backstage, his father and brother were getting ready to make their move. Could he let them do that alone? Take those consequences alone?

No. He couldn't. Not when there was still a small chance that he could stop them from doing whatever stupid thing they had in mind.

Lars opened the door to find Gustav and his father, and the strains of "Jailhouse Rock" boomed out of the auditorium, almost knocking him flat.

He could only hope that a real-life jailhouse wasn't in store for them.

Chapter 22

Jailhouse Rock" had finished up by the time Phoebe and Tony emerged from the backstage hallway into the lobby. The hotel security guards had seen Korean-looking guys who didn't seem to speak English and had steered them back up front. That had to be the Eklunds, but the guards didn't know what had happened to them after that.

Phoebe's phone rang, and she checked the display. *Chase.* Relief and worry shot through her. "Hey."

"Phoebe, where are you? What's happening?"

"I can't explain it all now. The Eklunds left the rally, and—"

"I know all that. Can't you wait for the cops?"

Phoebe heard the screech of tires in the background. He must be on the racetrack.

"Tony's with me," she said. "The cops are coming. And the FBI. And SWAT. We should have backup soon." She wished he were here at the convention center, being calm. It would be nice to have somebody besides Tony, who kept rolling his eyes like a wild horse about to bolt.

But Chase had the rally, his business, and his customers to take care of, and she couldn't ask him to do something he thought was both stupid and dangerous.

"*Cher.* I'm on my way. I'll be there soon. Don't do anything that'll get you killed, okay? Just…be careful."

"Okay," she said, her throat suddenly thick. "Thank you."

"That was Coach?" Tony asked, scanning the lobby, which was now nearly empty. "Is he coming? What's his plan?"

Phoebe sighed. "I don't know. He plays football, though, right? Maybe he plans to tackle them. Except, you know, bad knee."

Tony stared at her. "He was the *quarterback*. Quarterbacks don't tackle people. Although he tackled me once."

"See? You never know. Okay, let's focus."

"Right. The Eklunds. Where could they have gone?"

"They must be in the auditorium," Phoebe said. "They're not in the back, they're not in the lobby. They have to get close to the secretary. What are their other options?"

"Should we pull the fire alarm? Get the security guards?"

Phoebe shook her head. "Law enforcement is on the way. I don't want to lose them in the crush of people exiting the building."

"It would save the secretary, though. Probably."

"But not solve our problem." Phoebe took a deep breath. "I'm going inside the auditorium, see if I can find them."

"And then what?"

"I don't know. Talk them out of doing whatever they're planning to do."

"What do you want me to do?"

"Until the cops come, see if you can find somebody here to lock down the building. Conference security didn't listen to me on the phone, but maybe now they will."

She dashed over to the auditorium doors and slipped inside the darkened hall. Onstage, forty Elvis impersonators were finishing "All Shook Up." She didn't know how long they were supposed to perform—Harry said he had a solo, and she and Tony had already heard "Jailhouse Rock" from backstage—but if they sang two or three more songs, that gave her less than ten minutes to find the Eklunds and stop whatever they planned to do.

She walked down the darkened center aisle, searching the long rows for the Eklunds. Her progress was painfully slow. By the time the singers finished "All Shook Up" and launched into "In the Ghetto," she was only two-thirds of the way down the aisle, and her palms—and everything else—were sweating from anxiety.

"In the Ghetto" was Harry's solo, and she glanced up briefly to see him in a white jumpsuit decorated with sequins as the other impersonators stood behind and backed him up. Then she continued down the aisle, scanning faces for the ones she was looking for. The light was better toward the stage, and as she approached it, she moved more quickly.

Harry sang the final bars of the song, but before he hit the last note, the audience started clapping. Phoebe glanced up.

The secretary of state had come out onto the stage. She stood alone, applauding the performers. As Harry held the last note, the audience jumped to its feet, whistling and clapping like crazy.

"I want to thank the Las Vegas All-Elvis Revue for their wonderful performance," the secretary said. "In addition—"

But whoever else the secretary planned to thank would remain nameless. Phoebe saw motion from the corner of her eye, and she jerked her head to see Sven and Gustav rush the stage with guns drawn; Lars, who grabbed for Sven's sleeve, followed.

Oh, no. No, no, no, no, no.

Phoebe dashed after them.

The Eklunds moved so quickly that security was taken by surprise. In those first seconds, whoever was supposed to guard the secretary must have thought that overenthusiastic audience members had rushed the stage in their excitement. The audience, too, was transfixed.

The Eklunds pointed their guns at the secretary, who raised her hands in the air. The secretary's security detail, who'd been standing in the wings, dashed out and pointed their weapons at the Eklunds, and four Secret Service agents jumped onto the stage, their guns also pointed at the Eklunds. The forty Elvis impersonators crowded to the side.

"No! Stop!" Phoebe shouted, rushing up the stairs to the stage.

Two of the agents whirled around, pointing their guns at her.

Phoebe threw her hands up. This was what happened when you got Secret Service involved in the protection detail. Mistakes.

"Federal agent! Don't shoot! They don't speak English! I'm their translator!"

"ID!" one of the agents said.

"CIA," Phoebe said. "On leave. Contact Greg Peeling, assistant second deputy department director. He's aware of this situation and in touch with the FBI. Check your dailies! There's an alert."

One of the agents lowered his weapon and fished his phone out of his pocket. Everybody paused while he thumbed through it. Stopped to read. "Shit."

"They don't speak English," Phoebe said again. "I'm the translator."

Phoebe didn't turn her head to look at the secretary. "Madam Secretary, we're all focused on getting you out of here safely, so I'd like to request that the members of the audience don't try to play hero. In fact, maybe everyone in the audience could file out quietly. That's probably best."

She waited for a few seconds, and judging from the rustling she heard from the darkened auditorium, some people probably did leave. She didn't turn around to check. Those who were still here were probably taking selfies of themselves in the standoff.

"Okay," she said. "I'm going to talk to the Eklunds now, see if they'll tell me what they think the possible outcomes are here."

Phoebe turned to the Swedish-Koreans. "We're in a spot of trouble here," she said, switching to Korean. "Can you guys tell me what your plan is? And how we're all getting out of here without anybody getting hurt?"

Lars had been shocked when Phoebe came rushing up the steps to the stage. What did she think she was doing? But of course they needed her, because they didn't speak English, and as far as he knew, the secretary of state didn't speak Korean. Or even Swedish. So making demands of her would be... Tricky would be the polite way to put it. *Impossible* was more likely.

This is what happened when you didn't have a plan. On the upside, no one had been shot yet.

"There is no plan," he told her, trying not to sound bitter. "There used to be a plan, sort of, but it went to hell when we couldn't use the truck."

"Shut up," Gustav said.

"We were going to—" Lars said, ignoring him.

And then he told Phoebe everything from the beginning, back from when they were still in Sweden, to how they planned and then canceled the Empire State Building kidnapping, and why they were on the stage today.

Chase streaked into the convention center driveway, swerved around three bright yellow Venture Automotive sports cars with cones on the roofs, the support car, and an Indian-themed food truck that were parked at the curb, and jerked to a halt. He jumped out of the car, not waiting for the women, but he heard the doors open and Trouble, at least, bounded from the car. He couldn't afford to wait. Phoebe was in there, doing God knows what with terrorists.

"Hey!" the valet parking guy said. *"You can't park here!"*

"CIA!" Chase said, glancing back.

"No, you're not," the parking guy whined. "Not everybody can be in the CIA. I'm so getting into trouble for this." Then he recognized Chase. "Holy crap! You're Chase Bonaventure!"

"Yes, I am. And there's a national security emergency inside right now, so—" He didn't bother to finish the sentence, just kept running until he was in the building. Trouble barked once, and Chase glanced down, almost surprised to see the dog had followed him in.

"Sure," the parking guy said to Nattie and Kristin as they started after him. "National security. Nobody thinks to alert the fire marshals. Much less me. Why should I know what's going on around here?"

Kristin ignored him and kept going, but Nattie stopped. "It really is national security," she said. "And I'm really CIA." She pulled out her badge.

"Yeah, yeah," the valet parking guy said, waving the ID away. "Seen 'em all already. Go ahead. What do I care? It's just a job. Who am I to argue with national security? Go."

"Thank you." Nattie beamed at him and then dashed inside after Chase and Kristin.

Inside, Chase found Sanjay and met Uncle Boo-Boo and Brenda, who was wearing a bright sundress and astonishingly high heels. A nonchalant teenager was wearing pants that needed a belt.

"Sanjay, Uncle Boo-Boo, Brenda Renfrew—Phoebe's mom—

Kristin, and Nattie," Chase said, making brief introductions. "And the dog. Trouble."

"The police are not yet here?" Uncle Boo-Boo said. "What could be keeping them? We beat them here in a *food truck*. Although my nephew Sanjay drove like a crazed dervish, so that must be taken into account. Still, do I not pay my taxes?"

"I wish I had my tire iron," Sanjay said. "Or at least the pink umbrella. But they are in my taxi."

"Where's Phoebe?" Nattie said.

Kristin zipped over to the closed auditorium doors and eased one open. Then she dashed back to Chase.

"There's a standoff on stage," she reported. "It looks like Secret Service and the Eklunds at the O.K. Corral, with Phoebe holding down no-man's-land in the middle."

"Shit," Chase said. He saw a security guard hovering near the door and strode over.

"Jesus, Mary, and Joseph," the guard said. "You're *Chase Bonaventure.*"

"Yes, and I have to get backstage. Which way?"

The guard pointed. Chase banged through the door that led to a service hallway and looked left. He saw another door and yanked it open. A short flight of stairs led up, and there from the wing, he could see onto the stage. Four guys had weapons pointed at something out of his range of view.

Phoebe.

One of the agents turned and pointed his weapon at him.

"Whoa," Chase said, coming to a halt, putting out his hands. "Chase Bonaventure, CEO of Venture Automotive. I know these people. I can talk to them."

"Chase!" said Phoebe.

"Let him in," said a woman's voice, not Phoebe.

Chase came onto the stage to a scene that sent a cold wave of fear down his spine. Four agents had their weapons trained on Phoebe, who stood before the Eklunds. The Eklunds had their guns trained on the secretary and would have to shoot through Phoebe to hit their target.

"Phoebe," he said. *"Cher.* What's your plan here?"

"Well, I'd *like* everybody to put down their guns and talk

like civilized people, but nobody wants to."

"Maybe you could step aside."

"I can't," she said. "Somebody might shoot the secretary. Or the Eklunds. I think as long as I'm standing here between them, the chances of nobody shooting anybody are marginally better."

"Okay," Chase said. "Okay. Listen, everybody. I'm going to walk over and stand next to Phoebe. Nobody shoot, okay? Phoebe, tell the Eklunds."

Phoebe said something in Korean, and Chase edged across the stage to stand next to her.

"Seriously," he said when he got there, his mouth dry. "When we get out of here, we have to talk. This kind of thing has to stop."

Trouble barked and bounded on stage, and two agents whirled around, pointing their guns at him.

"Don't shoot my dog!" Phoebe shrieked. "He doesn't bite! He won't hurt anybody!"

"Phoebe?" Kristin charged out on stage.

The agents raised their guns.

"Crap! Don't shoot. Kristin Seiler. I'm with Chase and Phoebe."

"Hello?" Nattie edged out onto the stage, easing Kristin aside. "Nattie Wilkinson. Representing—ah, federal—the government."

"CIA." Kristin glanced over. "She's CIA."

"Yeah, we don't like to tell everybody," Nattie said.

"*Phoebe* tells everybody," Kristin said.

"She shouldn't, though."

"Holy crap," one of the agents said, looking hard at Chase. "You really *are* Chase Bonaventure."

"Yes," Chase said. "I really am. If I gave you an autographed jersey and a car and an all-expenses-paid weekend at my house, including an outdoor barbecue with members of the Rattlesnakes starting lineup, would you put down your weapon? That goes for all of you."

Two of the agents lowered their weapons.

"Agents!" snapped the third agent, and they raised their guns again.

"Sorry," one of them said. "Maybe—"

"Guns have to be lowered," Chase said. "Otherwise no weekend."

"Sounds like fun, though," the secretary said.

"You're welcome anytime, ma'am," Chase said.

"Nice play," Phoebe said approvingly under her breath. "Almost worked."

Chase's eyes were somber. "We have to think of something that *does* work."

Trouble trotted over to Gustav and stuck his nose into his crotch, sniffing and licking the fabric.

"Trouble!" Phoebe said. "That's very bad manners."

"I thought dogs did that only to women," Kristin said.

"What is this damn dog doing?" Gustav waved his gun at Trouble's head.

"Don't hurt him!" Phoebe said.

"You stuck the guns in your pocket," Lars said to Gustav.

"What?" Phoebe swiveled to look at him.

"Gustav," Lars explained with a grin. "We hid the guns in the steak tartare refreshments. Then Gustav stuck the guns in his pocket. That's what the dog smells. All that raw meat."

"Get him off me!" Gustav said, shoving at Trouble.

"Trouble, come here!" Phoebe said sharply. "Thanks for explaining that, Lars. Good to know."

At Phoebe's stern tone, the dog whined but went to sit next to her, looking anxiously back at Gustav.

"I'll get you a hamburger when we get home," Phoebe said, scratching his ears. "Forget about him now."

"What was that all about?" Chase asked.

"Steak tartare," Phoebe said. "Evidently that's how the weapons were smuggled past security."

"I'd wondered about that," the secretary said.

"Where's Phoebe?" came Brenda's voice offstage. "Through here?"

"You brought my *mother*?" Phoebe said, turning to Chase. "I can't believe you brought my *mother*."

"I had nothing to do with it," Chase said. "She came with Sanjay and Uncle Boo-Boo."

"Sanjay and Uncle Boo-Boo are here?"

"Somewhere."

Brenda teetered onstage in her ridiculous heels.

"Hi," Brenda said to the agents holding the guns. She turned to face the audience, shielding her eyes from the bright stage lights with one hand held to her forehead. She gave a little finger wave out to the crowd. "Hi," she said again, louder for their benefit. Then she turned back to the stage.

"What's going on here?" she asked of no one in particular.

"Think it's a bit self-explanatory, Mom," Phoebe said through gritted teeth. "Maybe you should get off the stage before you get hurt."

Brenda leaned into the nearest agent. "That's my daughter. She works for the CIA. I'm so proud of her. She got to college all on her own."

"Mom."

"Well, it's the truth."

"Hold on a second," Phoebe said. "I want to catch the Eklunds up on who everybody is." She turned around and spoke rapidly, pointing out Brenda, who gave them a little wave.

"Hi," she said again.

They all stared back. Lars gave a little finger wave. Gustav jabbed him in the ribs with his elbow. His gun swung wildly toward the ceiling and he fired a shot.

Phoebe, Chase, Brenda, Nattie, Kristin, the secretary, the Eklunds, and the Elvis impersonators—everyone except the agents—hit the floor. All the agents sighted down their weapons.

"Don't shoot!" Phoebe shouted. "It was an accident! Is everybody okay?"

Chase glared at Gustav. How careless could one idiotic Swedish-Korean terrorist be?

"Do you want to get us all killed out here?" he snapped. "Tell me why I should try to save your stupid ass!"

Phoebe cleared her throat. "Mr. Bonaventure says, please don't shoot," she told Gustav.

Gustav pointed the weapon in her face. "You do what I say!"

Chase knocked the gun aside. "Don't threaten her!"

Gustav pointed the gun at Chase. "I could kill you, too!"

"For heaven's sake, Gustav, killing us won't get what you

want!" Phoebe said in Korean. She glanced at Chase.

"How did you know what he was saying?" she asked. "He's speaking Korean."

Chase radiated fury. "I don't have to speak Korean to know what he's saying when he points a gun in your face."

"I fail to see what I could contribute to the many wiser people already on the stage," came another voice from backstage. "More persons in the line of fire can only be increasing the danger for everyone."

"*Crap*," Phoebe said. "There's Sanjay. I'm getting up now." She said something in Korean and then eased to her feet, brushing off her skirt.

"He and Uncle Boo-Boo came from the race in their food truck," Chase said, also standing. "With Brenda. And Justin."

"Who's Justin?" Phoebe asked just as Sanjay exploded onto the stage, staggering from a push. Two of the agents whirled and pointed their weapons at him.

"Don't shoot!" Sanjay shrieked. "I am merely a lowly taxi-cab driver!"

"Nobody's shooting." Phoebe glared at the agents. "That's Sanjay Agarwal, and he really does drive a taxi."

Sanjay righted himself, looking terrified. "I do not like having weapons pointed at me. I have quite enough of that in the taxicab."

"Stand over there," one of the agents said. "Next to those guys." He waved his weapon in Phoebe and Chase's direction.

"Very well. I will go because you are insisting." Sanjay eased over to their side of the stage and standing next to Phoebe. "Although this side looks to be seriously underrepresented in terms of weaponry."

"Where did Mr. Bonaventure go?" said another voice off-stage. "This way?"

"Uncle Boo-Boo," Chase said. "I met him out in the lobby. I wonder how he got that name?"

"So everybody, including my dog, is here, except for the cops?" Phoebe asked. "When are the cops coming?"

"Hey," said one of the Secret Service agents. "We're here. We're cops."

"Yeah, okay." She turned back to Chase and rolled her eyes. "I'm worried that these guys will get tired holding up these big guns and one of them will go off by accident."

"We won't get tired," one of the agents with better hearing said.

Phoebe sighed. "Sven Eklund was in the hospital earlier this week with a concussion, and I think he might like to sit down. Could somebody please get him a chair?"

"I'll get it," came from the side.

"Harry? Is that you? Would you mind? Thank you."

Phoebe turned around again and told the Eklunds where Harry was going. A door slammed and footsteps receded. Then, seconds later, the footsteps came back.

"I'm back," Harry announced as he eased open the stage door. "Nobody shoot."

Resplendent in his white jumpsuit covered with sequins, he walked onto the stage as gingerly as if he were walking across a minefield and handed the folding chair to Phoebe.

"Think of something to get us out of here," he said to her in a low voice.

"I was hoping you'd blind everybody with the power of sparkle. But that didn't work."

She opened the folding chair and edged closer to the Eklunds, reaching out to Sven. The Secret Service agents sighted along their guns.

Gustav stuck his handgun in her side. "Don't try anything."

"I'm just giving your father a chair. We'll all get killed if you shoot me."

Sven took the chair and sat down. Gustav eased back. The Secret Service marginally relaxed. Phoebe took a deep breath, reaching out for Chase's hand.

"Where the *hell* are the cops?" Chase said, squeezing her fingers. "Something is bound to go wrong with everybody pointing guns all over the damn place."

"I'm starting to think the cops won't be any help."

Just then the back door to the auditorium banged open and a crowd of black-clad soldiers swarmed into the darkened space, moving forward at a trot through the aisles toward the stage, pointing their weapons from side to side. At the same time, from the stage wings, local police and FBI stormed onto the stage and pointed their guns at the Eklunds. A collective gasp went up from the audience.

"About time." Chase glared.

"Getting crowded up here." Sanjay glanced around.

"It's just like the movies!" Uncle Boo-Boo said.

"Rudy at the bar will never believe this!" Brenda said.

"I don't think more guns will fix our problem," Phoebe said. "Hello, Detective Greenaway."

"Jesus Christ, Phoebe, this is a terrible mess."

"It's not my fault!" Phoebe said. "I've been trying to warn all of you for days now about the Eklunds, and nobody—"

From behind her, she heard the snick of a handgun as Gustav heard his name. Even in English, he could recognize that. In response, the Secret Service, FBI, and the SWAT team all raised their weapons.

"Don't shoot!" Greenaway ordered.

"Gustav already tried to kill me once," Phoebe said, sounding irritated. "I'm getting to the point where if somebody took him out, I wouldn't care that much."

"There'd be too much collateral damage." Chase gestured toward the audience.

"No lie," Greenaway said.

"Like me," Sanjay said.

"And me," Harry said.

"What about *me*?" Brenda said.

"*Anyway*." Phoebe said. "Here's what you missed, Detective. Lars said that after the Empire State Building plan went south, they decided to try again. So they followed the secretary when she came out here for this conference. That's as far as we got. But then more people got on stage, and the story got interrupted."

"They were behind the Empire State Building hullabaloo?" Greenaway asked. "There really was a credible threat?"

"Yes, but it was about the secretary, not the building," Phoebe said. "Let me ask them a couple of questions."

She turned around, focusing on Sven. "You have to realize this situation isn't good, but the secretary of state is giving you her full attention and she doesn't want anybody to get hurt," she said. "Please tell us your plan. Why did you want to kill the secretary of state?"

"We did not wish to hurt her!" Sven said, looking shocked. "We wish to *speak* to her! To ask—demand—that she help us."

"Really? Because I'm not sure this is the best way to go about getting a favor. What did you want to talk to her about?"

"My father is a prisoner in North Korea." He told the whole story, stopping to let Phoebe translate for the others. He talked about how at great cost, danger, and personal sacrifice, his father sneaked him across the border, bringing out family members one by one. Except he was found out. Disgraced. And now sick and— Sven feared—imprisoned and close to death. How no one in their own Swedish government could help them.

The stage had grown silent as Sven spoke.

"And now?" Phoebe asked quietly. "What do you want the secretary to do for you?"

"We want her to talk to the supreme leader of North Korea," Sven said. "We want her to negotiate the release of our esteemed ancestor. Or perhaps do a prisoner exchange. For humanitarian reasons. She has the power. She could set him free."

"The truck was to be our conference room," Gustav interrupted, his voice loud in the silence of the auditorium. "It has a couch and chairs. Water. We could have kept her there until she agreed!"

Phoebe cleared her throat, wondering if she should translate that last part.

"What did he say?" the secretary asked.

"They'd outfitted a truck with chairs and refreshments where they planned to meet with you," Phoebe said. "They'd made it as comfortable as possible."

"They don't understand diplomatic channels," the secretary said. "The United States doesn't have diplomatic relations with North Korea. But even if we did, I couldn't negotiate for Swedish citizens. They have to ask their own government for that. And according to what the senior Mr. Eklund said, they've exhausted their Swedish diplomatic appeals. In fact, the official link between the United States and North Korea is through Sweden. Even if I agreed, which I can't, I'd still be talking to Sweden."

"What do you want me to tell them?" Phoebe asked.

"Tell them the United States doesn't have diplomatic relations with North Korea. It's impossible for me to negotiate for them."

"Do we have any kind of solution?" Phoebe asked. "I'm afraid of the outcome with all these guns around."

"They have to surrender," the secretary said.

"No disrespect, ma'am, but I don't see that happening," Nattie said, eying the weapons.

"We'll make them surrender," FBI Special Agent Picone said.

"That's fine for you to say," Phoebe said, angry and upset. "You're wearing a vest. There's a lot of people standing on this stage who aren't."

"You didn't have to stand in the middle," Picone said. "Plus, I'm still not sure you're not in on it."

"Oh, for Pete's sake." Phoebe rolled her eyes.

"Are you sure he's not Secret Service?" Nattie asked. "He's dumb enough."

"Hey!" Picone and the Secret Service agents said.

"Hey yourself," Harry said. "We've got forty performers up here who aren't in on it, whatever you're trying to accuse Phoebe of. And we won't take kindly to being killed by the FBI and SWAT. Can't you people solve a problem without pointing a gun at it?"

"What is everybody saying?" Lars whispered to Phoebe in Korean.

"Ah, jurisdictional disputes," Phoebe whispered back. "Bureaucratic hot air."

"I would bet you on my honor that the reason the FBI was so late in getting here is because they were getting out their vests and their whatnot," Sanjay said. "Radios and sniper rifles and so on. We got here before they did, and we got here in a food truck."

"Perhaps our tax dollars should now be going to food trucks as a matter of homeland security, rather than to equip an agency that takes its leisure in responding to national security emergencies," Uncle Boo-boo said.

"*Hey!*" the Secret Service and all the FBI agents said.

"Hey," Phoebe said. "Can we all focus on our real problem?"

"By all means," the secretary said.

"The problem is that the Eklunds have to put down their weapons right now!" Agent Picone said.

"I believe *everybody* should put down their weapons right now," Sanjay said.

"Hear, hear!" Uncle Boo-Boo said.

"We're not putting down our weapons," Agent Picone said.

"I have an idea," Chase said.

Everyone on the stage turned their head.

"Magic," Phoebe murmured. "Abracadabra."

"*What is happening?*" Lars whispered.

"Chase has an idea to get us out of this mess," Phoebe whispered back. "You know he's a big sports star, right? When sports stars talk, everybody listens. They're like gods in America."

"What's your idea, Mr. Bonaventure?" the secretary asked. "Believe me, nothing is out of bounds."

"Dennis Rodman."

"Dennis Rodman?" Phoebe asked. "Who's Dennis Rodman?"

"Dennis Rodman!" Sanjay grinned.

"Dennis Rodman," the secretary said. "Hmmm."

"What do you think?" Chase focused on the secretary.

"It's beyond strange," the secretary said. "And, of course, there's no telling what the North Koreans will do. Or Dennis Rodman, either, for that matter. But—I think we should consider it."

"Who's Dennis Rodman?" Phoebe asked again.

"Retired professional ballplayer." Chase said. "Who has, ah, an eclectic personal style. Dated Madonna briefly. Goes to North Korea, plays exhibition games there, and—more to the point—gets meetings with the supreme leader."

"Holy cow," Phoebe said. "That's brilliant. Call him right now."

"I don't know him *personally*," Chase said. "He played basketball."

"Basketball, football, yada, yada. You can get him on the phone. I mean, you're *Chase Bonaventure*."

"Well, yeah, I could probably find him pretty quick."

"Okay! What do you think, ma'am?"

The secretary took in all the people on the stage and all the weapons. She nodded. "Call him."

"Great!" Phoebe sighed in relief. "Then we can all go home."

"Wait one second," Picone said. "These guys are still terrorists. They're still going to prison. And we're still throwing away the key."

"Could we do one thing at a time here?" Phoebe asked. "Get Sven Eklund's dad out of North Korea. That seems like a good thing to do regardless. What do you think, Madam Secretary?"

"By all means, make the call," the secretary said, "if it gets us out of this standoff."

"Yes, ma'am." Chase, looking amused, took his phone out of his pocket, tapped something into it, glanced at the result, and tapped out a number.

"Hello," Chase said into the phone. "Mr. Prince? Darren Prince? This is Chase Bonaventure, recently of the Las Vegas Rattlesnakes. How are you today?"

He nodded to the secretary.

"No, no, I'm not seeking representation, thank you for asking. Yes, the team's looking good. Coaches and players are working hard. I have an extremely urgent matter for you. I need to reach Dennis Rodman immediately. Can you put me in touch?"

Phoebe held her breath, waiting for the answer.

"It's a matter of national security. I have the secretary of state standing here with me right now. ... No, it's not a joke. I really need the number."

A second later, Chase made a writing gesture in the air. Uncle Boo-Boo pulled a small notebook from his breast pocket and handed it over. Chase pulled out the pen and wrote the number on one of Uncle Boo-Boo's business cards.

"Thank you, Mr. Prince," Chase said, hanging up.

"You got the number," Phoebe said.

"Trying it now." Chase glanced at the number on the business card. And a second later, Phoebe saw him smile. *Success.*

"Dennis, this is Chase Bonaventure, Las Vegas Rattlesnakes.

Your agent gave me your number. Listen, I need your help on an extremely urgent matter of national security. Would you be willing to go to North Korea on behalf of the United States and negotiate the release of an elderly man who is possibly a prisoner? … No, it's not a joke. … I know the secretary was mad at you the last time you went, but you shot your mouth off, what can you expect? This time she's fully on board. I have her standing with me right now. … Yes. Seriously."

He held out the phone to the secretary. "He wants to talk to you."

She took the phone. "Mr. Rodman? … Yes, I wasn't happy about your remarks at your exhibition game, but as Mr. Bonaventure told you, I'm in an extremely urgent situation right now, and we think the best way through this is if you would speak to the supreme leader through your informal channels. … At your earliest convenience. Tomorrow is not too soon, if it can be arranged. … Excellent. Thank you. I'll put you in touch with my assistant to work out the details. I understand you've talked before. … Yes. … Goodbye."

She disconnected and turned to the crowd. "He agreed," she said, breaking into a smile.

Everybody cheered.

"I'll tell the Eklunds." Phoebe turned around.

"Great news," she told them. "We've got a negotiator for your father. Have you ever heard of Dennis Rodman?"

"I have!" Lars said. "He would be even better than the secretary because he already knows the supreme leader."

"Great," Phoebe said. "Will you put your guns down now?"

"As soon as we get it in writing," Lars said.

"You do not speak for us!" Gustav said, turning to his brother, brandishing his weapon.

The SWAT team and FBI trained their weapons on Gustav.

Sven reached out and took his elder son's hand. "It's over now. We got what we came for. Put down the gun." He turned to Phoebe. "Although I do want the secretary's assurances in writing. That idea from Lars is a good one. I trust you to read it to us correctly."

"I will," Phoebe said.

Uncle Boo-Boo whipped out a boilerplate sales agreement, turned it to the blank side, and handed it to the secretary. She wrote a quick paragraph and signed it, Phoebe translated, and then the Eklunds put down their guns and SWAT swarmed the three Swedish-Korean investors, handcuffing them and leading them off the stage.

The standoff was over.

Chapter 23

Two days later, Phoebe packed her roller bag and box of books as Chase leaned against the doorframe and watched. She should feel happy. Everything had turned out exactly the way she'd wanted. The CIA had reinstated her. Greg had even flown out to Vegas to take credit for capturing the Eklunds. The secretary was fine and back in Washington, Dennis Rodman was in North Korea talking to the supreme leader, and Chase had hired both Dean Alvarez and Tiffany Bailor to defend the Eklunds.

Even better, Midnight Sun had decided to fund Venture Automotive up to one hundred million dollars.

Nothing could have turned out better. So why was she so depressed?

"You'll take care of Trouble." She roughed up the dog's coat, not looking up.

"Every day," he said. "He'll be fine. He likes my yard. And I'll take him to the plant. He fits right in over there."

"I'll miss him."

"Sure, but he's better off here."

Phoebe swallowed. Her throat felt too thick to talk and tears threatened. "I'm abandoning him." She buried her face in his fur.

Trouble, sensing something bad, whined and bumped Phoebe's leg.

"You're gifting him to me," Chase said. "He likes me better, anyway."

Phoebe snorted, coughing on her tears.

"We bonded," Chase said. "It's a guy thing."

"You be good for Chase." She rubbed the dog's head, not looking at the man she was leaving behind.

"*Cher.*"

Phoebe glanced up to see Chase uncoil from the doorway and enter the room. His walk, so graceful and powerful, was mesmerizing, and as she watched, he came to where she stood by the bed. He reached out and stroked her cheek, tucking a stray hair behind her ear. His touch was so gentle, Phoebe's insides cracked and shattered.

"You don't have to go," he said, his voice barely a warm breath against her skin, his eyes dark and clouded.

Barely breathing, she saw the desire—and maybe yearning, she wasn't sure—in his still face.

"I've worked so hard for this," she whispered, feeling awful as she said it. "The CIA is my shot. My ticket. I *can't* not go."

His fingers traced around her ear to the nape of her neck. "There are good jobs here."

She shook her head and leaned into his touch, tearing her eyes away. Longing to get more of him while she could, while he was standing here, wanting her and willing her to stay. "I can't be like my mom."

His hand traced that invisible pattern against her skin, weakening her resolve. His voice hardened, just a little. "You think if you stayed here, with me, that you'd be like her, chasing any guy who made promises."

That was exactly what she thought. She bit her lip, the ache in her bones so deep she thought she might fall.

"*Cher.* You don't want to try to figure out what we have here?"

"We've known each other only two weeks!"

"All the more reason. We haven't played this out. Did nothing in the past two weeks feel real to you?"

She closed her eyes. What she'd shared with Chase had *felt* real, but that didn't mean it *was* real. Brenda thought every guy was her true chance at happiness, and it never was. How could she know she wasn't exactly like her mother? Two weeks was *nothing*. She couldn't give up all those years of hard work and all her plans after knowing a guy only *two weeks*.

No matter how he made her feel.

Because feelings—yearning, wanting, aching feelings—didn't last. They changed. They evaporated. She didn't have to look further than her own mother to know that was true.

"I have to go."

"I'll do you a favor." He stepped closer, getting into her space. "That's what you promised me, back when you found this mangy dog and talked me into keeping him. You said you'd do me a favor. Now I'm calling it in."

She didn't want to meet his eyes.

"What do you mean?"

"You promised me a favor. *Any* favor. And this is what I want: I want you to stay. Stay six months. Then, if you think you're wasting your time, go back to the CIA. After this past week, they'll keep the job open for you."

She was tempted. But six months. She wasn't sure she could find a decent job in six months. What could she do for money? She couldn't accept Chase's charity. And what would she know after six months? Not much more than she knew now. Not enough.

She couldn't do it.

Sorrow and loneliness seeped deep into her bones and crept into her heart, her lungs, her belly, down her arms and legs, making her limbs heavy and her head thick and dull. Even so, she knew the sorrow and guilt and pain would ease in time.

As would his feelings, whatever they were, for her.

"That won't work. And Nattie's waiting. I have to go."

She snapped her suitcase shut and dragged it off the bed. Chase picked up her box of books. They walked to the front door, Trouble bumping her legs at every step.

Every step was painful and slow, like she was going to the guillotine. With each step, her body felt like it would shatter. That pieces of it would be left behind, strewn over Chase's beautiful polished floor.

There didn't seem to be anything more to say.

Nattie waited at the front door. The taxi waited outside.

Chase caught her up in an embrace. For the last time, she held him close, felt the beating of his heart, the heat of his body, the strength of his arms.

She tore away, tears streaking her cheeks.

"Goodbye," she said, not looking at him.

Trouble barked. And then she stepped out the door and closed it behind her on the two things that she cared about more than anything else in the world.

Chapter 24

C hase couldn't believe how fast it had happened, how quickly she had gone. One minute they were on the stage with guns pointing everywhere. And then it was over. The CIA offered Phoebe her job back. And she packed her bag and left.

Just like she'd said she would. Just like he'd known she would. Except that he'd thought she wouldn't go.

He'd thought they had something. Something special.

Now it was exactly three weeks and six days since they'd stood on that stage, and he still felt numb. If anything, he felt worse each day, not better.

And the house, always too big, felt like a prison. A big, lavish prison.

She'd emailed to say she got to DC. She'd texted him that she was sleeping on Nattie's foldout sofa. And that was pretty much it. Even though he'd emailed and called, but not so often that she'd think he was stalking her. She replied sometimes, but she never said anything personal. Not one "I miss you."

He didn't know why he was so damn disappointed. And hurt. In many ways, she was right. They'd known each other for only two weeks. No time at all, really.

Still.

He missed her. He tried to forget by spending long hours at the plant and exhausting himself with rehab, working out to a pounding beat. It didn't improve his outlook.

Trouble missed her, too. He was anxious all the time, watching the doors, sleeping in the room she'd slept in.

The dog wasn't happy right now, either. He whined and then barked, prancing at the closed door to the gym. The music was probably too loud for him.

He couldn't take his frustrations out on the dog. He got up, shut off the music, and opened the door to the hallway. Trouble bounded down to the front door. Clearly he needed to go out.

The doorbell rang, and Chase peered out the window to the circular drive in front. Sanjay waved by the open door of his cab. What was he doing here?

Chase yanked open the front door, and there she was, standing on his welcome mat.

Phoebe. Smiling tentatively. That damn roller bag sagging next to her and her box of books resting on the pavement.

"Hi," she said, looking a little shy. "When you didn't answer right away, I wasn't sure you were at home."

Phoebe. She'd come back.

"I was in the gym," he said. "The music was too loud. I didn't hear you."

Trouble leaped at her, banging against her legs, and she patted him roughly.

"Easy, dog," she said. "I missed you, too."

Trouble pranced between them, tail wagging eagerly, and she straightened to meet Chase's gaze.

Then he reached out for her, relief and joy so intense he felt weak with it, and she jumped into his arms, and he breathed her in.

For many seconds, too many to count, he held her, feeling that the world had righted itself, that she was here and real, that she'd come back. She felt warm and perfect against his body, like she belonged there. Her heart pounded erratically, and while her hair still smelled of lavender, he could feel the nervous tension in her.

He raised his head from where he'd buried it in her hair. "Does Sanjay have to come in?" He let her go but kept his arm around her.

"He wanted to make sure you were home." Phoebe waved to her friend, and Chase watched the cab take off.

"I missed you." Chase grabbed the handle of her suitcase,

one arm still wrapped around her waist. "Are you here to stay?" *Will you marry me,* he wanted to ask, but was afraid to scare her off.

If you still want me, Phoebe wanted to say, but was afraid that he'd changed his mind.

"For six months," she said instead. "Like you asked. I owed you that favor. I didn't want to welsh on the deal. But mostly, I missed you, too."

Chase swung the door shut, wrapped his arms around her, and kissed her. Phoebe kissed him back, his lips warm against her skin, feeling light and dizzy and terrified with risk.

"We have to talk a little bit," Phoebe said, breathless, and broke away. "Let's sit down."

She led him to the oversized sofa that overlooked the pool.

"Okay, I'm sitting," he said. "Shoot."

"When I got back to the CIA, it wasn't the same." She sat next to him. "And I thought I wasn't being fair to them, and I wasn't being fair to us, either. So I took a six-month leave."

"So now what? What about the money you owe them?"

Phoebe laid her head against his shoulder and shook her head, enjoying the friction. "Same as before. If I don't return after the six months, I'll be broke my entire life paying that back."

Chase shrugged. "I'll pay it."

Phoebe jerked upright. "*No.* I'll figure it out."

Chase tugged her scrunchie, freeing her ponytail. "We can argue about it later." He ran his hands through her hair. "Okay, six months. What's your plan? Freelance spy?"

"Pretty close," Phoebe said, feeling tingles shoot up her arm and down to her toes. "Detective Greenaway is retiring from the police force, and he's opening a private detective agency. He said he'd hire me as a PI in training. Doesn't that sound like fun?"

"It does." He raised her hand to his lips and nipped her fingers. The electricity zipped to her lower regions. "Anything else I should know?"

"Nothing that can't wait."

They sat for a moment. Phoebe leaned against him, loose-limbed, feeling happiness steal over her heart.

Then Chase cleared his throat. "It's a good thing you showed up when you did, because my physical therapist doesn't want me to fly yet, and now I don't have to catch my flight to DC tomorrow."

Phoebe jerked upright again. "You were going to DC?"

"I was. Suitcase is in my bedroom. Go look."

"I will." Phoebe snuggled back against his chest. She felt like she was home at last. "What else did your physical therapist say?"

"She said my knee needs a lot more therapy. A *lot* more. You want to help me with that, right?"

"I do. And the sooner we get started, the sooner that knee will be feeling better."

She slipped away from the heat and strength of his encircling arm and tapped him lightly on the shoulder, feeling joy bubble up.

"Race you," she said and pelted down the long passage to Chase's room.

Chase grinned, watching her retreating figure. A woman of action. He liked that.

He ran down the hall to join her.

The adventure continues!
Turn the page to read an excerpt
and see how Phoebe and Chase are...

Skirting Disaster

Available now!

SKIRTING DISASTER

Chapter 1

Phoebe Renfrew sat at the scarred picnic table in the one-room office and hoped to high heaven that she knew what she was doing. Did she really want to be a private investigator? Two months ago she had an important job that she liked and had worked years to get. The CIA wasn't perfect, but she'd used her brain to solve problems and, she hoped, help her country. She had a regular income. She wore suits to work. She had *benefits*.

That was before. Before the CIA suspended her. Before Las Vegas.

And before Chase Bonaventure.

She looked around at the fresh paint on the walls of the tiny office, her fingers clenched under the table, and wondered if she'd snag her tights on the picnic bench. One thing was for sure: she wasn't at the CIA anymore.

"I'm glad you're here, because a case came in and I could use your help," said Dave Greenaway, the ex-cop she'd worked with when she first arrived in Vegas. Now retired from the LVPD, Dave had opened a private investigator's office so he could, as he said, accept only the cases he wanted—preferably just the boring ones. "That is, if you still want to do this. It's not too late to back out."

Did she want to back out? The CIA had lifted her suspension, so she could return to work—and a big part of her wanted to. But the CIA was back in Langley, Virginia, and Chase was here in Las Vegas, Nevada.

She had six months to make up her mind. If she stayed, she wanted employment that used her skills. And that's where Dave Greenaway came in.

"Case?" she asked, stalling for time. "You have a case already?"

"Yeah," Dave said. "From your boyfriend. Vandalism at the car factory."

"*What?* What happened? He didn't say anything about it this morning."

Dave shrugged. "That's probably because he didn't know about it then. Last night somebody went into a secured parking area out there and damaged a bunch of cars that were supposed to be part of a fancy demonstration or conference or something—"

"Oh no! Not the Cars of the Future expo?"

"That's it." Dave nodded. "See? This is helpful. You got the inside scoop on everything."

"Not quite everything," Phoebe said. "How bad is the damage?"

"Bad enough that they can't be repaired and sent to the expo. All the cars in that lot were spray-painted, pounded with something—probably a tire iron, maybe a rock—windshields and windows broken."

Phoebe closed her eyes, feeling sick. Everyone had worked for weeks getting all the new models ready for the expo five days from now. If they had nothing to take to the expo, not only was the time, money, and effort wasted, but they couldn't get reviewed by the websites and magazines, wouldn't make any sales. The company's bottom line would take a huge hit. Maybe wipe them out.

She blinked. "Wait a second," she said. "Why did Chase call you? Why not the police?"

Dave let a hint of a smile cross his impassive features. "He called me because he thought I still *was* the police. He didn't know that today was the first day of operations for Western Private Investigations. I guess his girlfriend didn't tell him that."

"Who's that?" she said. "What girlfriend? Because I'm sitting right here."

"You mean you're not dating Las Vegas's most prominent citizen?"

"Dave, you're confusing me. I thought *you* were Las Vegas's most prominent citizen."

Dave laughed. "Touché. Yeah, Bonaventure is chasing me in the popularity polls. So anyway, I told him to call the cops."

"And did he?"

"He did. They went out there and said there wasn't much they could do. He filed a report. They dusted for prints. I put in a call to a buddy in the department, and I got the impression that the evidence collection was more a courtesy than anything else. Not that they won't run the prints, but they probably won't find anything definitive. Lots of people at the plant worked on the cars, so any prints they find won't mean much. It's basically a dead end."

"So then Chase called you back, and *you* said—"

"I might not be able to find out who damaged the cars. Probably won't be able to if the cops can't. But this little episode demonstrates that Venture Automotive needs a lot more security now. They're getting to be a big operation. They got assets to protect."

Phoebe hadn't been positive that working for Dave Greenaway would be a good idea. But now that Chase's business—and his hopes and dreams—were on the line, she had to help if she could. "So where do you see me in this?"

"Basically, I need a warm body, and you're right here already," Dave said, dispelling any notion she might have had that special skills were required.

"And I'm warm." Phoebe tried not to feel deflated. "Good to know."

Greenaway flashed a grin. "If this job turns out to be bigger than some stupid-ass kids messing with Vegas's most prominent citizen, I'll probably have to hire another couple of investigators no matter what you decide to do long-term with the CIA."

"Okay." Phoebe nodded. "Stupid-ass kids, huh? You think that's who did it?"

"No," Dave said, surprising her. "But anything's possible."

"Why don't you think it's kids?"

"I went out there to look at it. The fence is nine, ten feet high, topped with razor wire. So not that easy to get over, and there's no sign that anybody did. Wire's intact, not bent, and they didn't cut through it. Gate to the street wasn't tampered with. But there's two doors from the building right out to the lot. I think somebody strolled out there, banged up the cars, went back in, punched out, and went home. Unless Bonaventure is handing out keys to all and sundry, I think it has to be an inside job."

"An inside job? Chase will freak."

"You are correct. He is, as you say, quite concerned. And that's where you have an edge. You know everybody out there."

"Well, I know *some* people. They've been hiring like crazy to ramp up production. They got all that investor money, you know."

"I do know—largely because of you, is my understanding. Okay, you won't know all the new hires, but you have a reason to be there. People will talk to you because they'll think you have an ear to the top. Which they won't be wrong about."

"You're killing me here, Dave. But I guess we'll find out if people will talk to me. Where do we start?"

"We'll take a drive out there. Check out the damage. Assess what they need for security. But before we go, there's a few things we have to get out of the way if you plan to work here, even temporarily. First is pay."

Let it be enough to retire my CIA school loan. She'd accepted three hundred thousand dollars from the agency for her college education and follow-up training. That debt would be forgiven if she worked there for six more years—but if she didn't return, she'd have to pay all the money back.

"Fifteen bucks an hour right now," Dave said. "As we grow, you'll get more. Assuming you stick around."

"Okay." Fifteen bucks an hour was about half of what she'd need to earn every year for the next thirty or forty years to pay back her school loan. It wasn't nearly enough to pay off the loan. It was barely enough to pay rent.

But hey. It was a start.

"Now, about this job," Dave said. "It isn't what you're used to. Even if this were the biggest PI agency west of the Mississippi, which it sure as hell isn't, it still isn't the CIA. You'd be giving up a lot if you quit there. And you have a lot of work ahead of you if you're serious about becoming a PI."

Phoebe nodded. "I'm not afraid of the work, and I want to give it my best shot. Are you okay with a six-month commitment? The CIA gave me that long to decide if I want to go back or not."

"Sure, that works," Dave said. "Anybody else I hired would be provisional anyway. We'll call it a probationary period. You won't need to start weapons training right away, but—"

"Weapons training?"

"Yes," Dave said, an implacable glint in his eye. "Required for the PI license."

At one time she'd used a pink collapsible umbrella for a weapon, but Dave probably wouldn't be on board with that idea.

"Weapons training." She swallowed hard. "Check."

"The CIA didn't give you weapons training?"

"No. The CIA is about intelligence gathering, not law enforcement. I'm a language analyst. We wear suits and sit in cubicle farms and read stuff. No weapons required."

"Unbelievable what the government is coming to. Okay. Moving on. You might need to do surveillance for this gig. You'll have to use your own car, and—"

"Wait." Phoebe swallowed again. Dave wasn't going to like this, either. "You didn't know? I don't have a car. Or even a driver's license."

Dave shook his head. "I didn't know. No license. Of course not. Just because everybody over the age of sixteen in the United States has a license, and their biggest wish is to have their own wheels."

Phoebe didn't think it would help to tell him she got around on her bicycle. He probably thought she'd ridden it there for the exercise.

He sighed. "Can you get a license and a car? You can't do surveillance otherwise."

"I'm working on the license. I got my learner's permit. Chase took me out practice driving last week, and Sanjay is taking me again tomorrow."

"Sanjay—your friend with the taxi, right? A professional driver. Okay, that's good. The sooner all that happens, the better." He frowned, drumming his fingers on the scarred picnic table. Evidently the bad news was still coming.

"Here's the part that might be the hardest for you. Before you can get a license as a PI, assuming you want to do that after six months, you need to put in two thousand hours of supervised work with somebody who does have a license. That's me. Think you can handle that?"

"No problem," Phoebe said. Of course, Dave knew that she'd been in trouble with the CIA for—well, insubordination was probably too strong a word for what she'd done. But maybe she'd overextended her authority a little bit that one time.

"I'm asking because what I know of you demonstrates that you don't take orders that well."

"I can take orders!" Phoebe felt indignant. She could learn, anyway. She was learning everything else for this job.

Dave sat there, looking at her with those assessing eyes. *Oh, for Pete's sake.*

"The secretary of state would have been *kidnapped* if I hadn't acted. And nobody, not the CIA, or the FBI, or even the cops—no offense, Dave—would do anything. And who knows what would have happened to her?"

"I was thinking about the Empire State Building."

Oh. Yeah. The Empire State Building. The screwup that had caused the CIA to suspend her in the first place. Cops, SEALs, SWAT, tanks, robots, and drones had rolled in big time when she said a terrorist threat on the iconic landmark was imminent. Except then nothing had happened.

That had been a bad day. Really, really bad.

"Well, yeah, okay," Phoebe said, conceding the point. "It would have been better if more experienced personnel had been there to evaluate my decisions. But still, I wasn't all wrong."

"Everything worked out," Dave said. "But I want you to remember that our resources are more limited here. In this office, you've got only me for backup. And the cops, of course, should any situation come to that, which it better not. There won't be SEALs and SWAT teams at your beck and call. *This isn't the*

CIA."

Phoebe clenched her teeth. "I *know* that."

"So I don't want you to go off half-cocked," Dave said. "I don't want either of us to get killed or hurt. Not even *scratched.* I want a nice, simple, retirement gig here. I want to do background checks. Quiet divorce work. Maybe follow up on a couple of missing-person reports. I want desk work. Got that?"

"Sure." Phoebe shifted on the hard picnic bench. "Desk work."

"We're gonna go out to Venture Automotive and talk to Bonaventure and assess their vulnerabilities and install some security measures, and nobody's gonna get involved in shootings or kidnappings, is that understood?"

"Understood," Phoebe said, rolling back her shoulders.

"Two thousand hours is one year of full-time work," Dave said. "For one year, if you really want to become a PI, you do what I say. After that, when you get your PI license—if you get it—you can do what you want, I don't care. I'll do the background checks; you can go after the shooters. Until then, we're not doing anything dangerous. I had a bellyful of dangerous when I was with the cops, and I'm done with it. Got that?"

"Sure," Phoebe said. "Safety first. Got it."

"Are you *positive*? Because I don't want to get started on this and then have my license pulled because you can't follow the rules."

She leaned forward. "Dave, I don't know if I have what it takes to be a PI, but I will work as hard as I can and do my best for you. I worked at the CIA because I wanted to help protect citizens, just like you did as a cop. And being a PI falls right in with that. I know that I have a lot to learn and working here will be different than working at the CIA, but that's good! It'll be a whole new angle, and I'll learn a lot from you. And now that your first case is for Venture Automotive, I've got a personal stake in it. You know I'll go the extra mile."

"Okay. Well, we'll see. As long as you go the extra mile at the designated speed limit."

Phoebe grinned.

Dave didn't smile back. "One more thing."

What else could he say? He'd all but told her that her preparation was substandard and she didn't have the personality to be a PI. Maybe working for Dave hadn't been such a great idea. The CIA was looking better all the time. Or maybe bagging groceries. She could serve the public bagging groceries, too.

"What you did for the secretary of state—foiling that kidnapping," he said. "For a person with no police training, you got the job done, pretty much by yourself. The instinct you showed—you can't teach that. You'll be an asset here right from the start, and if you decide to become a PI, you'll be good at it."

That was the nicest thing anyone had ever said to her. She beamed at him, feeling a rush of pleasure.

"Thank you," she said. "I'll do my best not to let you down."

"I know," Dave said. "Because for some strange reason, you might rather be the number-two PI in a two-person office than work for the CIA."

"Call me crazy," Phoebe said, "but I think this might be more fun."

"And that's what I'm afraid of."

"Also, you don't intend to waterboard anybody."

Dave looked revolted. "Hell, no. And I thought the CIA didn't do that anymore."

Phoebe shrugged. "They don't. Of course not."

Dave assessed her again with those all-knowing eyes. She smiled back. She hadn't been part of the clandestine operations at the CIA, but she'd learned a few things even so.

"Any questions about all this?" he asked finally.

"Nope. I'm ready to roll." Phoebe slapped the rough edge of the picnic table. "But we have to do something about this piece of junk right away. No self-respecting client will believe it's a conference table. They'll be expecting us to serve hot dogs and lemonade."

"They'll be disappointed then," Dave said. "So if you're ready, let's head out. You drive. Don't kill us on the way."

ABOUT THE AUTHOR

Kay Keppler was born and raised in Wisconsin and now makes her home in northern California, where she lives in a drafty old house with wonky plumbing. If the duct tape holds, everything will be perfect.

Made in the USA
Monee, IL
10 July 2022